A scream, high- ...
stop. Another, ...
another. And ...
screaming as on...
she was screami...
appearing as she...
her seat by invisi... ....

Metal, ripping and tearing. Noise, louder and louder and louder; the terrible accompaniment to disaster. Thrown to one side, then the other, then whiplashed forward.

The carriage turning slowly over on its side, and then faster, hurtling towards the ground. The screaming was all over. An old woman freed from gravity, hurtling down the train, her face contorted by fear, her hands out in futile defence against the inevitable.

The jolt exploded through Annie's body. The walls seemed to turn to paper as they smashed and crunched and the noise filled everywhere until she thought her eardrums were going to burst. She was flung across the seat and up, a rag doll.

And then the darkness.

And then the thought: 'This is it. I'm going to . . .'

MARK CHADBOURN
THE ETERNAL

VISTA

First published in Great Britain 1996
by Victor Gollancz

This Vista edition published 1996
Vista is an imprint of the Cassell Group
Wellington House, 125 Strand, London WC2R 0BB

© Mark Chadbourn 1996

The right of Mark Chadbourn to be identified as author of
this work has been asserted by him in accordance with
the Copyright, Designs and Patents Act, 1988.

A catalogue record for this book is
available from the British Library.

ISBN 0 575 60062 4

Printed and bound in Great Britain
by Cox & Wyman Ltd, Reading, Berks

96 97 98 99   10 9 8 7 6 5 4 3 2 1

ACKNOWLEDGEMENTS

For my father, Gordon Chadbourn, who provided me with a quiet place to write when the real world got a little too close, and who provided enough coffee and doughnuts to give me a caffeine and sugar high for the rest of my life; astute editors Richard Evans and Jo Fletcher who kicked me into shape when my brain imploded (from all that caffeine and sugar); my agent Serafina Clarke for doing all the kicking on my behalf.

One final note (although this has become a cliché, it has to be said): the village of Riddington does not exist, although many of the other places mentioned in the book can be found on any good map of North-west Leicestershire. Strange things, however, *do* happen in that particular part of the world.

He fumbles at your Soul
As Players at the Keys
Before they drop full Music on—
He stuns you by degrees—
Prepares your brittle Nature
For the Ethereal Blow
By fainter Hammers – further heard—
Then nearer – Then so slow
Your breath has time to straighten—
Your Brain – to bubble Cool—
Deals – One – imperial – Thunderbolt—
That scalps your naked Soul—
When Winds take Forests in their Paws—
The Universe – is still—

EMILY DICKINSON

PART ONE

The First Step

A journey of a thousand miles must begin
with a single step.

LAO-TZE
Tao Te Ching

1

The darkness that enters everyone's life at some point came to Annie Boulton early, a few weeks before Christmas, on a train hurtling between Manchester and London. She had glimpsed it previously, from afar, but never so close, and like many people she did not recognize it for what it was until too late. There was no sound of giant, leathern wings in the night, no swish of a nicked scythe clutched by yellow-boned hands. The moment was filled with simple, pleasant sensations: the seductive warmth of the carriage and a gentle, rhythmic rocking; the flash of inviting lights from unknown towns out in the night; the sudden appearance of snowflakes on the window before their brief lives were burnt out by the contact.

No chill. No stomach-churning vertigo. No sudden, senseless terror. But death was close and it was drawing closer.

There was a soundtrack to the approaching dark, music from an archaic Walkman filling her head with relief from the bleak world. The Doors. 'Riders on the Storm'. After that there would be Iggy Pop with 'The Passenger', and then 'Move On Up' by Curtis Mayfield, some sixties' Motown, a dash of soul; timeless tracks from a different era, oddly juxtaposed but related in spirit, crying their message down the years.

Annie glanced out of the window and was taken aback by her reflection in the glass. She recognized the jolt of black hair, cut and styled only two days previously, framing the oval face and the slightly askew nose that gave her features their hard edge. But her naturally pale skin seemed ghost-white under the glaring carriage lights which also pooled deep shadows around her eyes; she looked like a woman in mourning.

She closed her eyes quickly so the music was all, drifting with the sound of rainfall that introduced the keyboards. The stress of last term was already starting to leave her, just three hours away from campus. No one had warned her that the pressures of her final year would be so great, the increase in lectures and tutorials, the spiralling reading list, the words *This is it! Make or break!* hanging ominously in the air. But although she had loathed the way the fun-loving atmosphere had faded like mist, another part of her had secretly relished the grind of preparing for those final exams. Charlotte, her best friend, had said she was too serious by far, digging out her Protestant work ethic and horse-hair shirt at every opportunity. Annie had tartly refuted her claims but she knew in her heart that Charlotte was right; she felt guilty having fun. The reason was so painfully obvious to her she sometimes wondered how many other people could sense the churning cauldron of doubts and fears within her. There was one point in the middle of a tutorial for Twentieth Century American Novelists when Annie'd had an overwhelming urge to grab some of the leaden faces around her and scream. On that occasion, the tutor thankfully took her ashen face for sickness and let her leave instead of recognizing the real cause: fear. Of the future, of change, of life in general. But somehow she kept going, burying everything beneath an acid tongue and a too-sarcastic demeanour. Only Charlotte acknowledged the truth. Not every day was a struggle, but there were enough that were, making her feel weary. She longed for a break from all the introspection and doubts, yet she couldn't see a way out. It was all Robert's fault.

The Doors started to fade away. Soon Iggy Pop would ease in.

Christmas would give her some perspective, Annie decided; her family, her friends; Riddington, as secure and warm and quiet and gossipy as ever. It was her favourite time of year and she would spend it with her favourite people in her favourite place, recharging the batteries, clearing the mind, preparing herself for the travail of her exams in the summer, and the vacuum that lay beyond.

She opened her eyes.

A smile, seductive. Eyes, dark, knowing, humorous, cruel, sexy. Black hair.

She closed them again hurriedly as if she had been burnt by the image on her retinas, but it remained scorched in place. The Doors were gone. *He* was there.

Annie opened her eyes once more, slowly this time. He had slipped into the seat opposite while she had been lost in her music. To complement that seductive glance, he was smiling broadly – at her. He moved his full lips lazily; up, down, and again. His teeth were white. She was transfixed.

It took a second before she realized he was speaking. Feeling uncommonly jumpy, she flicked off her Walkman and fumbled the headphones back from her ears.

'I said, to what are you listening?' The preciseness of his speech was both amusing and slightly jarring, the words made doubly strange by a faint, unusual accent which suggested Middle European or somewhere even further afield. From his appearance, Annie would have guessed Cyprus or the Middle East. His skin had a faint olive sheen and his shoulder-length hair was as black as crude oil, wavy and curly. A single gold earring glinted in his left ear (*Romany?* she thought), while a close-cropped beard and moustache added to his rakish look.

She gave up trying to pin down his origins and replied, 'The Doors. Do you know them?'

He nodded. 'An American rock group. Morrison, was it not? Van Morrison?'

'Jim. Van is a little less attractive, but just as talented.'

His brief laughter was measured, but rich and deep. 'I am out of my depth immediately. Popular music is not one of my obsessions. Although,' he added, 'I did know him.'

'Who?'

'Morrison.'

'Jim Morrison?' The moment the words left her mouth, the alarm bells started to ring, presaging a situation she had suffered a thousand times over the previous three years. Eyeing him suspiciously, Annie waited for the usual pathetic chat-up lines. His mouth was slightly open; his tongue darted out and touched the centre of his upper lip.

'I met him in Paris, shortly before his death. He was a very troubled man. We had a long conversation in a bar in Montmartre, about the meaning of life, the meaning of death. He took me back to his apartment to share a bottle of brandy and to continue our philosophical discourse.' He half closed his eyes in remembering and placed one long, manicured finger on his chin. 'Yes, a sad man. I hope my words did not disturb him too much.' A surface smile. 'It was a day or so later that I read of his passing. A drugs overdose, I believe. Or was it a heart attack? I may well have been the last person to see him alive.'

Annie wasn't convinced. Wryly, she said, 'You must have been quite young.' As she spoke, she realized she couldn't guess his age; more than twenty-five, but less than fifty. He smiled politely, but didn't give any clues.

'They are a strange breed, these rock stars. So serious about something as frivolous as music.'

'You've met others? I mean, apart from Jim Morrison?'

'I travel around a great deal. I have met many famous people. They are no different from you or I.' There was a wicked glint in his eye when he added, 'And if I had a choice in the matter I would prefer you.'

'Who wouldn't,' Annie replied acidly.

'Ah.' He was not in the least embarrassed by the put-down. He leaned forward, his smile now suggesting a sudden interest. 'You do not respond to flattery.'

'I don't respond to clichés.'

'What do you do when a cliché is the truth?'

Annie ignored his question. She could feel the flirtatiousness radiating from every inch of his body, but unlike the tawdry attentions she received from her fellow students, there was something here which intrigued her. Something deep beneath the surface, a complexity, a maturity. Perhaps it was even that hint of cruelty she saw in his eyes. She told herself not to be so perverse, but she felt a *frisson* of excitement nonetheless.

'Which other rock stars have you met?'

His brow furrowed in concentration.

'So many you have to think about it?' Annie mocked.

'I told you, they are just people. And I have met a lot of people.' He thought for a moment longer and then replied, 'Lennon? Is that his name?'

'John Lennon?' Now Annie knew he was playing games with her. He had met John Lennon and he couldn't be sure.

'Actually, I did not meet *him*. But I met the man who killed him.'

Annie raised her eyebrows in disbelief. 'Boy, these rock stars must hate it when you come along.'

'Chapman wanted to know the way to the Dakota Buildings. A spotty, unkempt youth. No dress sense whatsoever. But he had a book in his pocket so I presumed there was some small flame of intelligence flickering in the dark, empty caverns of his head. I showed him the way and hastily bid him well.'

'Let me get this right. You showed Mark Chapman to the place where he murdered John Lennon? So if not for you, Lennon might still be alive today?'

'Somebody would have ended his life sooner or later. One of those Government agencies perhaps. They hate lights which burn too brightly.'

Something crept and crawled around Annie's mind. 'Who are you?' she asked slowly.

He sat back in his seat and pressed his palms together like he was praying. 'Who am I?' He shrugged. 'A traveller on life's mysterious road. An investigator of the grandest secret of all. That sounds a little pretentious, does it not?' A pause. 'A seeker of pleasure.'

'What kind of pleasure?'

His full lips mouthed the reply softly: 'Later.'

Annie looked out of the window at the flurries of snow in the darkness. Her rational side told her to be wary; that it was unwise to talk to strangers on trains, and that this one had such a wild streak he could easily be unbalanced, if not dangerous. For a moment, she seriously considered making an excuse and changing seats, but then she looked into his face, and relaxed. She was amazed at the strength of his charisma, and more, she couldn't believe she was responding to it. There was something about him, so magnetic it made her feel hot in the pit of her stomach. Sex. Pure, potent sex. She wanted him, yet she felt embarrassed at herself for thinking it. He seemed to be so alive, it was oozing from every pore like lava. And his gaze was hard upon her, teasing and daring, even as she looked away.

'What is your name?'

She turned back to him. His stare was unwavering. 'Annie Boulton.'

'And you are a student?'

She nodded. 'Manchester University. Finals in the summer. Whatever happened to life?' She glanced back out of the window as the lights of another town flashed by. She wondered where they were in the darkness, how far it was to her stop, how soon before she reached the safety of Blackstone Cottage. *Safety? That was a strange word to think.* 'I'm going home,' she added, almost to herself. 'For Christmas.'

'And where is home?'

'Riddington. It's a small village in North-west Leicestershire.

Near Ashby-de-la-Zouch. That's where Sir Walter Scott set *Ivanhoe*.'

'I have been to many places in my life, but never there. Perhaps I will visit it one day.'

'No rock stars there for you to curse.' She smiled at him and he grinned in return; a bond developed. Across the aisle, two lovers butted foreheads gently and mouthed warm words. Somewhere down the carriage a child was crying, a warning sound that rose and then was suddenly snapped off.

'Is it a pleasant place, your home? Do you like it? Surely a small village is too quiet for you.' His gaze, almost hypnotic, never left her face.

'It's perfect.'

'Nothing is perfect in this world.' His eyes narrowed slightly and he rested his elbows on the table between them in a manner which was almost combative.

'Well, it's the closest thing to it. It was a great place to grow up – countryside, fields and all that. Friendly people. Everyone knows everyone else, and they all help each other. You don't get that in a city.' She shrugged self-deprecatingly. 'Our own little Garden of Eden.'

'Hmmm. It sounds like paradise.' There was an unmistakable note of sarcasm in his voice.

Annie bristled, but she tried not to show it. 'Maybe you have to be there to appreciate it. Where do you call home?'

He waved his hand in a circle. 'Oh, around and around. I have spent so long travelling there is nowhere I could really call my own. I never stay in one place for long. A few days. A week at the most.'

'That must be very interesting.'

'Some would find it so. There is not a country in the world that I have not visited. The bleak, snowswept wastes of Antarctica. The steaming jungles of South America. The lonely islands of the Pacific.'

'Very poetic.' She suddenly realized an important piece of information was missing. 'You haven't told me your name.'

He smiled like a tiger uncovered in the brush. 'To know someone's name is to have power over them, Annie. The ancients believed that very strongly. Only their closest and most trusted friends knew their true naming word. To everyone else

14

they presented an alias, thereby protecting themselves from attack by evil force.'

'But you know my name.'

He smiled.

Another train thundered past outside. Annie jumped. She felt strangely tense and there was a tingling sensation in her fingers and toes. 'That's not very polite. What am I supposed to call you?'

He leaned so far across the table his face filled her whole vision. 'You may call me Morrison.'

'As in Jim Morrison?'

'Yes.'

'What's your first name?'

'Jim.'

The game had begun.

The train rolled through the night and their verbal jousting began in earnest, each trying to draw secrets from the other; it was a silly game, but Annie found it intriguing. It wasn't simply about winning – she wanted to know everything about him. Morrison, as she had reluctantly agreed to call him, was an expert, spinning his words with such a poker face that she could never tell whether he was lying. He seemed to have a vast array of masks which he changed without warning: the urbane wit, the traveller with a thousand tall stories, the philosopher, the gourmand, the innocent. It didn't take Annie long to realize she was failing in the unannounced contest they were both playing. She responded too quickly to Morrison's subtle probing, providing information without gaining anything in return. He found out about her family, her friends, her likes and dislikes, even her lovers. And all she could get out of him was a string of tales so fantastical she was surprised he wasn't embarrassed to relate them. He discussed his exploits in the war, First, Second, Gulf or Vietnam, she wasn't quite sure; his bizarre meetings with the good and the great; the times he had romanced Marilyn Monroe, Louise Brooks and Clara Bow. Then there was his in-depth recall of every book he had ever read, and his encyclopaedic knowledge of ancient cultures. His stories were convincing, compelling, but she hated being the butt of the joke he was playing.

As one of his escapades rolled on, he suddenly broke off and said, 'You know, you intrigue me, Annie.' She waited for the familiar, slightly mocking grin to materialize, but for the first time she caught a glimmer of sincerity in his face.

'Why?'

'I can see something deep within you . . . something perhaps you do not even recognize yourself . . .'

'Very perceptive,' she mocked.

He waved his hand as if wafting away an unpleasant smell. 'No. No jokes,' he said, so firmly it was almost an order. Annie's smile slipped away. His eyes ranged across her, probing, hard, until she began to squirm. 'You are a great force for life, Annie. In all my wanderings, I have met very few people with that capacity. Most are so wrapped up in their own existence, their gaze never leaves the gutter.' He bit his lip. 'But those that have that force . . . that *essence* . . . have tremendous potential. Within you it is still an untapped resource. It will remain locked away until you accept its presence and release it. I feel it . . .' He closed his eyes. 'Hot . . . a furnace waiting for the blast of the bellows . . .'

'And here's me, thinking I was just a student.'

His voice hardened, 'You know, you should protect that resource. Some people may be jealous of it.'

'Yeah, well, there's a lot of sad folk out there.'

'But what is holding that potential back?' He spoke dreamily this time, and she was unnerved to see his nostrils flare, as if he was smelling her. *Like an animal*, she thought. A dog. Or a wolf. 'Ah, yes.' His eyes flashed. 'There it is! Unmistakable.' A vein was pulsing on his forehead. 'Darkness. Death.'

Annie shifted uncomfortably. Could he really tell? Was it that obvious? She shifted, hoping he would change the subject, knocked her headphones to the floor, picked them up, felt the heat rise through her cheeks.

'What is it?' His question seemed innocent enough, but Annie sensed a sadistic edge to it, as if he *wanted* to expose the rawness.

'It's nothing.' His silence was a vacuum which she felt she had to fill. 'My brother,' she added. Her throat had contracted to the width of a straw. 'Robert. He died before I started at university. How could you tell?'

Morrison smiled enigmatically and waved for her to continue.

'We were very close, although we fought a lot, all the time

really. He was a year younger than me. He'd saved up to buy a moped, one of the sporty ones that looked like a proper motorbike. He'd been dreaming about it for months. I came back from the pub one night with my boyfriend. We were a little drunk, too noisy, laughing. I walked into the lounge and it was like I'd stepped into a freezer. My parents ... their faces ... I thought they were dead. They were white as a sheet, just staring at the fire with this horrible expression, like all the muscles on their faces had been pulled taut. When I shut my eyes I can still see it.' She clasped her arms across her chest. 'Mum just said, "Robert's dead." She never looked at me. She just kept staring ahead.'

He was scanning every slight movement of her face, drinking in every emotion that traced a ghost hand across her features.

'He'd been out on the moped. Some driver ... some bastard ... had ploughed into him, smashed him over a hedge into a field. Hit and run. He was only found by accident. A couple out smooching saw him. His neck was broken. I miss him. I wish he was here.'

'Some years ago, and it still affects you so deeply?' he asked with little evidence of any sympathy.

'I've seen ...' She paused, wondering if she should tell him, but it was like she was on a steep slope out of control. 'I saw a therapist. Lots of times. Mum and Dad made me when I couldn't shake off the depression.'

'And did it work?'

She shook her head. 'Well, yes, the depression's gone. I can *live* now, for what it's worth. But it's still there, in my thoughts every day. The therapist reckoned it's not just Robert's death. That it's something deeper. He kept rambling on about Thanatos, the death urge, and lots of crap like that. As if it means anything. I had a sheltered, stable upbringing and when death came out of the blue like that I wasn't prepared for it – apparently.' She sneered. 'He said I just keep retreating from ... oh, Christ, I don't know. Mortality, maybe. Reality. That's easy for him to say; he was taking my dad's dosh all the time.'

She was letting her psyche do the talking, but she couldn't stop herself. She didn't want to stop. She wanted to tell him everything.

'And it still oppresses you – death. They would have loved you in the last century, Annie, trapped in a morbid mentality, just like the sickly Keats and all his cronies. You must remember, death is what makes people human. There is a reason for it.'

'I've tried that one,' she said sarcastically. 'And all the philosophies and the heart-warming homilies. None of them work.'

'Grief does strange things to people, but you will recover. Your brother's memory will fade. Life and all its petty little happinesses will return.' Morrison sounded almost bitter.

She was unable to give voice to her fear that she would never get over it. 'I can't understand why it happened. I can't see a reason for it. That's what makes it unbearable . . .' Her voice trailed off.

He shrugged nonchalantly. 'You are seeing only the tiniest fragment of an enormous picture. Trying to make sense of what happens in your little rock pool when the sea surges in and fills it with new life every day. Look at the totality, the massive, sprawling panorama. One death does not matter. Twenty deaths do not matter. Life goes on regardless, brutal and uncaring.'

'That's a very bleak view.'

'Not at all. I am merely pointing out that you cannot hope to work out life's dramas without any understanding of the rules and regulations that structure our existence.'

'What do *you* believe? Is there an afterlife? Will I ever see Robert again?'

Morrison mused for a second and then decided to go along with her questioning. 'Have you heard tell of the Black Cathedral?'

Annie shook her head.

He nodded thoughtfully and seemed to struggle for the correct words. At last, Annie had the sense that what he was saying came from the very heart of him. 'There *is* a place beyond death,' he began. 'Every culture, every society, every race since the dawn of man has believed that. Some scientists,' he pronounced the word contemptuously, 'would ascribe that to wishful thinking. Not true. The ancients were closer to the natural order than the people of this age are. They *knew*. Anyway, details of what lies in the land beyond are similar across cultural boundaries, and therefore more than the product of imagination. Near-death experiences, the accounts of spiritualists and mystics, all give a cohesive picture of an afterlife.

The evidence is there if one can break the boundaries of so-called rational thinking to perceive it.'

'So where does the Black Cathedral come in?'

'You will only know the truth when you see it, Annie.' His words were heavy and spoken with awe. 'The Black Cathedral, some say, is a spiritual edifice that lies on the threshold of life and death. All who die must pass through its giant door. It reaches up to infinity and its walls stretch from horizon to horizon – there is no way around it.'

'Sounds like the perfect symbol. Do you believe it actually exists? And what's supposed to happen inside?'

He shrugged wryly. 'Judgement, perhaps ... if you believe whatever Power resides there has the right to judge. Who knows? It is the place of all mysteries. The gateway to wonder ...'

'Or damnation.'

His smile was cold. 'Indeed.'

'That's all very intriguing, but it still doesn't do it for me,' Annie said apologetically. 'The Black Cathedral ... all this talk ... I don't know, it sounds too fanciful.'

His eyes narrowed slightly. 'Beware of the Black Cathedral, Annie.' His voice dropped to a whisper. 'You never know when you might visit it. Or what you will find there.'

Annie shook her head adamantly. 'All I want is some comfort in *this* world.'

'If you must try to comprehend death in limited terms, look at it as a student of literature: every life is a story. A story without an ending is worthless. Meaningless. Death allows the life's plot to be drawn to a close, the subtext finally to be understood. Death allows everything a person has done to be judged and weighed and put into perspective. Given some signification. Imagine, then, what it would be like never to die. Never to find any meaning in anything you do because there will never be an ending. Imagine the endless drifting, searching for something which can never be attained. *Imagine it.*'

There was fire in his voice when he stressed the final two words. Then he reached across the table and held her hand. The electricity of his touch jolted her alert. 'I am sorry you cannot find peace in yourself, I truly am. You may not believe that shortly, but it is the truth.' He stood up and started to button his brown suede jacket, swaying with the motion of the train.

'Where are you going?'

He smiled almost apologetically. 'I must take my leave now. I found our conversation very entertaining. I will not quickly forget it.'

Annie looked out of the window, puzzled, and then checked her watch. 'We're not scheduled to stop yet. We must be miles from the nearest station.'

He didn't bother to reply. Instead he stretched for her hand again. 'May I?'

Annie surprised herself by holding the back of her hand up to him. A shiver ran through her when his lips touched her skin as some unknown energy crackled between them. She felt the hairs along the length of her arm stand to attention, and the muscles of her belly contract. His breath was warm on her flesh. Then, for the merest instant, she felt the caress of the tip of his tongue in what was a base parody of a gallant gesture, an act of pure animal sexuality.

He stepped out into the aisle, still smiling.

'I don't understand—' she began to protest, but he hushed her with a raised hand.

'Farewell, Annie. Do not hate death so much.'

She started to say something else, but he was gone, moving towards the front of the train. He did not look back.

His smile, at once seductive and arrogant, and those predatory eyes, stayed with her after he had gone. Even the music no longer freed her thoughts; she was snared in his subtle web. She couldn't understand it. The majority of men she could take or leave. If the truth be known, she felt superior to most of the opposite sex. She certainly never *obsessed* about them. What was it about this one? Then The Clash came on the Walkman and launched into 'Stay Free' with a blare of guitars, chopping the image of him dead. There was no point in dwelling on him any further, she resolved. Even so, she couldn't resist glancing back along the aisle, just in case.

The train rattled on through the night. Annie checked her watch once again. Only half an hour to go and she would see her father waiting at the back of the crowd on the station concourse, the thick, fraying scarf that her mother hated twirled twice around his neck. Then it would be a short drive through the countryside to Riddington and Blackstone Cottage, a log fire, masses of shiny decorations and a Christmas tree draped with so many beads and baubles it was in danger of toppling over. Her mother didn't understand the meaning of the word 'overkill'.

Safety. Security. Escape.

She closed her eyes and drifted . . .

And in the darkness behind her eyelids, everything suddenly skewed. The night exploded with sound. She was hit by a terrifying rush of unfocused kinetic energy:

SKREEEEEEEEEEEEEEEEEEEEEEEEEEEEEEEEEEEEEEEEEE!

Shock snapped her eyes open. The air caught her lungs.

The carriage was magically lifting into the air and a feeling of weightlessness followed, like stepping off the high board at the pool. She saw a window imploding, the glass glittering and spinning through the air in daggers, deadly and beautiful. The face of the man sitting next to it disintegrating into red. A shower of blood, mixing with the sparkling glass, up, up, higher, then down. His hands rising. His head pitching forward.

A scream, high-pitched and reedy that wouldn't stop. Another, low and hoarse. Another. And another. And another. The whole carriage screaming as one, and Annie suddenly realizing she was screaming too. The weightlessness disappearing as she felt herself pressed back into her seat by invisible, monstrous hands.

Metal, ripping and tearing. Noise, louder and louder and louder; the terrible accompaniment to disaster. Thrown to one side, then the other, then whiplashed forward.

The carriage turning slowly over on its side, and then faster, hurtling towards the ground. The screaming was all over. An old woman freed from gravity, hurtling down the train, her face contorted by fear, her hands out in futile defence against the inevitable.

The jolt exploded through Annie's body. The walls seemed to turn to paper as they smashed and crunched and the noise filled everywhere until she thought her eardrums were going to burst. She was flung across the seat and up, a rag doll.

And then the darkness.

And the thought: 'This is it. I'm going to . . .'

Light, dark. Light, dark. Light, dark. Light, dark.

Her first thought – if the vague awareness she felt as she

crawled out of painful unconsciousness could be called that – was that she was alive. It seemed a miracle, but there was no jubilation; just agony.

Light, dark. Light, dark. She was floating in a black and white world: wherewasshewhatwashappening?

Her senses came back in fitful starts, like the jumps of a movie freed from a jammed projector, and it was then that she remembered there were worse things than death. A shattered spine, brain damage, a mind trapped in a body which would no longer do its bidding.

She whispered a prayer and attempted to wiggle her toes. There was movement. Her breath came out in a headlong rush of relief, followed by a burst of pain just below her left breast that made her yelp out loud.

In response, a moan echoed through the still air of the carriage. Annie ignored it, concentrating on her own small world of injury and shock. Probably a cracked rib, she thought. If that was the worst of it, she would go to church on Sunday. She would go for the rest of her life.

Enough of her confidence returned to extend her consciousness out beyond her own body. The carriage was on its side. Annie lay crumpled against the window which had cracked but not shattered. Another slice of luck.

The lights had gone out in the carriage at the same time as they had gone out in her head; the disorientating flashing was coming through the windows which now lay above her. It was accompanied by a crackle each time the light flared which made her think it was electricity intermittently arcing on to the tracks. It revealed in brief glimpses a scene of utter chaos: luggage, empty Coke cans, magazines and papers scattered over piles of bodies. They were everywhere. Hanging from the seats above her, limbs trapped, none of them moving. Could they all be . . .?'

She didn't want to think about that.

Annie twisted her head, and something warm, wet and sticky ran into her eye socket. She moved slightly and blinked it out. Blood. She guessed there was a hell of a gash on her head. *That's the modelling career out of the window*, she thought sardonically. Above her she could see a rectangle of dark sky.

An Intercity 125, British Rail's fastest train; the carnage must be unimaginable. *I've got to get out of here.*

All the repressed anxiety went flooding through her system, and Annie wrenched herself up in a frantic effort to get out into the night air. She collapsed back a second later, the pain in her right leg so great she felt as if an iron bar had been smashed across her shin. Broken. The tears finally came.

But so did the realization that another express could come hurtling along the line at any minute. There was no alternative. She *had* to get out.

Up and down the carriage she could hear a few signs of life, like prehistoric people emerging from the caves after a terrible storm. Grunts and scrapes, and someone sobbing weakly. Whenever the electricity flooded the carriage with its brief instants of light, she could even see some of the living – a woman trying to force herself upright, an elderly man leaning against what had been the roof – and that gave her hope.

Steeling herself, she took a deep breath and moved.

The pain erupted again in a fiery web which ran to her groin, but this time she managed to minimize it by relying on her other leg and hauled herself into a standing position. She was suddenly thankful for the days she had spent in the university gym. Her arms took the strain better than she could have expected and she was soon leaning against the top of the surviving seats, wheezing and nauseous. She closed her eyes and rested for a moment.

A scrambling and banging at the end of the carriage behind her jarred her out of her daze. It sounded like someone forcing open the electronic connecting door. She felt a surge of relief as a grind of metal told her they had succeeded.

'Over here,' she yelled, waiting for the next flash of light to reveal someone from the emergency services.

When the light did come, limning the rescuer against the open doorway, her breath caught in her throat.

It was *him*.

Morrison.

But he hadn't seen her yet. His attention was focused on those suffering near to him and Annie knew they needed his help first, so she contained the urge to shout.

Darkness returned.

Light.

He had reached the elderly gent who had slumped against the roof and was in danger of collapsing. Morrison was reaching out a friendly, supporting hand, brushing the old man's shoulder. There was tenderness there, a sensitivity that made Annie feel warm with humanity.

Darkness.

Light.

In that briefest instant, the focus of the scene had changed. Morrison's hand had moved past the man's shoulder and was heading towards his face. Annie watched in puzzlement. It looked like Morrison was trying to caress him.

Darkness. There were strange scuffling noises; a gasp, then choking sounds. Annie held her breath.

Light.

The old man was pinned against the roof. Morrison stood in front of him, one hand on each cheek holding his victim's head rigid. Pallid protests filtered weakly down the carriage, but Morrison's thumbs were poised over the old man's staring, frightened eyes. The thumbs jerked forward.

Darkness.

Annie felt a coldness drain through her body; she couldn't believe what she had seen. The image flashed on and off like a stroboscope in her mind. A trick of the pain and the flashing charges of electricity?

Light.

The old man was lost in the shadows behind a seat like discarded luggage. Morrison was loping across the carriage, oblivious to the debris, moving towards the female passenger who had half pulled herself upright.

Darkness. Annie wanted to call out a warning, but it was caught in her throat.

Light.

Morrison had the woman's head in his hands. She wore an expression of sudden fear, that increased as Morrison grinned. He was enjoying it. He held her head even tighter and then gave a sudden twist. There was a sickening crack. All Annie's emotions erupted at once in a short, sharp scream that cleaved through the stillness. Morrison looked up and saw her.

He smiled.

Darkness.

Don't wait for him! Move! Acting purely on instinct, she lurched forward, propelling herself from seat to seat, trailing

24

her broken leg behind her. Her body was a starburst of pain, but self-preservation had taken over.

Murder. Christ, murder!

Light.

Annie glanced behind her. Morrison had stumbled over a couple of the bodies in his path. He righted himself with a curse and then noticed that one of his crumpled obstacles was still alive. A low moan rolled out when his foot made contact. Annie knew he had seen the wincing, awkward way she was moving, and when he looked down at the prostrate form, she also knew he was thinking, *There's still time*. Sure enough, he dropped to his knees and rolled the body over. Then he flexed his fingers.

Darkness.

Annie almost cried out in triumph when she reached the end of the carriage. She dragged herself up into the waist-high doorway, nearly blacking out when her shin cracked against the wall. Fumbling in the dark, she realized the electronic door had jammed partly open. It was only a few inches, but she thought she could squeeze through. There was no way that tiny gap could accommodate Morrison though; she would be home free. She dived forward, head and shoulders first.

Thank God I never ate too much chocolate.

Her breasts caught on the doorway as she eased through. It was difficult to force them past the obstruction, and for the briefest moment she almost wished she were a man.

Behind her she could hear Morrison's breathing as he stumbled through the gloom, getting closer, coming to catch her.

That reminder did the trick. She shrank herself through the door and fell into the area between the carriages where she finally did black out for an instant.

When she came round scant seconds later, Morrison was at the electronic door. His face was pressed against the glass, the deformed features demonic in a flare of light like some medieval painting. Annie stifled a yell, levered herself up, and made for the open toilet door above her.

Morrison's arm had shot through the gap, brushing her jacket. His scraping fingers jolted her like a cattle prod and she heaved herself away from them.

'Annie!' The voice that had seemed so seductively warm before was now cold and hard. 'With her perfect village and perfect life. What do you think of this carnage, eh?' He was mocking, daring her to face him. More games. When she continued to retreat, he added venomously: 'The poor fool who cannot face up to death. Look around you, little girl. It exists. You cannot lock it away. It is a part of life. Of *your* life. Embrace it!'

'Why did you do it?' She didn't want to talk, she wanted to escape, but she had to know.

'I killed them because I could.' His statement was emotionless, but then the honey crept back into his voice. 'I find you very attractive, Annie. Hanging there like that . . . with those kicking legs . . . mmm, I could eat you up.'

Before she could express her loathing, there was a crash as the glass of the electronic door frosted. Then another, and another. He was hammering it with his fist or his head, or both, but the security glass held. She pulled herself towards the carriage door, the nausea so powerful she felt her vision blur. Dizzily, she glanced up at the door. The window was halfway down; she could see the cold night sky through it. It was close enough to reach.

The snorts and grunts from behind were growing louder, more ferocious, like a Rottweiler trying to tear itself free. Morrison had given up trying to smash the glass and now he was attempting to prise the door open. There was a grind as it moved an inch.

It was now or never.

Annie leant out through the open window. The outside of the door was freezing, and covered in snowflakes, but she registered only the grating sound and yell of triumph from Morrison as he gained entry into the corridor she had just left.

She swung her body out over the drop, fear giving her strength. She was almost clear of the carriage when there was a sudden burning pressure on her ankle. Morrison's fingers had snapped around it, his nails biting into the flesh.

'Come here, Annie,' he said in a sing-song voice.

He started to drag her back slowly as if he was reeling in a fish, and although Annie tried to grip on to the outside of the train, her fingers simply slid uselessly over the cold, wet metal. Until, on the verge of plunging back into the corridor, she stretched out and anchored herself to the door handle.

In that instant, her mind flashed back to the death of her brother. If she let go and was killed, would she see Robert once more? That floppy fringe that always reminded her of Oscar Wilde? That strange, screwed-up smile that he could transform into a mock sneer? Would he be there? The idea almost made her release her hold.

Give in, a voice in her head said. *Embrace death!*

Instead, she kicked out with the heel of her good leg and caught something pulpy yet hard.

There was a resultant yell from Morrison and his grip on her ankle loosened enough for her to yank her leg free, and then she was wriggling away like a worm, cracking her rib, ignoring it, cracking her shin, ignoring it, until she was out on top of the train in the freezing night air.

As she pulled herself up into a sitting position, she was suddenly transfixed by the eeriness of the scene. The only sound was the howl of the winter wind as it blasted between the cutting, hauling flurries of snow in its wake. Everywhere was white, an image of crisp Christmas innocence but for the wreckage scattered across the tracks. She appreciated, then, the extent of the disaster. The train was thrown at such an angle, smashed and distorted out of shape, that Annie found it hard to believe more than a handful had survived. One carriage was half buried in the bank. Bodies were lying where they had been thrown and some carriages had burst open like rotten fruit. Snow was dusting a veil over them.

The sound of Morrison scrabbling to climb up and through the window ended her reflections and with a sudden push she launched herself forward, sliding down what had been the roof of the carriage to land in a heap in the snow below. She blacked out again when her leg smashed into the ground, but the sensation of her face hitting an icy drift instantly shocked her back to consciousness.

Frantically, she looked around. There was no one to help her. Nowhere to hide.

She set off down the tracks, barely able to see ahead of her as the wind whipped snow into her eyes. The fire that erupted each time she put down her broken leg, the agony that burst each time she breathed, had pulled her within herself to her own hazy world. She was in a nightmare, and she might as well be stranded in the Antarctic wastes. Captain Oates heading into the snow to die.

I may be some time.

Through snow-stung tears she saw the dark shape towering above her, a pool of black in the surrounding white. She tried to recall a prayer she had been taught as a child, but all that would come was a line from a favourite film.

Wake up. Time to die.

She closed her eyes.

The expected blow never came. She opened them again and there was a hand in front of her face, offering help. The fingers were rough, calloused; they were not Morrison's. She was hauled on to her good leg where she teetered for a moment, before pitching forward into the dark pool which enveloped her, filling her senses with the smell of oil and dirt and the road. Arms folded around her back, and she allowed herself to give up the fight as her head found a secure place on a shoulder. The stranger let it rest there for only an instant, before he pulled her up into his line of vision.

His face was a locked door, but his dark eyes reflected a cold world of negative images: despair, anger, hatred, fear. Annie almost caught her breath at what she saw there. He was in his late thirties, slightly unshaven as if he had been travelling without rest. His long brown hair and square jaw reminded her of some rock star a few years down the line.

'Where is he?' An American.

She was lost to the pain for a moment and when she came back he was still staring into her face. 'What?'

'You're injured, you're frightened, and you're running from someone. In my book, that only adds up to one thing.' She started to fade back into the haze, and he shook her with a little more roughness than she would have expected.

'Ow!'

'Black hair, beard, swarthy skin, gold earring. You know who I'm talking about.'

'Morrison?'

'Yeah, if that's what he told you.'

Annie turned and pointed behind her. She was shocked to see Morrison standing exactly in line with her, grinning. His arms were folded casually, and he was seemingly oblivious to the howling snowstorm.

'Hello, Severin. We really cannot go on meeting like this. People will talk.'

Annie could feel Severin's body tense and when her good leg

28

suddenly grew weak and she fell to her knee, he did nothing to pull her back up. To her irritation, she was left like some weak, simpering princess clutching at the iron thigh of a barbarian preparing to slay her dragon-tormentor.

'Oh, come now. Cat got your tongue?' Morrison taunted the other man. 'After all the miles we have travelled since our last meeting, you should have *something* to say. No tales from the road? No aphorisms? No brief discourses about the weather? Or are you simply wracking your brain for a way to do me in? Severin, sometimes you remind me of a little dog that has its teeth in the trouser leg of a stranger and will not let go even though it knows it can cause no harm. Is that how you want to go through your exceedingly short life? Keep following me, by all means – I do love our brief encounters. But do not waste any of your precious mental energy trying to kill me.' Morrison licked at his own sneering words like they were sweets.

Severin's long, black coat billowed out voluminously in the wind. 'But I can hurt you, can't I, Wilde? And sooner or later I'm going to find a way to kill you; that's why you get scared when I get too close.'

Morrison, or 'Wilde', laughed, but Severin was already moving. He dipped his hand inside his overcoat and pulled out a sawn-off shotgun. Annie stared at it in disbelief, but when she saw Severin's face she covered her ears and ducked low.

Wilde's mocking humour turned to anger when he saw the weapon, but as he prepared to unleash another acid comment, Severin fired. The blast caught Wilde full in the chest, lifting him off his feet like a feather, and hurling him backwards into the snow.

Annie's jaw sagged. 'You've killed him, you mad, fucking bastard!' She wondered if the whole world had gone crazy.

'Oh Annie, you really do care!'

Wilde was sitting up and grinning at her, although once or twice his expression slipped into a grimace. His chest was a mass of flesh and blood and bone, leaking out on to the clean snow. The wounds were so deep it was obvious he should have been dead. Annie shook her head, not believing, suddenly very frightened. The world *was* crazy. As he continued to leer at her, Wilde absent-mindedly tried to press back into place a chunk of flesh that hung down his chest.

He then turned his attention to Severin. 'Guns now, Mr

Severin. How vulgar. You really are mixing in the wrong circles. Of course, you realize it is a penis substitute?'

Severin smiled triumphantly. 'It hurt, didn't it?'

Wilde ignored his jibe and clambered awkwardly to his feet, clutching his chest with red-stained hands. 'Do not try to use the other barrel. My temper does have limits.'

'Oh yeah, what are you going to do? Come over here and hit me? You've never let me within ten feet of you since this whole thing began.' Severin raised the gun once more.

Wilde looked at Annie and gave a slight, formal bow. 'You were very charming company, my dear. I hope you will believe me when I say our conversation was the most stimulating I have enjoyed in many years. Do not be too sad at our parting. I am sure we will meet again when you least expect it.'

'Go to hell!' Severin's growl was accompanied by the retort of the gun, but the pellets found only empty air. Wilde seemed to have melted into the sweeping snow.

Annie tried to search the black and white night for his disappearing figure, but it was like he had never been there. Strangely, she felt the slightest sense of loss.

Severin swore loudly and marched off in pursuit of Wilde, loading his gun as he broke into a run.

'Hey!' Annie yelled with as much energy as she could muster. 'What about me?' She toppled over into the crisp snow and lay on her side watching Severin's receding figure, wondering if she was going to freeze to death there on the tracks.

Severin stopped and turned round with annoyance. 'You got out this far, you get back yourself. I've got to follow Wilde. I can't give up now I'm this close.'

'Please . . .' Annie's voice trailed off into the wind.

Severin's dark face reappeared inches from her own. 'If I lose him I'll take it out of your hide.'

'Stop being such . . .' She had to take a deep breath before she could continue, '. . . a macho bore.'

He took her arm and supported her, leading her back towards the train. The shrill sound of sirens cut through the gale, drawing closer; over the top of the cutting she could see the glow of blue and red lights. Severin's roughness dissipated as they progressed and soon Annie was clinging to him as if he was her lover.

'What happened?' She looked at the twisted, jumbled wreckage. The smell of oil and burnt metal triggered her memory of that horrific moment of weightlessness before the crash.

'He did it.'

'Morrison?'

'Wilde. That's not his real name either, but it's the one I know him by.' His voice was hard and cold like a soldier who has spent too long on the front line. 'I don't know how. Maybe he got in with the driver, speeded up the train on the bend and derailed it. Who cares about the technicalities? All that matters is he's alive and laughing and everyone else is lying around dead.'

'But why . . .' Annie couldn't find words to reflect her sense of the atrocity before her. 'There's no reason for it . . .'

'He doesn't need a reason!' Severin spat the words out. 'He's a force that kills, he moves on, he kills again. The ultimate serial killer. There's no reason for any of the murders he commits, and believe me, I've seen enough of them.'

Annie looked at Severin askance, trying to see if he was as mad as Wilde.

'You don't believe me? I've seen him cause a plane crash, sink a boat, set fire to an apartment block. The more deaths the better. But that doesn't mean he can't get personal too, and do it one on one.'

Voices, nervous and fearful, echoed all around as anonymous figures scurried over the top of the cutting and slithered down the bank to the wreckage.

'If that's true, why hasn't someone caught him yet?'

'He's good. He doesn't leave witnesses.'

'I can't believe this! I can't . . . He must be completely psychotic.'

Severin laughed. 'He's as sane as you or me.'

Looking at her companion, Annie didn't find that very comforting. 'I think I'm going to be sick.'

She let Severin lead her to the train and they sat down while chaos erupted around them. The scene was swarming with ambulancemen, policemen, firemen, hurrying from carriage to carriage. As the injured were brought out on collapsible stretchers, Annie realized she was a member of a very small club. Only one or two lucky ones managed to walk away, clutching their heads or their arms. They would be counting the cost of this night for years, she thought. The worst rail crash in living memory.

Severin squeezed her shoulder. 'You'll be all right now. They'll be along to see you soon.'

'Where are you going?'

'After him.'

'Why you?'

He thought for a moment as if he had never considered the question before, but he didn't reply. Then he turned and trudged off into the snowy night. And soon he was gone, a patch of blackness swallowed up by the white.

Annie felt suddenly alone and tiny. The storm was getting stronger, but her thoughts were of the two human whirlwinds who had blasted into her life that night. They had made her feel insignificant, as if she had blindly intruded on to a huge stage where events of great importance were being played out. The central players had found the time to patronize her for a while, before discarding her as worthless.

As she sat there, obliquely observing the frantic activity and raw emotions of life encountering death, she was overwhelmed by a crushing feeling of bleakness and impotence. She looked past the hubbub to the cold whiteness that stretched across the tracks and up the bank a hundred feet away, past the sickly orange glow of an unknown town to the black expanse of sky devoid of stars or moon. She shivered.

Nothing would be the same again.

2

It was going to be a long, hot summer. By the end of June it had already been established that it was one of the hottest on record, with days ablaze, heat crushing down in yellow waves beneath a clear blue sky, and nights that were ovens, sweat-licked and uncomfortable, where even one sheet was too much and a breeze never stirred the trees. The pond at Taylors' farm which was home to the famous Riddington pike had shrunk from a large black oasis to a dirty puddle surrounded by cracked mud.

No one could find the energy to check if the pike was still alive; the sun had turned everyone into zombies, sluggish and glassy-eyed in their gardens or in their darkened lounges where the portable fans blew futilely, or in the snug of the Royal Oak where the icy pints could not be poured fast enough.

Riddington had weathered other extremes as it would weather this – the winter of '79, the gales of '56, the floods of '32. The village was immutable, like a fine, old English oak with roots that went down deep; and within its boundaries, its inhabitants took shelter against the vicissitudes of life, drawing strength from Riddington's unbending security. Where other villages starved and died in the wake of economic hardships, this one continued. Its residents knew they had to give something back for the security they drew upon and they fought, as only the middle classes can fight, to ensure their community's survival – badgering MPs, forming working parties and protest groups, conservation societies and Neighbourhood Watch. And so Riddington maintained a village shop, a newsagent's-cum-post office, a pub and even a village school, one of the last in a dying breed, independent and with a history that stretched back more than a hundred years. There were only four main streets, a small cul-de-sac of new executive houses and less than six hundred residents, yet the village thrived like a community four times its size, and each year the residents staged a fête to celebrate their continuing good fortune. The world might change, but Riddington would stay for ever.

Surprisingly in the blistering heat, the North-west Leicester-shire countryside still retained its verdancy. Whenever the grass threatened to start yellowing or the leaves on the oaks and elms were in danger of crisping brown, there would come a sudden downpour which had everyone believing the heatwave was over. The shower would always end quickly, refreshing the vegetation, but not lowering the temperature or restocking the dwindling rivers and streams. The local population would return to their gardens and lounges and pub, subdued.

Annie Boulton stood at the French windows at Blackstone Cottage waiting impatiently for another breeze to sweep down the garden. The route between the trees and shrubs was a wind tunnel in winter, but now there was barely enough draught to stir the washing on the line. She tried to ignore the uncomfort-able sensation of her sweat-soaked shirt; even her thin summery skirt seemed a layer too much. She would have stayed in her bikini all day, but Martyn would soon be here and she didn't want him staring at her breasts. Every time she saw him, he looked her up and down possessively as if they were still a couple. It annoyed her so much she wanted to punch him.

Her right leg gave its now familiar twinge as she turned and left the garden room for the lounge, a simple physical response which carried with it something more. It would never allow her to forget. For six months she had struggled with the horror of that night before Christmas, trying to find some way to reconcile the senseless slaughter with her view of a world that was sane and ordered. She *had* to reconcile it however long it took, because the alternative meant insanity. She had witnessed the rules of nature turned on their head. She had seen a man get up and walk away from a fatal gunshot. The one who had charmed her as Morrison and horrified her as Wilde. Whatever he was, man or monster, he haunted her nights and stalked her days. She had not felt safe since the emergency services had rushed her to hospital; not through her debriefing by the authorities, her recuperation, her return to university, and not even back here in Riddington where she had thought everything would be all right, as it had always been.

Her only hope, she had found, was to immerse herself in the mundane. Not to think or feel, just to *do*. As a solution, it was hopelessly short-sighted, but it kept her sane and that was all she could hope for until an exit presented itself. In Riddington, the mundane was easy to find.

She walked aimlessly round the lounge and then plucked the postcard from the mantelpiece and read the back for the fifth time: 'Glad you're not here, love Dad and Mum.'

She smiled; her father used the same pathetic joke each year. Briefly, she imagined them lazing in the sun in the South of France. A whole summer away, one of the perks of her father's job as a wine importer. There was always someone else to run the business. He feigned joy at escaping from his daughter's 'barbed wit and political arguments', but every year he asked her to go with them and always looked disappointed when she refused. That made her feel guilty, but holidays were never the same without Robert.

This year she told her father she had to think about the future, and that was partly the truth; she didn't have one. No plans, no job prospects, nothing, and she needed time alone to make a decision. She couldn't tell him the whole truth – that the world outside Riddington was too frightening a place to face. Still, she missed them both and the end of September seemed a long time away.

In the corner of the room sat a pile of her records, tapes and CDs, with more stacked in her room upstairs. She had always loved music, but it was her drug now; uppers when she felt too depressed, tranqs when her anxiety wouldn't let her sleep or think. Within that small collection were all her emotions, thoughts and memories, just waiting for a stylus or a laser to draw them out, and the old stuff was the best – whether it was *really* old like Sinatra or just slightly old like Teardrop Explodes, or Echo and the Bunnymen, or some other eighties band. She used to like new music just as much, but these days it seemed to unnerve her for some reason.

She selected one LP at random and saw it was Robert's favourite – The Stone Roses' debut, dog-eared and worn with a coffee cup ring in the middle of it – and suddenly the memories hit her like a train. At the graveside, a cold spring day with a wan light making everyone look sickly. Standing there, numb, staring at the coffin and thinking of Robert within. Wondering what had happened to their childhood, the horse-riding, the gymnastics, the quiet times, just chatting in the lounge after Sunday dinner, then falling asleep in front of the TV.

It wasn't just her brother that had gone that day; the part of her she thought was invincible had disappeared too. And now look at her; pathetic, weak; she hated herself. How did others cope? Why was she so different?

The knock on the door was slow and laboured. Martyn was there with his lazy, lopsided grin and sandy hair bleached even lighter by the sun, a few freckles that made him seem younger than he was and the coolest blue eyes that had first attracted her to him. She tried to give him attitude, but she didn't have the energy.

'You're late.'

'Gimme a break. In this heat I feel like I've run a marathon just walking up here.' Sweat patches stained his underarms and scrawny chest. He wandered past her and through to the lounge where he dawdled absently, picking up the postcard, reading it over and then making to return it to a different place.

'You're still as irritating, aren't you?' She took the postcard and put it back.

'You wouldn't have it any other way.' He flopped on to the sofa and draped his legs along the edge. 'Don't you get lonely here? You know, with your mum and dad away?'

'I'm enjoying a bit of privacy and peace and quiet. And if you're angling to sleep over *to keep me company*, you can forget it.'

Martyn held up his hands defensively. 'There was a time when you wouldn't have complained . . .'

'I was young and foolish then. Or maybe the word is stupid. We're friends now. You know what friends means?'

'Yeah. No sex.' He leant over the arm of the sofa to where she had piled her CDs and began to flick through them casually. 'I don't know what's happened to you in the three years you've been at that university.' He made it sound like an insult. 'You used to like cutting edge music. All this stuff is old – The Doors, Marvin Gaye, Teardrop Explodes, Velvet Underground. Since when did you start living in the past?'

Annie ignored his question. She was trying to recall what she was like a lifetime ago when she was a childlike eighteen-year-old and the ripe, wise, old age of twenty-one had seemed a distant, insurmountable peak. She had loved Martyn then, in that blind, unthinking way of someone who doesn't know any better. Looking at him now in his too tight t-shirt and his out-of-date jeans, she wondered how she had ever felt so strongly. In those days, Martyn Nash had been the prize catch in Riddington. He was cool in his own provincial way, rebellious and good-looking compared to the other thick-necked farmers' sons. Yes, Martyn Nash, so in demand he had stunned her, transforming her into a deferential, gooey-eyed follower. His word was law, but she didn't care because she was with him. But then Robert died, and university beckoned, and she had travelled a million miles through time and space. And now she'd returned, Martyn was still standing on the same spot.

'I'm glad you've come home, Annie.' His voice floated up from behind the arm of the sofa where he had taken it upon himself to shuffle the CDs out of their carefully arranged, alphabetically ordered regimen. Then he looked up and his eyes still held the sensitivity and innocence of old, and briefly she *could* remember, but it was a different feeling, tangled with

36

nostalgia; an affection for an old friend who had supported her through the most harrowing period of her life. It was a powerful force for her, but Martyn would never settle for it.

'It's nice to be back,' she replied noncommittally.

'You really have changed.' He was looking in her face, for once, with wide, searching eyes. 'You've grown up. When we were seeing each other, I always felt you were a little girl. Little Annie. Now, sometimes you seem like you're ten years older than me.'

She just smiled. He could never grasp what had changed her.

'It must have been very exciting. Up there. At university.' His words were measured. 'All those smart people sitting around drinking and talking about politics and philosophy. Very ... enlightening.'

'It wasn't quite like that, Martyn.' She grabbed his hand and pulled him to his feet. 'Come on, let's go. It's got to be cooler down by the stream.'

As she turned her leg twinged again and she grimaced.

'Does it still hurt?'

'Sometimes. It'll get easier with time, but the doctor says I'll never be completely rid of it.' She thought of all the weeks in a cast, losing last Christmas to a constant barrage of itching, then trying to get around campus on crutches.

And then she thought of the other things – his eyes, his smile. His hands twisting bone and gristle.

Her thoughts must have shown on her face, for Martyn was quickly at her side, a comforting arm around her waist.

'Do you still think about it?' he asked tentatively.

'Only when stupid shits like you bring it up.'

'I'm sorry ...'

'I'm joking. Yes, I still think about it, but not as much as I used to,' she lied. 'Now it only comes to me at night, when I'm trying to go to sleep. Sometimes I close my eyes and I can see it ...' Her voice trailed off.

'The wreckage?'

She nodded, but it wasn't what she meant. *His face*, that's what she wanted to say.

She stepped out on to the pavement and felt the oppressive heat beating down on her shoulders. The glare from the road and the houses gave her a permanent squint outdoors. Martyn was standing a little too close to her, and she jostled him to one side so she could lock the door. That was a hangover from her days in Manchester – in Riddington it had never been necessary.

'Do you still feel bad that they didn't believe you?'

Annie flinched; she did feel bad, even months later. To be met by such a wall of disbelief had been at first disconcerting and then dehumanizing. She knew what she had seen with her own eyes, but everyone from the ambulance workers through the reporters, and the police, to the Department of Transport investigators had treated her like some bimbo who barely knew what she was travelling on, never mind what had caused the crash. She could still feel the smart of their unconcealed sneers when she had said one man was behind it all.

'I can understand it.' She tried to hide her bitterness. 'It does sound unbelievable. One man, all those deaths. It doesn't add up. It's insane.' She looked round at the empty street, the thatched cottages, the old, jumbled houses with their quiet residents, but all she could see were broken bodies, twisted metal and bloodstains on the snow.

'Did the counselling help?'

'No.'

'You don't want to talk about it, do you?'

'For a hayseed who thinks Iron Maiden are the epitome of musical excellence, you're very perceptive, Martyn.'

'Duh. Was that an insult?' He put on a comic yokel accent. 'You educated folk with your big words. Hyuck yuck.'

He took her arm and for once she let him.

Their lazy route around the village eventually brought them to the church. St Martin's was on the outskirts, perched on a high point where it could overlook all its devout subjects and where they could see its stern reminder whatever they were doing. Colin Barnwell, the verger, was examining the cracked, ancient wood of the lych gate as they approached, his frown speaking of more repairs, more expense. Annie had always liked his humour and humanity, but she couldn't bear the questions she knew he would ask; she held Martyn back with one hand while she considered turning back or crossing the road.

'Ho! Annie Boulton!'

Too late. She smiled and hoped it didn't reflect the discomfort fluttering away in her stomach. *Why wouldn't people leave her alone?*

38

'Terrible weather, isn't it?' Barnwell said as he came over. There was a sheen of sweat on his ruddy face. He was carrying a bit too much weight, a result of his nightly trips to the Royal Oak. 'Listen to me! Moaning when it's raining, moaning when it's sunny. So how are you, Annie?'

'Fine, Mr Barnwell.'

'Been home long?'

'Not long. I finished my exams and I'm just killing time until the results come out. You know how it is . . . making the most of my last bit of freedom.'

'Ah, and then it's off to a wonderful job somewhere, I would imagine, leaving us all far behind.' Annie smiled politely. Barnwell tugged at his salt-and-pepper beard and Annie thought instantly, *Here it comes*. 'So will we be seeing you at church?'

'I don't really know what I'm going to be doing, Mr Barnwell. There's a lot—'

'You used to be such a regular. It was a joy to have you there, Annie.'

What could she say? That her faith went up in a puff of smoke with Robert's death? It was the truth. And after the train crash . . .

Recognizing that the conversation had taken a personal turn, Martyn hung back, allowing Barnwell the opening to move in closer. 'I don't know what's happened, Annie, but if you want to talk about it, I'm willing to listen. And I know Father Tony would too. Neither of us likes to see the change that's come over you. You used to be such a happy-go-lucky girl, always smiling, always cheering everyone up. Now . . .'

'Now I've grown up, Mr Barnwell.'

He bit his lip. Annie felt guilty at throwing back his offer of help. She could see the honest concern in his face, but it wasn't any of his business. It wasn't anybody's business apart from her own.

'Just do me one favour, Annie. Father Tony is having a coffee morning at the rectory tomorrow morning. It's nothing formal, just a little get-together for some of the villagers. We'd love you to come along too.'

'Who's going?'

'Well, it's really for Brian Swift,' he said with a sigh. 'You know Brian? He's, what, in his late thirties now? His mother was a bit domineering, kept him away from the girls. But she

39

passed away a few weeks ago, and Father Tony feels Brian may be taking it a little hard, feels it would do him good to mix with others who've lost loved ones over the last couple of years or so, just to see how they've coped. It might help him through this time of grief.'

'Well . . .'

'If not for us, Annie, for Brian. He needs us all now.'

Annie squirmed inside. It felt like a cheap shot for the verger to call on her sense of obligation, although she knew he hadn't done it consciously. There was no real choice, though.

'I'll see what I can do, Mr Barnwell.'

The Gilwiskow Brook ran through the section of the village known as The Hollows. As the name implied, it was lower than the area around the High Street and it always flooded in spring. But in the summer it was a godsend; cool and peaceful, tall trees lining both banks, channelling what little breeze there was.

Annie lay on the grassy bank, dangling her feet in the cool water and watching a patch of clear blue sky above the treetops; the relief from the heat had lulled her into a lazy, easy-going state where not even Martyn could irritate her. He was sitting nearby, flicking pebbles into the water, for once quiet and thoughtful. Perhaps he was recalling, as she was, how this scene had taken place so many times in the past when they had been younger and in love. A world away.

'Oh, for the lazy days of youth!' Annie recognized the rich, low voice immediately. It triggered instant memories of her childhood, of fantastic stories told on a bright summer's day in the shade of the Miller barn, snippets of magical information which she treasured and had retold a hundred times.

'George!' she cried, rolling on to her stomach and jumping to her feet. George Newton didn't look as she remembered, even from a few months ago, but his grey eyes still sparkled and he still had the friendliest smile she knew. He had been ill, she had heard on the village grapevine, packed off to the hospital in Burton for many weeks and then confined to home. No one knew quite what had been wrong with him, but his wrinkled face now bore a few more lines and his cheeks had turned from chubby to hollow.

He grinned and lifted the old floppy hat he had been wearing for as long as she had known him. 'And how are you, my dear? I heard about that awful thing you were involved in.'

'Forget about me – I'm fine. How are *you*?'

'Remarkably spry and jolly for eighty-two!' He took her hand and patted the back of it. His manner brushed away any suggestion of ill health. 'And look at you – the prettiest woman in the village. Whatever happened to that little girl who used to pester me for stories about ghosts and witches and bogles?'

'Oh, she's still here. She's just a bit taller.' Annie gave his hand a warm squeeze. She was amazed at how happy he always seemed. His life had been far from easy: years of excruciating labour down the pit, soaked in water for so long his spine had started to crumble; losing the young wife he doted on and never having any children of his own to warm his twilight years. George had plenty to moan about, but he never did, never seemed lonely, always thought of others and greeted them sunnily. *What's your secret, George?* Annie thought as she looked into his eyes.

'Come and sit down for a while,' she said, eager for his company. 'Tell us some of your tall stories. I haven't heard one in years.'

'Sit on the grass at my age? No thank you, young lady.' He rested on the wooden stick with the wolf-shaped handle he had carved before Annie was born. 'And what's all this about tall stories? Every word I told you was the truth and nothing but the truth.'

'Oh, of course, George! The Willesley werewolf, the vampire in Measham, the ghost at Staunton Harold. Everyday occurrences.'

'Ah, my dear, you've spent so long in the city you think the world of bank managers and shops is all there is.'

'Too much reality does that to you.'

'It does indeed. Stranger things happen hereabouts. They call this the haunted country, you know – Leicestershire, Derbyshire and Staffordshire.'

'Oh?'

'That's right. The old ways still carry on.'

'I suppose you're going to mention Croxton now?'

'And why not? If something odd or haunted is going to happen, it will happen in Croxton. They've been plagued for years. They just accept it as normal now.'

'Years of interbreeding, that's all it is, George.'

'And there was that explosion at the pit up the road . . .'

'But that was an accident!'

'They never did find the cause. And there were other funny things happening round there at the time.'

'George!' Annie burst out laughing and clasped her arms around him. George laughed too, surprised by her show of affection.

He raised one hand and quoted theatrically: '"While yet a boy I sought for ghosts, and sped Through many a listening chamber, cave and ruin, And starlight wood, with fearful steps pursuing Hopes of high talk with the departed dead."'

'And who would that be?'

'So much for education today,' he tutted. 'I thought you studied literature up there in the cold North. Why it's good old Percy Shelley, of course. "Hymn to Intellectual Beauty."'

'So how are you, Mr Newton?' Martyn had wandered up to them while they were hugging.

'Well, young lad. I hope you're looking after my favourite little girl here.'

'Doing the best I can, but you know how Annie is . . . she likes to stand on her own.'

'Yes, very independent, our Annie Boulton,' George replied, winking at her. 'She was always that way, even when she was a little lass. The brightest spark in the village, that's what we used to say. Bursting with energy, full of beans, and always looking for something exciting and new. It's a good job you grew up or I would have run out of stories and then where would my reputation be?'

'George . . .' Annie cautioned light-heartedly.

Martyn shuffled awkwardly, feeling like an outsider. Annie could see what was on his mind: *I wish this old git would hurry up and go*, and she hated him a bit for it. George was special to her. As a child his tales had instilled in her a sense of wonder that sent her flying. In a village where people kept their horizons close to them, he had taught her to dream of the wondrous world beyond. She felt a sudden pang of guilt that she had in some way let him down.

'Well, I better be on my way,' he was saying, giving her a supportive pat on her arm as if he could sense her thoughts.

'You young folk don't want an old man like me hanging around. I must be away to seek out more strangeness.'

'You won't find much of that in Riddington,' Martyn said with a laugh. 'Dull as dishwater, this place.'

George's face darkened as he looked past them upstream. 'Oh, we've had our share of strangeness.'

Annie's blood ran cold as she turned and followed his gaze, over the slow, soothing water that gurgled peacefully past the clipped lawns of the large homes that backed on to The Hollows, past the gnarled, ancient trees, to the sun-bleached brick bridge.

The Loving Bridge was old – 'first built in 1690', the village history book said – and it had a quaint, reassuring solidity for anyone who didn't *know*. Rebuilt and modernized down the years, the bricks were still old and carved with the initials of lovers who had first kissed in Annie's great-great-great-grandparents' youth. It was bald and bright in the sunlight, but Annie's eyes were automatically drawn to the seething darkness that lay beneath it, where the pleasant waters became black glass and disappeared into the shadows.

She shivered, remembering, as everyone in the village would remember for the rest of their lives.

'Let's all pray,' George said quietly, 'that that kind of strangeness never comes back again.'

George Newton pulled his hat down low as he turned along Colthorpe Road into the sun. He felt weak and his legs and arms ached unceasingly. The illness had taken a lot out of him, and he didn't have long to go; he knew that in the same way that he knew when a storm was blowing up or when the first snows of winter would fall. And recently he had had the strangest feeling that winter was coming early with dark days and cold nights, despite the heat of mid-summer. A wind rustled through the treetops, and he paused and looked up. There were bad vibrations in the air.

The school lunch bell was followed a minute later by a cacophony of voices as the children tumbled out into freedom. Annie watched them lazily, aching for that innocence which separated her from childhood. As her thoughts flew back down the days to when she had played kiss-chase and tag in that very same playground, she noticed near the railings a young woman trying to get her attention.

Jane Sutherland was eight years older than Annie, but they had hit it off during a games night at the Royal Oak two years earlier. They had kept in touch ever since, enjoying a shared belief in open-mindedness in a village of entrenched views. Annie was the only person to know of Jane's affair with Tim Huxton-Smith, a big-boned, big-bellied pig of a man who farmed his land without thought for anything apart from maximizing his profit. He had polluted the stream several times with his slurry and pesticides. Annie couldn't understand what Jane saw in him, nor why she had taken up with a married man, but she kept her doubts silent when Jane said she was in love.

Annie left Martyn dozing in the shade and walked over to the school gates. Jane looked cool and demure in a billowing silk dress, her long brown hair pulled back from her face.

'I see the wild horses dragged you back,' Jane said with a smile.

'I'm hooked on boredom. Boredom and gossip. If I don't get that Riddington high, my life is meaningless. So how's you? How's love?'

'Same as ever. Snatched moments. I'm an expert at having sex in a Land Rover without putting my back out.' Then Jane shook her head. 'Sometimes I think he flaunts it. I reckon he likes the danger. You know how perverse men are. The more chance there is of his wife finding out, the more he loves it. How about you? Any new men?'

'Oh, I'm too intense,' Anne replied, thinking she should say *These days I don't even try.* 'And too smart. And too beautiful. Maybe one day.'

Jane swung open the gate and took Annie's arm. 'Come on, there's something I want to show you.'

No one saw them as they slipped along the edge of the playground and through the iron gate. It was only a small school, even for a village; just three classrooms in the dark-brick building which hadn't changed in a century. Inside, Annie had another sweeping feeling of nostalgia at the familiar smells, the chalk and wood, and the stale air warmed by sunshine through the big, dusty windows.

'What is it you want me to see? Dirty pictures drawn by 2B?'

'You'll see. You're not really moving back for good, are you?'

'I don't know.' Annie looked away uncomfortably. 'I feel safe

44

here. Charlotte, you know my pal Charlotte, she thinks I'm crazy. She wants me to move to London, share a flat.'

'So why don't you?'

'I love her to bits. I really miss her. She was the one who made university bearable during those first few weeks when it was a bit rough. But I don't know . . . London . . . it's not really me, is it? And she's got this steady boyfriend. I'd feel like a gooseberry.'

'Sounds to me like you're making excuses. You should do it, have a great time. You don't want to be stuck here with the zombies. Tim was asking after you, by the way.'

'He's probably worried about his reputation as a hard man.'

They looked at each other and burst out laughing. Even a year after it had happened, Annie knew Huxton-Smith was still smarting over the childish prank she had played on him in the Royal Oak. It was shortly after he had been caught polluting the brook again and had escaped, as usual, by doling out bribes in the appropriate areas. Most people in the village seemed to accept his wilful disregard for the environment as some mild eccentricity – being a major landowner and a mainstay of the community helped him cover a multitude of sins. But Annie had always hated his contempt for everything but cash, and she'd felt his latest outrage had deserved some revenge. While he was regaling a crowd in the bar with his bravado she had stuck a piece of paper on his back which said: *Pesticides give you a limp dick – official.*

At the same time she had pinned up a poster in the bar with Huxton-Smith's head superimposed on the body of an Aberdeen Angus with the legend, The Real Cause of Mad Cow Disease, printed beneath it. It was a work of art courtesy of Martyn's design skills, which had certainly seen their finest moment.

When Huxton-Smith finally traced the cause of the merriment which had trailed him around the pub, he pretended to see the funny side, but Annie could tell she had made an enemy for life. Still, it marked one of the few times in the last three years when she had felt like her old self, and for that reason alone it was worth it.

Their female laughter echoed lightly along the empty corridor, releasing old ghosts from the child-worn walls. Halfway along, Jane paused at a classroom door and said, 'Have you noticed anything odd?'

'Odd like what?'

'It was something Tim said yesterday. About his sheep acting funny. They keep trying to smash their way through the fence into the next field. They even ignore his dog. They just keep trying to batter their way out like they're scared of something.'

'Perhaps it's all those pesticides he sprays on his crops.'

'That's just what I was thinking. He keeps going on about how unnatural it is. "Sheep don't do that." So it must have disturbed him. And then when this happened ... well, it made me think some pollutant had got into the water supply or something. Look.'

Jane swung open the door and pointed to a row of five cages on a table. There were hamsters in them, each one rattling away on its little wheel so that they sounded like small electric turbines in action.

'Yes, Jane. Hamsters,' Annie laughed. 'Getting exercise like all good hamsters should.'

'No, you don't understand. They've been doing that all day, and all yesterday, and all the day before. Without a break. They haven't eaten or drunk anything. I take them off and show them their food pots, but they just get back on again.'

Annie looked closer. Their beady black eyes were starting to roll and there were traces of white froth on the fur around their mouths.

'They're dying, Annie. It's like they've got some disease that forces them to keep on the move.'

'Maybe they're running away,' she said absently. There was something about the desperation in their frantic movements that made her feel queasy.

The cages rattled in unison, tiny paws clattering on metal, legs pounding unceasingly. The rodents had gone insane.

'Oi! Watch where you're going.'

'For Christ's sake, it's a little boy, not some teenage thug,' Annie said sharply to Martyn. The sight of the dying hamsters had disturbed her. She was still too hot, and her temper was growing shorter by the minute. She should be inside, alone, not with company which would soon feel the sharp lash of her tongue.

'Bloody kids get everywhere.'

'I shouldn't have to remind you, Martyn, that this village is particularly protective of its children.'

He fell silent. She didn't have to say any more; the horror was so close that Riddington people only alluded to it in cryptic comments and dark hints. It was as if to speak about it would suddenly bring that time flooding back.

There was a group of people standing on the pavement at the end of the jitty; some were animated, others shaking their heads mutely, all wearing expressions of concern. Among them Annie recognized Hartley Williams, parish council chairman, bald head red from the sun, and Bill King, fat and muscle merging into one hideous mountain of local builder made very good.

'We could get a JCB over. Dig a few ditches around the fields. That would keep them out.' Annie thought Hartley Williams was going to have a seizure.

'It's private land, Hartley,' someone said. 'We can't go around . . .'

'If we follow the letter of the law, we're lost,' Bill King snarled. 'Once they get on that land, they're there for days, maybe weeks.'

'Well, what do you suggest? Vigilante groups?'

King thought for a moment, unperturbed by the sarcasm, and then nodded and grinned broadly. 'Aye, why not? We've got to protect our community any way we can.'

As Annie tried to squeeze by, Hartley Williams turned to her and pressed sausage fingers around her upper arm.

'What do you think about it, young lady?'

'Think about what?' she replied, shaking herself free.

'Surely you've heard! There's a convoy of those awful New Age Travellers moving to the village. One of the local policemen tipped us off last night. Apparently they were moved on from a site near Loughborough – and they're coming to Jack Tarrant's land. The bloody fool thinks they're harmless, so he's offered 'em space. Before he knows it, they'll be robbing him blind, and us too, defecating in the hedgerows, loud music blaring out at all hours.' He spluttered to a halt.

'I'm sure they're not as bad as all that, Mr Williams,' Annie said reasonably. 'They just have a different lifestyle . . .'

'They're thieves and scroungers living off taxpayers' money,' he snapped and rudely turned his back on her.

As Annie pushed by to join Martyn, she felt the sly eyes of

King and Williams on her as she walked, igniting memories of the times they had stopped her in the street when she was a teenager, improper suggestions lurking just beneath the chat. King, drunk from the pub one lunchtime, had wanted to give her a little kiss and she had allowed him to peck her on the cheek, dodging away before he could work his way around to her mouth.

'Those morons are going to cause a disaster,' she said caustically. 'I can just see Bill King leading a torchlight parade of uptight parishioners.'

'They've got a point, Annie.' Martyn adopted his *I know best* tone, which always irritated her. 'Those travellers don't belong here. They don't follow the law and they don't care about anyone apart from their own group.'

'You know, do you, Martyn?' Annie said tartly. 'I look at it this way . . . we live in a free land where people are free to live as they choose. These people don't want to follow society's rules – well, what's wrong with that? The country isn't going to come crashing to its knees.'

'They're allowed to be free as long as they don't bother anybody else. And they do.' A note of exasperation had crept into his voice.

'Some of them do. Not all of them. And some pensioners go shoplifting in Tesco's, but you don't confine the whole lot of them to senior citizen concentration camps. There are good and bad people in every group. You punish the individual, not the collective.'

'You really are a student, aren't you,' he sneered. 'You're even talking in the language now. Why don't you —'

'Martyn . . .' She spun on her heel and pushed her face into his. '. . . you're really starting to piss me off. Why don't you quit while you're ahead. And while you still have your testicles.'

She left him in no doubt she didn't want him to follow. After she had gone fifty yards, she heard his voice float after her.

'I won the argument.'

That really did annoy her.

Blackstone Cottage was still unbearably hot so she ran herself a tepid bath, poured a glass of orange, and slipped in for a long, relaxing soak. She tried to read, but her eyelids soon grew heavy, and her pristine Armistead Maupin almost fell in the water so she laid it on one side and rested.

In that hazy half-world, the dream images flickered in and out of her consciousness until her mind had difficulty telling what was real and what was not. Her brother was there, funny and sharp and irritating. She could even smell him, the Aramis aftershave he was convinced would help get him a girlfriend. '*What are you doing, Black Head? Get out of the bath.*' His soft voice floated through time, reminding her of his games and taunts, love and antagonism rolled into one. There he was in his favourite leather jacket that he secretly thought made him look like James Dean. She had spied him acting out a scene from *East of Eden* before his bedroom mirror one night when he was preparing to go out. And there was his motorcycle helmet . . .

No. Not that.

. . . the orange one with his name written on the back. Annie remembered how proud he was the day he'd bought the fourth-hand 50cc Honda, symbol of his passage from boyhood to being a man. There he was, putting on the helmet, the smoky plastic obscuring his face.

Don't go, Robert . . .

There he was, heading out of the kitchen door to the bike parked on the yard outside. One last turn, a hidden smile, a wave . . .

Annie hadn't really been there to see him go that night, but she had played it over so many times in her mind that she almost believed she had been; it was so lucid. That familiar swell of blue emotion, claustrophobically intense, started in the pit of her stomach and began its slow, clawing takeover.

She tried to think of something else, and for a moment it worked, but then Robert was there again, still turning and waving, trapped in his own time loop.

Only this time it was different. Something jarred in that mistily focused image, a shadow hovering behind him, out in the yard near the bike. Annie tried to pull details from the umbra, and slowly a head, features, began to coalesce.

Black hair, beard, moustache. Olive skin. A gold earring. Black, piercing eyes.

The figure beckoned to Robert, holding out the keys to the

bike, and Robert went to him happily, slapping him on the back as he mounted the shiny blue Honda.

And then the figure turned and beckoned to Annie.

Water gushed over the edge of the bath as Annie submerged and then fought her way to the surface, gasping and flailing as she was jolted from her doze. There was a second of panic and then she calmed herself.

'Jesus,' she muttered. Her mother had always warned her about falling asleep in the bath. Slowly, her breathing subsided, but the daydream would not go away. She remembered Robert.

And she remembered the other.

For the first time that summer, she shivered.

'Thank you for coming, Annie.' Father Tony Aris sipped his coffee and surveyed the lounge. The chink of spoons in saucers and the soft mutterings of conversation filled the room.

'That's OK, Father Tony,' Annie replied graciously. But it wasn't OK; it seemed like she had a steel bolt lodged in her throat. She had felt uneasy the moment she had stepped into the rectory to be greeted by Tony Aris and Colin Barnwell with their simple, unswerving faith. Annie envied them their lack of doubt, the way life seemed to wash over them without buffeting them even slightly. Always a smile, always a warm handshake. The truth was, the rectory, the church, the dog collar, the cross, it all reminded her of Robert's funeral. There was something about religion that was always connected with death; it wouldn't let you forget the end was always near. Who wanted to be reminded of that every day?

The others in the rectory that morning did little to dispel her thoughts. There was Brian Swift, the reason they were all there, looking emotionless, an enormous owl blinking away behind his too-thick glasses as if observing some alien civilization. And others, touched by death, from a couple who had lost their baby son to cot death – or Sudden Infant Death Syndrome as the doctors called it now – to a woman whose senile father had died more than a year ago, and a man whose fiancée had been killed in a hit-and-run. Annie knew them all, the sad stories that had taken over happy lives.

Father Tony was wandering around the room shaking hands and smiling. She heard him mumble, 'Even though we are in life we are in the midst of death.' As if that made it all right. And although she guessed it might comfort someone, all she wanted to do was shout out *Shut up, you miserable git!* And then she felt guilty, and the guilt bred black thoughts and the whole cycle started again.

Colin Barnwell came over and touched her forearm. 'How are you, Annie?'

'You know what this place needs, Mr Barnwell?' she said. 'A clown with shoes that squeak and a flower that squirts water.'

'Oh?' He raised his eyebrows questioningly.

'Are you happy, Mr Barnwell? Here in the village, in your life?'

His eyebrows started to rise again, but then he seemed to see the truth behind her question and he nodded thoughtfully. 'I am, yes. Not blissfully, of course. No one is all the time. *Content* would probably be a better word. The family's under no great pressure. We've got a holiday to look forward to . . .'

'Don't you worry about dying?'

He tried to meet her eye, but she let her gaze wander around the room, resting on nothing in particular. He chose his words carefully and then replied, 'Why worry about that? There's too much to do today. Every day.'

'Sure.' It sounded more sarcastic than she intended.

'Annie,' he began sagely, 'learning how to cope with death is all part of maturing as a human being. The society we have doesn't make that easy – it's true to say that a veil is drawn over the whole process. The Victorians had the right idea. Grief was public and monuments to the dead were huge so no one could lose sight of them. Much healthier, I think. Now we spend all our time and energy trying to fool ourselves that we are immortal. Children cope with death the best, but somewhere down the line we lose that ability. Children have an innate understanding . . .'

'That's because they have no doubts about an afterlife,' Annie interjected. 'You believe everything you're told at that age.'

'Do you have doubts, Annie?'

Her attention had wandered. Colin Barnwell followed her gaze to a woman who stood apart from the others with her three teenage daughters and a younger boy. The Cockburns. They had a reputation for being low-lifers. Everyone in the village had been afraid of the drunken bully-boy of a husband until he had died in a fall at home a year ago. Even though he was no longer around, everyone still treated the family as outsiders. Perhaps it was the way they looked; the children all wore cheap clothes and the mother had a wild-eyed look offset by unkempt, badly dyed black hair. As Annie stared she realized what had caught her attention: there was something wrong with the woman. She was swaying from side to side and staring glassily into the middle-distance.

Suddenly she dropped to her knees with a shriek. Her hands were in her hair pulling at it furiously while alternately cursing and sobbing. Her voice produced a strange wailing, like an air-raid siren, while her fingers left red nail marks on the white skin of her face. The son dropped to his knees to help her up, but she threw him backwards.

While everyone else looked on aghast, Annie moved quickly to Mrs Cockburn's side. Her arm went round the woman's shoulders and this time Mrs Cockburn did allow herself to be helped up and led out to the kitchen; Mrs Cockburn didn't seem to know Annie was there.

Embarrassment forced the others in the room to return to their conversations as if nothing had happened, although Father Tony did venture towards the kitchen before Annie waved him away. After a minute, the children trailed through and while the girls crowded round their mother, Annie dropped to her haunches before the young boy who, she guessed, was around nine or ten. He had a mop of sandy-brown hair, and sharp, intelligent eyes, but where he should have had an easy, open smile to match his youth, there was only a deep seriousness which wouldn't have looked out of place on a man of fifty.

'What's your name?' she asked gently.

His eyes darted worriedly from her to his mother. 'Peter.'

'Peter, is your mummy all right? Does she need to see a doctor?'

He shook his head. 'She's been like this since Dad died, on and off. She just needs to lie down for a bit.' For a moment pride hardened his features. 'We'll look after her. We always do.'

Before Annie could ask any more, Peter thanked her in a strangely formal manner and then he led the girls and their mother quietly out of the back door; Mrs Cockburn looked like a hunched, old crow.

Annie realized she couldn't take any more. She went back

52

into the lounge and said goodbye to Father Tony and Colin Barnwell, hurrying away like a small black cloud as soon as she had done so.

Riddington lay slumbering like an overweight dog in the baking heat of the day. Nothing moved in Church Street, where little Amy Skinner had died in 1986 when a teenage driver ran into the horse she was riding. In Colthorpe Road, where Con O'Sullivan was found dead in the gutter after celebrating his 75th birthday with a three-day binge in 1967, the only sound was the occasional tinkle of wind chimes in the porch of Forge House. And in The Hollows, where the unidentified body of a two-day-old baby girl was discovered floating in the stream in 1952, there was just the rustle of leaves on the avenue of trees. The village was as constant as the turning of the seasons; babies were born, old people died, but the village lived on, unchanging, guarding its secrets jealously, harbouring hidden grudges and unwise romances, secure and safe and protected.

At St Martin's Church, the Reverend Tony Aris emerged from the coffee morning and stood in the shade of the lych gate near the yew while he fanned himself with a folded copy of the *Daily Telegraph*. He had experienced hotter weather, during his time with the navy sailing off the coast of Africa, but this heat was irritating in a different way; it seemed to wrap itself around his head and burrow into his lungs so that he had trouble breathing. He looked across the graveyard to the fine old church he had been proud to call his for ten years that summer. It had a sense of history and power that came from years of worship, and in that he found his security. The heat would go soon, but the church would still be there.

Although he tried to fight it, his eyes were drawn to that one particular corner of the churchyard where the grass was never cut, and the weeds multiplied and choked the shiny black granite of the gravestone as if trying to obscure it for ever. No one ever chose to visit that corner, and if anyone strayed there by accident, they would invariably come to their senses with a jolt, and then hurry away without a backward glance. Clinging to those few square feet was an absorbent atmosphere that was like the feeling in the coldest, darkest prison; it radiated up out of the ground in black waves. Tony Aris would not go there either.

At the same time, up in The Green House on Starling Lane, Hilly Pitt was sneaking up to the small room and her now worn collection of photo albums, hoping her husband would not find her and shout at her to forget, to let it go. How could she? Every day, at different times to fool him, she went there to cry about a life that might have been and to wonder why. Her grief was a cold rock that would weigh her down for ever.

And in numerous homes throughout the village, parents of a certain age still flinched when they saw their younger neighbours pack their charges off to school, still shook their heads when they saw the children laughing and playing in the street while the mothers stayed at home and the fathers went to work.

And in the Royal Oak, Alexander Alcock had hung a picture on the wall of the lounge so that people would never forget. But no one ever looked at it, although everyone knew it was there, and the table beneath it was always empty. Alexander Alcock never was a good judge of human nature. People didn't need to be reminded; the details squirmed in their minds like maggots in a carcass.

On the main road into Riddington was a wooden post bearing an ornate frame from which hung a sign that flapped in the breeze. It said: 'WINNER – BEST KEPT VILLAGE AWARD'. For Riddington *was* kept very nicely. The verges were trimmed and straight and no litter stayed on the streets for long. The gardens were a joy to behold, a beautiful, colourful, scented mass of honeysuckle, clematis, roses, wisteria and more; everyone tried to outdo each other.

Yes, Riddington lay slumbering in the baking heat of the day, and deep within the cool, dark private places of its homes and businesses, it kept its secrets carefully.

3

They came just after dawn, rolling through the village from the direction of Loughborough, a rebel army convoy heading for the front line. Pole position was borne by a black single-decker bus of fifties vintage, still bearing the dust of Stonehenge and the mud of Glastonbury. The windows were blacked out and only the driver was visible, an unshaven twenty-year-old with dreadlocks. Other vehicles followed, plucked from history and given a new life through sensitive mechanical surgery: lumbering lorries with strange machinery in the back covered by tarpaulins; squat bug-like vans; elephantine trailers that would suit a movie star; discarded ambulances; a renovated hearse; all of them trundling slowly in line.

At first there were only a few to see the arrival; the milkman who greeted them with a cheery wave and who received one in turn; the assistant at the village shop who stared with growing horror; the newsagent who swiftly got on the phone.

Soon others were out, drawn from sleep by the deep-seated rumble or by a flurry of anxiously ringing telephones. Bleary-eyed, they peered from behind bedroom curtains or stumbled out of their front doors as they tried to make sense of this harsh disruption to Riddington's usual tranquillity.

Martine Alcock only just prevented her husband from running out of the pub to brandish his shotgun as 'a show of strength'. Instead he had to be content with yelling obscenities out of the spare bedroom, his voice lost in the grind of the labouring engines.

George Newton was chewing on a piece of toast in front of the fire as he always did at that time of day; sleep seemed less and less of a necessity. He went out into the early light and stood in the garden until the last vehicle had long gone. Their passage had awakened memories of the wonderment he'd felt as a boy watching the processions of proud miners from the surrounding coal villages as they celebrated hard labour and good life. The parades had disappeared with the pits, and George had lost something from his life too. There, in his front garden, he briefly sensed it again; a feeling of freedom and pride, and of love of life. It was just a whiff and then it was gone, but as he wandered back inside to his toast he thought that for one more time he really ought to seek it out again.

Hartley Williams thundered at his wife with such scarlet rage she thought he was going to hit her. She ran to the kitchen and started to prepare breakfast with much clattering of pans although it was almost three hours until they normally ate. After a few minutes her husband's anger subsided to a quiet seething which she knew from experience was infinitely worse.

He was plotting something and she didn't expect it would be very nice.

Martyn Nash slept, dreaming fondly of his former girlfriend. And Annie Boulton stirred once as the convoy passed by Blackstone Cottage; she was also dreaming dreams, yet hers were dark and strangely exciting.

Eventually, the disparate group of ageing vehicles completed its journey along the High Street and trundled off in the direction of Jack Tarrant's farm. When it had gone, the birdsong started once more.

Annie had only dropped into the newsagent's to buy a *New Musical Express* to read in the garden's shade before the heat of the morning grew too unbearable. She hadn't anticipated running into a congregation of the busiest bodies in the village *en route*. Rather than get dragged into their midst, she turned back, only to be confronted by Martyn, leaning, arms folded, against the post box.

'You've heard the news then?' He grinned and nodded in the direction of the mêlée that was blocking the path to the post office.

'How could I miss it? The Martians have landed. Riddington is about to be invaded.'

'You know this place, Annie. It was big news when Tom Roper painted his front door pink. Next to that, this *is* the Martians landing.' He hooked an arm through hers and she shook it off. 'So what shall we do today?'

'Why don't you go down to the Job Centre?' she replied with an acid smile.

'No point,' he said cheerily. 'No one wants a loser like me.'

'You said it.' Then she added thoughtfully, 'Let's go up to see the travellers.'

Martyn looked at her as if she had gone crazy and instantly she felt irritated; that same expression had punished her too many times when she was younger and weaker. 'No fraternizing with the enemy,' he said.

'That's just what I'd expect from you, you conservative bastard. You're turning into Hartley Williams. For God's sake Martyn, they only want to be free and have fun. Are there any of those words you don't understand? Like *freedom* and *fun*?'

Martyn shrugged at her sarcasm, which irritated her all the

more. 'You know how I feel,' he said. 'They're scroungers and crooks. They'll leave rubbish everywhere. They'll cause disruption and then they'll move on. It's not just me who thinks this, Annie.'

'The narrow-mindedness in this village must be catching. You've just soaked up the propaganda.'

'And you're just a typical student. Latching on to a trendy cause and ignoring what's happening in the real world.'

Annie looked at him and wondered how they had ever been close. 'I'll go up there by myself. I fancy spending time with some real people.' She saw the conflict on his face as she started to walk off, but he couldn't bring himself to follow her.

There was a snap of hardness in his last words. 'Don't come crying to me when they attack you.'

As she marched down the High Street in the direction of the travellers' camp, Annie's annoyance was stifled by nature's obvious charms. With the blue skies lofting above the green fields, and the doves drawn out by the sun to coo in the trees, there was a pastoral innocence that was reassuring to someone who had spent months in the inner city. Thoughts of Martyn faded quickly as her step speeded her away from the last few houses.

The travellers' camp was bigger than she had expected. There were around thirty vehicles parked on the hillside at the end of a long lane and locked into a single community: a village on wheels that could uproot itself then settle back down miles away in exactly the same formation. Next to many of the vehicles were tents, some of them big enough to house a family, while on the edge of the camp Annie could make out a couple of Red Indian teepees. A black flag with a white 'A' in a circle fluttered over one of them. There was a central space where preparations had been made for a large fire; logs cut and stacked neatly. To one side, an ageing generator chugged and coughed, churning out electricity for a huge sound system mounted at the back of a lorry; some bass-heavy track throbbed from the two man-size speakers and electric lights had been strung all around. There was a strong smell of cooking, something heavy and musky, but behind it Annie occasionally caught the flowery whiff of marijuana.

As she stood there on the outskirts of the camp, she wondered why she had come. She was an outsider – they wouldn't want anything to do with her – and for a moment she almost turned back. Yet there was something about the jumble of vehicles which ignited a spark within her; it drew her on towards the music. She recognized the lazy, sunshine beat of Soul II Soul's 'Keep on Movin'.' Where Riddington was dusty and repressed, the camp seemed colourful and potentially volatile, just as relaxed, just as secure, yet vibrant.

A few travellers eyed her suspiciously as she approached and eventually a couple of them hurried into a black bus painted with a yellow peace sign. They emerged a second later with an unshaven man in his late twenties, his hair a cluster of black dreadlocks. He was wearing a black boiler suit open to the waist and scuffed Doc Martens. The dreadlock man and his compatriots – a youth with bleached hair and a bad case of acne, and a girl in combat gear – marched straight over to Annie to halt her progress.

'Hello,' she said. There was a nervous tension in their body language. Annie guessed the kind of welcome they were used to. 'I thought I'd come up here to see how you were getting on. You know, a neighbourly gesture.' She shrugged. 'Actually, I'm just plain nosy.'

The tension eased a little. 'Are you from the village?' The dreadlocked man jerked his head in the direction of Riddington.

Annie nodded. 'You caused quite a stir when you drove through this morning.'

'We cause a stir everywhere,' the youth said bitterly. 'People don't like us.'

'Because we frighten children and burgle houses,' the girl added sarcastically. 'And eat human flesh.'

'We've had a lot of trouble recently,' the dreadlock man interjected. His voice was calming and confident, his eyes sharp and bright; Annie knew he was trying to tell from her face if she was an *us* or a *them*. 'Two weeks ago we were parked near a village up in the Peak District. Some local vigilante group decided they couldn't wait for an eviction order so they thought they'd *advise* us to move on. Two of us are still in hospital. And they burned out one of the vans. We had to dump it.'

'Couldn't the police do anything?'

The girl sneered. 'They probably helped plan it. The fucking cops hate us even more than the locals. When we left the Peaks, they set up road blocks, kept moving us off the main routes all the time, trying to break up the convoy, shifting us from lay-bys. Just generally fucking harassing us every step of the way. We weren't hurting anybody. We just wanted to find a place to park up and rest, get some food. A democracy! Don't make me laugh. It's a fucking police state.'

'Freedom only if your face fits,' the youth added.

Annie looked around the camp. 'You seem to have things well sorted here.'

'It's a good community,' the dreadlock man said, following her gaze. 'We look after each other. All we want is to be left alone. We could care for ourselves pretty well if we didn't get bother from dawn to dusk.' He looked back at Annie and said tentatively, 'Cup of tea?'

The girl bristled, but Annie ignored her. 'That would be nice.'

She followed them to the black bus where the acned youth lit up a small Calor Gas burner and started to boil some water. He did it quietly and without being asked; it seemed to be one of his tasks. The blacked-out windows kept the interior of the bus dark and musty and the rear portion had been curtained off. In the front the seats had been ripped out and replaced with bean bags and large cushions. Patterned cloth hung from the walls like some Arabian prince's tent.

'My name's Tommy,' the dreadlock man said as he slumped on one of the cushions. 'That's Angela and that's Fox. We don't use surnames. They're just restricting.'

'I'm Annie.' She flopped on to a bean bag opposite him. Angela continued to stand, watching Annie with unconcealed wariness. 'Are you staying long?'

Tommy shrugged. 'As long as people let us, which shouldn't be too long. We heard about this land to rent on the travellers' network. The farmer's a bit of an old duffer, but he seems all right. It's a bit harder for them to shift us when we've got permission to stay. A bit harder, but not much.'

He stretched out languidly and closed his eyes. The smell of hash hung in the air, and Annie felt cocooned in the warm gloom.

'What's this place like?' Tommy asked, his eyes still shut.

'It's OK. Just normal, I suppose, same as anywhere else. Quiet, cliquey, conservative.'

'They'll love *us* then,' Fox cackled.

'So what are you doing here? Slumming it?' Angela stared coldly and threateningly.

Annie couldn't hide her irritation any longer. 'I told you why I was here. Which words didn't you understand?'

'You . . .'

'Cool it,' Tommy said. 'Let's stay mellow, Angela.' It was not an order, but his words seemed to carry weight. Angela bit her lip, glared once more at Annie and then walked out. Fox made a face behind her back and laughed before following her.

'What's her problem?' Annie asked.

'Angela's always the same with outsiders. She's had some bad times since she joined us. Beat up by a farmer down in Devon. Had a dog set on her. You learn to live with it, but it makes you a little defensive.'

'What are you going to do if they cause trouble for you here?' Annie suddenly thought of Martyn and his irrational opposition; and he was one of Riddington's more liberal residents.

'Same as we always do. Soak it up for a while and then move on. There's no point being confrontational. I know people only give us a hard time because they're afraid of us 'cos we lead different lives to them. You can't hate them for it.'

'Can't you?'

He shook his head, then sucked thoughtfully on his tongue. 'No, not hate. There's anger, certainly. Sometimes it's like the whole world's against us. You've got Tory MPs raging in the House like we're a threat to the nation, and that's from the party that appeased Hitler. This Criminal Justice Act has made life hell for us. They can break up a gathering of ten or more if they feel it's liable to cause a breach of the peace, and you can't get much more nebulous than that. It's one of the most anti-democratic laws passed in Britain, yet everybody seems to have been blinded by the propaganda. Don't they realize it gives the police the power to break up garden parties and car boot sales, as well as peaceful protests and strikes? The country's traded off a vital piece of national liberty because a bunch of crazy MPs who like to dress up in women's clothes and feather their own nests have convinced them we're the enemy.'

'You don't have to preach to me. I'm the converted.'

'I'm sorry . . . I'm not preaching really, just angry. I just want a quiet life, you know. I want to sit at Stonehenge and watch the sun come up on the solstice. I want to drive around the country and have a different back garden every day. I don't want to overthrow the government or cause trouble for anyone. Yeah, I know there are a few rotten apples who dump litter or nick things or play their music too loud, but we do our best to control them.'

'You said it . . . people are frightened of anything different—'

A loud, wailing scream erupted somewhere nearby. Annie's first thought was: *They've started already*. But before she could give voice to her fears, Tommy had jumped to his feet and was scrambling out of the bus.

Outside there was no sign of Bill King's bully boys, but a crowd of travellers had gathered near a garishly painted transit. Annie kept close behind Tommy as he pushed his way through to the front.

Sitting against the wheel of the van was a youth in his late teens with a shaven head apart from a tiny ponytail at the back. There was a traveller on each side of him, gripping his arms tightly. The youth's eyes rolled wildly as his contorting face shifted through degrees of panic. Annie recognized the signs of a bad trip.

'I told him to lay off that brown acid we picked up in Worcester,' the bearded traveller holding his right arm said. 'After Gil had a bad trip, I knew it was a rotten batch.'

The tripper's eyes focused, unfocused, focused on things no one else could see. Suddenly he started thrashing his arms and legs like a wild animal in a desperate attempt to get away. The travellers holding him pinned him to the ground with their bodies so he couldn't hurt either himself or them.

'Coop, it's Michael,' the bearded one said, stroking the tripper's head rhythmically. 'It's OK. I'm here. You're with friends, Coop. Chill. Listen to my voice. Follow my voice. It's Michael.'

The thrashing continued, but Michael remained calm, repeating his name over and over again until Coop grew still and his gaze snapped back to the real world. In that instant, Annie had the sensation that he was looking directly at her.

'He's coming,' he said in a breaking voice. 'Down the roads, across the fields, over the hills. His eyes are open graves. There's a fridge inside him. I can see his hands . . . they're falcons. Everlasting . . . never escaping . . . none of us are safe. Look after me, oh, look after me. The wings are beating. Oh God.

I'm frozen in ice. I can't get out. Wings . . . wings . . . as sharp as razor . . . oh God!'

His body erupted in another mad thrashing, more frenzied than ever, and it took all of the other two travellers' strength to restrain him.

'Coop! Stay calm! I'm here. Listen . . .'

Michael stopped mid-sentence at the power in his friend's sudden stare. Slowly, Coop's eyes moved across the assembled group.

'He's coming.'

A feeling like winter came over Annie. She looked around at the travellers. No strangers to bad trips, their faces were worried, some almost fearful. They felt it too.

Michael and the other traveller fell backwards as Coop convulsed violently. His face turned ashen in seconds and then he vomited down himself. He continued to retch, barely pausing to catch breath, until his body turned rigid and he lay face down in the contents of his stomach.

The frozen watchers were suddenly galvanized. A couple dashed forward, turning Coop over, wiping his face, checking his pulse. Annie felt fingers close tightly around her wrist and she looked up into Tommy's concerned face.

'We need a hospital.'

'Burton's the closest. About eight miles. I'll show you how to get there.'

Coop was lifted into the back of a van and Tommy leapt in next to the driver, with Annie close behind him. The driver looked at her guardedly, but before he could say anything, Tommy barked, 'She's OK. Do what she says.'

The engine roared, the wheels spewing grass and dust, and then the van skidded across the field towards the road. As they hurtled through the outskirts of the village, they passed Hartley Williams. For one fleeting moment his eyes settled on Annie and widened in surprise before he was lost behind them.

'What was he talking about?' Annie asked, pointing to Coop.

'Just a bad trip,' Tommy replied. 'Who knows what was going through his head.'

But Annie felt him shift uncomfortably in his seat as he spoke, and she knew Coop's words had disturbed him too.

4

John Claridge stopped to wipe the sweat from his forehead and to look at the fat, red sun as it slipped slowly behind the cranes, chimneys and factories that were growing black against the early evening sky. The heat wasn't abating. Stoke baked like one of the potteries that had made the town's name; too hot to move on the streets, too hot to stay indoors.

Claridge had hoped it would be cooler down by the canal, but against the oily water where flies buzzed in clouds amid the smell of petrol fumes and rotting garbage, he felt almost faint.

'Come here, Pike,' he called out half-heartedly as his dog bounded along the towpath towards the thick shadows beneath the bridge. How could the damned thing have so much energy? It should be on its way to a heart attack running around in all that fur.

A pebble looped out from Claridge's toe and plunked into the murky, still water. His shoes were dusty, he noticed; he might clean them tomorrow, but without even the slim prospect of a job interview there seemed little point. And in this heat, no task should be done unless it was absolutely necessary.

The sickly stillness was disrupted as a train thundered by thirty feet away, beyond the tangled mass of scrub. Fleetingly, Claridge wished he was on it, moving off to other places and another life, but it passed quickly. One life, no escape.

'Come on, Pike,' he snapped with new-found irritation. 'Get back here.'

'Dogs, eh. They cannot be trusted.'

The voice made him jump; it seemed to come out of nowhere. Glancing round, Claridge saw the speaker sitting amongst the dry, yellow grass and willow herb, beneath an emaciated ash. Claridge wondered how he had not seen him before. The man was dressed in a black sweater and black Levis despite the weather, but from his skin tone and curly, dark hair, Claridge guessed he was used to the sun.

'All right?' Claridge greeted him politely.

The man nodded in response. 'Nice day, is it not? Do you always walk down here?'

'Oh, aye. It's the only way I can get any bloody peace. Have a bit of time to myself to think.'

'I apologize if I have ruined your stroll.'

'Don't you worry. It was getting a bit too quiet anyways.' The dog scurried back from the shadows of the bridge, snuffling and snorting in the undergrowth. He cast one eye at the man and continued to Claridge's feet. 'Here we are then.'

'What a nice dog. Pike, is it?' Claridge nodded. 'Here, Pike.'

The man rubbed his fingers and thumb together and the dog responded instantly. He sniffed the stranger's fingers and then allowed his head to be scrubbed.

'You're honoured. He's normally wary of strangers.'

'Animals like me,' the man replied distantly. 'I used to be a farmer.'

'What made you give it up? Too many early mornings?'

'Something like that.' His voice drifted away and for a moment he seemed lost in his memories as he stared into the canal. When he looked up his eyes were sharp and bright. 'What is your name?'

Claridge was a little taken back by the question, but his natural politeness shone through. 'John Claridge.' A pause. 'And you?'

The man smiled. 'Gaye. Marvin Gaye.'

'Don't get many folk called Marvin round here.'

'No. No, I do not suppose you would.' Gaye tweaked his beard and smiled at some joke Claridge couldn't grasp. 'Tell me, John. Are you happy?'

It seemed a strange question, and if it was anyone else Claridge might have made his excuses and returned to his journey, but Gaye had a magnetic quality; Claridge had difficulty breaking his gaze. 'Ah, well, no, not really,' he began hesitantly. 'No job, you see. It's tough without work. Bloody dole doesn't go far. Stuck around the house all day ...' He ended his sentence with the shrug of someone who had given in.

Gaye weighed Claridge's words for a moment and then rested his head on the dog's neck, scratching his back affectionately. 'Come on, Pike. Time to go,' he whispered. 'There are rabbits under that bridge. Rabbits!'

The dog's ears perked at Gaye's urging and then it bolted back along the towpath and out of sight. Gaye watched after it, smiling. 'Nice dog.'

'Hey!' Claridge protested.

'Do not worry, John. He will be back.' Gaye stood up and stretched like a cat. His body was strong and supple and he towered above Claridge's stooping, overweight frame. 'Do you know, John? I am bored now. I find I need constant stimulation to maintain my interest. A wandering mind is a heavy burden to bear in this life.'

Before Claridge could ask him what he was talking about, Gaye's arm stretched out quickly. Rigid fingers snapped into an unbreakable hold around Claridge's throat, and then, with only the minimal effort, Gaye lifted him off the ground. Claridge thrashed like a fish on a line, but Gaye's arm held true and eventually Claridge's eyes began to bug out as he gasped for breath. His nails dug into Gaye's wrist until the blood flowed freely, but he could not ease the grip at all.

Gaye watched him intently as he died, drinking in every fleeting expression, every emotion, the surprise, the fear, the despair, the whole tide of his life rushing out of him; Gaye noted it as coldly as a scientist in a laboratory. Eventually, Claridge's legs stopped, gave one, final, violent kick, and then stopped again.

Gaye shook the body. It lolled like a rag doll. Satisfied it was all over, he walked forward and dispassionately dumped it into the water.

When the ripples had subsided, he dropped to his haunches to welcome Pike who loped back up the towpath, wagging his tail with unrestrained affection. The dog licked Gaye's hand and rubbed against him.

'Good boy, Pike! You deserve much better. I would expect a clever dog like you knows his way home, am I right? And there will be someone there to look after you? Good boy, Pike.'

He tapped the dog and it set off back from where it had come. Gaye watched fondly until it disappeared and then his face darkened and he turned back to the water where Claridge's body floated face down, like a bag of old clothes someone had discarded.

The flat, unhealthy silence of the canal was broken once more as a bus rumbled over the bridge, heading out of town. Two ten-year-old boys were yelling the name of a football team out of the window, trying to impress the girls further down the coach. They had harsh haircuts, shaven at the sides, and blank, stupid expressions.

Gaye waited until they had gone and then he concentrated on Claridge's corpse. For five long minutes the scene was frozen; Gaye's body was so rigid, passers-by would have thought him asleep. Inertia lay heavily across the polluted waters.

Slowly, Claridge's body began to move.

It was only the faintest tremor at first, just a brief stirring that could have been attributed to a non-existent breeze ruffling his hair and shifting the weight in the water. Except the movements were too rhythmic. A muscle twitched on his neck. An elbow banged against his ribs. The black water started to lap at the canal sides. And gradually the twitching increased until Claridge's corpse was thrashing like a flounder on the deck of a trawler.

And then the corpse rolled over, awkwardly, as if Claridge had only been sleeping. It lay on its back, pallid, bloated from the water, now an alien fish from the unlighted depths.

Gaye stood up and clicked the aches from his joints. With a theatrical flourish, he raised his hand and passed it across the body.

Claridge's eyes snapped open as if they were steel-sprung, a cold look within them.

The shadows around the canal were growing long. The heat was turning from blazing to suffocating as the sun fell lower, its glaring redness somehow dismal. Gaye smacked his lips like a hungry man preparing for a feast and then said, 'Welcome back.'

A globule of water and saliva erupted from Claridge's mouth. When it had cleared, his awkward lips formed the words, 'It hurts.'

'Life is painful, is it not? Death is so much more comforting. Tell me,' his face grew serious and suddenly seemed very old, '. . . what is it like?'

'It hurts.'

'Please do not carry your stupidity with you to the other side. What is it like in death?'

A brief pause. Then, 'Warm, soothing. A bright light. My . . .'

'Your family is there. Your friends are there. Do you know how many times I have asked the question? Millions upon millions. Billions. Yet the answer is always the same. Insubstantial. Superficial, suggesting a womblike existence. I cannot believe that is all there is, John Claridge.' His bitter laughter

66

trailed off into the growing dusk. 'If I let you go too far, when I bring you back there is something missing. The essential humanity is gone, replaced by a machine mind that can tell me nothing before it slowly deteriorates. Not far enough and all I get are honied words. Somewhere there is the right point, the threshold of the hereafter where all horizons are clear, where all knowledge is open to me.'

The air was thick with midges dancing in the remaining red light. The smell of petrol and cats' urine was everywhere. Gaye watched the midges for a second, trying to recall the first time he had ever seen such a sight, but it was lost in the black halls of memory along with every other forgotten first experience.

'I have killed a lot of people, John Claridge,' he continued introspectively. 'Once I had a reason for what I did. My first kill was born of rage – that I do remember. The second was cold and clinical. He was a good man and that was reason enough to wipe all trace of him from this planet. I do not like *good*, John Claridge. I abhor anything that bears the fingerprint of God. Once I moved among the great and the good and took great pleasure in eliminating as many of them as possible. These days that is no longer so easy. A clumsy kill could draw attention to me quickly. I have already been punished enough – a lifetime's incarceration would be too much to bear. And so I content myself with the little people, who, although good in only tiny ways, are still part of The Great Plan. People like you, John Claridge. Your death will seem like an accident; and so I will be free to carry on as I wish. Oh, yes, occasionally I get the chance to destroy a musician or a painter or a writer – those fumbling to communicate God's voice to the masses – but it is never enough. Now, I try to content myself with quantity, not quality. I kill when I can. I destroy wantonly and if, along the way, I can gain an insight into that final mystery, then that will be my reward.'

A train thundered by, white faces pressed against the glass, staring out into the twilight. When it had passed, Gaye laughed and clapped his hands together.

'Enough! The road still rises, John Claridge. A world before me, a world at my back. Which path should I take? No, that question was not for you. Close that idiot, gaping mouth. For six months, I have drifted. Now I need a campaign.'

Claridge moved up and down in the water, still staring. 'Here is a joke for you, John. What do you call a fat man in the water who has just died a meaningless death? Bob. Get it? Well, that is resurrectionist humour for you, John. Not many laughs, and you have to live with the punchline for all eternity.' He smiled cruelly.

There was a twitch beginning at the corner of Claridge's mouth as if he was growing distressed.

'Do you want to go back?' Gaye looked at him contemptuously.

'Yes.'

Gaye toyed with the idea of leaving him floating there in half-life, but it could never be. There had to be no obvious signs of his own passing if he was to carry on his way unhindered. That was the rule, there were no others. He passed his hand over the body once more, and this time it seemed to grow darker as if some faint luminescence had been extinguished. The eyes fluttered slowly shut and the limbs grew limp until they sagged back in the water into that formless bundle of clothes.

Gaye stepped back from the edge and looked both ways along the towpath. Claridge was already forgotten, an insignificant distraction on his endless journey.

He selected his direction at random and started to walk. There were other people to meet, other questions to be asked.

5

Every joint and muscle throughout his body ached, but after five years of using the nearest hedgerow for a bed, John Severin had got used to the unpleasant sensation. At least the night had not been too cold, and the morning sunlight had taken some of the edge off the numbness that had permeated to his bones.

Most of the time he didn't like England, but today there was no rain again, thankfully, and the heat of the sun reminded him faintly of home, although he tried not to think about that too much. He breathed in the clean air fresh with the smell of hedgerow flowers, felt it fill his lungs, hinting at distant days, buried memories.

Brushing the dust off his clothes, Severin crawled out of the dry ditch that had been his resting place, and stretched as he surveyed the countryside. Exhausted from the previous day's tracking, he had slept too late. Wilde would have a head start on him, and he moved too fast as it was. Pulling his long coat around him, he felt the weight of the shotgun thump against his leg, reminding him, if he needed it, that hedgerow flowers and sun-drenched mornings were no longer part of his life. There was just the hunt.

As he climbed a gate and strode across a field of idle, masticating cows towards the thrum of traffic, his body slowly clipped into life like the machine he had made it. Deep in his head, the compass twitched and turned, the radar bleeped. Unerringly he turned and faced the direction of Stoke. Across his range of vision a wood pigeon swooped and soared and for a second he almost remembered what it was like when he was simply a man, but Wilde's filthy stain across the land drew him back to his new life. Now he was more, like Wilde was more, and he would keep on driving himself until he had enough within him to scrub Wilde's blackness from the face of the earth.

He emerged at the side of the road in the petrol and exhaust fumes, watching the cars zip by. It was busier than he had expected which was a relief; he certainly didn't feel like spending all morning trying to hitch a lift. Nobody offered rides any more, they were too worried about picking up some psycho. You never really know who's out there. He stuck out his thumb and hoped.

Surprisingly his first ride of the day pulled up next to him after only fifteen minutes, some kind of record. It was a blue Nissan Primera, unwashed for three or four weeks, with a couple of scrapes down the side. Severin guessed the driver was a travelling man.

The window rolled down. 'How far are you going?' The speaker was in his mid-forties with sandy hair and a bushy moustache, striped shirt pulling uncomfortably across a bulging stomach.

'As far as you can take me.'

'Any particular destination in mind?'

'Nope. I just need to keep going thataway.' Severin pointed into the glaring distance ahead of them.

The driver flicked the door handle for Severin to climb in. It was warm in the car and smelled of sweaty feet and flatulence. Severin had to ease the passenger seat back a few notches to accommodate his long legs.

Radio 1 was playing 'Nowhere to Run' by Martha Reeves and the Vandellas a little too loudly for conversation. The driver turned it down, and glanced at Severin with an open, smiling face. 'Paul Carmichael,' he said, sticking his right hand sideways.

Severin took it. 'John Severin.'

'American, right? You're a long way from home.'

Severin didn't feel much like making small talk, but he couldn't clam up after being offered a ride. 'It's been a few years since I've been home. I've been on the road, travelling.'

'Sightseeing?'

'Something like that.'

'I spend a lot of time on the road myself. I'm a sales rep. Pet foods. Boring product, I know, but I love the job. On the go all the time. Never the same scenery. Never stuck in one place. I think I'd go mad if I had to work in an office all the time.'

Severin felt almost envious. Once he had been similar, days steady as you go, no surprises, no excitement, yet no shocks either. *Flatliners*, he called people like that, wandering through their existence with no peaks or troughs and no knowledge of the horrors he now experienced on a daily basis. Side by side, the incongruity was almost laughable. Carmichael in his cheap suit and cheap aftershave, with his soft, scrubbed body and smiling, open face. And there was he, wrapped in an overcoat for warmth; drab clothes; hair, long and greasy; five-day stubble, his body hard, trained, filled with power. A man and a more-than-man.

'Where are we headed?' Severin peered through the dusty windshield into the sun.

'The next big town's Stoke-on-Trent. Not very picturesque, you might say, but the locals are nice and friendly. I wouldn't put it at the top of your sightseeing list.' Wilde was there! Severin could sense him, scurrying through the streets like a rat in a sewer, a thick cloud of malignancy following overhead. Severin was sure he was getting closer, if only by a few seconds each time. Soon they would confront each other.

'How are you finding England then?' Carmichael asked.

'Nice place, what I've seen of it,' he lied. 'I've not been here long.'

'Where were you before?'

'Europe ... Italy, Austria, Germany, Spain.' Eventually the countries all blurred into one, an endless succession of roads and fields, cheap flophouses and low-life characters. Only his single-minded determination had kept him going. Five years. Five long, wasted, weary years, never knowing a home, never seeing the same face for more than a few days. He had to fight back his emotion.

'You've certainly seen life then! I'd like to do that myself, take a few months off, but I've got too many responsibilities. Should have done it when I was younger, I suppose. No family yourself, then?'

'Once. A few years ago. They died.'

Carmichael shifted in his seat uncomfortably. 'I'm sorry. Is that why you keep on the move?'

Severin nodded. It was funny. When Marj and Matty went, he couldn't imagine life without them, but his mission had kept him going. One of life's little ironies. What would happen when it was all over?

'How much further to town?'

Carmichael shrugged. 'Ten, eleven miles.'

He would soon find out.

6

It had started off as a couple of drinks and somewhere down the line it turned into an endless stream. The pubs had grown increasingly seedy as Annie and Charlotte Ames wound their way around Leicester city centre, but neither of them cared that the smart clothes of the nightclub set had given way to Union Jack t-shirts and tattoos, and the CD juke boxes to an over-loud karaoke machine.

A man with a neck as wide as his thighs was bawling 'King of the Road' into a microphone with a rough voice that wanted to be Joe Cocker but sounded like a dying man growling for more cigarettes. Opposite them a hideously fat woman sat on the lap of a skeletal man with blue skin and planted huge kisses over his skull-like face.

'We do go to all the best places,' Charlotte said. She couldn't help the supercilious expression which crawled on to her face whenever it was relaxed, and it had made Annie laugh from the moment she had met her three days into her first university term. Charlotte now leaned forward so her long, dark hair fell across her face, hiding the fine-boned features which Annie had always told her were too pretty by far.

'There's art and humanity in true squalor, and don't let's forget it.' Annie lined the Pils bottles across the centre of their table to keep the rest of the pub at bay. She was drunk and happy; no dark thoughts or maudlin moments could survive in her alcohol-rich system. It almost made her want to stay drunk for ever. Charlotte had as much to do with her mood as anything; Charlotte, her best friend. 'I'm so glad you stayed over in Leicester on the way to Douggie's,' Annie told her.

'I couldn't pass through the wasteland that is the Midlands without seeing my best pal, could I? Besides, I'd forgotten what the DTs were like.' She played with her glass for a second and then said, 'So have you thought any more about London? We'd have a great time in a flat, you know we would.'

'Yes, I know, but . . .' She took a deep breath; she hadn't even convinced herself she was taking the right course. 'I'm just not ready for it, Charlotte. I need to get my head together, like the hippies used to say.'

'Well, Riddington is certainly the place to get away from it all.'

'You should see it at the moment. It's a seething pit of passion.'

Charlotte smiled sardonically. 'Right. Sure. The new Sodom and Gomorrah.'

'I'm serious. A bunch of travellers have set up camp on the outskirts of the village. Naturally, everybody's up in arms. You'd think the apocalypse was pending.'

'The travellers aren't hurting anybody, are they?'

''Course not, but you know what village mentality is like.'

Charlotte finished her beer and then said, 'You know you're hiding there in Riddington, Annie.'

'No, I'm . . .' She paused. 'Yes, I *am*.' There was no point in lying; Charlotte knew her better than she knew herself.

Charlotte gave a sympathetic sigh. 'You're still having problems? Why don't you try the therapy again?'

'I just can't face it. It's like turning over too many stones. It's not even just about Robert any more.'

'So what is it about?'

Annie didn't reply. She wanted to tell Charlotte about Wilde but since her brutal treatment at the hands of the crash investigators, she had learnt to repress her memories of that night.

'You're looking tired.' Charlotte sensed not to push her question.

'Thanks. I must remember to compliment you some time.'

'You've had it rough these last few months.'

'Life's a bitch.' Annie threw back her head and emptied the remains of her Pils down her throat. 'Boy, I wish someone would teach me how to be a lady.'

'You don't fool me, Boulton. Why don't you talk about it?'

Annie pinched the bridge of her nose and focused on the beer bottles. There was so much she could say, but the same two words were always at the forefront of her mind.

'I'm afraid.'

'Of what?'

'Everything. Afraid of the future, taking risks, meeting new people, building any kind of relationship, facing up to the world. Christ, how long have you got? I don't know who I am any more. Weak Annie, strong Annie, miserable, happy, light-hearted, serious. Sometimes I feel like I can't go on with all this not knowing. It's like, when Robert died, somebody coshed the real me on the head. Sometimes I think I'm going crazy.'

'Of course you're not!'

'Riddington's the only place where I feel safe and secure. Yet it bores me, can you understand that? Martyn's decent, but he bores me too. I know it's all too cosy and conservative, but I love it and I feel safe there. Shit, I must be pissed!'

'What you need, Annie, is the love of a good man.'

'No, what I need is the love of good *men*. A couple would do for starters. At the same time, preferably.'

Charlotte mugged an expression of shock and Annie laughed loudly. 'You know you'd love it too, you old slut.'

Charlotte laughed conspiratorially. 'It always takes the demon drink to pull out the truth.'

Annie started to play with a silver ankh on a chain around her neck. Charlotte leaned over and examined it closely. 'Been out spending?'

'It's the Egyptian symbol of eternal life. It was Robert's. He was into all that mystical shit – you know what teenage boys are like. I was in his bedroom the other day and I saw it lying on the side. I don't know what it was doing out – Mum's normally obsessive about tidying everything away. I haven't seen it since before he died. It was a bit of a shock, brought back a few memories, but I just fancied wearing it.'

The room grew quiet as a man in a too tight football shirt vacated the small stage at the far end of the pub. The woman in charge of the karaoke called out for the next victim, but there were no takers; everyone waited expectantly.

Annie suddenly felt excited. 'Come on,' she said, pulling at Charlotte's arm.

'What? Up there? You've got to be joking!'

'I think one of us is being a stick-in-the-mud here, Charlotte, and it's not me.' A smattering of applause rippled round the room as Annie stood up, and in the focus of attention Charlotte had to follow.

The walk to the stage was nerve-racking, but exhilarating; Annie loved the feeling of all eyes upon them. They chose their song quickly – 'Road to Nowhere' by Talking Heads – knowing they could perform it in their brassiest voices. The single spotlight was glaring, but Annie was too drunk to care. She glanced at Charlotte and they laughed their secret us-against-them laugh once before the music started. Annie let herself go for the first time in months. Their dance was stupid but sexy, their vocals belting then harmonizing with tongues firmly in cheek, and the crowd loved it. A group of men at the bar were calling for more after the final chorus, so Annie dragged Charlotte back and thrust the microphone at her.

Before they could launch into a new song, Annie's attention was drawn by three women near the door. They were leaning against each other in a tight huddle as they watched the stage. One was ancient, wizened and hook-nosed, another was matronly and in her forties with doughy cheeks, while the third was a beautiful girl in her teens. Behind them, through the window, Annie could see the bright, hypnotic moon.

'Annie . . .?'

Annie suddenly became aware that her head was aching. She rubbed stubbornly at her temple which was throbbing and getting worse, but the ache just seemed to spread until she felt fuzzy and weak. Her vision was affected. There were flashes and wavy lines like a sudden, debilitating migraine attack. She tried to focus on the monitor showing the song lyrics, but her eyes moved back to the three women who now seemed to be moving slowly in a circle, back to back. As each one appeared, her gaze locked on to Annie unblinkingly until the turn broke it. Charlotte was speaking, but Annie couldn't hear the words; even the hubbub in the bar faded slowly into the background until there was a void of silence between herself and the women.

'. . . song?' Charlotte's voice broke through.

'You choose,' Annie replied; her words were slurring, but not from the alcohol.

Charlotte disappeared from her field of vision and a moment later the music started. Annie didn't recognize the song, but it was only two bars old before it disappeared completely.

In that instant, everything in the pub altered. It seemed like she was suddenly seeing it in a negative image, black and white people moving in slow motion through a monochrome setting, while flecks of white drifted down slowly like snowflakes from the ceiling. It was beautiful and terrible, and she caught her breath at the wonder of it.

The scene was dominated by the three women, still turning, but now resembling an ancient marble statue in a starlit garden. The moon glowed so brightly through the window behind them that Annie could not look into the face of it.

It seemed to stay that way for hours and hours; Annie was lost to it. And the women, staring at her all the while, without ever moving their lips. Trying to communicate, failing, trying again.

Trying to warn her.

And still they turned, slowly, a moonlight waltz of grace and power. Annie stretched out a hand; she wanted to be with them.

Then it ended. There was a roaring like a jet taking off and the music and the colours rushed back to her consciousness. Charlotte was singing alone and nudging her to join in, but

Annie felt giddy. She looked around, disorientated, but now there was no sign of the women.

As the music cranked out loudly around the seedy setting, Annie recalled the startling beauty of her vision and felt a sudden wave of sadness. She must have imagined it all, yet it was there in her head, an image so powerful that everything else seemed insignificant. *I am going mad*, she thought.

Annie finished the song half-heartedly and then dragged Charlotte from the stage as insistently as she had pulled her up there.

'What the hell happened to you?' Charlotte asked worriedly. 'I thought you were going to flake out on me!'

'Too much booze,' Annie replied. 'I had the strangest sensation . . . spacy . . . like I was somewhere else.'

'Yeah, you wish. Come on, I'd better get you to the taxi rank.'

'Did you see those women?'

'What women?'

Annie shook her head dismissively and laughed. 'No, forget it. For a minute there I thought I'd flipped into the Twilight Zone. Do-doo-do-doo, do-doo-do-doo!'

Outside, in the sweltering city night, Annie still couldn't shake off the feeling that something important had happened. She felt special and changed. There was just her, her best friend, and the moon. Whatever lay ahead could stay in the shadows. For that night, she was happy.

7

The next day was just as sun-drenched as all the others in recent memory, but all Annie could see was the moon. It cast its silvery illumination across her thoughts as she ventured out into the heat, whispering reassuringly on the edge of her consciousness. In her head was an image of three women offering supportive hands, turning slowly, hypnotically, and she felt an echoing response from deep within her; something had changed in her head or her heart, just slightly, and although she couldn't tell exactly what it was, she knew it had happened on a fundamental level. Annie still didn't know if she had really experienced her bizarre vision or if it had been some wild hallucination brought on by the booze, but at least if she was mad it was a cosy madness and she felt better than she had done in months.

Her euphoric mood, she soon discovered, was not reflected throughout the village where things seemed to be going from bad to worse. In the store where she called briefly to buy some milk and then at the post office where she sent a letter to her mother and father, there was a level of tension that almost made her feel queasy. The arrival of the travellers had disturbed everyone. People were nervous, afraid of attacks at night, robberies, gigantic raves attracting the youth of three counties. Annie tried to calm the worries of one woman in the store, but she met with such instant suspicion that she realized it was better to keep her own counsel.

The disturbing atmosphere made her fear some of the more volatile members of the community might try to cause trouble at the camp and she decided it was best to warn Tommy so the travellers could pre-empt any clash. Dropping off her milk, she took a leisurely walk up to the field, scuffing her Doc Martens as she booted stones lazily into the hedgerow. She was pleasantly surprised when she was greeted by a few waves and shouts as she stepped into the circle of vehicles. A handful of travellers came over to talk, thanking her for her help in getting Coop to hospital after his bad trip. He had recovered, they said, and he'd like to thank her himself at some point. Apparently, she had been discussed at length in her absence. There were a few who treated her with some resentment, but many others told her she was welcome to hang out with them whenever she wanted. For the first time since returning to Riddington, she felt at home.

Tommy seemed particularly pleased to see her. He surprised her with a hug and then ushered her into his bus where he listened intently before dismissing her fears. The villagers' reaction was normal, he said; the travellers were used to it and knew how to cope. Then he disappeared into the shadows at the back before returning with a couple of cans of Red Stripe.

'You should come with us when we move on,' he said. 'It's a great life. No rules except the ones you make yourself. Getting close to nature. You'd fit right in.'

His words stirred a complex mix of emotions in Annie; the idea sounded perfect, just what she really wanted, yet it frightened her: insecurity, danger. She smiled and mumbled some half-hearted reply and was happy when Tommy didn't probe any further.

'I hear Coop's recovered,' she said, changing the subject.

He nodded and swigged down a mouthful of beer. 'His trip was bad news, though. Some folks are worried about the things he was saying. All that about someone coming . . . falcons . . .'

'It was just the acid talking. Wasn't it?'

'Maybe. Maybe not. One or two reckoned he was having . . .' he looked at Annie askance, '. . . a vision.'

'What? Like a premonition? I didn't realize you were a superstitious bunch.' She smiled, but Tommy didn't return it.

'We believe in the power of the mind,' he said after a moment. 'We're a mixed bag – Wiccans, pagans, druids, tree worshippers – but we're all clued up enough to recognize when the subconscious speaks.'

'It was weird, yes,' Annie said.

'Well, if you come back tonight you'll find out more.'

'How?'

He smiled enigmatically. 'Come back and you'll see.'

The camp smelled of woodsmoke and flowers and was filled with the deep rumble of percussive music when Annie returned. It was nearly 10 p.m. and although the sun had disappeared, the sky was still light, though quickly turning a dark blue in the East. Tommy was naked to the waist, lean and muscular; when he gave her another hug in greeting she felt his sinews tighten beneath her hands.

'Are you ready for a bit of magic?' he asked.

'Just what my life needs,' she replied.

'Good. You've been deeply honoured. A few of us are going to carry out the Ritual of Determination, and everyone agreed when I said you should sit in. It's not heavy or anything. You might even enjoy it. You game?'

'I might be. What is it?'

'It's based on an old Native American ritual. Young braves used to go through it as part of their passage to manhood. It put them in touch with the Great Spirit. They were supposed to learn all about themselves, and sometimes they were given a glimpse into the future too.'

Annie felt apprehensive. 'I'm not too keen on that ... the future ... knowing myself ... it's ...' Her words tumbled out uncomfortably.

'Don't worry. You're among friends. We'll take care of you. And really, it's nothing wild. We've done it before whenever we've had bad times, real crises a few of them, and the ritual just gives us an insight to the right path. Don't expect the earth to move. It doesn't work like that.' He laughed. 'You never know, it might do you good.'

Reluctantly, she allowed herself to be led to a makeshift hut erected on the edge of the camp. The roof was covered with turf cut from the hedgerow and the walls smeared with some kind of pitch. Tommy called it the sweat lodge. At the door they were greeted by a group of six men and two women who would all be taking part in the ritual, Tommy explained. Annie was happy to see Angela wasn't one of them.

They hugged each other supportively and then trailed into the gloomy interior. There was a small hole in the roof which allowed enough light to filter through for Annie to see that the hut was filled with the cushions and drapes she had earlier noticed in Tommy's bus. The atmosphere grew tense the moment the door was closed and they each sat down.

A big-built man with a thick beard and straggly, long hair like a caveman lit a pile of kindling in the centre of the room, and once it was blazing away, he heaped on branches from a pile in the corner. White smoke thickened and fanned out instantly; little of it seemed to be going through the tiny roof-hole.

Annie caught a lungful and coughed until she thought she was going to be sick. Through streaming eyes, she saw Tommy lean over. 'Don't worry. You'll get used to it,' he whispered.

Once the fire was at full blaze and the temperature in the hut had risen considerably, the travellers began to peel off their clothes. Annie watched nervously for a moment, and then followed suit. She would not have done so in front of any other strangers, but everyone else made it seem so natural, completely unsexual. Even when she was naked she didn't feel any cooler; the sweat was streaming between her breasts and collecting in her navel, and the air was so clogged with smoke it seemed to

79

press the heat into her pores. By the light of the fire, the nine bodies around her glistened orange and almost seemed to melt as the smoke coiled around them, obscuring then revealing.

Her observations were disturbed when Tommy thrust a small metal box into her hands. It seemed to be filled with black twigs and leaves.

'What is it?' she asked.

'Psilocybin. Mexican,' Tommy replied, munching slowly. 'The sacrament. This is the pathway to the worldmind, the god-zone, whatever you want to call it.'

She glanced back into the box. 'Mushrooms?'

'They're considered sacred by cultures across the globe. They open up the mind, straight to the heart of the subconscious. They'll link our psyches.'

'I've had them before,' Annie said dismissively.

'Not like these. Very powerful. There are other drugs we could use, but we prefer these. The Native Americans like peyote. And there are tribes in the Brazilian rainforest who use a drug called ayahuasce. They're not fun drugs, not recreational. In fact, they make you sick to the stomach. They're used for spiritual reasons – it's a religious event.'

'Is that what this is?'

He nodded.

She dipped her hand into the box and pushed some of the mushrooms into her mouth. They were dry and rubbery and tasted a little musky, but they went down easily.

The heat and smoke made the wait unbearable, and the first stage of the trip didn't start to register until about twenty minutes later, but then the experience became easier. Each lick of flame in the fire glowed radioactively and the hut was filled with the sound of its crackling; Annie found herself staring deeply into the heart of the blaze with fascination. Without looking, she knew Tommy was smiling at her and she turned and smiled back. They laughed together.

Time seemed to disappear.

It took an eternity for one globule of sweat to trickle from her neck to her belly.

An aeon later a woman's voice floated through the smoke: 'It's starting.' This was followed by an appreciative giggle from someone else.

Annie felt a rush of sheer joy and exhilaration like she had not felt in years, if at all. She was in tune with everyone and she smiled at all the open faces in turn. Who cared if they didn't discover any secret truths? It was a party and they were having fun.

It took a second or two for her to realize reality was changing, and almost a minute to understand that it was not happening in her mind. It should have been disconcerting, but the hallucinogen made it seem completely natural. Or perhaps it *was* in her mind, in all their minds at once, a joint vision.

The world was melting; the air above the fire where the smoke was thickest appeared to be opening out upon itself, like a flower, she thought at first, but then she decided it was more like a vagina. It was opening and curling, opening and curling, revealing layer after layer of reality. Sparks of molten brass were fizzing out of it and bursting in bolts of incandescence upon the ground.

This isn't like a trip at all, Annie thought.

The smoke was so thick it should have been difficult to breathe; her lungs were on fire, but there was no discomfort. And now her body was melting. Her essence ran out of every pore and coated her with a sheen of humanity.

I could love if I wanted to, she thought. *I'm a criminal that never broke the law, and now my lifetime's piling up.* And then: *Where did that come from?*

Tommy was beatific, swimming behind his closed eyelids. The fire licked his slick skin red and gold, defining his taut muscles in lines of darkest charcoal.

Annie was outside herself, yet so far inside she could barely see the world. The air was still unfolding, but the crackling of the fire had disappeared to leave a chiming silence waiting to be filled.

'Show us,' someone said. The call was taken up by two others.

A second later the hut was filled with the beating of wings like hundreds of doves taking flight at once. Annie covered her ears, but couldn't keep the sound out. The beating grew deafening, thrashing madly, no longer doves, but mighty pinions.

'It's never been this good before,' the man on the other side of Tommy said breathlessly. 'It's never been so close.'

'Something special,' a woman with blonde dreads replied.

81

'There's big shit happening. There must be to cause this. It's brilliant!'

The sound of the birds departed, the brass sparks showered once more and were gone. And then it was just the ten of them waiting in stillness for something to happen.

At first Annie wanted to laugh, but the urge quickly drained out of her as the room filled with uncertain anticipation. Annie watched the smiles fall away from the faces of her fellow trippers one by one. The tension turned black; something was going to break.

Tommy opened his eyelids. 'Shit!'

He pitched backwards like he had been smashed in the face with a baseball bat, crumpling on to the cushions with his eyes wide open but unseeing. Everyone tried to move at once, but no one could shift from the spot; Annie felt her legs had melted into the ground.

A few seconds later the man on Tommy's right keeled over. He too lay unconscious with his eyes open. The woman with blonde dreads shrieked, but even before the sound had died away, the next man went down, and then another and another.

Annie watched the movement in horror as it worked its way around the circle. When it came to the blonde she closed her eyes and waited for the invisible thunderbolt, but strangely it passed her by and focused on the man next to her who collapsed mid-scream. Soon only Annie and the two other women were conscious and waiting in terror for what was going to happen next.

'Oh goddess, please get us out of here,' the blonde sobbed.

'Shut up,' the other woman snapped. She was in her late thirties with coarse brown hair streaked with silver. 'We've been chosen. Can't you feel it?'

Annie could certainly feel *something*. The atmospheric pressure in the hut increased so rapidly she felt someone had wrapped their arms around her chest and was squeezing the life from her. The air hummed. There was a vacuum in the space above the fire and whatever was coming was rushing into it.

Her sense of smell flared into life so that every passing aroma was so powerful it was almost paralysing. Behind the woodsmoke and the sweat, she soon caught a whiff of something animal; the potent musk grew so strong she gagged. And then it was hovering above the fire like a shadow slipping through a

82

crack in a door: insubstantial and mixed with the smoke. Annie thought she saw the head of a horse, but then it shifted and became a tusked boar; then that was gone and there was a yelping dog. Behind it all, though, Annie could sense one mind, wild and alien.

A lump had settled in her throat and would not go away. She felt her heart might stop beating at any moment.

'Speak to us!' the coarse-haired woman called out. 'What do we need to know?'

The shifting shapes seemed to coalesce into a dark figure which drew itself up to the ceiling and spread out along it. Beneath it, other things were appearing in the smoke. Annie was horrified when she saw a human face screaming, quickly followed by another and another until the entire centre of the hut was writhing with the constantly shifting features of scores of humans in agony.

'Oh my goddess!' the blonde hissed. 'I'm going to be sick.' The vomit erupted out of her mouth and on to the ground next to the fire.

Annie's breath caught. For one instant she thought she had seen the face of the old man who had been murdered on the train.

'Wilde,' she whispered.

'Show us a sign,' the coarse-haired woman continued breathlessly. Her eyes were wide in wonder.

Suddenly, and for just a second or two, Annie saw a face at the top of that dark shape. It was bone-white and so terrible that her mind automatically snuffed out the image. With it came a voice like bones being crushed: '*When the door is opened, call his name.*'

Annie's head snapped backward, then forward like an epileptic; she no longer had control of her body. 'What have we done?' she said weakly.

The faces in the smoke had gone now, but something else was taking their place. Slowly Annie's own face and body appeared, as if she was looking into a warped mirror. She felt an overwhelming distress. This smoke image of herself was white with the lustre of death, and showed her hands clawed in a last spasm. She was seeing herself as she would look in death, only she didn't look any older than she did now.

The shock hit her full force. Death. Her death, as she had always feared.

'Is this it?' Her voice trembled. 'Is this what's going to happen? I'm to die? Soon?' Annie wanted to scream, but her mouth wouldn't respond.

The image of her corpse hung in the smoke, stirring a deep, arctic dread in the heart of her. As she stared in horror, the eyes of her sister-reflection bulged and then burst open and two red roses erupted from the sockets and grew upwards, the thorns tearing at the dead skin of her forehead.

Death. Her death.

With that final glimpse, the fire was extinguished with a whoosh and the hut was plunged into darkness.

Annie was almost stupefied by the premonition of her death, but she eventually managed to crawl out into the night with the other two women, shaking with shock. The men were already waking, rolling unsteadily on to hands and knees, mumbling things that didn't make sense.

'What did we do back there?' Annie asked again, pathetically.

No one answered.

Unable to regulate her breathing, she felt on the verge of an anxiety attack. The night was hot, but it was still cooler than the blanketing heat of the sweat lodge. They all lay on their backs looking at the sky while they tried to calm themselves, and for a long time no one spoke. A plane crawled slowly across their field of vision, its lights winking dispassionately, and that finally seemed to restore some sense of reality.

'Shit,' a voice sang out. 'What happened?'

'We touched a higher power.' It was the coarse-haired woman; her voice was awed. 'The time must have been right. The mood, the people, everything. We broke through the barrier. This must have been what it was like for our ancestors, when everyone was close to the earth and the gods.'

'Its voice was so terrible,' Annie whispered, her own voice trembling at the memory.

There was a long pause, then the other woman said, 'I didn't hear any voice.'

'Nor me,' spoke the blonde woman next to her.

Tommy rolled over on to his side and looked at her. Annie

suddenly felt self-conscious about her nakedness. 'What did it say?' he asked.

She flipped over on to her stomach. 'It said, "When the door is opened, call his name." Does that mean anything to anyone?'

There was a murmur of disagreement, but no one could say for sure. Exhaustion and stress had taken away all sense of reasoning, and for a time all they could do was huddle together like Neanderthals waiting for the night to end.

Eventually Annie gave voice to what they were all thinking: 'It was a warning. Something terrible is going to happen.'

She remembered the swirling, agonized faces in the smoke. *Wilde*, she thought. *It was a warning about Wilde.*

She saw her death-image once again, and when she closed her eyes she felt she was plummeting backwards into the void; she had to hook her nails into the dry earth to stop an involuntary spasm. *I'm lost*, she thought. *It was telling me I'm going to die.*

A shuffling started on the edge of the circle and then they all moved inwards until everyone was touching someone else.

'What's going to happen?' The blonde's voice was verging on hysteria; Annie wanted to slap her.

'We have to be ready,' the second woman replied. 'We're facing a time of crisis, that's what it means. I could see death there, and destruction. The death of all of us.'

Annie looked so deeply into the night sky, she saw through it, into the heart of reality; it was cold and completely unreasoning, just an insane chaos.

Yes, death was drawing near; she could feel it in the air.

8

Birmingham was laid out before him, a rabbit warren of factories, tower blocks, council estates, and in the distance the glass towers of the city centre, black against the angry red of the setting sun. He breathed deeply of the thick evening air, smelling the grimy, sweaty odour of the city in summer. The breeze was not fresh, but it cooled his face as he rested on the ledge of the attic window of the cheap flophouse in Moseley.

He thought of the past as he watched the subtle shift of colour while the sun trailed down the sky. Nostalgia was a dangerous trap that he tried to avoid at all costs, but when he had time on his hands, it was easy to get sucked in.

Behind him, the room was dark and smelled of vinegar. He had been in it for half a day, after meeting some of the flophouse's residents begging for spare change near New Street station. The girl had been easy to seduce. Eighteen years old with a child and a heroin addiction to support, the scent of power and money around him had proven too much.

He teetered dangerously on the ledge without any fear. She was still naked on the bed from their love-making session, her thighs wet with his semen. Her hair was dyed black and teased upwards and outwards. The heavy mascara around her white, staring eyes had run slightly; black tears on one cheek.

'Poor, witless sheep,' he muttered.

The piece of rubber tubing that had been tied around her upper arm lay on the sheet next to her. A blackened spoon was on the bedside table, beside the syringe which he had used to administer her fix, a loving act to bond their relationship for ever. He had watched her face intently, moving in closer to catch her creeping realization that he had made the shot too strong.

'I'm ODing,' she had croaked, wide-eyed with terror. 'Help me.'

So he had held her hand and supported her across the threshold.

Somewhere beneath him, the waiting calm of the building was disturbed by voices raised angrily. A woman bawling, a man barking, two members of the boarding house's itinerant population colliding before ricocheting off into the void. A door slammed and silence descended once more.

'I never even knew your name,' he said, sitting at the end of the bed.

'Julie,' a flat, cold voice replied. The body didn't move, her peaceful expression undisturbed.

'Julie,' he echoed, nodding thoughtfully. 'It is French, did you know that? The Gallic form of the Italian Giuliana. Names are so poetic when you examine them closely.' He paused and then asked, 'What is it like, Julie?'

The air buzzed as he waited for her response. 'Cold. Lonely. I can hear voices . . . in the distance. Someone is screaming.'

He nodded approvingly. 'The Dark Side. I am sorry to have to put you through this, Julie, but I need to know. You have to tell me more. You have to go further.'

Silence. Then: 'A building, like a cathedral. I can't see the top of the spire. It's made of huge stones, as black as the night. There's a big door. It's got an iron knocker on it.'

'Everyone must pass through the Cathedral, good or bad. Go on, Julie.'

'The door is opening. There's a wind rushing out . . . a hurricane . . .'

'Enter, Julie.'

The sun had almost set and the streetlights were winking on in the road outside. The red glow that had suffused the attic finally disappeared, leaving a wintry gloom. Julie's face glowed white like a ghost against the headboard.

'Julie?' Nothing. 'Come back now, Julie. Are you there?'

'*Yes.*'

'What did you see?'

There was a sound like phlegm in her throat, and then '*L'arrghl sssterm plataw . . .*'

'Enough.' He shook his head wearily and sighed. He thought the drugs might have fortified her for her return, but she was the same as all the rest. Too weak. Too pathetic. Too damn human.

He returned to the window and looked at the city lights, and the time flashing on and off at the top of the *Post and Mail* tower.

'Ah, well, Julie,' he said without turning round. 'There is no sense in being disappointed. After all these years, I am nothing if not resilient. There will be other occasions, other tests. You will not be the last.'

He grew silent as he looked out into the growing night, sensing smoke in a small room but not really knowing what the vision meant.

'Sometimes, Julie, I feel as old as the earth itself.' His voice sounded taut in the gloom. 'Once my life was like yours, finite, too brief, yet with the promise of the ultimate reward, the great, shining Beyond through the doorway of death. My punishment seemed like no punishment at all until I began to grasp its monstrous implications. I cannot die, Julie. Ever. Heaven, Valhalla – call it what you will – is denied me. What I have here, the power I administer, is no substitute. I have experienced everything, every possible sensation, every piece of knowledge, however small and insignificant. Nothing is new. The only mystery is death and to what that leads. I *must* know what lies beyond the Black Cathedral. It is the only thing left me.' He laughed without any trace of humour. 'I admit, Julie, it has become something of an obsession. Tell me if I go on . . .' He laughed again. 'And so I try to experience it vicariously, through others who have had the joy of going before me. What a sad man I am, having to be content with second-hand experience like a lonely bachelor hooked on pornographic films.' His voice grew bitter, all pretence at humour gone.

'You see, Julie, death gives life meaning, and without it I have a meaningless existence, a banal soap opera that continues to the end of time. You cannot imagine what it is like to live with no direction, constantly making random choices with no hope of resolution. And so I have tried to find my own motivation, something to keep me warm in the night of my life, and it is a simple one: revenge. For my punishment, for all my suffering. That is what I do, Julie. Do not take your death personally. It is simply a sign to show that I am still defiant, that I will bow my head to no one.'

Above him, he could see the red and white lights of a plane coming in to land at Birmingham International Airport. 'Where next, Julie? You shall decide for me. Europe, perhaps?'

'*Yes.*'

'Or shall I stay on the trail here, in this fading land that was once fit for heroes?'

'*Yes.*'

He laughed coldly. 'Oh, Julie, what are we to do with you? You young girls are so indecisive.'

A noise drew him to the yellowing cot in the corner of the room. The six-month-old baby stirred in its sleep and then grew still once more. 'Perhaps I am doing you a favour, little one. You may stand a better chance without the feeble ministrations of such a deplorable mother.'

He watched the child quietly for a moment and then turned back to the dead girl. The room was now pitch black, but he could still make out her unblinking eyes.

'Talking like this has reminded me of someone, Julie – a girl on a train who lived in Eden. Perhaps I could look her up. What do you say?'

'*Yes.*'

'Annie Boulton,' he whispered. 'I remember her name. How surprising.' He grew thoughtful; curiously, he could sense smoke again. 'She was a very special person. Perhaps even unique in this day and age. Down the years I have met a handful of people who have been gifted with the power, the life-essence. I could see it in her, burning like a hot, white light, but she had no sense of it herself.' He paused. 'I would have liked—' He cut off the sentence and shook his head.

'I have a life that goes far beyond the furthest reaches of loneliness, Julie. No one can know the smallest part of my experiences, because no one can be by my side, in my terms, for more than the blinking of an eye.'

He looked back at the girl on the bed with contempt. 'You are nothing compared to what I saw in her. I *liked* her; now is that not foolish?'

He turned back to the window. The night had closed in completely.

'And that is why I will have to kill her.'

9

The pub was just a stone's throw from Stoke railway station, down a dingy side street where the thunder of the passing Intercities still managed to rattle the glasses behind the bar at regular intervals. Like so many similar inns, The Travellers' Rest was filled with an odd mix of itinerants and locals – sales reps overnighting in cheap suits and bad aftershave, businessmen meeting clients and flat-capped regulars who had steadfastly refused the encroaching gentrification. It smelled of sour beer and stale tobacco and no one could be motivated to repair the slashed seats in the corner.

Searching for the taint of Wilde, Severin glanced round the room slowly, taking in the browning wallpaper and the beer-puddled, ash-strewn tables, the flat atmosphere of decay. He felt nothing, but nevertheless something tugged at him to stay and so he marched up to the bar and ordered a Jack Daniel's. His throat was dry from too long on the road and his eyes were sore and heavy, but he could not afford the luxury of relaxing. He was so close. He could sense it as if a flame was burning next to his cheek.

'Quiet night,' he said after downing another short.

The barman looked twenty years older than he probably was, his face revealing in each burst capillary where the profits were going. 'S'always quiet on a Tuesday,' he grunted.

'I guess you get a lot of people passing through, being so close to the station.'

'You're right there. People like a drink after a long journey.'

Severin nodded and smiled, but it didn't feel comfortable so he let the expression drop. 'Maybe you've seen a friend of mine. I know he's in town at the moment. Tall, black hair, beard and moustache. Got one gold earring. Magnetic personality. You'd remember him if you saw him.'

'Doesn't ring a bell, mate.'

Severin sipped his third slowly. 'Don't worry, it was just a shot in the dark.' He left his drink at the bar and went over to the archaic juke box which, to his pleasure, was filled with oldies. He slipped 50p into the slot and made his selection. Sinatra was crooning 'Come Fly With Me' before he had made it back to his seat.

Subconsciously he slipped his hand inside his coat and felt the thinness of his wallet. The cash was running low again; he would have to call his bank when he got the chance. How much longer would the insurance from Marj last? And what would he do when it finally ran out? Give up? Get a job? Go back to being a normal person with a normal life? Those bridges had long been burned.

To distract himself from thoughts that always led to a bleak depression, he leaned forward and plucked a copy of the *Evening Sentinel* from the end of the bar. But it was so different from his own local rag that it obliquely triggered a feeling of great loneliness. He wished he was back home in Nashville with Marj and Matty and all the boring, everyday things that made life happy and secure. England seemed cold and dark, even when the sun was shining.

As his eyes scanned the front page, his attention fell on a small item at the foot, and suddenly the alarm was crashing through his head: BODY PULLED FROM CANAL.

With tingling nerves, he read on. *Police have identified a body found in a city canal. He was named today as John Claridge, an unemployed sheet-metal worker. Investigations are continuing into the death, but a police spokesman said that at present there were no suspicious circumstances.*

There never were, Severin thought.

He noted the location of the canal from the few remaining paragraphs, and then he finished his drink and rose, energy crackling through every sinew, his mind alert once more.

The canal towpath *smelled* of him. Maybe it was some psychic after-image, but the presence of Wilde was unmistakable. Severin dropped to his haunches and stared into the black water. Away in the night, he could hear the rustling of rats in the undergrowth and the hum of the nearby railway lines.

Another death. One more faceless corpse in a long, long line that stretched back into history. How many? Severin wondered. And still no one had a clue that he was culling humans so mercilessly. A one-man industry of funeral pyres and charnel houses.

Severin closed his eyes. The bond was as strong as always, since the accident; he wondered if it would ever fade. Absently, his fingers eased into his shirt and closed on the corroded metal bracelet that hung around his neck on a leather thong. There was a hiss and a whisper in his head. In his mind, he saw the nameless killer rising on the canal towpath and finding the right pressure point that would crush the life from the luckless Claridge. Severin even felt Claridge's too-late click of realization that his life was about to end, and the fizz of elation that bubbled up through the murderer.

There was more, but he didn't want to picture it. He opened his eyes and fought a momentary destabilization that threatened to pitch him forward into the greasy water. The echoes were still strong; the trail burned the ground away into the distance. Slowly, he started to walk, following the lines of force.

'I'm getting closer, you bastard,' he said under his breath.

10

Annie was shocked awake by the dream, which was not really a
dream but a memory playing over and over, a memory of the
future, and she was trapped inside that memory. Her face,
shining with the pearly lustre of death. The lankness of her
black hair. Her eyelids closed, but not in sleep. She looked
down on it like she was floating over it, detached somehow, but
aware she had lost everything. And then came the mounting
terror that manifested itself with a howling in her ears as she
felt herself dragged away, up and out, into the void.

She clambered on to the edge of the bed and rubbed her face
awake, trying to expunge the image. It was 7.10 a.m. and the
room was already hot from the sunlight which streamed
between the curtains. Sweat slicked her skin and her throat was
unbearably dry. Stumbling from the bed, she stood for a
moment or two in the golden shaft of light and tried to bring
herself together.

Just the drugs, she told herself. *Don't be silly.*

It didn't work. However much she tried she couldn't destroy
the memory of the premonition; she could only try to bury it
deeply.

As she showered, she realized she missed her mother and
father desperately and wished they were back, filling the place
with their familiar sounds and scents, even though she would
undoubtedly end up arguing with her father and the usual
claustrophobia would sweep in from nowhere. An insatiable
desire to escape filled her, but the only place she could think of
going was the travellers' camp, where there were no walls and
the horizons were always open.

The journey was slow-going in the heat which pressed down
and deadened all life in the village and the surrounding countryside. There was no breeze to dampen any noise, and before the
camp was in sight Annie could hear the sound of trouble.
Someone was screaming, 'Bastard! You bastard!' while someone
else howled like an animal with its leg in a trap. Annie broke
into a jog. She had known it was only a matter of time before
somebody came here to vent the hatred that had been seething
away in Riddington; she was only surprised it had not happened
sooner. There had been a meeting in the village hall with

Hartley Williams practising his favourite 'Blackshirt' speech, and various mobs had been plotting in corners in the Royal Oak. The word had gone out on the village grapevine: *drive out the scum*.

Annie hurried up the dusty, rutted track to the camp as fast as she could, fearing the worst. The next thing she knew she was crying out in shock as a rock appeared from out of the blue and crashed against her shoulder blade. She ducked behind a hedge and it took a couple of minutes for her to realize she had been an accidental target.

Peering over the hedge, she saw a small crowd had gathered, looking like an oil smear against the green of the field. The gravity of the situation had pulled the confrontation into a tight nucleus where the opposing voices were making enough noise for an army. Annie recognized some village know-it-alls: Gordon Wilson, a signwriter; Caroline Curtis, a campaigning member of the local wives' group; a couple of teenagers and four others. Then, away from the confrontation on the other side of a barbed wire fence, she caught sight of Bill King and Hartley Williams talking conspiratorially and pointing.

Annie hurried forward and as she neared the crowd, she saw another familiar figure standing on the periphery. George Newton looked frightened. When he saw Annie he waved her over to a spot out of missile range.

'Bloody hell,' he said. 'I don't know what's come over everybody. One minute, they were in the shop on about the camp and the next minute they'd decided to march over here. Now look at them!' He waved his walking stick at the crowd with a trembling hand.

At that moment, Gordon Wilson lurched forward and grabbed the most belligerent traveller, a teenager with so many chains and rings piercing various parts of his head that he rattled when he was pulled off his feet.

'I've had about all I can take from you, you dirty layabout,' Wilson bellowed. 'Now get off this land!'

The teenager struggled to break free and accidentally kicked Wilson hard on his shin. The response was instant: Wilson's head ducked, snapped upward and smashed into the teenager's face. The youth went down like a puppet whose strings had been cut.

There was one second where everything was in stasis and

then the two sides flew at each other. Caroline Curtis was screaming, hands flashing up and down before her face, nails raking like a cat. Wilson had blood all over him; Annie couldn't tell if it was his or the teenager's. He was punching out randomly. One of the travellers brandishing a stick caught a village youth on the side of the head and the stick exploded with a crack.

Annie suddenly saw George was no longer at her side. He was already lurching into the thick of the fight with surprising sprightliness. 'George! Leave them alone!' she called out, but the old man ignored her.

Without hesitation, he pushed into the brawl and threw his body between the opposing forces. The last Annie saw of him, he was trying to pull Wilson off a traveller whose head was getting pounded, then he disappeared beneath the thrashing bodies.

There was a lump in Annie's throat as she sprinted forward. No one seemed to care about the crumpled shape at their feet. She plunged among the bodies, her foot catching Wilson on his upper thigh just an inch away from his groin, while at the same time she managed to overbalance a couple of travellers. It gave a space for her to shriek, 'Look what you've done!'

The edge in her voice cut through the anger, and everyone around her slowed like clockwork toys winding down as they seemed to see George on the ground for the first time. Annie dropped to her knees and unbuttoned his collar. He was unconscious and deathly pale. At first she thought he'd had a heart attack until she saw the slight rise and fall of his thin chest.

She looked up angrily. 'You're all acting like animals! For God's sake, there's no need for this!'

'Call a doctor,' someone said. And as if glad to get away, a suddenly embarrassed Gordon Wilson ran in the direction of the phone box on Colthorpe Road.

One of the travellers proffered a well-worn hip flask. 'Whisky,' he said.

Annie took it and poured just enough to moisten George's lips. After a few seconds his mouth started to work and eventually his eyes opened. He looked disorientated.

Annie pushed her face into his line of vision. 'George, you stopped the fight.'

'With my bloody head, it feels like.' He managed a weak smile. 'I knew I still had it in me.'

'You rest a while,' Annie said. 'The doctor's on his way.'

'Yes. I think I'll do that.' He closed his eyes again before adding, 'He'll be bloody sick of the sight of me.'

Annie held George's hand until Doctor Evans trundled into the field in his car. After checking the casualty over, he helped him into the passenger seat. Annie gave the old man's hand a final squeeze; she was frightened by how pale he looked, almost deathly.

When she turned back, the villagers and travellers had all slunk off, leaving her with a bitter feeling that she no longer recognized the people who had been her neighbours all her life.

Tommy came out to see her before she could walk off. He looked a little wary, but his clothes seemed pertinent to the day – combat trousers, a black army surplus t-shirt wearing to grey, and Doc Martens. Angela was at his side, her expression combative.

'All dressed up for war?' Annie said tartly.

'We didn't start it! They came here looking for trouble. I managed to keep most of our lot back, but a few hotheads slipped through the net.' Tommy took a deep breath and scanned the hedgerows and fields for the enemy. 'Will the old guy be OK?'

Annie nodded. 'George is pretty resilient. Look, I'm sorry for snapping at you. I guess you didn't provoke anything.'

'That's very generous of you,' Angela sneered.

'What's your problem?' Annie could barely contain her contempt. In that instant there was something about Angela that reminded her of Hartley Williams; narrow minds were everywhere.

'My problem is that *your* people are trying to drive us away and they don't care who they hurt in the process. It's the same wherever we go,' Angela continued. 'We're supposed to be the troublemakers, but it's always the ones who claim to uphold the law who throw the first punch. They're the ones who have no respect for others.'

'Well, I'm not one of them,' Annie said defiantly.

With another contemptuous sneer, Angela spun round and marched back towards the camp. Tommy watched her go and then said, almost apologetically, 'Come and have a cup of tea and a chat.'

He led her to his bus where he brewed up on the primus and then they sat on the steps in the sun and drank slowly. He told her tales from the road, and of how he'd first dropped out of society, giving up a home, a good job, everything, for a taste of freedom. His easy-going nature and his lazy speech soothed Annie, drawing out the tension until she felt she didn't want to leave.

As they spoke, Annie's attention was caught by the sudden appearance of the coarse-haired woman from the sweat lodge. She was watching intently. She came up a minute or two later and held out her hand.

'Hello, I'm Miranda. We didn't get the chance to talk before. I'm sorry,' she said, sitting cross-legged next to them. Compared to Tommy, she seemed anxious, almost fraught. She repeatedly chewed on the nails of her forefingers, and tugged at one braid of hair. Annie felt uncomfortable in her presence; it seemed like Miranda was studying every contour of her face as if searching for some hidden code.

'What's wrong?' she said. 'Have I got a spot coming up?'

'No . . . I'm sorry . . . I just had to be sure.'

'Sure of what?'

'After what happened in the sweat lodge, I've been trying to find out what was wrong . . . what the threat was. It scared me. The whole vision was too powerful. I believe in magic, but I never imagined anything like that. I've been carrying out certain rituals . . .'

'Miranda's a pagan,' Tommy interjected.

'That's right! I worship the Triple Goddess, Maiden, Mother and Crone, all the aspects of femininity. I felt her presence in the sweat lodge that night more powerfully than ever before.' She turned and pointed to the far side of the camp. 'Over there we've made a small stone circle with a fire-pit at the centre for our rituals. Late last night I tried to call on Her to clarify . . . to help me to see the threat properly. I decided to invoke Her as the Crone, the one who lays out the dead and greets us in Summerland, the resting place before we are reborn. It seemed right somehow.'

Miranda was clawing nervously at the earth, struggling with something inside her, and her anxiety was starting to transmit itself to Annie. Eventually she seemed to reach some conclusion, for she looked up, her eyes like glass reflecting the startling blue of the sky. 'I cast the circle with the sacred knife and entered the realm between the worlds of matter and spirit. She came, not just in spirit but in form. For the first time. It was like a howling wind blasting from the depths of space. And she showed me things.' She paused. 'She showed me *you*.'

'Me?' Annie jerked forward, slopping her tea on to the ground.

'You've been chosen. I saw your face.' Miranda stretched out a hand to touch Annie's cheek, but Annie swung her head away, shaking it vehemently, although she had no idea what she was denying. 'You've got to oppose whatever it is that's coming. It threatens Nature. Life. Everything. You're the one. You've been *chosen*.'

'I'm not a pagan. I'm a Christian.' Annie looked to Tommy for support, but he seemed as baffled by Miranda's words as she was.

'But you're a woman, with power. You're one of the sisterhood. The Goddess looks over us all.' Miranda reached out again and this time Annie didn't shy away; she was drawn by the pagan's eyes. When fingers brushed her arm, something like electricity rushed between them. 'Can't you feel it?' whispered Miranda.

Annie almost could, if she let herself. 'A couple of days ago . . . I was in a pub . . . there were three women . . . there, then not there.'

Miranda nodded eagerly. 'That's it! The Goddess. Mother, Maiden, Crone. You were chosen.'

Things started to click into place in Annie's mind. The strength she had found, the vision that had spoken to her in the sweat lodge. Could it be real?

'You'll know what to do when the time comes. Trust in intuition. Trust in the feminine things, dreams, visions. Our time is coming.'

'What possible threat could I have been chosen to face?' Annie felt a chill race through her the moment she asked the question. The experience in the sweat lodge was a warning about Wilde, she was sure of it. The faces in the smoke, *his* victims.

'When it arrives, you will know.'

Wilde! No, she couldn't face up to him. Her stomach turned at the very thought. He wasn't human. He was more like a demon who walked the earth.

Annie could have lost herself in Miranda's swirling crystal eyes and it took an effort to snap free. Having done so, she was speechless.

Miranda smiled and started to walk away. She turned after a few paces, her face relieved as if a burden had been lifted. 'You've embarked on the Spiral Dance, Annie Boulton. Life, Death and Rebirth. The cycle of Nature, of all existence.'

When she had gone, Annie collapsed back on to the steps of the bus. 'What the hell was all that about?' She started to turn it into a joke, but the words stalled in her throat. Instead, she listened to the beating of her heart, pounding like the drums of war.

Annie chose the only place where she could be at peace with her thoughts. Everything seemed to be whizzing out of control when all she really wanted was stability, and the place which summoned that up was the church. Although she had always been a regular churchgoer, Robert's death had changed everything she felt about religion, destroyed all its meaning for her. Yet, confusingly, the church was also the place she felt drawn to when she was at her weakest. She wished she understood herself more.

In the shadows of St Martin's, she paused briefly to appreciate the comforting solidity of the huge stone building behind her. Slowly she looked around the graveyard in search of understanding – the yews along the perimeter, the long yellow grass in the corner where people never seemed to venture, the neatly tended graves and the white, grey and black of the stones.

Hesitantly she stepped on the path that wound through the neatly tended grass to Robert's grave. She was glad he had been buried here. It gave her somewhere to go to talk to him, almost as if he was still around.

At the graveside she stopped and bowed her head, more out of habit than out of any real desire to pray, and then her hand automatically went to the ankh at her neck.

'I suppose the church would call this a pagan symbol, Robert. Father Tony never really agreed with you wearing it. But you always thought it was important, didn't you?' She remembered, and smiled. 'You know, this is the first time I've been here and not cried. It's weird, isn't it? What with all the bad shit that surrounded the train crash, and the mad things that seem to be happening now, I should be in the loony bin. What do you reckon, Robert? Is there more than all this? Is there such a thing as a man who can shake off a gunshot like a bee sting? Is there something in all that pagan stuff that you used to talk about? A Goddess? I wish I'd listened more.' She closed her eyes dreamily and then looked back at the stone with renewed force. 'In a way, I hope these strange things *are* real. Because that means the laws of science can't explain everything. And if they can't explain everything then there *could* be a place where we go after we die. And you ... and you ... could still be around somewhere ...'

A movement on the other side of the churchyard broke her chain of thought. She looked across and saw a young boy hurrying towards the perimeter, a bag slung loosely over his shoulder. She recognized him instantly as the lad whose mother had collapsed at the rectory coffee morning. Peter Cockburn, that was his name. Why wasn't he at school?

When she turned back to her brother's grave, the moment was gone. She bowed her head once more and when she looked up she said, 'I hope you're watching me, Robert. I hope you're keeping an eye on me and wishing me luck.'

And with that she turned and walked away, feeling the weight of her unanswered questions pressing heavily on her shoulders.

School was forgotten for the day, the sun was out and there was plenty to do before bed. Peter Cockburn, older than his nine years, had everything he needed in the compact rucksack hanging off his shoulder: a creased and torn copy of *House of Mystery* comics from the 1970s which he had unearthed on a market stall, his Gameboy, a few copies of the Page three pin-up from the *Sun* in case he got bored, a can of Shandy ('with real beer!'), and a giant packet of cheesy Quavers. The village was quiet as he made his way up Church Street, but at the gates of the church he still paused to double-check there was no one around; there was a woman down at one of the graves, but she didn't see him. He didn't want to take the risk that anyone would follow him to his quiet place. With three sisters it was hard for him to get time on his own at home and the churchyard was one of the few places he could be really alone.

He scooted up around the perimeter wall, taking care to avoid the haunted area, and quickly made his way to the south-eastern corner. There was an old elderflower bush there which provided natural cover. He scurried under it through the long grass into the hollow area he had created by breaking a few branches and flattening the weeds. When he had settled in, he watched the woman walk away from the graveside and head towards the gate. Alone at last.

Lying on his stomach, he had a good view of the whole graveyard on this side of the church. Many of his friends wouldn't visit it under any circumstances, especially alone – they were afraid of the village's famous bogeyman – but Peter didn't mind. He had a taste for the macabre. These days he had moved even further apart from his friends; nothing could scare him, no ghosts or vampires or werewolves. When you've killed somebody it gives you a special power over fear.

He opened the comic, instantly losing himself in a story by his favourite artist, Berni Wrightson. There was a swamp, dark and mysterious, and a dead thing that rose out of it to terrorize an innocent couple. In the end, a kid saved the day. That gave Peter a warm swell of pride.

When he emerged from the four-colour world twenty minutes later, he looked up and discovered he was no longer alone in the graveyard. A woman was transfixed before a grave on the other side of the yard near the gate. Peter recognized his mother instantly. These days she always walked slightly hunched like someone was sitting on her shoulders, and she rarely bothered to do her hair so that often it stuck out from her head as if she'd had an electric shock. Karen always lost her temper when her mother let it get like that, but Karen was sixteen and she never left the house until every hair had been combed into place. Sometimes she combed for hours, over and over again, humming quietly to herself, and once she had done it for a whole Saturday until their mother ran into Karen's bedroom, yelling. Then her comb was thrown away.

Why had she come to see his grave? Peter thought bitterly. *Couldn't she forget him like everyone else?*

Peter instinctively touched his cheek, just below the left eye, where the bruise never seemed to fade. He couldn't remember the time he had been to hospital, but Karen had told him about it and he had created his own horrific scenario to replace the lost memory. The things his father had done to Karen and Julie and Ruth had been much worse, his mother said, but Peter had never seen any bruises on them.

His mother suddenly fell to her knees and pulled at her wiry black hair before hammering her fists over and over again on to the baked ground. Her strangled sob was snatched by the breeze and Peter trembled when he heard it. She sounded like an animal caught in a trap.

Part of him wanted to run down there and put his arm around her and tell her all the bad stuff had ended that night eight months ago; for once the future was going to be happy. But another part of him was scared of her. She hadn't been the same since they had moved his father's body and concocted the plan that would make everything all right. Something had got lost within her.

As her torment welled out of her in shrieks and sobs, the tears streamed down Peter's cheeks. He hated himself for not comforting her, but he was pinned down by the weight of what he had done. He loathed his father.

After a few more minutes his mother rose, her figure black and spindly like a scarecrow against the sun-bleached landscape. Peter waited until she had disappeared through the gate before dragging himself out of his hiding place and running across the churchyard, still crying silently. At his father's grave, he snatched up pebbles from the ground and pelted them at the headstone with unrestrained venom.

'Leave us alone!' he yelled as each missile found its mark and careered off into the air. 'I'm glad you're dead!'

It took five full minutes before his anger dissipated, leaving him drained and flat; there was no point going back to his hideaway – he didn't feel like being on his own any more – and, anyway, it was getting close to lunch, so he turned sullenly and stepped on to the path. He hadn't gone more than five paces when he heard something, or thought he did. It had seemed like his name, or perhaps it was just a breeze through the yews. He glanced around him, and his attention was caught by the haunted area, a patch wild with long, yellow grass and viciously curling brambles that stood out from the rest of the neat, clipped graveyard. Had it come from up there? Peter felt a slight tingle of excitement tinged with fear. He wanted to see.

His father forgotten momentarily, Peter traipsed up the slight incline until, in the midst of the untouched zone, he could just make out the black marble of a headstone. Nonchalantly, he began to swing his foot to flatten the grass. The brambles were more of an obstacle, but he stamped them into the ground. As he drew closer, a compulsion came over him, growing with each second until his entire body buzzed nervously. Suddenly it was not just a passing fancy; he *had* to see *it*.

And then he was before it, half crouching, sweeping the choking weeds aside so he could read the inscription. It leapt out at him, the name as sharply defined as the day it had been chiselled:

LAURENCE LUCAS

Peter's stomach did a little flip and then tightened up on itself. No message, no dates, nothing. It was like a canister that had been labelled for opening at a future date. Peter remembered the tales he had heard whispered by the grown-ups, twisted and coloured in by the children. He understood why the under-growth had been allowed to grow so wild. No one in Riddington wanted to remember Laurence Lucas, and he guessed everyone would be happier if nature rose up and sucked the grave out of sight for ever. A monster, that's what he had been. A monster even worse than Peter's father.

There it was again! The noise. He glanced at the yews nearby, waving slightly from side to side. The wind seemed to be picking up; he could hear it moaning, drawing closer. Was that what he had heard?

But it had sounded like his name.

He looked down at the grave now, suddenly afraid, and for a moment he had a startling sensation of an alien mind touching his. Of something watching him, through shards of rotting wood, and stones and roots, and six feet of soil.

Peter didn't wait to feel any more. He turned and sprinted down the incline as fast as he could without once looking back.

Just before he reached the lych gate, as the blood pounded in his ears, he heard it again, as clear as a bell.

'Peter.'

*

It was 8.30 p.m. and the hot day seemed like it would never end. Annie was wearing a long, baggy t-shirt, a pair of briefs and nothing else. Her hair was pulled back into a scrunchie, but she was still sleeked in sweat. It seemed like nothing would ease her discomfort.

She tried to muster some interest in the TV, but every channel seemed flatly uninteresting. She couldn't concentrate anyway; two opposing forces seemed to be thundering across her mind, one lost in a silvery-white light, the other swathed in shadows, and both of them slamming together.

Miranda's words were at the centre of that disturbance: *You have been chosen.* That frightened her because it implied a mission, and she had a terrible fear as to what that mission might be.

Somewhere out over the fields the drone of a tractor rose and fell as a farmer eked out the last, weary hours of the day. Annie closed her eyes and listened to it as she massaged her temples where the first stage of a tension headache had started to thud. Other noises began to impinge on her consciousness as she switched off her thoughts and listened: the whine of a motor-cycle disappearing into the distance, the hum of the TV set behind its muted sound, children shouting and playing, and birds, so many different bird calls she was surprised at the cacophony. Doves cooing on the telegraph pole across the road. Wood pigeons venturing out from the trees on Jack Tarrant's land. And something else, harsher, more . . .

A sensation of utter cold came from nowhere and swept through her, as if someone had tipped a bucket of icy water on her head. Her eyes snapped open with the shock. As she looked down at her forearm, her skin contracted and prickled into a wave of massive goosebumps which ran up and down, sucking the cold deep into every pore.

The cry of that bird grew louder, outside the house now.

A change was coming over the room. Shadows flew in from nowhere to spread across the walls and everything suddenly seemed so sharply defined it made her eyes ache.

And the bird, so loud now it hurt her ears.

The TV screen froze in an image of a high-powered car. Annie's eyes fixed on it involuntarily, and whatever she did, she could not break her stare. A core of panic began to rise inside her.

Then came a voice that sounded from both inside her head and outside too, booming loud from every corner of the room.

'He's getting closer.'

And suddenly the bird was in the room, although she couldn't see it; the shadows of its mighty wings were beating across the walls, and the cry of a raptor hungry for meat echoed shrilly all around. A falcon, she thought. It was a falcon.

Before she could double-check, there was a shift in reality and the whole experience ended as suddenly as it had started. Slumping back, Annie felt strangely drained as if she had spent an hour in the gym. She glanced round the room. No bird, no shadows. The TV was behaving normally. Everything was as it should be.

The heat, she thought. *It's screwed up my mind.* But more of Miranda's words came back to her. *Trust in intuition. Trust in the feminine things, dreams, visions.* And then the panic spread.

The knock at the door made her spring forward as if a hot poker had been pressed against her skin.

Martyn was smiling sheepishly, expecting her usual acid tones and a quick exit, so when she grabbed him and pulled him in, he was nonplussed.

'Sorry? Is this the house of Annie Boulton?'

He could tell from her face that it wasn't the time to joke, so he allowed himself to be led quietly into the lounge where she gave him a big hug.

'What is it?' he asked.

'I don't know what's happening to me, Martyn.'

He could see she was upset and scared, but he saw something else too. For the first time in three years he recognized a glimmer of the old Annie he had grown up with, and loved.

'Have you been thinking about Robert? Or the train crash?'

She shrugged. 'No . . . yes . . . well, that's part of it. But there's more . . .' She looked into his sympathetic eyes and knew instantly that they lacked any comprehension of what she was going through; she couldn't tell him. 'Oh, don't worry,' she said with a faint smile. 'I'm just going crazy in the house on my own.'

He wasn't convinced, she could tell, but he didn't push her further. Instead, he pulled her down on to the floor and sat next to her with his arm around her shoulders. It reminded her of the old days. They stayed there quietly while he bathed in the warm glow of happier times.

'I may be a thick yokel, but I know Annie Boulton,' he said softly. 'Something's changed you. It's like you're coming out from under that dark cloud that's been following you around.'

'I'm not out yet,' she replied. 'But I think . . . maybe . . . I'm getting there.'

'Let's hope,' he said, and gave her hand a squeeze.

'There's something else that's bothering me now,' she said without looking at him. 'I keep having this premonition. That . . . that I'm going to die.'

'Don't be silly,' he said. 'I'll be here. I'll look after you. I always said I would.'

His words didn't really comfort her, but she jabbed him playfully in the ribs, and the strained atmosphere eased back to normal. 'I'm glad you're around,' she said.

'Does that mean sex is back on the cards?'

'In your dreams, Martyn.' She laughed softly. 'In your dreams.'

They lay there, hugging each other and talking quietly for an hour or more, until Annie heard Martyn's breathing grow steady as he dozed in the heat. In the growing twilight, she stared up at the ceiling and thought how isolated she felt from him, from all the people in the village. It was as if each strange experience took her one step further away, into another world where anything could happen.

11

Birmingham roasted; the concrete sizzled and the tarmac steamed. Its too bright world of glass and steel shimmered, and there was dust in the breeze. He stood on the overpass above the speeding traffic and looked along the Aston Expressway towards Spaghetti Junction shimmering in the heat haze and the petrol fumes.

She was in that direction. His internal compass never lied.

He always felt the faintest tingle of excitement whenever he had a destination in mind, the last vestiges of what he used to be and what he used to feel. He was surprised he still felt anything at all. After so long, so much. Someone in a Parisian bar had once told him that experience bred maturity and spiritual fibre. He had laughed until wine came down his nose.

There was another sensation too; an eagerness to see her that was so alien he felt disturbed by it. He had thought about her many times over the last few hours, remembering her face, her figure, her hair. He knew, perversely, he was drawn by that power inside her. Life and vibrancy were attractive however much he tried to deny it, but there was something more about Annie Boulton which had its hooks in him. Paradoxically, the attraction was a threat. The only thing he could do to stop it growing was to eradicate it at source. Destroy the thing that it grew from, psychologically. Break her.

Then kill her.

He didn't have a watch, but he could tell from the position of the sun that it was about noon. He couldn't afford to stay in the city much longer. They would never be able to trace any of the deaths to him, but soon that irritant Severin would be buzzing around like a fly on a corpse. The American was blind and ignorant, but there was always a chance his eyes would open, and then there would be trouble on the wind; his own freedom would be severely curtailed.

He walked along to the slipway, down to the Expressway, and watched the vehicles trundle past, choosing *the one* carefully. He could sense it before it rolled into view.

And there it was.

A battered black van chugged and missed as it came off the roundabout and began to build up speed along the slipway. 'Hammerlock' was sprayed on the side against a red-and-gold sunburst. He held out his hand. There was an instant when it seemed it would pass him and then the driver slammed on the brakes and crunched to a halt with a slight skid. A youth in his teens with long blond hair, he turned to say something to whoever was sitting in the back. A second later the side door slid open and three heads hung out. They were grinning like monkeys, all of them long-haired. One wore mascara. Another was bare-chested and tattooed.

'Where you going, man?' the mascaraed one said.

'That way.' He jerked his thumb. 'Wherever I feel like going.'

They looked at each other and laughed. 'Hop in, guy. You're

one of us.' The tattooed one stuck out an arm and pulled him aboard.

When the door slid shut, the van became as hot as an oven and was suffused with an overpowering smell of hairspray, hash, sweat and feet. He looked around and saw the back was packed to the roof with amplifiers and flight cases.

'We're Hammerlock, man.' A weak hand was offered by the one in mascara. 'The best fockin' rock band on the road.'

He nodded and smiled. 'Musicians.'

'Too fockin' right. What's your name?'

He opened his mouth and then paused. He had had his fill of dead musicians from the latter part of the twentieth century. He searched the vast libraries of his mind and came up with another name.

'Rimbaud.'

There was a moment of silence and then they looked at each other like naughty schoolboys and burst out laughing.

'Shit, man, great name! But where's your headband? Come on, show us your muscles!'

He looked at them inquisitively, shaking his head.

'Rambo, man. From the movies. Sylvester Stallone. Blowing all those people away in Afghanistan. You know?'

He smiled and nodded blankly.

The fourth member, who wore leopard-skin trousers, leant forward incredulously. 'You must know him, man. Big explosions. Guns. He kills people.'

'Ah, yes,' Rimbaud replied. 'That would be me.'

12

The building rose up four storeys from the grey street, each one radiating death. Severin could sense the foulness left by *his* passing as if the entire edifice had been contaminated.

'How did she die?'

He let the question drift out, directed at no one in particular. A girl barely more than sixteen sitting on the front steps started and seemed to see him for the first time. Despite the weather, she was dressed in black, voluminous folds of skirt and coat that hid her frail body. A chain of tiny silver bells hung around her waist and jingled nervously when she moved.

'Did you know Julie?' she asked from behind a mask of panstick make-up and thick mascara.

He ignored this and continued to look up at the pollution-blackened building, feeling more than seeing. 'When did it happen?'

'Two days ago. Luxa – that's her baby – had been crying solidly for four hours, and when someone went to see what was wrong they found her.' She bit her lip. 'Can you spare some change? Normally I wouldn't ask, but . . .'

He gave her a couple of pounds and helped her to her feet. She was ecstatic, a response far beyond the value of the money.

'Can you show me the room?'

She nodded, anxious to please. 'You must have known her well. Were you one of her regulars? She had a lot of, you know, acquaintances, but there were one or two who always looked after her. She used to speak of them really well. You one of them?'

'Yes,' he lied to shut her up. He wanted to concentrate. The house stank; damp permeated everywhere, but there were worse smells behind it. They climbed the stairs slowly, the girl wheezing like an old woman; twice she had to rest, but eventually they entered the room at the top. It was still filled with all the dead woman's gear as if she had just stepped out for a moment. There was a pair of handcuffs on her bedside table.

'She was a good one,' the girl said emotionally. 'She always treated me right. We had a lot of bad times here, but she helped me out when things were rough.'

'Do you remember a man being with her on the day she died?'

She nodded. 'She met him down at New Street. We'd been hanging out there all morning. He'd just got off the train and he came over to talk to her. Ignored the rest of us completely, but that was Julie. She attracted people, you know? They could see something in her. She was so full of life, like a light in the dark.'

'What was he like?'

'I thought he was a bit creepy when I first saw him. Like an undertaker, you know. But when he got up close he was really sexy. Charming, like someone out of an old film. Anyway, they started talking and decided to come back here. She must have ODed after he left.'

Severin sat on the window-ledge and surveyed the room, trying to imagine the scene. The honied words. The easily won trust of a person short of comfort and desperate for warmth. The usual moment of horrific realization. Each time Severin hoped he would stumble across some clue that would reveal *why* he did it; death after death and all of it so meaningless, like a hobby to pass the time.

His thoughts must have shown in his face for the girl suddenly looked uncomfortable and asked, 'What is it?

'He killed her.'

She shook her head. 'Julie ODed.'

'You're telling me she wasn't experienced? That she didn't know how strong her drug was?'

'The police never said anything.' She thought for a second and added, 'They probably don't even care, not when it happens to the likes of us.'

Dispassionately, Severin suddenly appreciated how comical she looked, as if a tennis ball had got stuck in her throat. 'I know the guy who did it. He's done it before.'

'Why Julie? She had a little baby. She was nice. Everybody liked her.'

'That's probably why. He's the ultimate sociopath. He hates people, all people, and he kills without conscience.'

'You're talking like he does this all the time.'

'He does. It's second nature. Hundreds of times. Thousands. More.'

'Then why haven't the police . . .'

'Everyone looks like an accident or a suicide. He's clever. There are crashes and drownings and bodies found at the foot of the stairs with broken skulls. Happy, contented human beings found hanging in their attics. Lonely souls who fall from deserted motorway bridges. No witnesses. No clues that anyone else was involved.'

'How do you know?' she asked in a voice that wanted to sound defiant.

He ignored her question. The buzz had begun, the faint magnetic pull that constantly carried him along in the killer's wake.

'Thousands?' she asked queasily. 'When he came over to talk to Julie . . . listening to him, I fancied him. If she hadn't got in first . . . it could have been me.' She looked at Severin and then at the bed.

He nodded. 'No one is safe.'

13

'I'm surprised to see you back, Annie. I thought you'd deserted me.' Gerard Poulson led Annie across his dark, luxurious office to the marshmallow leather chair in the centre of the room.

'I didn't seem to be getting anywhere at the time. It just felt like we were talking in circles, you know?' She took a deep breath, steadied herself. 'But over the last few weeks, things have been playing on my mind. I need to get them straight.'

'Therapy isn't a quick-cure business, you know.' Poulson settled behind his oak desk which looked as big as a double bed. The size of it in such a small room convinced Annie he should turn some of his therapy on himself. 'You have to invest a lot of time and effort to get results.'

'I know. Maybe I'll keep it up this time,' she lied.

'OK.' He rested his elbows on the table and pressed his fingertips together to form a triangle through which he watched her. 'Where shall we begin?'

The small office could have been considered gloomy with its dark furniture against walls that were a deep claret, but Annie found the sombre interior cocooning. The tall window behind Poulson's desk was a counterpoint of glaring light; it looked out over Ashby's Market Street three storeys below, abuzz with the sound of slow-moving traffic and the morning throng of a bustling small town.

The office had almost been a home from home for a while – after Robert's death, when her parents feared she was sinking into a cycle of black depression. Week in, week out, trying to express feelings which she didn't understand herself. Poulson was a good listener, but Annie couldn't shake the belief that she shouldn't be there. She had always been the good girl, well balanced, liked by teachers and neighbours, and then, just like that, she couldn't cope. The therapy made her feel weak when she knew she was strong, even though she understood it was just another part of the healing process. And when she had convinced herself it wasn't working, she simply stopped.

The truth was, by that time Poulson had already helped her open a seething can of worms and Annie was afraid of what else lay inside her: all those fears and doubts waiting to come out and make a joke of the life she had led before.

'I don't know where to begin,' she said hesitantly. 'It seems so long since I've done this kind of thing.'

'It is.' Poulson was in his late forties with jet black hair streaked with grey and swept back with a touch of hair oil; Annie always thought it made him look like an ageing rock 'n' roller. He wore a charcoal pin-striped suit which seemed a little ostentatiously expensive to her, but his manner always seemed caring enough and it hadn't taken Annie long to feel at ease around him. And he had pretty good credentials; the diploma on the wall said he had trained at the university in Zurich.

He swivelled round on his chair to look out of the window which Annie had quickly noted was one of his tricks to make her feel she wasn't being observed. 'Are you still having the nightmares?'

'About Robert? No.'

'A different kind of nightmare?'

'Yes.'

Wilde's face, grinning.

'And do you remember what we agreed the last time you were here?'

Annie felt like an infant before a teacher, but she took a deep breath and composed herself. 'I know it isn't just about Robert's death.'

She remembered their last conversation clearly. All she had wanted was somebody to make her feel happy again, but Poulson insisted, quite rightly she grudgingly admitted, that she had a deeper problem with the acceptance of death. 'In denial,' he had said. *In denial, in denial, in denial*, until she was sick of those two words.

'I know I'm retreating from mortality or whatever you want to call it,' she continued. 'That's easy for you to say. I can't just flick a switch and change it.'

111

'That's why you were coming here. To find for yourself the way out.'

'Are you going to have a go at me now for quitting?'

'No.' He turned his chair slowly and looked at her sympathetically. 'You have to be ready to heal yourself. Perhaps the time wasn't right then.'

'So what do I do?'

'You know that.'

She sighed. They had been over this point so many times. 'I have to come to terms with Robert's death first before I can deal with death in general. That's right, isn't it?'

He nodded.

She glanced at the clock. Time was ticking away; Poulson was getting richer and she wasn't getting any closer to the real reason she had come. All the talk about Robert and death was a blind, a point of reference for Poulson so he wouldn't think her crazy when she started to talk about what was really on her mind.

'Tell me,' she began tentatively, 'If I said I had a vision . . . of three women . . . one young, one middle-aged, one old . . . what do you think that would mean?'

'Well . . . it could mean many things . . .'

'You're a Jungian, aren't you? Could it be something in my subconscious coming out? An archetype?'

Poulson laughed in surprise. 'You've been doing some reading, haven't you, Annie!'

'I had to do a psychology course as an option for my English degree.' That was true, but what she had learned hadn't seemed so relevant then.

'Don't you want to carry on talking about Robert?'

'No. This will help.'

He nodded and smiled, humouring her. 'Yes, I was trained in the Jungian discipline. I was always attracted to his theory of the collective unconscious. Do you know about that?' She shook her head, playing dumb. 'Jung suggested there was a huge well in the mind which stores the memories or mental patterns shared by all human beings, a well that could be internal or external, something we all tap into from time to time. He came up with this idea to explain recurring delusions in patients with different backgrounds, but also common themes in dreams. And, as you rightly say, the archetypes, universal ideas which appear in similar myths in cultures right round the globe. The language of the unconscious and subconscious is symbols – an image that means something else.'

'So what is my subconscious mind telling me with this vision, Mr Poulson?'

Poulson laughed. 'Well, that's the sixty-four-thousand-dollar question, Annie. It's *your* deep mind speaking to *you*. You have to work it out for yourself. There are no pat rules about what these things mean. I suppose it could be linked to the female archetype which Jung described as a woman with a timeless quality, who looks young, but seems to have experience beyond her years. She's wise, but not overpoweringly so. There's always a sense that she contains some secret knowledge and she may have within her great power, but she normally has two aspects, light and dark. If you had seen two women that would suggest that duality, but three? I don't know. When you're talking about the mind, you can't simply say, "Here is *a*, therefore it means *b*." It doesn't work like that. Proper understanding involves a lot of talking and weighing of evidence until the solutions start to present themselves. It takes time.'

That wasn't what she wanted to hear; in her heart she felt time was one thing she didn't have. 'Can't you give me anything to go on?' she pleaded. 'Something to go away and think about?'

He shrugged. 'Do you feel your femininity is under threat? Are you having problems competing in an all-male environment?'

'No more than normal.' She sighed. 'Mr Poulson . . . it was so disturbing.'

'These things normally are. Lots of people have them though, Annie. You're not alone here. The mind is incredibly complex.' He hummed thoughtfully for a moment and then added, 'You see, Jung also identified the existence of the feminine aspect – the anima – in men and the masculine aspect – the animus – in women, and these two sides of the mind often come into conflict. This vision may be indicative of some internal battle which you are fighting unbeknown to your conscious mind. I think the best thing would be to make some appointments so we can consider all aspects of your life. If you just see my secretary at the end of the session, she'll sort something out.'

Annie felt deflated. She had wanted Poulson to say her visions, even her premonition, were all in her mind, just a more extreme sign of the problems she had carried inside her for the last three years. She would even have settled for him saying she was crazy because that, in comparison, was an easy way out. Then she could just walk away and return to her sad, sour little world. But all Poulson ever wanted to do was talk. After six months would she know any more? Would she still be alive?

Poulson tugged uncomfortably at his collar and added, 'Is it me or has it grown very stuffy in here?'

He spun his chair round and grunted as he threw up the sash window to allow some fresh air to circulate. Although it seemed remarkably still outside in the morning heat, a sudden gust of wind surged through the gap and blew a pile of papers from his desk across the room.

'Oh no, there goes my essay.' Poulson muttered some curse under his breath and got down on his hands and knees to collect the pages.

Three had blown squarely on to Annie's lap. Disinterestedly, she picked them up and cast her eyes over them. On the first page, in the therapist's wild scrawl, one underlined section leapt out at her: *A collective image of woman exists in a man's unconscious. He projects it on to the various women he meets.* (*See Jung's* Two Essays on Analytical Psychology.)

The second page on her lap had only one paragraph on it: *There are no coincidences. Everything happens for a reason. Jung's principle of synchronicity, stating that coincidences are linked to the unconscious mind, has the underlying message that the subconscious mind already knows the implied meaning behind those coincidences.*

And the third ... was a photocopy of an old engraving. It showed a woman lying on her back with her arms folded on her chest ... and roses growing out of her eye sockets. Annie felt her forearms lock in place and suddenly the piece of paper seemed as heavy as lead, but she couldn't let go of it. It was the image of herself she had seen in the sweat lodge. The premonition.

A rush of cold tore through her. 'What's this?' she asked in a small voice.

Poulson plucked the paper from her rigid fingers, glanced at it and then spoke dismissively, 'Just something to illustrate the

114

essay . . . if I ever get round to finishing it, that is. It's about symbolism and how symbols speak to the unconscious mind.'

Annie wanted to ask what it meant, but she was afraid. She had the feeling that she was an insect in a maze, thinking it was choosing its own direction while all the time an invisible giant was secretly herding it towards an inevitable destination. Her skin crawled.

'Shall we continue?' Poulson asked with a clinical rationality which suddenly seemed very hollow.

'No,' she replied weakly. 'I have to go now. Another time . . .'

It was speaking to her. The Beyond. It was telling her to believe. *There are no coincidences.* And it was telling her in no uncertain terms that there was no escape.

Annie felt uneasy as she made her way along Market Street and through The Mews towards the car park. The world had turned into an unfamiliar place, like a play with things moving unseen behind the backdrop. She shivered despite the heat. She remembered from her university course Jung's belief that coincidence piled upon coincidence at times of great crisis, and that was when visions began. He himself believed he had been warned about the horrors of a world war through synchronicity and a waking dream of a sea of blood.

A middle-aged woman strode by with a pinched, mean expression. She was talking to her friend who was fat and ruddy faced with enormous, drooping breasts. 'There was blood everywhere,' Annie overheard as she passed. 'I told her not to use the knife like that, but you know how she is. She always knows best.'

At the end of The Mews and to the right, there was a building which had stood in a state of disrepair for years. It was finally being converted; scaffolding had been thrown up overnight and dusty builders were marching in and out of the front door with planks and buckets. There was a sign hanging from the scaffolding and Annie was irked to see it was Bill King's firm that was carrying out the conversion. She was even more chafed when she saw him standing at the side of the house talking animatedly with Hartley Williams, as ruddy faced as ever. Every time she saw King she realized how much she despised him, and she

wasn't particularly wild about Williams; they represented everything she was starting to feel bad about in the village.

As Annie stepped towards the kerb, hoping the reptilian eyes
of King and Williams wouldn't fall upon her, she heard a tumult
behind her and before she could turn someone almost ploughed
into her back. Whoever it was shifted at the last moment and
threw himself in the direction of the builders.

'Stop him!'

The cry came from behind her. Bewildered, Annie spun
round. A greengrocer was running up The Mews, his striped
blue apron flapping wildly. He was chasing the person who had
almost crashed into her, a long-haired, unshaven traveller in
shabby army fatigues who was trying to sprint away, but who
was hampered by a pair of oversized combat boots. The
runaway had his arms pulled tight against his chest to protect
what seemed to be a pile of fruit.

The greengrocer stopped at the end of The Mews, breathless
and scarlet-faced. 'Stop him!' he yelled again. 'He's nicked my
stuff!'

King broke off from his conversation with Williams to check
on the disturbance. A quizzical look passed briefly across his
face as the traveller ran in his direction and then realization
dawned. He took a step forward and smiled.

The traveller was too concerned with getting away from the
greengrocer to spot King ahead of him until the last moment.

King's fist shot out just once, so rapidly it was almost a blur.
It caught the traveller full in the face and he went down like he
had been poleaxed, apples and oranges tumbling into the gutter.
Annie thought King's reaction had been extreme – he was half
as big again as his scrawny prey – but he hadn't finished there.

While Hartley Williams laughed fit to burst, King pulled the
semi-conscious traveller to his feet; his nose looked broken and
his face was a mess of red. King turned to the builders who
were grinning nearby and shouted, 'Come on, lads. Let's teach
this bastard a lesson.'

Four of them surged forward and with King's help dragged
the now struggling youth back towards the house. His face was
framed for a second against the dark doorway, his eyes wide
with fright, before one of the builders lashed out with his steel-
toecapped work boot against the victim's knee. He crumpled

116

once more and disappeared into the darkness a second before the builders piled in after him.

Annie was briefly frozen in horror and then she launched herself forward, desperate to help. The traveller might be in the wrong, but he didn't deserve to have King's Neanderthals turn him into mincemeat. His cries were stomach-churning and punctuated by the meaty sound of kicks and blows, but before Annie could enter the house, Hartley Williams had inserted his portly frame in the doorway.

'Now, dear, where do you think you're going?' he said as if talking to a child.

'Let me by! They're killing him!'

'Now I know you've got a soft spot for those dirty layabouts,' Williams continued, placing a chubby arm out to stop her at the same height as her breasts. 'I saw you fraternizing with them up at that camp. I suppose it's a bit exciting for a nice little middle-class girl like you. But this one's a thief. He's broken the law and he can't be allowed to get away with it.'

Annie wasn't going to start arguing. She tried to push by, but as she did so her gaze fell upon the diamond-black window of the lounge on the left of the door. There was an electric *frisson* that turned her skin instantly cold. Reflected in the glass were the three women she had seen in the pub in Leicester, their arms stretched out to her.

In the background, the blows grew heavier, the youth's struggles weaker; a piercing cry rose up in his throat, but it sounded strange, like he was gargling soup.

'And,' Hartley Williams was saying, '. . . watch those travellers. They'll only be after your young body.'

Annie snapped round to see the spot where the women should be standing if the reflection was true. There was nothing.

Her heart started to thump – lub-dub, lub-dub – matching the rhythm of the kicks and punches. The youth was silent now.

'. . . your mother say if she knew what you were doing . . .'

The faces were still in the glass. Chalk-white skin, crazy eyes. Summoning her with their hands. Ghosts. They wanted her to join them. They wanted *her*.

Coincidence upon coincidence, vision upon vision . . . It was closing in on her, herding her.

Next thing, Annie was running, the traveller forgotten, her only urge to get away. She threw herself along The Mews as

117

fast as she could, afraid to look back, afraid to glance into any shop window in case she saw those faces staring at her.

And then someone was in her path, and she tried to throw him off before swinging a fist at his chest, but he grabbed her wrists until she stopped struggling and focused on his face. It was George Newton, trying to mask his concern with a broad grin.

'Bloody hell, lass!' he said. 'I thought the devil was after you.'

The café was in a converted warehouse overlooking Rushton's Yard, a quiet Victorian precinct away from the main shopping street. Annie and George took a window seat on the first floor where they could sit in the sun and look out on the tranquil setting. There was a welcoming lull which meant they could talk without raising their voices.

'You better tell me what that was all about,' George said as he stirred three heaped spoons of sugar into his tea.

Annie sipped at her cappuccino and avoided his eyes which were gentle and warm. She was afraid to tell him; she didn't want George, of all people, to think badly of her. 'I'm afraid you'll think I've gone funny in the head, George.'

'There's no such thing as funny in the head – just people who have different views on life. Now you tell me who was after you, and we'll see what we can do.'

Not who, Annie wanted to say. *What.*

She weighed up the pros and cons and then she told him everything – about Wilde on the train and what she'd seen afterwards, the vision in the pub, the premonition at the sweat lodge, the general madness that was crowding into her life. As she spoke she stared at the table and tore her paper serviette into tiny pieces before screwing it all back into a tight ball.

'Now that's an interesting brew,' George said when she had finished. He rubbed the grey bristles on his chin thoughtfully.

'What's the verdict then? Should I order the straitjacket now?'

'You don't want to spend too long talking to that therapist johnny. He'll rot your brain. You're as normal as me, lass, though that isn't saying much.' He chuckled throatily. 'A lot of people think they're going barmy when they see things they can't explain because all those stupid scientists tell us *everything* can be explained.' His face grew serious as he continued. 'I've seen some funny things in my life, Annie. Some of them still give me bad dreams. The world's a bloody strange place and not at all like the scientists tell you, and as soon as you appreciate that it all starts to make a lot more sense. Now I can't help you out with that thing on the train except to say I heard of something similar when I visited Burma just after the war. But the other thing . . . Now why don't you believe what that traveller woman told you?'

'Because . . .'

'Because it sounds mad? Well, there's plenty of people who still have pagan beliefs. In fact, some would say that's the original religion, the one that was around for thousands of years before Christ was nailed up on the cross. Why, most of our churches were built on pagan sites, did you know that? Perhaps even our own St Martin's . . . The old religion couldn't be destroyed so it was taken in by Christianity. "Assimilated", I think the word is. That's a thought, isn't it? Under all those churches, there's a place of worship that owes its allegiance to another. There's a lot of power in belief, Annie, and if you think you saw something that represents that power, well, who's to say you didn't?'

'I don't know . . .'

'You're not the first person to go through something like this, lass. The poet, Robert Graves, wrote a book called *The White Goddess*. It's all about the Triple Moon-Goddess, the same thing you've been on about. She was a symbol all over the world in different mythologies, a powerful religious force that represented all womanly ways – dreams, intuition, magic, because magic is a woman's thing. Any bloke knows that's true.' His laughter was a weak attempt to ease the tension he saw in her face. 'Anyway, after hundreds of years another cult grew up, run by men, to do with sun worship and Apollo, and over a time that beat back the women's religion. Christianity followed on from that sun worship naturally. It was based on men's things – strength and logic and all those things men think are important, but aren't really. But the old way hasn't gone, lass. It just went into hiding. The point I'm getting to is that the power of the Goddess spoke to Graves in the same way that it's speaking to you. When he was thinking about the book, he was surrounded by coincidences that led him in the right direction, to more knowledge about the cult. Once when he was stuck for a vital bit of information, a book fell off his shelf – for no reason at all – and fell open at the right page with the information he needed.

'And it didn't even end there. The first publisher he offered *The White Goddess* to rejected it, then died of a heart attack. The second bloke who rejected it hung himself dressed in women's clothes. The third one accepted it – T.S. Eliot – and not only did he do well out of the book, he also got the Order of Merit in the same year. Now if a great man like Graves understands all that, why shouldn't you?'

Annie had been listening with increasing wonder. 'How did you come across all this, George?' she asked incredulously.

'What's the matter? Don't you think an old miner can read books? I'm interested in anything that makes sense of this mad world, Annie. You have to keep learning to find your way through the dark.'

'What happens if I don't want to be *chosen*, don't want a pagan power addressing me?'

There was a cautionary note in George's voice when he replied. 'All I would say is this: fate rules folks' lives, Annie. You can go against it for so long, but sooner or later whatever makes those rules comes looking for you.'

Annie finished off her cappuccino which had grown cold as they talked. Her life had been complicated enough before, and now it seemed completely out of control. The thought that there was some outside power which wanted to influence her left her with a feeling of icy dread.

'I'm frightened,' she said quietly.

George nodded sagely. 'That's a good way of facing it.'

They tried to talk about more mundane things then, but a strange weight had settled on both of them, and finally they gave up and went to pay the bill.

Downstairs a radio behind the counter was playing a local station. The music stopped as Annie opened her purse and the news began. '. . . Four people were killed when a transit van crashed on the A42 just outside Ashby-de-la-Zouch this morning. The dead were all members of the Birmingham rock group Hammerlock. Fans of the band have vowed to hold a candlelit vigil at . . .'

More death, she thought coldly. *It just won't stay away.*

*

120

That night Annie had a disturbing dream. She was in total darkness, so deep she might have been entombed far underground, yet she had the feeling she was out in the open somewhere; she could feel a faint breeze on her skin and smell fragrant vegetation. She wandered around blindly for a while, wondering why she couldn't see.

And then she suddenly had a powerful sense that there was someone nearby, shadowing her but always just out of reach. She didn't feel threatened by the presence, but she felt very strongly that it was trying to communicate with her.

'Who's there?' she called. 'Speak to me.'

Her voice rang out, but there was no reply and eventually she felt the presence fade away.

When she woke in the bright, warm morning, the dream stayed with her unlike any dream she had ever experienced before.

It almost felt real.

14

In Riddington there were few places to be really alone. The streets often looked deserted, but eyes always stared from the darkened windows, people taking notes in silence, ready to spread any gossip. Many times during the early days of her romance with Martyn, they would sneak off for a kissing session in some private place, only to hear about it a day later from somebody or other. Annie had learnt to be secretive, like everyone else in the village. In fact in the last few days she had started to appreciate just how much of Riddington's true nature was kept deliberately in the shadows, and she was disturbed at how wrong her childhood perception of 'the perfect place' now seemed.

Tarrant's Wood was still a favourite bolt hole. No unwanted eyes penetrated the thick greenery where the oaks and ash and sycamore stood densely together and where the sunlight was transformed into gloomy chlorophyll rays that kept the interior cool and secret. Annie picked her way among the sporadic patches of bracken, remembering the numerous journeys she had made to the wood's dark heart. In the stifling heat, it had become the only place to go.

But it was more than that, wasn't it? She wanted to recapture the days when life was happier and simpler; the wood's hoard of memories was waiting to be unlocked, if she could find the right key. Was she running away? Perhaps. Only twenty feet into the wood and she felt she had entered a different world. The suffocating heat that blanketed the surrounding countryside had gone, replaced by a refreshing coolness that reminded her of a deep cave. The sound of her footfalls seemed intriguingly different; the echoes were crisp as if she was walking on hoar frost. Even the air smelled unique, perfumed with moss, leaf mould and fern spore.

There was the hush of a cathedral under the towering trees and for the first time in days, Annie felt a simple peace descend upon her. It seemed like nothing bad could touch her; no dark thoughts of death within, no inhuman killers or visions without. She was free.

Pausing briefly by an ancient oak, she rested her hand on it for support before sudden realization forced her to snatch her fingers away as if they had been burned. She glanced around and saw the tree's compatriots, nine hunched old men in a circle, the weird heart of Tarrant's Wood. A chill ran through her, as it had done every time she had seen them, ever since she was a little girl. She smiled to herself at her instinctive reaction, an adult still ruled by the tale of 'The Old Men of Riddington'. She remembered the rich voice of George Newton rumbling on about the ten oldest trees in the centre of the wood which reputedly turned into deformed humans under the light of the full moon and stalked the countryside by night looking for children to eat. She had never been able to pass the wood since without thinking of what might be locked under all that bark.

And now, here she was, alone with all the Old Men. And there was the old hut which Tarrant used as a base when he was coppicing, or cutting up firewood. Annie still recalled its singular smell of wood mingled with petrol from the chainsaw.

Sauntering over, she rubbed the cracked window and peered into the dark interior. Nothing had changed in nearly four years. And when she entered, the smell hit her like the voice of the past.

She could see the two of them: herself on the floor, nervous but trying to seem confident; Martyn on top, the same. All those smooching sessions when sex had crept a little nearer each time, and then the big one, when the burden of her virginity was finally shaken off for good. The sex had never been great, but the aftermath was always wonderful, hugging each other tightly while twilight drew in, listening to the animal noises from the wood as the undergrowth started to come alive, promising they would love each other for ever, never part.

Annie watched the ghost images and felt she was watching strangers. How long ago it seemed. She left the hut wistfully and shut the door on the past, feeling a profound sense of loss as the spectres slipped back to their own hazy, golden time. But with her back pressed against the hut door, she closed her eyes and enjoyed the moment, the cool, the peace, the smells and sounds of nature.

The crack of a dry branch, unmistakable in the stillness, disturbed her. Somebody was out there. *It's only Jack Tarrant, or a poacher looking for rabbits.*

There was another break of wood, closer this time. Annie searched for some sign of movement and eventually caught sight of two suspicious figures among the trees in the distance. For some reason, they kept stopping and ducking down before heading off quickly. Decisively, she turned and pushed off through the undergrowth in the opposite direction.

The atmosphere in the wood had altered. A vacuum had been created in which she suddenly couldn't hear any birds singing. To Annie this was as jarring as any warning sound.

Trust in intuition.

Run for it.

She thought of the Old Men of Riddington, shifting uncomfortably in their bark prisons to look at her. She thought of Wilde, sitting up and grinning as his blood splattered the snow. She thought of all the dark creatures that had ever slipped and slithered through her psyche, and suddenly they were all real. The rational modern world was gone and she was in a medieval mayhem.

She hurried on, no longer wanting to be alone, but as she pulled into one of the thickest areas of the wood her nerve endings burst into flame and a voice rang out in her head.

They're coming.

123

The sense of anticipation became electric, and Annie found herself giving in to her subconscious fears. Her heart was beating unnaturally fast. She changed direction, ran a few yards, then switched back. Her limbs felt heavy, her vision distorted. What was happening?

They're coming.

She had to move more quickly. Whatever it was, was coming for her.

They're here.

Three women stood in the greenery ahead of her. Like ghosts, yet somehow substantial. *Three women.*

They were just like she had seen them in the pub in Leicester, bathed by the moonlight and reflecting its silvery-white luminescence: an old hag, wizened with so many wrinkles her skin had taken on the consistency of tree bark; a middle-aged woman with piercing eyes which had no one colour; and a young girl in her teens, with flowing black hair and a clear complexion, eyes, too, that seemed to stare right through Annie. She was the most beautiful, but they all had an inner beauty which left her breathless.

Ice froze her spine as she stared at them. Three women, but not women. Something else, something so terrible her mind could not give it form.

Annie sensed the tremendous power coming off them, and knew that she had been granted a vista on a different world.

Mesmerized, she recited to herself, 'Maiden. Mother. Crone.'

The Triple Goddess.

They were side by side, dark clothes merging, their hands in their wild hair as each opened her mouth in a silent scream of pain. Annie wanted to close her eyes to blank out this terrifying sight, but they were locked on to the vision.

She fell to her knees. They were ... it was ... trying to communicate with her.

The silent screaming continued and then, like a subliminal flash on a TV screen, Annie saw the premonition once more. Herself, in death, eyes closed, then open, as the roses erupted out and grew upwards.

She did the only thing she could. She turned and ran blindly, letting the branches lash her face as she barrelled through the undergrowth. Faster, faster, no longer caring if she fell. Pitching forward, she hurled herself over the lip of a bank and down into a hollow, the sides slick with leaf mould. The world was whirling, but her eyes focused and froze on what lay at the foot of the bank – a gin-trap, the jaws prised open on a powerful hinge, ready to snap shut at the slightest contact.

She threw up her arms to protect her face, knowing there was nothing else she could do.

Something caught her upper arm and yanked her back so roughly she thought her shoulder would dislocate. The world whirled again, and then she slammed into the top of the bank like a dead weight. Winded, she looked around for what had saved her.

A man stood a few feet away silhouetted against the sun breaking through the tree tops. A patch of billowing black against the light. As if a flock of ravens were surging on one spot.

Annie had one brief instant of panic. She thought of dark curly hair and a secretive, seductive smile. She thought of death.

Nervously, she shielded her eyes and the figure shifted away from the light. She relaxed a little; it wasn't *him*, not quite. It was the other one, the man who had saved her that night on the railway tracks. Severin. He didn't look quite so imposing out of the glare. His black clothes were shabby and dusty from too much travelling and his hair hung lankly against hollow cheeks. But there was still an air of strength about him.

As he watched her pull herself to her feet, Annie saw a glimmer of recognition in his face. She brushed herself down and glanced below at the gin-trap, suddenly realizing how close to extinction she had been. Snatching up an old branch, she threw it towards the trap; it hit the release mechanism and disintegrated in the smashing jaws. It could have been her leg.

Annie felt nauseous. She covered her mouth and at that moment, through the trees, she glimpsed the two figures she had seen earlier, only this time they were close enough to recognize. Bill King still wore his building-site clothes, and next to him, with a big sack slung over his shoulder, was the imposing figure of Tim Huxton-Smith, the farmer. They took a few more paces then dropped down to their haunches and opened the sack. King took out another gin-trap and set it.

'What the hell are they doing!' Annie said aghast. 'They'll kill someone!'

Her voice must have carried for King and Huxton-Smith jumped to their feet nervously. She watched the farmer put a finger and thumb in his mouth and give a piercing whistle.

Immediately, there was the sound of paws, punctuated by low snarls and snaps. The dogs erupted from the undergrowth on either side of King and Huxton-Smith and hurtled towards Annie. Two Dobermanns as big as pit ponies crashed onward with the saliva from their bared teeth spraying the greenery.

Annie slipped to her knees; Severin stood his ground.

The first dog roared up and threw itself towards his throat. Severin braced himself and at the last minute his arm snapped into action in a blurred arc. His fist smashed heavily against the side of the dog's head and the Dobermann spun yelping in the air before carouselling down the bank.

The second dog was upon him too quickly, breaking through his defences. It hit him like an express train, then it had him pinned to the ground, head flashing from side to side as it worried a way through to his throat.

Annie watched in horror as the second dog recovered and bounded up the bank to join in the attack on the downed quarry. It slipped forward and sank its teeth into Severin's forearm. She waited for the agony to explode on his face, but there was nothing. The only sign of emotion was the throb of a vein on his forehead as he strained to hold his own against the dog thrashing madly above him.

Annie ran forward and kicked the second dog, but although it jumped sideways with a snarl it didn't loosen its grip. While she looked around for a branch to batter the Dobermanns, she saw Severin draw on some remarkable reserve of strength and start to lift himself off the ground. It didn't seem humanly possible, but he continued into a sitting position while holding the wilder dog with his hands around its throat and using his elbow to ensure the other dog didn't reach his face or neck.

He gave one brief facial twitch and then his fingers played a virtuoso flurry across the first dog's neck, ending with a sudden jerk. Annie heard its neck snap with a sickening crack. Severin flung its carcass to one side and stood up with the other dog still hanging from his arm by its teeth. He brought his arm back and then cracked it like a whip. The Dobermann flew against a tree where it slid to the ground and then slunk off yelping.

'Jesus!' Annie ran forward and snatched at Severin's forearm to examine the wound. There were deep teeth marks, but surprisingly no blood. He seemed oblivious to any pain as his eyes searched the wood for King and Huxton-Smith.

'They've gone,' he said dismissively.

'What are you, Superman?' Annie asked incredulously. 'Doesn't it hurt?'

'I'm tough-skinned.' He slid his hand over the teeth marks and pulled his sleeve down.

'Jesus,' Annie said again, looking at Severin and not daring to voice the obvious question.

In his eyes she could see him weighing something up, and then he said simply and quietly, 'Yes. He's here.'

Annie's head was spinning. She allowed herself to be led blindly out of the wood. As they emerged into the thick noonday heat, she noticed obliquely that the trees abutted the field which held the travellers' camp. In her heart, she knew why King and Huxton-Smith had been laying the gin-traps. Not for animals.

By the time they had made it down to Colthorpe Road, she had composed herself enough to talk, but Severin refused to discuss anything until he had had something to eat and drink. There was no point in arguing; he simply ignored her. He was so silent, his movements so fluid, Annie felt she had a shadow walking next to her.

The Royal Oak's bar was filled with the lunchtime crowd, so they took their drinks to a table in the lounge where Severin could watch the door. Annie thought she had maintained a placid exterior, but the hand that held her glass gave her away, as it shook.

'What's going on?' she demanded.

His answer was interrupted as the barman brought over the all-day fry-up. Severin took it without smiling and drained half his pint. He cast half an eye on her as he turned to his food and said emotionlessly, 'You're in great danger.'

'Don't beat about the bush, Severin. Why don't you just tell me straight.' Feeling better for her sarcasm, she snatched at her glass and swigged down a mouthful of vodka. Her hand was still shaking, but she didn't even try to hide it as she slammed her glass back down on the table. Anger and irritation cut through her fear; she felt confused and powerless and that always made her annoyed, and Severin was the only target she could find for what she felt.

'You've saved my life two times now—'

'Three,' he interrupted distantly, wiping egg from his chin. 'At the train, from the trap and from the dogs.'

'The dogs wouldn't have killed me,' she snapped. He shrugged. 'But that's not the point. I don't like it—'

'You don't like being alive? I'll bear that in mind next time.'

'There won't be a next time.'

'Tough talk.' He crunched up some bacon and glanced around the room distractedly.

Annie felt herself responding to his baiting and she had to make a concerted effort to control herself; her nerves were shot and her emotions a mess, and she knew it would be best if she thought before she spoke. She took another drink to calm herself before continuing.

'Wilde is looking for me. He's somewhere in the area, that's what you're trying to tell me. Why?'

'It's because he wants to kill you. If you mean why does he want to kill you, the answer is, because you're there.'

'Because I was a witness to what he did on the train?'

'That too.'

'You don't sound very sympathetic.'

He shrugged; beer swilled out of his mouth.

'And you eat like a pig.'

'Pigs get meals every day. I don't.' He paused mid-drink and looked at her curiously as if he was examining some new life form, and then he put his glass back on the table. 'OK, I'm sorry. I forget what it's like sometimes . . . what you're going through. When you deal with this shit every day it becomes the norm. Here's the bottom line: Wilde won't give up until you're dead. You can stay here and try to fight him with me or you can run away and wait till he tracks you down, and in the meantime kills all your loved ones in a fit of pique.'

Annie clenched inwardly, then she forced a laugh of denial.

'I'm not joking,' Severin said coldly.

'You expect me to believe that this freak of nature even remembers me? And that he's taking time out to come and hunt me down? It's almost flattering.' Her attempt at bravado came out weaker than she expected.

Severin chewed on his lip for a second and then said simply, 'You saw what he can do.'

The images flashed into Annie's mind before she could stop them. The most lingering was a clear snapshot of the sadistic glee on Wilde's face as he'd crushed the life from her fellow passengers on the train.

'Now tell me you're brave enough not to listen to what I have to say.'

Annie tried to keep her mocking smile, but it wouldn't stay in place. 'Go on.'

'I didn't know he was coming back for you until I saw you in the wood and then it all fell into place. He doesn't like loose ends. I should have guessed it was only a matter of time before he tracked you down.'

'Did you follow him?'

'In a way. From a distance.'

Over in the bar, some man was shouting, 'Give her a kiss for me!' over and over again and punctuating it with a burst of rough laughter. Others joined in like a pack of hyenas howling at prey.

Annie thought aloud, 'I should go to the police . . .'

'Your choice. But you'd be wasting your time. Did you tell them what happened on the train?' She nodded. 'Got a good response, right?'

'So I should throw up the barricades, get myself a shotgun and sit there like Elmer Fudd for twenty-four hours a day?'

'You could, but that won't do any good either. You saw what he can take.'

Severin firing the shotgun. Wilde getting hit full square in the chest. Flesh, bone and blood splattered everywhere. Wilde grinning, pressing his body back together. Getting up and walking away.

Annie shook her head and grimaced. 'What *is* he?' she whispered.

Severin looked as though he was trying to make up his mind about something. After a moment of silence, he said, 'He's not human, you know that. You saw.' He let the words hang in the air as he watched her reaction. 'It's the truth.'

'He can't be killed, he survives gunshots, plane crashes, explosions. He looks pretty rough afterwards, but he heals within hours. He's rumoured to have lived for hundreds of years, maybe thousands.'

Annie looked in his face for some obvious sign of lunacy, but if it was there he managed to hide it well. She felt cold; as insane as it sounded, too many strange things had happened to her to discount what he was saying.

'But where did he come from? What does he want? Why does he kill?'

'I wish I could answer. I've been tracking him for five years now. I've seen at first hand what he's capable of. I don't know what he is, but I do know no *man* can live through the things he's experienced. When I was following him across India, I was told about a living legend that matched Wilde's description. "The man who could not meet God." That's what they called him.'

The laughter in the other room had grown uncomfortably raucous now, with only the occasional barked word breaking through the din. 'Kiss! KISS!'

It suddenly went silent as if everyone in the bar was listening to their conversation. Annie's voice grew small. 'Five hundred and seventeen. That was the death toll from the train crash.'

His smile was humourless. 'A drop in the ocean to him. He's killed so many he's like a force of nature gone wrong. The first time I met him was on board a plane. He brought it down. Everyone died apart from him and me. I got lucky. If you read of some disaster in the papers, some fire or explosion, there's a good chance he's behind it. And I've seen the results.' Severin's intensity was disconcerting.

'You're taking this very well,' he said.

'What am I supposed to do? Go to pieces? That won't do me any good. If I face up to it I can find a solution.'

'Smart girl.'

'Don't patronize me.'

'I'm not. You are smart. You could laugh in my face here and walk away. And tomorrow or the day after, or the day after that, you'd be dead. Or you could believe something that sounds crazy and stand a chance. Most people would have gone for the former.'

'Yes, well, I'm definitely adaptable,' she said ironically. 'But if he's killed so many, why haven't I heard of him? Interpol, the FBI. Jesus, every cop in the world should be on his tail!'

'He's twisted, but he's not insane. He loves to do it, and he's too smart to get caught. If anyone tells you evil doesn't exist in this day and age, don't believe it. He's the definition of evil. Killing without rhyme or reason, every few days, one or two here, a handful there, interspersed with the occasional big one, right across the globe. Take your train crash. Everybody thought it was an accident, right? And that's how he gets away with it. The cops are too hard-pressed to look into accidental deaths if there are no glaring incongruities hitting them in the face. That goes for New Delhi or New York.' He paused. 'And he doesn't leave witnesses.'

'Apart from you and me.'

'Right.'

'And who the fuck are *you*?' Annie homed in. 'You could be as bad as Wilde for all I know. You turn up out of the night blasting away with a shotgun like you're Clint Eastwood and you can kill a dog with bare hands. As a curriculum vitae, that doesn't look good. All I know is you're American, you're called Severin and you've got a big gun in your pocket.' She smiled tightly at the innuendo.

'That's about it.' He turned to his food and added, 'I may be no angel, but I'm on their side. You'll just have to trust me. I don't care if I'm looking for him on my own or with you. But you'd be safer with me.'

Annie *did* trust Severin on a gut level; there was something about him, beneath the rough trappings, which suggested a deep-rooted honesty, and Annie had always considered herself a good judge of character.

'OK, you're telling me he's immortal. What have *you* got to equal that?'

'I've got certain abilities.'

'Like?'

He didn't answer.

'Very mysterious,' she said irritated. 'I see before me a long-haired drifter in dirty clothes. And I'm supposed to believe he can offer me more protection than the police? Pull the other one, why don't you?'

Severin ignored her while he finished the rest of his food. Then he wiped his mouth with the back of his hand and leaned back in his seat. 'OK, get this. He's scared of me.'

'In your dreams.'

'He taunts me, he threatens me, but he won't come near me. And I think it's got something to do with this.' He slipped his hand into his shirt and pulled out a corroded iron band about half an inch wide which hung on a leather thong around his neck.

'What is it?'

Severin shook his head. 'He had it with him when we met on the plane. I was struggling with him when the plane went down and it got caught around my wrist. When I woke up in the wreckage, I was still holding it and he was gone. Every time I catch up with him, I see his reaction. It scares him that I've got it. I don't know why, but I plan to find out.'

'But it's just a dirty old piece of iron,' Annie said incredulously.

'Maybe. Maybe it's more than that. You've got to remember we're dealing with different rules here. This isn't the world of science and industry. This is the world you always feared existed when you were a little kid in the middle of the night. And it does exist, take my word for it.'

She took a deep breath, but couldn't take her eyes off the bracelet. 'What are you saying? That it's magic?'

'I'm saying that it's got some kind of power which is tied up in everything that he is.'

'Here, let me see.' She held out a hand and Severin slipped the bracelet from his neck and held it dangling by the cord, spinning hypnotically. Annie was transfixed; up close there was something fascinating about it. The first thing she thought as her fingers closed around it was that it didn't feel like iron. It was warm and soft, almost like skin. The second thing that struck her was the whispers, tiny, conflicting voices babbling incoherently that suddenly erupted in her mind. She could almost make out individual words in the insistent hum, and for a split second she had the strangest sensation that the bracelet was trying to talk to her. She snatched her hand away and the mind whispers ceased immediately.

Severin looked at her curiously, but he didn't say anything as he laid the bracelet gently on the table. Annie could see it had once been quite ornate before the corrosion of years had taken hold. There seemed to be an inscription on the inside, but she couldn't read it without picking it up.

'What does it say?'

'I don't know. It's not in English.' Severin nonchalantly hung the bangle around his neck again. 'But somehow, this is the key to getting him.'

'*Getting him*? Murder?'

'I'm prepared to do that.'

'Hmmm, nothing like male logic. You believe he's a man who can't be killed, yet you want to murder him. If you hadn't helped me out after the crash, I might start to think you're a dangerous combination, Severin – judge, jury and executioner, with a gun and no concept of reality.'

'I'll cover the area until I locate him. He'll be lying low somewhere, getting the lay of the land. A derelict property maybe, or a boarding house – he likes to be around people. But he won't stay hidden for long, and when he does surface, I'll get him.'

'Right. Interesting plan. Do the words "needle" and "haystack" mean anything to you?'

'You know the area. You can guide me.'

Annie suddenly felt that although she might be coming apart at the seams, she had to fight back and here was her chance. 'We're going to beat him.'

The defiance in those five words had a palpable effect on Severin. For the first time, she felt the beginnings of a bond building between them.

Perhaps that was why she noticed immediately when a strange expression crossed his face, and he glanced curiously around the bar until his eyes alighted on the framed photographs that lined one wall.

'What is it?' Annie asked, following his gaze.

'I don't know.' He sounded troubled. 'I felt something . . . I get that sometimes, a feeling, a hunch . . .' He walked over to the photographs and started to examine them closely.

Annie moved in behind him. 'They're all snapshots from village history. There's nothing important here. There's one of the fête last year. The church. The Lovers' Bridge. The medieval lock-up. That fat bloke is Hartley Williams, the parish council chairman. Possibly the most pompous man in Riddington.'

'Who's that?'

Severin pointed to a photo near the bottom. It showed a grinning boy in his teens, handsome with the energy of youth, freckles that hinted of innocence, and a floppy fringe that fell over one eye. The snap had the garish colours of a sixties movie.

'Laurence Lucas,' she replied. 'The village bogeyman. They put his picture up here so no one will forget what he did. Nobody really talks about it any more, but we all know. He's our one guilty secret.'

'He's only a kid. Looks no more than nineteen. What did he do?'

'What's age got to do with it? If you're born bad, that's the way you are.' Annie dropped her voice. 'He killed children. Three of them, all local. He was the son of the wealthiest family in the village, charming by all accounts, very, very smart. He was educated at a private school nearby and had a place at Cambridge waiting for him. The pride of the village. I don't think anyone knows what made him do it. Just a pervert, I suppose. Anyway, there was a big outcry about it in the sixties, and a massive police investigation. It was in all the papers. Somehow the trail led back to Lucas. I think the police found him with the body of his third victim. Doing things to it.' She broke off; that bit always got her. 'He gave them the slip, and when they caught up with him again he'd killed himself. The coward's way out. He's buried in the graveyard here. The whole village tried to stop it, said it was an affront to the parents of the children he killed, but you know how it is – money speaks. His family pulled all the strings and got him a plot up there. Your hunch, was it something to do with him? He's long gone.'

Severin spoke with a strange note of worry in his voice. 'I don't know.' He returned to their table. 'Wilde would have liked him,' he said.

'At least he doesn't know where I am,' Annie said. 'That gives us some time, doesn't it?' It sounded unconvincing even to her own ears.

She shifted down a gear to negotiate a bend and then glanced over at Severin who was staring out of the passenger window. He gave no sign that he had heard her.

'How much further?' he asked.

'It's just at the end of this lane,' she replied. 'Jack Tarrant's farm is pretty isolated, he's become a real recluse. And he's not the most popular person in the village at the moment after renting his land out to those travellers.'

Severin couldn't understand why she had insisted on a detour to warn Tarrant about the gin-traps that had been planted in his wood, but Annie knew she wouldn't be able to live with herself if someone got hurt.

She punched a tape into the outmoded cassette machine wired up beneath the dashboard. 'Keep on Running' crackled out of the speakers.

'This is before your time, surely?' Severin stretched out his long legs and hung one arm out of the open window. 'The Spencer Davis Group. Reminds me of summers when I was a kid.'

'I like the old stuff. It makes me feel secure.' She turned the music up a notch and they bumped over the potholes in the road without talking for a while. Annie let her thoughts drift back and forth.

Tarrant's farm was a secluded huddle of run-down buildings at the end of a long lane. It had fallen into disrepair after the old man had semi-retired and sold off his herd; the roofs of the outbuildings sagged and gaped and ivy had crawled everywhere, even obscuring some of the dusty windows.

Annie parked next to the hulk of a rusting farm machine of indeterminate use. It was still oppressively hot, and clouds of fat flies buzzed in the air.

'Hello?' Her voice bounced off the walls of the farmhouse and surrounding outbuildings.

'Maybe he's out in the fields mending fences or whatever farmers do.' Severin leaned against the wing of a primer-splattered old truck with a flat tyre while Annie banged on the farmhouse door. When no one came she proceeded to peer through the filthy windows.

There was no one in the kitchen. Dirty dishes and pans were piled on the drainer and there was a pair of Wellington boots abandoned in the middle of the floor. Stained towels hung on a line above the old range. Annie moved on to the lounge window and then the dining room at the end of the building. She saw movement before she pushed her face close to the glass.

'They're in here,' she called to Severin.

Tarrant was sitting at the table, digging his fork into a pile of mashed potatoes and spreading it around his plate. Vegetables and gravy had spilled out across the place mat. He was staring at his meal with the blank gaze of a drunk or someone in shock.

His wife stood on the other side of the room, seemingly preoccupied by a row of ornaments on the mantelpiece.

Annie watched this dazed tableau curiously before gently rapping on the window. There was no response so she tried again, harder, a little concerned by the rudeness of her action, but sure Tarrant would understand. The farmer continued to play with his food while his wife remained motionless at the mantelpiece.

She tried one more time, three sharp raps in a row. For a few long beats, nothing changed, and then slowly Tarrant turned his head to look in her direction. Behind him, his wife began to inch round in a laborious shuffle like some clockwork mouse.

Annie waved cheerily and pointed to the back door, but their eyes were so cold and empty that the smile froze on her face. Slowly her wave wound down and came to a dead stop. The Tarrants stared at her without acknowledging her presence, their faces set in stone, and then gradually they returned to what they had been doing.

A movement on the table caught Annie's eye. A fat black beetle had dropped from somewhere up in the rafters and was skittering towards Tarrant's plate. It climbed over a piece of carrot on the place mat, and then mounted a lump of potato, before levering itself up on to the china. The farmer watched as it progressed to the centre of his plate where it became mired in the gelatinous gravy, and then he moved with a speed that belied his previous lethargy. His fork came down suddenly and impaled the beetle, crunching through its carapace. Just as quickly, he whipped it up and opened his mouth to jaw-cracking width. Annie's stomach clenched in disgust, and she threw herself away from the window.

'What's wrong?' Severin asked as she hurried over.

'Nothing's wrong with *me*.' She screwed her face up in distaste, unable to bring herself to repeat what she had seen. 'But I'm starting to think there isn't a sane person left in this village.'

She took an old notebook from the glove compartment of the car and scribbled a quick message about the gin-traps before slipping it through the letter box. She felt a sense of relief that her duty had been done and that she could once more concentrate on her own problems.

'What now?' she asked once they were back in the car and trundling down the lane.

'I want to get to your cottage and make sure it's secure.' He checked the position of the sun in the sky. 'Before nightfall.'

15

When they arrived at Blackstone Cottage, Severin spent the next hour rattling windows, examining door locks, looking at the thick hawthorn hedges which surrounded the garden. His actions seemed half-hearted, Annie thought, as if he was doing it just to keep her mind at rest rather than because he thought it would really keep Wilde out.

After that he showered and shaved, and then they sat in the kitchen and talked. Annie could smell the green apples of her shampoo on his hair, and surreptitiously she examined him. His chest was naked as he sat with the towel slung around his shoulders; she could see his muscles, lithe and hard from his life on the road, and his fingers, uncommonly long and artistic. He was a far cry from the men who had followed her around during her university days.

For the first time in months, Annie relaxed and she felt almost sad when the conversation inevitably turned to Wilde and how he could be found. The moment his name was mentioned a shadow seemed to fall across them both and everything else was forgotten. Their options seemed limited – a laborious search of the area, hoping they could get to him before he got to them. *Hope*, Annie thought as the sun slipped down towards the horizon. That was all there was left.

Hope and faith.

'We've got to take a stand somewhere. We can't keep running for ever.'

The heat from the roaring campfire burned Angela's face, but the sensation was lost beneath her anger. To her, the others were all so submissive, stupid sheep blind to the threat.

'That's the nature of our life, Angela,' a voice chimed up from the other side of the fire. 'We're *travellers*. We keep on the move, follow life's rhythms . . .'

'At our own pace.' Her whiplash reply stung the dissenter into silence. 'I'm sick to death of being driven. We spend so much time looking over our shoulder, we can't see where we're going. You all heard what happened in the sweat lodge. You all know about those stupid, fucking villagers who caused the trouble! This is a dangerous time. We can't sit back and do nothing.'

The eyes of all the other travellers were on her as she addressed the gathering with hands on hips, her temper as hot as the fire. The air was filled with smoke and sparks and in the background was the continuous thud of the sound system.

'What do you suggest?' It was one of the old ones, a greying hippie who always insisted on talking about the flowering of the culture in the sixties. Angela had never liked him.

'We fight them. With everything we've got.'

There was some laughter, a few sighs, which made her face burn all the more.

Tommy finally stood up, swaying a little, and Angela reluctantly sat down in deference.

'I think we all share Angela's feelings about wanting to live our own lives. That's why we joined the tribe, right? To be free. But fighting, y'know . . . confrontation . . . it goes against everything we believe in. We go with the flow.'

'Right on,' the old hippie interjected.

'On top of that there's the simple fact that we can't win. They've got the law on their side. If we try to fight, we'll just get crushed. So, the way I see it, we've just got to wait until they start to come round to our way of thinking. And they will, you know. They'll recognize how shallow their own lives are, and they'll see the example we set. We've just got to be patient.'

'Bollocks,' Angela said quietly, but loud enough for those in her immediate circle to hear.

Somebody else backed up Tommy's views and most of those around were nodding and murmuring approval, trying to hurry up the serious stuff so that they could party. Angela couldn't take any more; she stood up pointedly and walked away from the circle into the shadows among the randomly parked vehicles.

Away from the fire, the night was cooler. There were no clouds, and with no streetlights to spoil the ambience, the sky was filled with a thousand glittering stars surrounding a full moon.

Her anger subsided a little as she walked, but she still knew she was right. How could everyone else be so laid back?

She stopped on the edge of the camp where she had a view down the sloping field across the moonlit countryside. Her skin tingled at the sheer beauty of the silvery landscape spreading out to the hills in the distance. This was why she didn't want to live in a house in a street in a town, where the skies were always cloudy with pollution and you couldn't see the horizon. She took a joint from her pocket and lit it, drawing in the smoke deeply until it added to the clarity of the scene before her. So beautiful. Why couldn't the townies realize what they were missing?

Stoned or not, her attention was drawn by a half-seen movement out of the corner of her eye. In the light of the moon, she could see a solitary male figure walking through a field nearby as if it was as clear as day, and there was something in his slow progress through the corn that made her skin feel icy. Why was he avoiding the roads and footpaths at that time of night, she wondered? And where was he going? There were no houses nearby, no reason for him to be there at all.

When he reached the centre of the field, he stopped. The hairs on Angela's arms prickled. Then he slowly turned around and looked in her direction.

Right at her.

It could have been the dope, but paranoia swept over her. She suddenly found life in her heavy limbs and scrambled back into the security of the camp. She didn't stop until she had reached the fireside.

The church clock said 12.30. Colin Barnwell, the verger, could see it from the bedroom window of his house on Starling Lane opposite the churchyard, illuminated by the light of a bright, full moon. He pulled his dressing gown tightly around him as he scanned the countryside. Despite the heat of the day, it seemed uncommonly chill in the bedroom as if winter was hinting at an early return.

As usual, he had gone to bed at eleven, joining his wife who had already been there for half an hour, but something indefin-

139

able had snapped him out of sleep. Not a noise or a flash of light, more something tugging at the inside of his head.

The dark of the bedroom made the view from the window clear and unmuddied by dazzle. To his right, Riddington slumbered under a sprinkling of stars, with only a couple of lights in Partridge Cottage on the High Street signifying any life. Nothing moved. All was peaceful, all was serene.

Barnwell gave another cursory sweep of the area and, noting everything was as it should be, put it all down to a bad dream. He felt tired and the warm bed was beckoning. Yet as he turned to return to his wife, there was an insistent tug which drew his gaze back to the window.

He looked around again. Where was it? The churchyard? Something was not quite how it should be down there among the pooling shadows and splashes of white stone. And then he glimpsed the vague movement near the foot of the church. At that distance, it was impossible to make out what it was, but he opened the window cautiously, and across the still of the night he could just make out the indistinct mumble of a voice.

With irritation, he cast a fleeting, rueful glance at the bed and then turned to dress. They had had this kind of trouble before. Children with too much time on their hands and not enough discipline. The last time – when was it? Two years ago now? Four graves were disturbed, the stones upturned, one of them smashed beyond repair. Youths from the school down in Ashby, experimenting with black magic rituals and scaring each other silly, turning in the end to mindless vandalism when they grew bored with their mock conjuring.

As he left the house, Barnwell picked up a walking stick leaning against the back door. Just for protection, he thought. If drugs were involved there would be no telling how the troublemakers would react to his sudden appearance. Familiar with the creak of the gate into the churchyard, he was careful how he opened it so he didn't disturb them until he caught them in the act. The element of surprise would help to teach them a lesson.

Carefully, he stepped off the path, ghosting among the aged stones as unobtrusively as possible. The shadows were thick in the bright of the moon and it was difficult to get his bearings; he struggled to reconcile the view from the bedroom window with what he could now see on the ground. With no sound apart from the rustle of the yews against the perimeter wall, there was nothing to tell him if the intruders were still there. Pausing against a lichen-coated cross, Barnwell waited for a sign.

There was no movement, yet strangely he felt uneasy as if someone was watching him. He glanced up at the moon beyond the church steeple, and wondered if it was its cold eye which made him feel so tense.

The voice took him by surprise. It came out of nowhere, a deep muttering that materialized when the breeze changed direction. He couldn't make out the words, but he registered that it was not a child and his uneasiness went up a notch. A group of silly children he could cope with, but he had no desire to confront anything else in that dark, isolated churchyard. His sense of duty, though, would not allow him to turn back. In the absence of the vicar, the protection of the church and grounds was his responsibility.

Subconsciously, he stooped to merge in with the surroundings and felt his heart pound faster than it had done in years. *Drunks*, he told himself. *Resting after the pub.* And then, *An amorous couple finding a daring spot for their love-making.* He couldn't quite convince himself.

As he drew closer to the dark hulk of St Martin's, the voice rode over the breeze, clearer and stronger. There seemed to be just one man, talking to himself. The voice had confidence and no taint of alcohol, and even more curious was the things it was saying. *No,* Barnwell thought, *Surely I've misheard?*

It was easier to pinpoint the source now, and Barnwell scurried forward, like a soldier in the bush. The voice was emanating from the newer section of the graveyard, close to the east wall. Now he had him! Nervously he peered around a bone-white tomb.

The man was standing with his hands behind his back, staring up at the moon and stars; he seemed to be humming to himself. Barnwell's first thought was that he was a stranger; his swarthy skin had the hint of foreign lands and there was something almost dashing, well-travelled, about him. He didn't look dangerous.

Barnwell was about to ask what he was doing when he noticed what was happening nearby. *No. I'm getting old,* he thought. *Not seeing right.* But as he watched, the breath slowly caught in his chest, and when he could no longer deny the hideous thing, his mind started to fold in upon itself and retreat.

Dear Lord, the verger thought.

Dear Lord!

The stranger had stepped back and was making a sweeping gesture with his arms. After a brief pause, there was a sound like thick soup bubbling in a pot. The sucking noise grew louder.

The scene had become monstrous.

Barnwell felt madness start to swallow him and he lurched out from behind the tomb, looking to the stranger for some support, anything.

Wilde turned and Barnwell was suddenly transfixed by a pair of eyes which seemed to be filled with golden stars.

'Good evening,' Wilde said with a tight smile. 'I do not believe we have met. What is your name?'

The words leapt from the verger's mouth without conscious thought. 'C-Colin Barnwell.'

'Hmmm.' Wilde nodded. 'Your church?'

'I'm the verger. I . . .' He brought himself to his senses sharply. 'What have you done?' His eyes wanted to flick back to the nightmarish thing, but he couldn't allow it.

'Now, now, Mr Barnwell. Courtesy, please. I am about to grant you a tremendous honour. You believe in this whole religion thing?' He waved his hand towards the church. 'Yes, yes, of course you do. You believe in an afterlife, I presume? A God? Of course. How would you like to go on a journey? Just a short hop, from here to there, but what wonders you will see! And then I hope you will come back and tell me about them. It has been quite a while since I sent someone with your particular perspective. Perhaps this time I will be lucky!'

Barnwell felt he was suspended in space; his home, his wife, all forgotten. There was something hypnotic about the man in front of him, something charming yet strangely reptilian too; he was attracted and repulsed at the same time. For one instant, he wondered if he should run away and find help, but the thought was gone almost before it had arrived.

Wilde beckoned to him and smiled. 'Come here, Mr Barnwell.'

Barnwell took a step forward. Now he couldn't run if he wanted, his limbs were so heavy he felt sedated. And his peripheral vision seemed to be shutting down until all he could see were Wilde's eyes, charged with electricity, gold sparks on black.

'Good man, Mr Barnwell. You come here now.' Still smiling, friendly, charming.

Barnwell was before him, looking up into his eyes, entranced. Wilde placed his hands on the verger's shoulders, and, slowly, through the haze, Barnwell had the creeping feeling that all was not right. The smile wasn't friendly, it was malicious. The eyes weren't welcoming, they were . . .

Barnwell's head was pulled forward until it rested on his chest, and then Wilde clasped his hands around it and gave a sudden twist.

A sound like breaking wood echoed across the churchyard.

By 2 a.m. Annie knew it was futile trying to sleep. She climbed out of bed and walked out on to the landing. The house had the peaceful, ghostly stillness that only an old house in summer can have. She didn't really know what she was doing, just that she had to do something, so she paused at the top of the stairs and stared at the door of the spare room, trying to imagine Severin inside, on his bed, sleeping. She knew every creak of every floorboard in that house, and she was sure she hadn't made even the slightest sound, but a second later his door swung open and he stood there brandishing the shotgun at her, limned by the moonlight.

'Jesus! You almost gave me a heart attack!'

'Sorry. I heard a movement. I had to check.'

He glanced up and down the landing, and satisfied no one else was there, stepped back into his room and left the door open for her. Her heartbeat speeded slightly as she followed.

'I can't sleep, and I keep thinking about Wilde,' she said as she closed the door behind her.

'Yeah, I know how you feel. I haven't slept so good for a while.' He had walked over to the window and was looking out across the village. The moon was framed above his head.

Annie took up a position on the other side of the window and followed his gaze across the rooftops to the black expanse of Tarrant's Wood. 'It's hard to believe that he's out there somewhere,' she said.

'It's hard to believe he's anywhere in this world.'

143

'Tell me seriously, what chances have I got of getting through this?'

There was a long pause, and then Severin replied, 'He'll make his move soon.'

Annie looked up at him. The moonlight seemed to bleed out the hardness in his face, leaving a man who was caring and concerned, and fearful for the future.

'You haven't told me how you got involved in all this,' she said.

'It was five years ago, I had my own business, providing computer software for security systems – pretty successful, too. I was based down in Nashville. That's not where I'm from . . . I was brought up in Monterey, California, but it was Marj's home town and I relocated there after we got married. I was always pretty carefree. You know, when money came in, I spent it. We had a pretty good life. But all that changed when Matthew – Matty – was born. I suddenly couldn't just drift along any more. I started working hard, nights, weekends, and the business was doing better and better. I was talking about expanding it, setting up a place in Silicon Valley and up in New Jersey. Marj kept nagging me to have a holiday because I was pushing myself so hard, so in the end I booked us a couple of weeks in Palm Beach, down in Florida. It was great, just like the old times. Sun, sea, sand, lots of laughs. Matty loved it too – he was five by then.'

In the still of the room his voice echoed hollowly. Annie had the feeling he had forgotten she was there; his memories had claimed him.

'It made me realize how much I'd been missing,' he continued. 'Work takes over your life. You lose perspective. I decided I was going to adjust all that. When we got back home.' There was a moment of silence which covered up a whole host of thoughts. 'I met Wilde on the flight back to Nashville. Marj and Matty had seats on one side of the aisle and I was on the other. Wilde came in and took the seat next to me, maybe a minute before take-off. I remember I didn't like him as soon as I saw him. It was a gut reaction; he made my skin crawl. But after we got talking, we got on just fine. He intrigued me. He drew me in so I wanted to know everything about him. He was fascinating.' He looked at Annie. 'You know what I mean?' She nodded.

'He introduced himself as Oscar Wilde, but he didn't seem to mind me laughing. He said his parents had a strange sense of humour. I tried to work out his age, but it was impossible to tell. His skin and the way he acted suggested thirties, but his eyes . . . They seemed like they belonged in a different person.'

'I remember thinking that.' Annie saw Wilde's face in her mind's eye and she twitched involuntarily. 'He didn't seem to be any age.'

'Back then, I was easy-going – I'd speak to anyone – but Wilde would have had me hooked even if I was the most anti-social guy in the world. He was interesting, funny, you name it, and he had the best stories. I even invited him to come see us when we got back to Nashville.

'About halfway through the flight, he suddenly made his excuses and stood up. He didn't say where he was going, but naturally I thought the john. Where else could he go, right? I looked out the window, and the next thing I knew people were screaming. Wilde had grabbed a stewardess at the front of the plane. Her eyes were all bugged out like she knew what he was going to do, and there was no way she could stop him. She was yelling, and he was grinning like it was the best thing he had ever seen. Maybe if I'd moved quicker . . . but you just don't expect people to act like that. Not people you've been talking to normally just a few minutes before. My brain . . . it was still trying to work out what was happening. I stood up, and Wilde looked at me. I swear he winked. Then there was this horrible crack. He'd snapped that poor girl's neck. He threw the body in the aisle like a bag of junk he was discarding, and then he headed for the cockpit.

'There was screaming and everything, but nobody was doing *anything*, and I thought, *What if he gets to the pilots?* I felt myself step into the aisle and start after him like I wasn't in my own body.

'I looked back at Marj and Matty was crying and I knew I had to save them. I wasn't a physical kind of guy back then – I mean, I went to a gym, but I spent most of my life in front of a computer screen – but somehow I managed to catch up with Wilde and drag him back. But he was strong, very strong, and I knew I wouldn't be able to hold him for long. I kept using my weight to try to pin him down, hoping someone else would help me, but I could see them all standing back. Wilde was a madman. He was punching me, blow after blow, but I kept

145

holding on. Then my fingers caught on something, the bracelet which he had on a thong round his neck. He suddenly looked frightened when he saw me holding it. It was just for an instant, but it was there – *fear*. I looked down at the bracelet, trying to work out what had disturbed him, and in that moment he head-butted me again and I went out. What a fucking wimp.'

Annie could hear his back teeth grinding together. 'What happened then?'

'Then,' he continued bitterly, 'my whole life fell apart. I woke up and I could feel the sun on my face, and there was a smell of gasoline. I was in the wreckage of the plane. Wilde must have got through to the pilots, done to them what he had done to the stewardess. They obviously knew there was some disturbance on board because they'd been trying to make an emergency landing at some local airport when the plane went down. God knows how it didn't turn into a fireball. It broke up into pieces, lots of pieces. The fuel tanks were found a field away.'

'Your wife and boy . . .'

Severin breathed in a deep lungful of air before he carried on. 'Dead. Everyone was dead except me. You can't imagine what it was like. I stood up on my little section of fuselage and looked around. It was like hell. Bodies everywhere. Some of them in pieces. The plane was scattered over a wide area. Some of it was burning, sending up thick clouds of smoke. I can't remember much after that, just watching the smoke float up into the air. The paramedics said I was wandering around the wreckage like a zombie, talking to myself, trying to find Marj and Matty. I never did see them. That's probably a good thing. I got sedated in the local hospital. It was four days before I was told they were dead, along with everybody else.'

'How did you survive?'

'Just unlucky, I guess.' He slipped his hand into his shirt and pulled out the bracelet. 'Maybe this had something to do with it, I don't know. I was gripping on to it when the paramedics found me. And it was the last thing I held on to during that struggle with Wilde. That's my only answer.'

'What happened to Wilde?'

'He wasn't in the wreckage. I told the authorities all about him and what happened, but they couldn't find any trace of his body. His name was on the airline manifest so they knew I wasn't totally delirious, but if they did believe he was responsible for the crash, they never showed it. They went for mechanical failure and all that bullshit.

'The day after I was lying in a hospital bed watching the sun set through the window. They'd got me pumped full of junk to control the shock. Anyway, there I was just thinking about killing myself when the door opened. It was some orderly coming in to clean my room – I glimpsed the uniform, but I didn't look at him. I just kept staring at the sunset, wishing Marj was still there to watch it with me. Slowly, I got this prickly feeling and I realized the orderly was staring at me. It was Wilde. He had this huge How Ya Doin' grin on his face like we were long-lost buddies. I struggled to reach the call button, but I was so out of it and, I don't know . . . it was like he was *doing* something to stop me moving. "Hello, John," he said in that oily voice of his. "I never expected to see you again." Seems he'd read about my "miraculous escape" in the local paper and he'd come to finish the job. I wasn't scared of dying, not after Marj and Matty. But I needed to know *why* he'd done what he had; how he'd managed to walk away.

'He pulled up a chair like we were old friends and told me he did it because he *could* do it, and because there was no one to stop him. He didn't sound crazy, just smart, cold, like he didn't care about anybody or anything. I thought he was a serial killer or just a total sociopath, but then he did something which showed me what I was dealing with. He had a switchblade with him. He put the point of it up near his elbow and opened the inside of his arm down to his wrist.

'I guess if I hadn't been so drugged up, I would have been horrified, but all I remember is being fascinated. Like, *so that's what the inside of an arm looks like*. It hurt him, I could see that, but he was still grinning. He held the wound in front of my face and while I watched it started to heal. The flesh pulled together, the skin knit. It took about fifteen minutes in all, and by the end there wasn't even a scar.

'That's how I walked away from the plane crash, John,' he said. 'Nothing can hurt me for long. Nothing can kill me.' I could see in his eyes that it was over for me. "Time to die, John," he said, and brought his switchblade up to my neck. Then he changed, suddenly, just like that. His grin had gone and he was looking past me at the bedside table. "It's here!" he said. "I thought I had lost it in the wreckage."

147

'It was the bracelet. I'd kept it with me for some reason. I don't know why, but I didn't want to let it go. He backed off quickly like he'd been burned, right up to the door. His grin had come back, but it didn't seem the same. "Not this time, John," he said. "Maybe a month from now, or a year from now. Maybe . . . who knows?" And then he was gone.'

'Just like that? After threatening to kill you?'

'Just like that.'

Annie's mind was racing as she looked out into the night. 'So he was scared of it?'

'I guess. I can't see why.'

'What happened after that?'

'That visit from Wilde changed me, psychologically. It saved me, and maybe it damned him. When I got out of hospital, I wasn't thinking about killing myself like I had been before. I had one thing on my mind – to get that bastard and make him pay. I sold up everything, the business, the house, and invested the cash so I had a living, and then I planned to track Wilde down. I just *had* to do it. Then, one night, I was watching TV in a motel room just outside Nashville, trying to decide where to start, when a news report comes on about a fire at some flophouse. Everyone inside had died. I felt this buzzing that started at the base of my spine and ran up to my neck. I knew Wilde was involved. I got my ass down there that very night, talked to the neighbours, and one or two of them had seen someone matching Wilde's description. *That* was my starting point.

'And that's when I realized I'd changed physically too. Somehow between the time I was up in the plane and recovering in hospital, something inside me had altered. I'd become psychic. Not in any flash-bang way. Just in a way that meant I could *sense* Wilde, wherever he was in the world, like there was this bond between us. And that meant I could follow him. I couldn't narrow him down to a house or a street, just areas, but it was enough. And when I reached a spot where he'd *done* something, I could sense that too. That was horrible.' He paused for a second or two before continuing. 'There were other changes too. I was stronger, had more stamina. Pain doesn't bother me too much now.'

'Maybe some of what he's got has rubbed off on you.'

'That's what I'm afraid of.'

148

Annie reached out and touched his hand; he didn't pull away. 'That's a very sad story.'

'Don't think I feel sorry for myself. It's all gone now. Wiped away.'

Annie looked at the granite expression and the dark eyes and knew he was lying, to himself more than to her. She slipped her hand under his hair on to the back of his neck and gave it a squeeze. He didn't flinch. Annie felt a sudden fluttering in her stomach; she surprised herself by deciding to go with it.

Her fingers massaged his skin briefly, and then she exerted a slight pressure, easing him towards her. Severin turned stiffly, sliding his arms around her waist. Annie felt exposed in the thin material of her nightshirt, but it merely added another tingle of excitement. *What am I doing? This isn't me.* She leaned forward, smelling his hair and his skin, and then she kissed him, forcing him to respond. He didn't need much encouragement. His hands slid down from her waist, over her curves on to her behind. She didn't care if anyone could see them against the window, she just wanted to get on to the bed. She began to lead him away from the window.

The mood was broken by an electric burst of tension which crackled through her fingers as they brushed the bracelet hanging around his neck and she recoiled instantly. It had felt like burning skin, and those chattering voices had erupted inside her head once more. Incoherently. It was speaking to her. The bracelet was *speaking*.

Annie pulled away from Severin and retreated, her mood distorted by sudden fear. 'I'm sorry,' she said. 'I can't. The bracelet . . .'

Confused, he pulled it out on its thong and examined it. 'What about it?'

Annie shook her head, her mind fizzing from the alien contact. She felt panicky at the thought of staying in the room. 'I've got to go!' She turned and almost ran back to her own bed. Under the duvet, she hugged herself. Terrified.

Heat, thick and oppressive, beneath a big sky ablaze with a thousand shining stars and a crescent moon. A wind like sandpaper. An alien environment.

The sand beneath her feet was still baking from the blazing

warmth of the day. It crushed up between her toes, reminding her of summer holidays, but it was coarser than beach sand.

So hot. It was almost impossible to breathe. Her t-shirt was sodden with sweat and clinging to her body. Throwing back her head, she looked up at the magnificent vault of sable sky. No man-made light dulled the illumination from the heavens, but the stars looked odd, not how she remembered.

I'm dreaming, she thought obliquely, and then let that thought drift away on the scorching wind.

She turned round in a full circle. The sand stretched as far as she could see, a white desert broken by the rippled shadows of dunes. Against the lighter sky, the silhouette of an enormous pyramid rose up. All perspective was lost in that landscape; it could be on the horizon or just a mile away.

Annie sensed the presence behind her rather than heard it. The roaring wind leeched all sound from the vicinity apart from its own white noise. Annie turned, fear becoming apprehension becoming mild curiosity, and then back again.

A man stood on a dune. He looked uncommonly tall, and his dusky skin was highlighted by a flowing white robe. There was a loose belt around his waist with an ornate gold clasp and another clasp at his shoulder. His long hair was black and pulled back tightly, and there seemed to be mascara around his eyes.

He's beautiful, Annie thought, with his fine features and wrought cheekbones, and huge, dark eyes. But he looked as if everyone he had ever known or loved had died, and as if that pain was indescribable.

Slowly he raised his arms towards her in a pleading gesture. Annie almost started to walk towards those outstretched fingers, but then reminded herself, *You're dreaming. Don't go.*

Suddenly she became afraid. The tall, sad man continued to plead with his outstretched arms, and as he realized she was not going to respond he started to speak. His full lips formed words precisely, but they were plucked from his mouth by the wind and lost to the night. All Annie could see was his mouth opening and closing and his eyes calling to her; it filled her entire vision.

And then the wind grew bolder until she was forced to shield her eyes from the stinging sandstorm, trying to make out what the man was doing, but the sand rose in clouds between them, and slowly he was lost to it, mouthing silently, calling something to her, until all was sand and the unbearable roaring of the wind.

Annie woke suddenly. Her memory of the dream was bright, and she knew it would stay with her. It raised many questions, but they were all lost when she felt the dampness of her pillow against her cheek and realized she had been crying. Without opening her eyes, she stretched in the bed and slowly recalled something had woken her, a sound, or just some sixth sense. She felt it once more, a tingling in the pit of her stomach telling her something was wrong. She opened her eyes.

The face was only six inches away.

A scream caught in her throat and in a shock reaction she thrashed out with her right arm and rolled to one side, but she connected with thin air. There was nothing there.

A nightmare, she told herself. She looked up at the ceiling she had know in minute detail since she was a little girl and tried to calm herself with comforting thoughts, of her parents, then of Martyn, and even more surprisingly, of Severin.

The chuckle echoed across the room like the rustle of newspaper.

Annie went cold. Suddenly too scared to move or utter a sound, her eyes darted about the room madly until she saw him, sitting cross-legged on the floor next to the chest of drawers.

Wilde's grin was white against the surrounding gloom.

Annie desperately tried to scream out for Severin, but all that would come was a pathetic strangled sound barely louder than a whisper. Her arms, her legs, her entire body felt like it had been welded to the bed; she couldn't move an inch.

Slowly, never once taking his eyes off her, he began to crawl across the floor towards the end of the bed. He was like a cobra, sinuously stalking the prey he had hypnotized. On to the bed now. Annie felt it shift beneath his weight. Over her feet, his body pressing down on her. The duvet and her t-shirt so thin, they might not have been there. She could feel his contours, the map of his body. Over her knees, her thighs, rubbing against her groin, her belly, and then he stopped when his face was once more six inches away from her, filling her whole vision.

'Hello, Annie.'

His voice made her feel dizzy.

'I told you I would see you again! Did you miss me? Well, worry no more – from now on, I will be with you until the end.'

He moved even closer and rubbed the tip of his nose on hers. 'We are two sides of the same coin, you and I. I am filled with darkness, you with light. Opposites attract. But it is a strange attraction because hidden inside it is the need to destroy – opposites cannot bear each other either.'

He smiled icily. Annie desperately tried to wriggle her way out from beneath him, but the only movement she could muster was so slight it barely disturbed the duvet.

'We're going on a journey, Annie, just the two of us. A night journey. And you will learn many things before we reach the final destination. I want you to see the world as I see it. I want you to realize there is no hope, no justice, no faith, just decay and degradation. In short, I want the goodness in you to be tainted, because I cannot abide goodness; it should not exist.'

He moved back slightly so he could see her entire face. Slowly his eyes ranged across her features, as if he was recording them for his memory. His face was cold and hard, but then, for the briefest second, she thought she saw tenderness suddenly break through. It was so incongruous, it was shocking. He must have felt it too, for he quickly looked away and when he spoke again there was anger in his voice.

'You will have time to prepare yourself. It took your God seven days to make this rotten concoction and how could I hope to equal Him?' His laughter was acidly sarcastic. 'Eight days, Annie, and on the ninth I will seek you out.'

She felt she was teetering on the edge of a deep, dark well. Gently, he stroked her cheek and moved a stray hair from her forehead; his fingers were hot. Then he leaned forward and kissed her. Annie didn't respond, but couldn't fight him off. At first his lips were pliant, a lover's kiss, but gradually they grew harder and harder, sucking at her breath, forcing the life from her, crushing down on her, crushing . . .

It could have been a minute or an hour later that she awoke. The panic flared instantly and she leapt from the bed, her limbs as light as feathers. The room was empty. But as she glanced around, she noticed that the chest of drawers had been opened. Investigating, she discovered her five-year diary and her Filofax, her most personal items, were missing.

Her lips were swollen and she couldn't shake off the dirty feeling of having been abused. Slowly, it crept up on her that Wilde's visit had been *real*. His presence was still there, like a bad smell, seeping everywhere. She felt sick and she started to rub absently at the places where he had touched her. Then came fear. She realized nowhere was safe.

Dazed, she drew back the curtains and sat in the middle of the bed, a small girl again, praying for the sun to come up.

PART TWO

The Road Rises

Does the road wind up-hill all the way?
    Yes, to the very end.
Will the day's journey take the whole long day?
    From morn to night, my friend.
CHRISTINA GEORGINA ROSSETTI
Up-Hill

16

In the dingy reception room, Annie was greeted by an over-weight policeman who looked as if he had been pumped into his uniform. He had kept her waiting for ten agonizing minutes while her temper had flared between beats of fear. When the window did finally open, she didn't know whether to explode in anger or beg him to protect her.

'Yes, madam?' he said.

Annie took a deep breath to compose herself. 'Someone broke into my home last night. He's threatening to kill me.'

'You better come through and talk to one of the detectives.'

He led Annie along a yellow-washed corridor with a flickering striplight into a bland interview room dominated by a cheap desk and a *Have you seen this man?* poster featuring a rat-faced youth with too wide eyes. Through a small window Annie could see a dingy courtyard. Someone nearby was hammering a piece of metal with an insistent but irritating off-beat.

The detective entered a couple of minutes later, a tall, thin man who introduced himself as Detective Inspector Pearson and Annie felt as if he thought he recognised her.

She repeated what she had told the desk sergeant. Pearson nodded attentively. 'Do you know the man?' he asked.

'I met him on the one-two-five which crashed at Christmas. You know the one . . . he was on board . . .'

Pearson looked as if he'd seen the light. 'Now I know you! You gave a statement saying that one bloke had caused the crash. The media had a field day with that, didn't they?'

'It was true.'

He folded his hands on his stomach. 'And this is the same bloke?'

'Yes. We got talking on the train. I told him where I lived and now he's tracked me down.' Her lips had dried out and she tried to moisten them, but her mouth seemed dry as well.

Pearson was making her uncomfortable by the way he was looking at her and it brought back unpleasant memories of how she was treated after the crash. 'He's completely insane,' she continued. 'He'll do anything. He says he's not going to stop until he's taught me a lesson, and then he's going to kill me.'

'How did he get into your house?'

'I don't know.'

Pearson raised one eyebrow. 'We'll look into it.'

'Don't you want a description? My address?'

He shrugged. 'OK.'

'Forget it.' Annie stood up with such force that her chair flew back and fell over. Her sudden movement took Pearson by surprise and the clatter made him leap to his feet like a startled animal, but Annie was already out of the room and marching back towards reception. She burned with a dull, red anger which had beaten the fear back.

She was on her own.

The heat made driving hellish. Sweat pooled in the small of her back and soaked into her Levi's and even with all the windows open, there was no respite. The M5 was packed with summer traffic, holiday-makers heading down to Cornwall and too large lorries on a run to the ports. She should have warned Charlotte, called to say she was on her way, needing somewhere to lie low for a few weeks, but she couldn't bring herself to return to Blackstone Cottage where *he* might be waiting. In her disillusion after the police station, she had just leapt into her car and headed for the one place where she could escape. Her best friend's home.

Annie indicated and slowed down as the next motorway service station came up. A break was what she needed, a can of Coke, some junk food, and maybe a little sleep. Although the car park was mostly empty, she parked up close to the other vehicles. Inside the main building she ate in the café and enjoyed the security of people moving around her, before heading to the call boxes. Charlotte's number was engaged the first two times she called, and then it just rang unanswered. *Silly cow, you've missed me*, Annie thought. *It'll have to be a surprise.*

Back in the car, it didn't take her long to drift into a light sleep. This oblivion lasted until an explosive crack outside snapped her back to life. A car backfiring. The sudden awaken-

158

ing disoriented her and for an instant she thought Wilde was staring at her through the windscreen, before her eyes drooped shut once more.

The knock at the window may have come as little as a minute or as much as half an hour later, but this time she rose to wakefulness sluggishly. Someone *was* peering in at her, rapping on the glass. Tanned face, crew cut, several shaving nicks.

Rubbing her eyes, Annie wound the window down an inch. The man manoeuvred so he could speak through the gap; his front teeth had been knocked out of line.

'Are you on your way to see Charlotte Ames?'

'Yes.' *How did he know?*

'A bloke told me to tell you there's been a message from her. It's in that van over there.' He pointed to a dirt-streaked Luton van in the far corner of the car park.

'She doesn't even know I'm here,' Annie replied, puzzled.

The man shrugged and lurched away from the window. 'I'm just passing on a message, love.'

She glanced at the van again and when she looked back, the man had started to walk off towards the main building. Annie opened the door and called after him, 'Who gave you the message?' but he didn't give any sign that he had heard her.

For a moment, she watched the van intently, weighing up her options, but there was no real choice. Slipping out of the car, she approached it in a wide, cautious arc, hesitating every now and then in an attempt to peer through the dusty front window. There seemed to be a pool of stillness around it.

Annie felt a tingle run through her head as her subconscious spoke to her, a whisper at first, then a scream. She paused for a while on the edge of the still zone, but the pull was too great.

By the time she was ten paces away, it was obvious something was wrong. The windows of the van were opaque, almost as if a dark sheet had been laid across them. There was an odd smell in the air too, an acrid mix of burnt metal and smoke. And behind it something stronger, meatier.

Steeling herself, Annie marched up to the driver's door, her legs tense and ready to break into a run. 'Is anybody there?' she called out feebly.

No reply. The window was high so she put one foot on the step and grabbed the door handle to haul herself up. She hadn't noticed the door wasn't latched and when she put her weight on it, it flew open and sent her sprawling back on to the hot tarmac. The impact winded her, but as she lay there recovering, her breath caught in her throat.

Through the open door she could see the inside of the windscreen was covered with blood. More blood than she had ever seen before. It had smeared almost all the glass, running down on to the dashboard and pooling on the floor.

Her first reaction was to run away, but somehow the horror of it held her in its grip and instead she found herself moving tentatively forward. All she could focus on was that incarnadine sea. The smell that drifted off it was like a butcher's shop.

A man was sprawled across the seats, the chalk-white fingers of his right hand clutching a pistol. He was twisted awkwardly, his thighs under the steering wheel, while his upper body and head rested on the passenger seat. Only he didn't have much of a head. Annie had never realized that a handgun used at close range could be so brutal. It hadn't been a car backfiring that had woken her.

Suicide. That was what it was supposed to look like, but Annie knew who had done it.

Staggering back, then pivoting on the spot, she tried to see where he was hiding. The only human movement she could see was up near the main building. Slowly, she backed further away, feeling the blood pound in her head. Wilde intended this to be a warning. He knew she was fleeing to Charlotte's. He had her fax, her diary, all the addresses and phone numbers of her friends and relatives. He was probably following her everywhere she went with a hunter's eye for the perfect moment.

That thought brought such panic she couldn't help but break into a run and only when she was back in her own car with the doors locked and the windows up did she breathe a little easier. The relief didn't last long. A sudden ringing jolted her like an electric shock and she dropped the ignition keys.

On the passenger seat was a mobile phone. It was slick with blood and Annie was afraid to touch it, but it kept ringing and ringing like an alarm and she thought someone might come over to see what was wrong.

Frantically she snatched it up and punched a button to stop the awful sound. When she brought it up to her ear, the blood trickled across her wrists and down the pale skin of her arm.

Stay calm, she told herself. *You're losing it.*

'Good afternoon, Annie.' Wilde's voice was as clear as if he was in the car with her. She peered into the back suddenly, just to make sure. Wilde laughed. 'No, Annie, I am not there, but I *can* see you. I can always see you!'

Fearfully, she glanced around. *Where was he? How close?*

'What is it like to speak into a dead man's phone, Annie? Oh dear. And now your fingerprints are all over it, and our luckless driver's blood has stained your pretty skin. What will people think? That you stole it? Looted a corpse? Better start the engine, Annie. Get away before anyone catches you.'

Annie felt she was swimming through oil. There was an iron taste in her mouth and the steak-sweet smell of blood in her nose. She retrieved the keys, slipped them into the ignition and pulled away. The phone was cradled between her ear and shoulder, the blood sticky on her cheek and in her hair.

'Drive out into the carriageway and at the next exit leave the motorway and find your way on to the other carriageway. Go back the way you came.' Annie didn't even think about disobeying. 'Here is a joke for you, Annie. What do you call a woman who gambles with her life? *Bet!* No, not funny, I know, but I am *trying* to cheer you up. What? Nothing to say? You have picked up some very poor manners from our good Mr Severin.'

Annie drove the car slowly in the inside lane, half mesmerized, still holding the phone to her ear. Soon she was back on the northbound carriageway, as instructed.

'I have already started my work in your village, Annie. Did you know that? I would not want you to miss anything so please do not try to leave again. As the song says, there is nowhere to run to, nowhere to hide. Now I fear I must sign off, but do not deviate from your route, I will not be far behind. Oh, and I have arranged another little surprise for when you get home. Be seeing you.'

Annie let the phone fall from her shoulder. She could see in the rear-view mirror that she had blood smeared up the side of her face as if she had been beaten up. But it didn't matter. Nothing mattered any more. She put her foot down and headed back towards Riddington.

The police car parked on Starling Lane outside the church was such an incongruous sight in Riddington that child after child reported it to the village shop and post office as they made their way to school, and it didn't take long for various adults to make their way up to St Martin's to see the scene for themselves. Martyn Nash heard the news while sitting outside the village hall waiting for a reasonable hour to call on Annie.

Justine Alcock held court over a group of children nearby, dismissing her sweet-sixteen sullenness for just long enough to spread the news. 'A grave's been disturbed up at the church! Black magic, they say. And they've found something else that they won't talk about, but I reckon someone's dug a body up. Can you believe it? Here in Riddington!'

There was still an hour at least before Martyn could drop in on Annie without raising her wrath, so he decided to wander up to the church gates with the others to kill time. When he arrived, there was already a fair crowd rubbernecking and gossiping about the excitement. A nervous policeman hovered just inside the churchyard as if he expected the villagers to storm the church at any minute.

'What's going on?' Martyn asked.

When the policeman shook his head and looked away, Martyn realized it was worse than he had expected. He felt a shiver of curiosity slicing through the dullness of his days. Since he had lost his job as a graphic designer at a print shop in Ashby almost a year ago, his time was spent waiting for something to happen. In the last couple of months, the TV and the village had become his whole existence. Only Annie had provided some excitement, and some real life, and it was that which drew him to her as much as his feelings.

'Is it the vicar?' he persisted, but the policeman was starting to grow irritated and Martyn knew he would get nothing out of him. As he turned to ask someone else, he noiticed Tony Aris standing in the doorway of the church, rubbing his hands together over and over again. He was wearing his dog collar, but he hadn't shaved and his hair was unkempt.

There was a brief flurry of movement in the crowd around the gate as a grey Mondeo pulled sharply out of a drive across the lane and stopped outside St Martin's. This was obviously what the vicar and the policeman were waiting for. Two men got out, detectives Martyn guessed, and held open a door for a woman in her fifties with silvery-blonde permed hair. Martyn recognized Mrs Barnwell, the verger's wife, despite the fact that she was as white as snow and had the glazed, vacant expression of a drunk. One of the detectives took her arm, while the other eased a path through the churchyard. There were a few murmurs of shock among the onlookers, but Mrs Barnwell seemed unaware there was anyone else in her world.

'She looks terrible,' Martyn said to himself in a hushed voice.

As she passed close by him, a sudden uneasiness fell on him. He needed to know more. He forced his way out of the crowd and moved quickly to the perimeter wall where he could clamber into the graveyard without being seen. While the detectives were leading Mrs Barnwell into the back of the church, now accompanied by Tony Aris, Martyn slipped in through the smaller door which opened into an annexe next to the altar. The inner door was ajar so he had a good view into the nave.

A morbid chill filled him when he saw a paint-splattered dust-sheet covering a shape on the floor. The uniformed policeman who stood guard over it was like a grim-faced statue.

Mrs Barnwell was led reluctantly up the aisle like some skittish animal. She raised her hand to her mouth in slow motion and held it there, her glazed expression suddenly replaced by a terrible awareness.

The vicar mumbled some comforting words to prepare her for what she was about to see, then one of the detectives nodded and the policeman pulled back the top part of the sheet.

Martyn could see that Barnwell's face was purple and bloated, and there appeared to be a ligature still trailing from his neck. Mrs Barnwell's eyes grew wide and frozen, and she almost pitched forward on top of her husband's corpse. The detective caught her arm and motioned impatiently for the policeman to cover up the hideous sight.

'Yes, it's my Colin,' Mrs Barnwell managed. 'Please tell me what happened,' she pleaded in a voice only just louder than a whisper.

'Mr Aris found your husband,' the detective began hesitantly. 'He was hanging from that light fitting there.' He pointed upwards. 'He obviously stood on the altar and . . . well . . .'

'And is it true? What he was wearing?'

The detective flickered his eyes to the others present as if hoping someone would save him. After a few beats he nodded to the policeman again, who carefully eased up more of the sheet. Barnwell was naked beneath it apart from black stockings and a suspender belt. Martyn didn't think Mrs Barnwell could get any paler.

'Yours?' the detective asked.

She nodded.

'Did he . . .?'

'No! Never!' She took a deep breath. 'He was quite, quite normal. He never showed any sign of this . . .' She paused and then said hazily, 'Last night . . . I half woke. I thought there was someone in the room, going through my drawers . . . a dream . . .' She waved a hand at the body as if she was trying to drive it away. Then she added forcefully, 'He was a good man. A good husband and a good father. My God, this will destroy the children!'

'Was he depressed?'

Mrs Barnwell shook her head a few times too many. 'He was happier than he ever had been. We were talking about going away for a few days.'

'I think that's enough for now.' Tony Aris stepped in and put an arm around her shoulder. He looked shaky himself. The second detective took over and led her back down the aisle, trying to stop her looking back.

When she had gone, the other detective eased a little. 'Nice woman. She shouldn't have to go through something like this.'

'I can't believe that he did it,' the vicar said. 'Old Colin could be a little dour at times, but he seemed at peace. And he was so strait-laced.'

'Those are often the type, Father. They keep things bottled up so tightly that when they do come out there's a real rush.'

'Poor Colin. All the good he has done in his life, and it'll be forever tarnished when this gets out. People won't remember the tireless service. They'll just think of a pervert who killed himself in women's underwear.' Tony Aris sighed as if all the air was rushing out of his body. 'The village will suffer too, of course, and the church. Things like this make folk cynical.' He shook his head wearily. 'It will take a lot of work to restore faith.'

'There's still the matter of the graves . . .'

'Yes, yes.' Aris looked flustered. 'I'm glad you didn't mention that to Mrs Barnwell. It's all too much.'

'If he did that, he really *was* a sicko.'

'Did you check how much damage was done?'

'A few stones knocked over. The topsoil's been turned over on four graves like he's been digging there.'

'How far down ...' Aris paused and placed a hand over his eyes to steady himself. 'How far down did he go?'

'Not *that* far, if you get my drift. It's desecration though, and somebody better talk to the relatives. Do you know the names?'

'Most of them departed in the last two years. Ah ... Simon Elliott, parents Christopher and Katy. Bill Cockburn, ah, you probably know the family there. Eunice Swift, son Brian is the man to see – go easy on him. Malcolm Hughes, used to own the Old Mill. No known relatives. And Laurence Lucas.'

'Lucas?' The detective's attention snapped up from his notebook.

'The only old grave. When he was originally interred it was away from the main section of the burial ground. A sensitive issue, as I'm sure you will appreciate.'

'Out of sight, out of mind?'

'I suppose. In the intervening years, the spare ground has been mostly used up, so the Lucas grave is now on the edge of the most recent plots.'

'Hardly worth me chasing that one up, is it? Even if I could find his family, they wouldn't want to be reminded about him.'

'No, I would think not.'

The detective finished scribbling and for a second he glanced up at the altar, as if picturing the dead man still hanging above it.

'Tell me, Father,' he began. 'How do you figure a man like Barnwell?'

Aris shook his head as if through insistence he could deny what had happened. 'I thought I knew Colin as well as my own brother. When something like this happens, it shakes you. You think you're a good judge of human nature, and all of a sudden ... He was a good man, that's how I'll remember him. Nothing can shake that.'

The detective made as if to say something else, but the look on the other man's face made him think twice. He nodded thoughtfully a couple of times and then trudged down the aisle, leaving Aris to slip into a pew and bow his head in either prayer or despair.

Martyn backed off quietly until he was standing in the shade outside. Climbing into the churchyard had seemed like a good idea at the time, but now he regretted it. Barnwell's distorted, purple face would haunt him for days, if not longer, and he was left feeling extremely queasy. This was turning into one hell of a bad day. Checking his watch, he decided it was high time to make that call on Annie.

Annie had barely been in the house two minutes when the phone rang. She didn't feel like talking to anyone, but the caller was persistent and she gave in. Her father's voice was as clear as if he had been in the next room which made the note of anxiety sound even sharper.

'Annie. Thank God! Are you all right?'

'Of course ... sure ...' Puzzlement made her tongue leaden. 'Dad, what's wrong?'

'We had a call, from a friend of yours. He said you were in terrible trouble, out of control. We should come home immediately. Are you really all right, Annie?'

'Yes. Of course.'

'Be honest with me.'

'Dad, listen to my voice. Do I sound out of control?'

'You don't sound too good.'

'I'm fine, really.'

The line went quiet for a second or two. Her father was muttering something, a prayer, thanks. Annie felt dizzy.

'Dad, who called?'

'I didn't catch his name. He sounded very sincere, Annie. Are you ...'

'It was probably one of my friends playing a game.'

'Well, it gave us a real turn. How did he get the number anyway?'

'Oh well, I gave it to one or two people, you know, in case of emergencies,' she extemporized. Wilde's *little surprise*; another guarded threat. It was obvious what he was saying: *I can reach your parents too.*

'Don't worry about me, Dad. I'm a big girl now.'

'Not to me, you're not.'

'Look, call later, tomorrow, whenever, if you don't believe me. I can even get Martyn to give you a full appraisal of my wellbeing, if you like.'

'I'd rather not, thank you.' He put on his mock-grumpy voice and they laughed together.

'Now, you get back to the beach or whatever you're doing and have a good time. And I'll go and prepare the cottage for the rave . . . oops, what a giveaway!'

'Annie . . .!'

'See you, Dad.'

The smile fell from her face the moment the receiver hit the cradle and she swore aloud, only to see Severin standing in the kitchen, his face sullen and closed.

'Where the hell have you been?' he growled.

'*He* was here, last night. I got scared stupid, ran to the police and got nowhere like you said. Then I tried to run away.' She sighed heavily. 'That was the old me proving it was still around. I've been running away for the last three years or so and I thought I'd finally shaken the habit, but when it came to the crunch I reverted to type.'

'Understandable under the circumstances.'

She could feel his eyes on her as she moved around the kitchen to make coffee. He was trying to tell how deeply she had been affected by Wilde's appearance and if she had the stomach for the job ahead. *And if I'm going to be a burden*, she thought.

'I'm OK, Severin,' she said as she poured boiling water into two mugs. Even with her back to him she could feel his mood lighten.

'Yeah, I'm sure you are,' he replied honestly. He took the mug from her and slumped into a chair. 'When I woke up and you weren't around, I thought something bad had happened. I went out to check the village to see if anyone had seen you. I know how you felt, but don't do it again, right?'

Annie gave his shoulder a quick squeeze. 'Thanks for looking out for me.'

'That's—'

At that moment, the door burst open and Martyn breezed in, looking excited and flushed from the heat. He froze on the threshold when he saw Severin and then his eyes fell on Annie's hand on the American's shoulder and his expression darkened perceptibly.

'Sorry,' he muttered. 'I didn't realize you had company.'

'It's OK, Martyn. This is a friend. John Severin.' Martyn nodded noncommittally while Annie continued, 'You look like you're about to blow a gasket. What is it?'

Martyn promptly garbled out everything he had seen at the church, paying particular attention to the lurid details of Barnwell's death and the desecration of the graves.

Annie's shock at the verger's awful death was confused by a growing feeling of dread. She flashed a questioning glance at Severin who nodded in reply. Martyn saw their secret look and shifted uncomfortably.

'What do you reckon?' Martyn said when he had finished. 'Old Barnwell a pervert? It's unbelievable.'

'Yes, it is unbelievable. Completely.' Annie looked at Severin again, but the American was lost in thought. 'Martyn, can you come back later,' she said, slipping her arm around him and leading him towards the kitchen door. 'I want to talk to you, but it'll be better when we're alone.'

'Well, tell me when he's leaving so I'll know when to come.'

'He'll be staying a few days . . .'

'What, here?' Martyn looked at her incredulously.

'Yes, here.'

'Do you mind if I—'

'Not now, Martyn.' Annie manoeuvred him into the doorway so his only option was to step out.

He muttered something under his breath, but stomped away. He turned at the garden door and said moodily, 'I'll be back later. Later today.' It almost sounded like a threat.

Annie returned to Severin and said bluntly, 'Was it him?'

Severin nodded. 'It's exactly how Wilde operates. He hasn't just killed the body, he's perverted the memory too.'

Annie stared into space. 'But why Colin Barnwell? *I'm* the target.'

Severin sluiced his coffee round his mouth, then ventured softly, 'You'll soon realize that when Wilde arrives in town, he brings a lot of suffering in his wake.'

She took Severin's words to their logical conclusion, 'My friends, the neighbours . . .' She paused, then added, 'And it's my fault. I brought him here.'

'It just means we've got to track him down as quickly as possible, for everybody's sake.'

'Eight days,' she said fatalistically. 'Last night he said it would take him eight days to do whatever he has to do, and then he would come for me on the ninth. This is day one. The countdown starts here.'

Severin stared into the depths of his empty coffee cup for a long moment and then said, 'Two years ago I was tracking him across India. It was the closest I'd got to him for a long while, thanks to a few lucky breaks. I'd almost lost him when we were passing over the Karakoram Mountains into Kashmir, but there was such devastation in Bombay when he caused a blaze in a slum that it was easy to locate him again.' He closed his eyes. 'It's like one death is a whisper in the dark, but when there's more . . . when there's hundreds like it was that day . . . it's like screaming in my ears.' He took a long, deep breath before continuing. 'He commandeered a boat from Bombay to Goa where he played havoc with a few old hippies and then he set off cross-country for Calcutta. He probably thought he had more chance to shake me in a city like that. It almost worked. I had trouble sensing him . . . There were so many people, crushing in every street, all the voices, the thoughts in my head, the death . . .

'He holed up for a few nights in one of the darkest, poorest quarters. There was filth everywhere, rats the size of cats, so many beggars, people with limbs missing, open sores, all sorts of diseases. It was like he had come home. I was walking through the streets when I suddenly sensed something more powerful than I ever had before – it was like an alarm ringing out. I ran as fast as I could, smashing through the crowds, knocking people over, and eventually I got to this tiny courtyard at the back of these delapidated buildings. There was an enormous bonfire blazing away with all these people standing round staring at it silently. It was the eeriest thing I'd ever seen. And then I heard . . .' His voice seemed to dry up.

'What?' The word caught in Annie's throat.

'A strangled, awful scream. A terrible, terrible sound . . .' He shook his head. 'From the bonfire. I thought, "My God, they're burning somebody alive." I tried to get near the fire, but when they saw what I was doing they grabbed my arms and held me back, and all the time there was that scream in the background, until it was cut off and there was just the roar of the fire . . . and all you could smell . . . There was one guy there who spoke English. Not very well, but enough to tell me what happened. He said the body they had burned was already dead. Had been for two days. It had disappeared from the family home and when they finally found it after a search of the neighbourhood

169

it was lying naked on a table in an old warehouse. But when they got close to it ... it spoke to them. He said it moved its mouth and spoke, and the things it said were terrible.'

He looked deep into her face, but Annie couldn't read his eyes at all. 'Why are you telling me this?'

He shook his head. 'I don't know. Maybe just to show you what we're up against. There are so many myths that follow him around. You never know what's true and what's a lie. The simple fact is, we don't know who he is or where he came from or what he can do. All we know, and I guess all that matters, is that he kills.'

17

The mood of bleak resignation seemed to fill every corner of the Royal Oak like the grey-blue cigarette smoke that normally clouded up over the bar. Everyone had heard of Colin Barnwell's shocking, untimely death and the rumour factory was in full flow as it plumbed the depths of imagined perversities and dark desires. It seemed everyone had turned out to hear the wheels of the village mill turning, as they always did in times of crisis or excitement. On the day the travellers had first arrived, the pub had filled to capacity by 7 p.m., just as it had done when the news broke that the village school was threatened with closure. The Royal Oak was the time-honoured place to go on such occasions. But with Colin Barnwell's death, there was none of the usual hubbub, just a sea of blank, uncomprehending faces.

Annie and Severin fought their way through the crush at 7.10 p.m. and managed to snatch a table near the stone fireplace. Annie knew she had made the right decision the moment she saw the crowd. If they wanted to find out if anyone had seen Wilde, this was the place to be. After Severin had bought their drinks, he set off on his rounds, breaking into conversations without any embarrassment, reeling off Wilde's description time after time. Annie watched him.

Severin had only been gone a few minutes when Martyn

hurried up and slipped into his seat, slopping his beer on to the table in his eagerness.

'I thought I'd catch you here tonight,' he said guardedly. 'How's your friend?'

'Severin? He's fine. He wants to find an old acquaintance who's just moved to the area, so he's asking around.'

'Bit old for you, isn't he? As a friend, I mean.'

'Not as old as George Newton, Martyn.' She tried to keep the irritation out of her voice, but she had no energy left to deal with Martyn's immature jealousy. 'And Severin is just a friend.'

'Never heard you mention him before.'

'Oh look, there's Bill King and Tim Huxton-Smith.' She peered over his shoulder as she changed the subject. 'You know, I saw those two bastards laying gin-traps in Tarrant's Wood to get at the travellers. Can you believe it? They're Neanderthals. I hope Jack Tarrant has cleared all the traps out by now. And there's Hartley Williams talking to Alexander Alcock,' she added sarcastically. 'The whole sick crew.'

'Well, you should have guessed they'd be here. The conscience of the village, and its muscle. Somebody should tell Williams he's not as important as he thinks he is.'

'He thinks if he shouts it loud enough, people will believe him, and, let's face it, some people do.'

Despite the subdued atmosphere of the pub, Williams was demonstratively noisy as he held court at a table near the picture display with loud claims about how 'his people' would deal with 'that traveller scum'. King was backing him up, drunk and flushed, while Huxton-Smith sat back with a sly grin. Standing away from the seated men were their female partners. The wives of Huxton-Smith and King were not there, but their mistresses had filled the vacancies.

'I've been saving up my money,' Martyn ventured cautiously. 'I thought we might go away for a few days next month. Nothing heavy, like. Just as friends. What d'you say?'

'Maybe. We'll see.' Annie looked past Martyn, into the crowd, trying to see Severin. How could she tell him that next month seemed a lifetime away? Out of the corner of her eye, she could see he seemed a little hurt by her half-hearted response, but the hard, cold present was the only thing that concerned her.

At that moment, the door swung open and a woman marched

in pulling a red-faced boy behind her. Annie recognized Julie Connor who lived just across the road from the pub. The boy was her son, Simon. Annie had looked after him a few times when she had helped out at the nursery at the village hall. There was fire in Mrs Connor's eyes as she pushed her way through the crowd until she found Hartley Williams.

'Mr Williams,' she said furiously.

The laughter at Williams' table trailed off and the men watched her approach suspiciously.

'Mr Williams,' she repeated. 'Something has got to be done.'

'What's that, my dear?'

'It's those travellers again. One of them attacked my Simon.' Her voice rose to the edge of hysteria.

'Calm down, Mrs Connor. Tell us what happened.' Williams jumped to his feet and took her hand with an obvious lack of sincerity.

The woman gulped air and continued. 'Simon was playing down near Blacksmiths Lane and one of them tried to drag him off. Look!' She held out Simon's arm to reveal raw scratches on his wrist. 'He pulled himself away. Lord, I daren't think what would have happened if—' She bit her lip, and Bill King drunkenly pulled her down to a chair before there was any greater display of emotion.

'Don't worry. Your boy's safe now,' Williams said. 'And we're not going to rest until that scum is driven away from our village.'

Simon, who had obviously forgotten his fright, had drifted away from his mother and was examining the pictures on the wall. One of them caught his eye and he yelled out excitedly, 'That's him! He's the one who grabbed my arm!'

Everyone gathered round the picture.

'Laurence Lucas,' Huxton-Smith said in a dry, quiet voice.

Williams reacted first to break the tension, and then he scrubbed Simon's hair. 'He's dead, young man. A long time ago.' There was a ripple of nervous laughter.

'No, it was him!' Simon protested. 'I recognize him. He wanted to take me away. He said he wanted to have some fun with me.'

The whole room fell into a queasy silence. Simon's mother attempted to pull him away from the picture. Bill King drained his pint in one go.

'It *was* him, Mummy.' Simon looked up at his mother with tearful eyes.

She smiled wanly, but didn't say anything. The atmosphere had suddenly become uncomfortable, adding another layer of pain on top of the one caused by Colin Barnwell's death.

'Come now,' Williams said, trying to buoy everyone up. 'Let's not dwell on the past. We have more pressing problems.' He smiled like a tiger. 'Those travellers really do have to pay for this.'

The noise level suddenly surged as the tension passed. A few smiles broke out first, and then the conversation turned to football and TV – anything mundane in direct counterpoint to what had gone before. Annie watched Williams milk the occasion as he took Mrs Connor's hand once more and led her and her son to the door.

She told Martyn she was going to the toilet and then she weaved among the huddled groups until she found Severin involved in a conversation with a lad who worked as a farmhand.

'Any luck?' she asked when he eventually broke off.

He shook his head. 'We just have to keep trying. Someone somewhere will have seen him.'

They discussed the attack on Simon Connor in Blacksmiths Lane. 'Do you think it could be him?' she asked. 'Simon thought his attacker was young and looked like Laurence Lucas or something, but you know how kids are. He could have been confused.'

Severin shrugged. 'It doesn't sound like Wilde's thing, but you never know. We could check out the area where it happened tomorrow. I'm open to any lead.'

Blacksmiths Lane was a potholed, dusty road that led past the turning to the travellers' camp and up to Jack Tarrant's farm. It was also the demarcation line between the village and open countryside; only the Old Mill lay just beyond it, and after that there was a vast expanse of green fields and woodland, but no habitation for a few miles.

No one to call for help, Annie thought with a crawl in her belly. *And nowhere to hide.*

It was 10.15 p.m. and Annie felt uncomfortable that there was nothing she could do. She had to content herself with making small talk with Martyn, but the only time their conversation reached any real level was when she got tearful over Colin Barnwell and even then she couldn't explain that her emotions were those of guilt. She had attracted Wilde to the village. How many more people had she damned? How would she be able to live with herself?

There was another thought which had been preying on her mind. 'You said some graves had been disturbed?'

'So the coppers said. I had a quick look, but it didn't seem much. Just like the soil had been churned over by a plough. And a couple of markers had fallen down.'

'Was Robert's . . .?'

'No, I checked.'

At least that was something, she thought.

The door opened, then closed with a bang and the crowd near the bar suddenly fell quiet. All heads turned to see who had entered. The new arrival was hidden from Annie beneath the shoulders of the drinkers, but as the crowd parted for someone to pass through, Annie was surprised to see Mrs Barnwell, head held high, overcoat pulled tightly around her. She was smiling, but it was fixed, and there was a dazed look about her like some punchy boxer. When she turned to the bar to order a drink, her coat fell apart and Annie saw the white silk of her nightdress beneath it.

'My husband used to have a drink here, you know.' The room had grown so still her voice could be heard right across it. 'He used to have half a pint of bitter, and not in a straight glass, and that's what I'll have please.'

Mrs Barnwell took her beer and went to stand near a pillar where she hummed quietly to herself. Everyone looked away in embarrassment. They could see what grief had done to her – and they were unable to cope with it.

'Colin?' she enquired of the space next to her. 'What are you doing?'

Alexander Alcock flinched and started to edge his way out from behind the bar while the drinkers near to her suddenly found interesting things to see in the corners of the room.

A cough at the back of the room broke the spell, and Mrs Barnwell looked around anxiously for her husband. There was a moment of panic when she realized he wasn't there, but then

174

she drifted into her dream world once more, talking quietly in a singsong voice to the ghost imprinted in her memory.

Just before Alcock reached her, she stopped mid-sentence. Her face held its dreamy quality for just another second and then her eyes grew wide with horror. She was looking at something beyond Annie and her reaction was so intense Annie had to check over her own shoulder. There was an instant of staring silence and then Mrs Barnwell started to scream.

The landlord leapt forward to try to restrain her, but she thrashed out blindly and raked the side of his face with her fingernails. He stumbled backwards and jolted two other men into life who managed to grab her arms and hold her still. Even then her screaming didn't stop.

'What is it?' she howled, her voice raw. 'What's it doing here? It's coming for us all! Oh my God, my Lord! It won't rest until we're dead!' Then she took a deep breath and intoned, 'The first blood is spilt. The sheep have no shepherd.' She mumbled something else inaudible and then she added loudly, 'The black river runs and never stops. He calls in a voice like a clown. Beware – small feet never dally.' Her eyes rolled and slipped in and out of focus until they came to rest on Annie's face, and there they suddenly locked.

Annie felt she had been punched in the face. *Can she see it's all my fault?* She found herself swimming in Mrs Barnwell's mesmerizing stare. The world pulled out of shape like plasticine, then did a flip, and Annie was staring at herself, the alabaster-skinned premonition again, as powerful as it had been in the sweat lodge.

Before she could cry out, what she was seeing changed again, and now it was Wilde, grinning rakishly, pushing his way past Mrs Barnwell, through the crowd towards her, getting closer, a murderous glint in his eye . . .

Annie jumped to her feet. The crash of her chair on the floor shattered her hallucination, and everything was back as it was apart from the prickly cold of her skin and the churning of her stomach. The men were steering Mrs Barnwell through to the landlord's private quarters. Her screams still echoed long after the door had closed.

'Are you OK?' Martyn asked with concern.

'Jesus.' Annie blinked back her tears.

'I wonder what she could see.' Martyn looked ashen. 'You

know everyone's always said she has a touch of second sight. It used to really bother Mr Barnwell because he couldn't reconcile it with his religion. Suffer not a witch, and all that malarkey.'

Annie looked out of the window, but saw only her reflection which looked unnervingly like that recent death-image, too-white skin framed beneath jet black hair. Bleakly, she toyed with the ankh around her neck which caught the light and glowed white like the moon. She felt she was like a soldier as he went over the top into no-man's land.

'For Queen and country,' she said quietly, raising her glass to her reflection. 'We who are about to die give thanks.'

18

The flies seemed to come from nowhere, sweeping into the village early the following day in clouds so thick that for one moment they blocked out the sun. People looked up with joy and thought the rain was finally coming, not really wondering what was the source of the buzz that sounded like the irritating drone of overhead power cables. For a while they hovered above Riddington as if checking their destination, and then they dropped and separated, beginning their occupation so surreptitiously no one noticed them at first. They were not there, then suddenly they were everywhere, hovering in back gardens, buzzing against windows, crawling over uncovered food, haunting the graveyard. *Everywhere*.

The fat meat flies which moved as if they were bloated were the ones which irritated Annie the most. She watched them bumping stupidly into the apple tree above her head, their whine so loud it was impossible to ignore. At irregular intervals they would alight on the bare skin of her arms and legs. Even when she moved her limbs they didn't fly away and she was forced to lean forward and swat them disgustedly.

She could have gone indoors, but it was even hotter in there and there were just as many flies. When she had come downstairs that morning after a few, troubled hours of sleep, there had been fifteen or more, battering against the kitchen window.

She had used the can of fly spray until the kitchen stank of chemicals and although the bodies piled up, their number never seemed to get any smaller.

It was only the ringing of the phone which finally distracted her from their attentions. She brushed two flies off her leg and hurried indoors to answer it.

'Annie?'

'Charlotte?'

'You're so difficult to get hold of.' Charlotte was pumped up with her usual exuberance, but Annie also detected an off note in her voice. 'I've been trying for—'

'Is something wrong?'

'Apart from the fact that I've split up with Douggie, no.'

'Oh, Charlotte. What happened?' Annie asked sympathetically. Charlotte and Douggie had been close ever since they had met on their course, and in the last few weeks before finals, Annie had even heard marriage mentioned.

'Oh, he was just a shit. I'm better off out of it.' Charlotte sounded blasé, but there was a vein of hurt which Annie could sense immediately. Besides, Charlotte would never have spoken about Douggie like that unless he had done something really bad.

'Do you want to tell me about it?'

'Not now. I'm all talked out. I thought I could go into all the gruesome details up there. I know your mum and dad are away, and it'd be nice to spend some time together.'

Annie held her breath. What could she say? *Actually, Charlotte, I'm having a few problems with a serial killer at the moment. Maybe another day.*

'What is it?'

'This isn't a very good time, Charlotte.'

There was a long, hurt pause. 'I really need you now, Annie.'

Annie felt crushed, but she couldn't invite Charlotte to Riddington and put her life at risk. Wilde had won again.

'Maybe in a few weeks,' she said. 'It really *is* difficult now.'

'Right. Well. OK.' The pauses were worse than anything she said. 'I'll call you then.'

'Look after yourself.' It sounded icy compared to what she should be saying, but if she allowed Charlotte the opportunity to question her she was afraid she would break down and tell

177

everything. Then Charlotte would want to help, and that would make her a target.

'And you.'

A wave of depression swept over Annie as she hung up, but she knew she had done the right thing.

'Problems?' Severin was leaning in the doorway, towelling his hair dry after his morning shower.

'I've just lost my best friend. Score another one for Wilde. When he sets out to destroy a life, he doesn't do it by half measures.'

He nodded understandingly. 'Any chance of a coffee?' Annie pointed to the kettle on the side and he took the hint. As the water boiled, he replaced Wilde's bracelet round his neck.

He looked at it for a second and then said, 'Does this still disturb you?'

She eyed the bracelet warily across the kitchen. 'There's something weird about it, that's for sure. It screws up my head, and I keep thinking I hear voices when I touch it. Sorry about . . . you know . . . running away from you the other night, but it spooked me and I had to get out.'

'Maybe you're just a little spacy after everything that's happened.' He touched the bracelet, saying, 'So, are you ready?'

'As much as I'll ever be.'

'Scared?'

'Terrified.'

Annie had her own destination in mind when they entered the graveyard and she left Severin to wander among the stones looking for the desecrated plots. She made her way quickly to the edge of the disturbed area and she was relieved to see Martyn was right: Robert's grave had not been touched. But as she drew close, she saw something *was* different.

She knelt to examine it, and that was how Severin found her a few minutes later, her face drained of blood.

Annie looked up at him and then back at the thing on the grave that served as a base parody of loving remembrance. Jammed in the soil not far from the headstone was a single rose, its petals turned black through some corruption she couldn't quite envisage. It seemed to be alive, whole, yet rotting.

'Wilde left this here for me . . . another little twist of the knife,' she said bitterly as she snatched up the unclean bloom and threw it across the graveyard. 'This is my brother's grave.' She paused as her fingers momentarily went to the silver ankh. 'I told Wilde about Robert. God knows why, but I did. And now he knows exactly what hurts me.'

Although she didn't mention it, there was something else about the rose which disturbed her, and that was its warped parallel with her premonition of the roses sprouting from her dead eyes. She bolted that thought down inside her as she asked Severin, 'Any luck?'

'I can't feel any vibrations of substance. He was here, that's a fact, but he's managed to hide the reason why.'

'There's no point staying any longer then,' Annie said firmly. 'We better get moving.'

As they walked down towards the lych gate, a breeze seemed to spring from nowhere and when it rushed wildly among the headstones behind them, it sounded oddly like laughter.

It was only a short hop in the car from the church to Blacksmiths Lane where Simon Connor had been attacked. They had divided the circle on their Ordnance Survey map into six segments – one for each of the days Annie had left with one day spare (*to panic*, she thought) – highlighting deserted buildings and other likely locations. Annie didn't want to think about what would happen if they had drawn a blank by the end of that sixth day.

They drove in silence but as they pulled off Colthorpe Road into Blacksmiths Lane, Annie felt Severin stiffen beside her. He was looking past her, through the clumps of oak and ash to the dark brick of the Old Mill which could just be glimpsed beyond.

She followed his gaze, 'What is it?'

'That building. Is that one of the empty ones you pointed out on the map?'

'The Mill? Yes, it's been empty for a while. Why?'

'I don't know . . . I just felt something.'

'Do you want to stop?' She slowed the car down to a crawl so he could have a better look, and through the trees there was the faint lub-dub, lub-dub of the water wheel turning slowly, like the beating of some giant heart.

'No, it's not that strong. Another time.'

They carried on a little further and then Annie pulled the car over. 'Well, here we are, Sherlock.'

They climbed out and entered a field that whisshed and

179

shusshed as the breeze swayed through its golden crop. The footpath ran round the outside of the field, and then plunged into another, before disappearing into the trees. The air was suffused with the sweaty, choking odour of rape from the other side of the lane, an alien crop that cast its pall over the whole countryside. At that moment, Annie saw the landscape with new eyes: isolated, inhospitable, desolate. Dangerous.

Severin strode out ahead, his black coat swirling around him like a cloud of ink, but Annie was soon at his side, unable to prevent herself scanning the flowing corn for suddenly emerging figures.

After a minute or two she spotted a movement in the field ahead and tugged at Severin's sleeve. A male figure was ploughing a path towards the trees, head down, insistent, trying to get to the shadows.

Wilde?' she asked.

Severin squinted into the sun. Can't tell. Let's check him out.'

He started to jog, his boots thudding heavily on the dry, packed earth, and Annie wondered how he could move so quickly, in those clothes, in that heat. Even though she was wearing a light t-shirt and shorts, she was soon slick with sweat.

It took them nearly five minutes to reach the point where the walker's path broke out of the corn on the edge of the trees. Ahead, Annie could hear the trickle of the Gilwiskow Brook which flowed out of Riddington into the open countryside.

'Do you feel it?' Severin asked.

She knew what he was talking about instantly. In the village, it would not have been so easy to pick up, but in the clear background of the country it leapt out from its surroundings; a jarring sense of discord that made Annie's heart beat faster. There seemed to be a trail of whatever it was, an airborne and invisible slug-path of blackness that picked up the track from the corn and headed into the trees.

'I don't like this,' Annie said. 'What is it?'

'I don't know. But I'd say we're on the right lines.'

It was barely cooler in the shade, although the stream gurgled noisily, cutting a deep bed between banks lined with brambles and overhanging trees. There was a loud splashing to their left as if someone was walking through the water.

Severin jerked his thumb in the direction of the noise and then ghosted off through the undergrowth. Barely a blade of grass quivered at his passing and Annie felt like a lame rhino in comparison. As they moved, the black psychic stain grew stronger until it had the potency of a gas; Annie had to fight to control her negative emotions.

The splashings, which were slow and laboured, grew closer and once or twice Annie caught a glimpse through the foliage of the man they were pursuing. Only the back of his head was visible for a second or two, but it was enough to realize it wasn't Wilde. That knowledge should have calmed her, but for some reason it pushed the tension up a notch.

The splashing stopped a few yards further on, and Severin brought Annie to a halt with a hand on her shoulder. She tried to listen to whatever the man was doing, but all she could hear was the pump of blood in her own brain. After a minute Severin motioned her to stay where she was before he eased round the trunk of a tree and disappeared.

Left to her own devices, Annie let her thoughts race wildly, but reclaimed them when Severin called out her name. Cautiously, she peered round the tree. Severin was standing in a clearing at the top of the other bank, beckoning to her without any sense of urgency. She first jumped the stream, and then hauled herself up the other bank using the grass for leverage.

'He's gone.' Severin pointed through the undergrowth to the fields on the other side. 'He finished what he was doing here, and then he set off again while we were waiting.'

'Aren't we going to fol—' The words caught in Annie's throat as she suddenly saw what was around them. The smell hit her a second or two later. 'God!' she said with distaste.

Several poles like the kind used to support saplings had been hammered into the ground at various points on the perimeter of the clearing. Each one bore a grisly trophy.

The decomposing head of a badger, its eyes long gone, stared at them blankly from the nearest pole. At the next one there was a cat, impaled through its anus, its face hideously frozen in terror. Then a rabbit, its flesh mostly gone; a wood pigeon, its wings pinned back and tied to a pole with barbed wire; a fox, beautiful even in death, hanging limply; another bird, larger and black – a crow? Some of them had been partially dissected. Cut open with a knife to see how they worked?

'How sick can you get?' Annie said.

'This isn't Wilde's work. The atmosphere – it's worse here,

can you feel it? It's like the guy who did this is leaving some kind of trail.'

Annie's hand went to the ankh subconsciously, a comforting action which she found she was doing with increasing regularity. The moment her fingers brushed the silver, a thought leapt into her head and ran straight to her mouth. '*An abomination. Nature is rebelling.*' She looked at Severin. 'Whatever ... whoever ... did this isn't playing by the rules. That's what we can sense – Nature crying out.'

Something caught her eye under a bush on the edge of the clearing. She moved forward, pulling the foliage back to investigate. Hidden underneath was a mongrel, its eyes tightly closed.

'Leave it. It's dead like all the others,' Severin said dismissively.

'No, I can see its chest moving slightly,' Annie corrected. 'I think it's injured. We should get help.'

Gently, she stretched out her hand to stroke its fur. But instead of feeling the warm resilience of muscles, the fur gave like a paper bag filled with nothing. A second later, the dog erupted with flies. They ejected like bullets in a rapid-fire swarm of droning black from its jaw, nose, eyes and anus, hundreds and hundreds of them pelting into Annie, into her face, into her mouth, until all she could see was a thick cloud.

And every time she spat some out, others crawled in; fat meat flies hitting her like stones, and leaving her no air to gulp. She toppled over backwards, and still they would not go away, and then Severin's hands were on her, dragging her from the carcass. After a few feet, she pressed her face hard into the grass and the buzzing began to diminish. Eventually, she looked up, gagging and fighting back the shock.

Severin helped her into a sitting position and put his arm around her shoulders. The flies had disappeared, but Annie could still hear them buzzing sickeningly among the trees.

'That wasn't natural,' she gasped. 'It was like they were *waiting*.'

'I know,' Severin said coldly.

She could still glimpse the dog under the bush, but now it was almost flat, the fur hanging loosely over the bones.

'Flies don't do things like that,' Annie continued, as if the real sense of it would suddenly come to her. 'What's going on?'

There was something underneath the carcass. Against her

182

better judgement, and feeling her stomach churn, she crawled on her hands and knees until she was close enough to use a stick to lift the dog. The fur and the bones slid back into an unrecognizable heap.

'What is it?' Severin asked.

'There's a hollow underneath the dog. And there's something in it.' Warily, she crawled closer. 'An old tin . . . really rusty . . . and an old pen-knife.'

She pulled out the two items and flung them halfway between her and Severin as if they were hot coals. When the tin hit the ground, it burst open and a book fell out.

Severin retrieved it and turned the pages gingerly. 'It's a diary.' He flicked to the front. 'The diary of Laurence Lucas.'

Annie went cold. 'Laurence Lucas? *The* Laurence Lucas?'

'Yep. Nineteen-sixties vintage. The ink has faded pretty badly and,' he lifted it to his nose, 'boy, does it smell. Must have been here a while. Only, get this . . .' He turned to the untouched pages at the back. 'There's a new entry.'

He held the diary up to show her. The writing was fresh, blue fibre-tip, yet on occasion shaky and almost illegible, and at others, fully formed.

'This is too much,' Annie said. 'What kind of creep would do that?'

'Maybe he's got a fan.'

She spoke nervously, 'What does the entry say?'

Severin began to read. '"We're poor little lambs who've lost our way. Baa! Baa! Baa! We're little black sheep who've gone astray, Baa-aa-aa! Gentleman-Rankers out on the spree, Damned from here to Eternity, God ha' mercy on such as we, Baa! Yah! Bah!"'

'That's Kipling,' Annie interjected curiously.

Severin continued. '"The farmer thinks he's in control, but he's dealt with the uneducated and the weak for too long – never anyone like me! I can feel the power within me the same as it always was! I burn with life and passions! I saw the others, dull by comparison, and they'll do his bidding, but he'll never control me. Not me! The Lover Boy will dance the fine, old dance and we'll whip up some fun in this dismal place. And let's leave the farmer with the sheep. Ha! That's a joke! He should never have killed the shepherd all those years ago – he ought to be sick of sheep by now! I don't know when he plans to send them back, if at all, but I won't be going with them. I never want to pass through that Black Cathedral again. What's on the other side is ..."' Severin held the diary up and peered incomprehensibly at the writing. 'There are a few more lines, but I can't make any sense of it. It's like it's gone into gibberish.'

'What does it mean?'

'No idea! But then other people's diaries never make a great deal of sense. Some nut who's got an unhealthy interest in Lucas and wants to be him? Whatever, it doesn't help us very much.'

Annie wasn't wholly convinced. She was hearing voices in her head, the ones that had been there that night in the pub in Leicester with Charlotte, and they were screaming at her, but the connections would not come. 'So we're no closer to finding Wilde,' she said. 'We just stumble across other nuts instead. Riddington used to be such a *nice* place. Now you can't move without falling in a cesspit.'

Severin pocketed the diary. 'I know what you mean. Death ... pain ... this is so Wilde ... but not him. Perhaps he's got a protégé,' he joked.

Annie nodded. *Coincidences. Synchronicity.* Suddenly she wanted to get out of the clearing. If anything, the atmosphere of unease was getting stronger. Glancing round at the animal corpses, she said to Severin with a shudder, 'Remind me never to go walking in the countryside again.'

When they made it back to the car, the seats were like hotplates; they had to leave the doors open for ten minutes before they could even think about climbing in. Their next destination was the travellers' camp along the lane.

A minute after the car pulled up to the edge of the camp in a cloud of dust, it was surrounded by a crowd of dirty-faced children hammering on the windows. Severin managed to open the door enough to squeeze out.

'Hey, kids, get off the fuckin' car,' he said.

'Yeah? Whatcha gonna do about it?' a ten-year-old sneered, hands on hips.

Severin whipped open his coat and half drew the sawn-off shotgun from the pocket in the lining. The children ran off hooting and screeching, although the ten-year-old paused long enough to flick a few Vs before disappearing among the vehicles.

'Big man,' Annie said.

'Sometimes it's got to be done.'

She was surprised to see a faint impression of a smile on his face.

En route to the centre of the camp, they passed the sweat lodge and Annie gave an involuntary shiver. It held an almost mythic status for her now. She explained what had happened there, and she asked Severin whether he thought what she had seen then, and since, could have been real.

'I'll believe anything,' he replied. 'Because if you don't believe, one day you're gonna get caught out when that alien spaceship lands on you.'

'There was something else,' she added. 'A premonition.'

'What did you see?'

'Me. Dead.' Annie turned to Severin who was looking at her strangely. 'I can't get it out of my head, day or night. I'm going to die, soon, and Wilde's going to kill me.'

'Come on. Don't talk like that.'

Severin ushered her onwards and they found Tommy and Angela arguing quietly near the smouldering campfire. Whatever they were talking about was obviously not for general consumption. Annie introduced Severin to Tommy and ignored Angela whose frostiness turned to an arctic blast in her presence.

'I wanted to ask you a favour,' she began. 'We're looking for someone. He's a wanderer, a bit of an outsider. Tall and very charismatic, curly black hair, clipped beard, one gold earring, slightly swarthy skin. You'll remember him if you see him.'

'Sure, I'll put the word around,' Tommy said. 'What's he done?'

'Let's just say he's trouble. You want to keep out of his way if you come across him.'

'People say that about us,' Angela said.

'In this case, it's true,' Annie replied tautly. 'I tell you, he's dangerous.'

Angela sensed an opening and took it. 'Maybe he's just had some bad press. If he's an enemy of yours, I'd certainly give him the time of day.'

'And I'd say you're welcome to everything you'd get, but I wouldn't wish that on my worst enemy.' Annie turned back to Tommy and handed him a piece of paper. 'Here's my home address and phone number. I'd appreciate a call if anyone comes across him. It's important.'

Tommy took the paper with a smile. 'Consider it done.'

On the way back to Blackstone Cottage to grab some lunch, Severin started to dip into the Lucas diary, reading an entry, flicking through a few pages, reading another. Annie could smell it in his lap like rotten offal and wanted to fling it out of the window into a ditch; it seemed tainted on a much more basic level than its smell.

After a minute or two, he came across an entry which seemed to capture him and he read intently for a while, but then his attitude suddenly changed and he coughed and stifled a noise in his throat before slamming the diary shut and shoving it under his seat.

There were a few people scattered around as they crawled slowly into the High Street, and then slid smoothly up the hill towards Blackstone Cottage. It was then that Annie slammed on the brakes so sharply Severin had to brace himself against the dashboard.

'What have you seen?' His eyes darted around as his hand automatically went to the hidden shotgun.

Annie laughed weakly and buried her face in her hands. 'I'm sorry. This tension is getting to me. I'm going crazy.'

She pointed to a run-down house across the road. The windows were dusty and a few tiles were missing off the roof. 'A man called Brian Swift lives there. He's a bit of weirdo, to tbe honest, but he's always been OK to me. He's in his late thirties and he's lived alone with his mother all his life so I suppose I can forgive him. Anyway, his mother died recently and left him on his own. I went to some do up at the rectory which the vicar arranged to cheer him up. Stupid idea, but that's our vicar for you.'

'Yeah? And?'

'I could have sworn I just saw his mother standing at the bedroom window.'

I'm running away, Jake.'

In the shade of an elm tree at the end of the jitty, Simon Connor was oblivious to the late afternoon heat as he flicked a football with surprising dexterity for a six-year-old. He was wearing his favourite Leicester City shirt, royal blue with the team name on the back and fox logo on the front, and a pair of loose tracksuit trousers.

Jake Samuels could barely tear his mind away from his own problems, but Simon's bravado piqued his interest. How could someone else consider running away when he was so desperate to stay *with* his parents? He had heard his father mention the *divorce* word the other night and he had been living in fear ever since.

'There's not long before school's out, Simes,' he said. 'Things won't seem so bad in the holidays.'

'I'm definitely running away.' Simon was adamant. He tried a mighty flick to get the ball on his head and swore when he failed. 'My mum keeps having a go at me. All 'cos that man tried to grab me.'

'She's probably just worried about you.'

'Nah, she hates me. She wouldn't let me watch *Star Trek* the other night, an' then she screamed at me for spilling my milk. An' she won't let me go out and play after school.'

'So when are you off?'

'Now. I've got some sarnies for if I get hungry. It'll be great!'

Jake wasn't convinced.

'You can come too, if you want.'

'No, thanks. *Star Wars* is on this weekend.'

'Oh.' Simon sounded like he hadn't considered this important detail, but it was too late to back out. He paused at the entrance to the jitty and looked down the High Street past the pub towards the fields and hills. For a moment, he seemed to be having second thoughts, but then he grinned, punched Jake on the shoulder and yelled, 'See ya!'

Simon ran until he had crossed Colthorpe Road and found the public footpath that would take him across the fields to Measham. When Riddington disappeared from view behind the trees, he decided to have the first sandwich from his backpack, kicking his football ahead of him at the same time.

The path ran along the side of a cornfield and then past a thickly wooded area. When he reached the copse, Simon rested on the trunk of a fallen tree and ate his packet of crisps. His lunch box was quickly becoming depleted.

As he munched away, he gradually became aware of the loneliness in the countryside. There weren't any houses and the slight afternoon breeze caused waves to ripple across the corn, rustling the branches of the trees and echoing in his ears.

The corn looked like the sea, didn't it? And there were

monsters beneath the sea – he had read about them. His gaze fixed on each ripple as he imagined something swimming through the gold towards him. The hairs on the back of his neck prickled.

Simon looked round quickly into the trees and bushes, but there was no one there. There were flies, lots and lots of them, but no people. No friendly faces or comforting voices. Just a strange, lonely world.

He peered into his crisp bag and decided he didn't feel like any more. He screwed up the top of the packet and returned it to his bag. He was feeling a little scared now, and had to tell himself to be brave. Like the X-Men. Perhaps he should put off running away until another day. After *Star Wars*, that would be good.

Something wet dripped on his head. He scrubbed it and then checked his hand to see if it was the white of bird droppings. His hand was clear.

Another splash. This time it dribbled down his forehead. It couldn't be rain; there wasn't a cloud in the sky.

Simon looked up. There was something above him, something hideous which might have been human, but which looked more like a giant bat. He heard a voice which at first sounded like a clown, but then like the roaring of some monstrous beast. He had no time to consider what it was saying before its owner released itself from the branches and dropped.

He had one second to raise his arm and then the darkness folded around him.

Annie and Severin spent the afternoon searching the first segment on the map without any luck and when they finally returned home, exhausted, the sun was already low on the horizon. Annie realized then how laborious their work would be before her time was up.

They left the car on the road and walked to the back of the house. Warning signals started ringing in her head the moment Annie laid her fingers on the handle of the kitchen door. It was open, although she distinctly remembered locking it.

It took Severin only a few minutes to check the house was empty, but when he returned to the kitchen Annie was looking traumatized. 'He was here,' she said, pointing to where a mobile phone spattered with dried blood stood in a charging unit plugged into the socket next to the cooker.

'It's the one Wilde left in my car at the service station,' she continued. 'I threw it out of the window after I pulled off the motorway.' For her, it was an extension of Wilde, his malignant psyche given plastic shape and it had now got into her home, her sanctuary.

When it suddenly rang, Annie jumped a few steps as if it was a giant insect that had suddenly started to chirrup and flex its mandibles. She looked at Severin, who nodded in the direction of the phone, giving her no choice.

'Hello?'

'Hello, Annie.' His tone was honied, but the menace behind it was unmistakable. 'Do you like your little present? I thought it would be an excellent way for me to be near you. You know how it is ... old friends need to hear each other's voices to remember all the good times they shared together. And I do think it would be in your interest to keep in touch with me, Annie, because every bit of information will help in your search. Yes, I am quite aware of what you are doing. I watch you ... where you go ... what you do. You have no secrets from me, you should know that by now. It seems to be shaping up into a nice little game of cat-and-mouse, and I do so like to play. I have no problem with you and Severin wasting your time. However, I should warn you that if you bring my existence to anyone else's attention, there will be a price to pay.' He sighed playfully. 'My plans for you and your quaint little village are starting to take effect quite nicely – you should see the results very shortly. Keep your eyes open, Annie.'

The line went dead and Annie immediately repeated what Wilde had said.

Severin nodded thoughtfully. 'We should keep the phone. He thinks he can't be beaten, but you know how it is with arrogant bastards like that ... they always make mistakes. There's a chance he might let something slip when he's talking to you ... something we can use ...'

'I suppose you're right,' Annie said reluctantly. Somehow she would have to live with the knowledge that there was nowhere to hide any more.

*

'504, 505, 506 . . .' Karen Cockburn counted aloud each time the brush ran through her long, golden hair. It was a mantra for peace and forgetfulness, soothing away the black memories that inhabited every waking hour. She was sweet sixteen and never been kissed – by anyone who wasn't family – yet most of the time she felt sixty.

'512, 513 . . .'

Peter was hiding in the attic with his comics. *House of Secrets. From Beyond the Unknown. Strange Adventures.* Bizarre, dark little stories that probably made his own life seem normal. He had suffered terribly, Karen thought, but he had probably suffered the least; all his scars were on the outside and, after eight months, the bruises and the cuts had healed. Oh, it probably still preyed on his mind, she knew that, but it was not like it was with her, or Julie, or Ruth. Every time they smelled beer they had a sudden, whirlpool image of foul breath blasting into their faces, of the weight on their limbs, of the pain, and that dirty, stinking feeling of guilt and self-loathing.

'537 . . .'

Her image hovered in the three angled mirrors of her dressing table. *Beautiful.* She could hear his words as if he was in the room speaking them. *My little princess.* And now his face was there. Karen cried out as she hurled her brush venomously across the room and covered her face with her hands to press back the tears.

She was glad he was dead, and she wished he was there.

In the next room, she could hear her mother singing in her high-pitched, whining voice, sounding like a dog who had been chained up too long. Karen hammered on the wall. 'Shut up!' she screamed. 'Shut up!' There was a second of silence and then the singing started again.

The clock next to her bed said 11 p.m. Icy fingers tickled her spine. She would never forget that time. *11 p.m. Tuseday night.* Her night. Bang. Crash. Belch. Slam-slam-slam up the stairs. Thump, thump, as he hit his fist against the landing wall with each step. And then the sound outside her door, of laboured, drunken breathing, the wait that seemed like an eternity for the handle to turn . . .

There was a knock on the door. Karen cried out instinctively and jumped back against the headboard, but when the door swung open it was only Peter, worry turning his tiny face pale. He remembered the time too.

'Can I come in?'

'As long as you don't bring any of those comics in here. They all smell of damp.' She thought about adding that he smelled a bit too – his personal hygiene had deteriorated over the last eight months – but thought better of it. It wasn't the time.

Peter crawled on to the end of the bed and hugged his knees, and at that moment Karen thought he looked his real age, not the one that had been thrust upon him. 'I'm worried about Mum. I think she's going a bit mad. I saw her down at his grave the other day. She was hitting the ground and screaming like she was ready for the loony-bin.'

Karen nodded. Their mother *was* going crazy. She was trapped in a dizzying spiral: guilt for not doing anything before when she knew what was happening, and then guilt for standing back while they solved the problem themselves in the only way they could find.

'I'm scared she's going to say something to the vicar. Confess or something.' Peter fiddled with the bedspread nervously.

'I don't think the vicar can do anything if it's said in church. Or is that the Catholics?'

'Well, you don't have to worry. You didn't kill him.'

'We all killed him, Peter. You pushed him down the stairs, but we were all in it together.' She put her hand on his arm. 'You were the hero. You saved us all.'

Then he started to cry, big, racking sobs, built up over months, and she had to put her arms around him to comfort him. 'I didn't want Daddy to go, Karen. I just wanted him to stop,' he gasped.

Karen held back her own tears. 'I know, Pete. I loved him too. And I hated him as well. He would never have stopped, though. It would have gone on and on . . .' She caught her breath. 'It's best he's gone.'

As if on cue, the back door slammed, reverberating throughout the whole house. Karen had locked it before she had come to bed.

'Who's that?' Peter asked. They both held each other tighter, pressing the memories back.

Crash. Someone had stumbled into the kitchen table. A chair screeched on the lino floor as it was pushed out of the way. In the room next door, their mother's singing was strangled in her throat.

Bang, went the kitchen door. Then there was a moment of silence before they heard the slam of a work boot on the bottom step, followed by another one, slowly and laboriously, as the intruder maintained his balance and struggled to make his way. *Slam*. Silence. *Slam*. Silence. *Slam*. To the top of the stairs.

Hysterical crying erupted from the twins' room across the hall, Ruth and Julie's wailing intermingling into one terrified howl. And their mother joined in, her reedy voice a notch higher. Karen and Peter held their breath, closed their eyes and prayed.

And then came the thump-thump-thump along the wall of the landing, until it stopped outside the door. Karen watched the handle.

And waited.

19

The night was thick and dark beneath an uncertain cloud covering which trapped the heat of the day and stifled any thoughts of sleep. Besides, Hartley Williams had much to concern him in his role as Riddington's foremost citizen and most pressing was the threat of the travellers which nagged him so much that he was likely to lose his temper at any moment. He regretted hitting his wife, he really did, but she had the unfortunate habit of saying the wrong thing at the wrong time.

He poured himself another large Scotch and looked out into the gloom of the garden, feeling the reassuring security all around him. Riddington had been home to him all his life, like it had to so many of the village residents. It was a refuge from the buffeting storms of the outer world and a place where he could truly be himself – that was surely something worth fighting for. But now he felt the enemy was camped just beyond the walls, ready to storm the gates and destroy everything he valued. Their entire lifestyle was a danger, threatening to smash the rules and regulations that provided the very foundations of society. Someone had to take a stand. Was he strong enough? He looked deep into the amber glow of the whisky and hoped he was.

Although he never mentioned it to anyone, least of all Bill King or Huxton-Smith or that buffoon Alexander Alcock at the pub, sometimes he felt riddled with insecurities. His wife knew it, of course, and he found it hard to forgive her that. Those creeping doubts and worries had been a part of him since childhood, and to this day he remembered lucidly the incident which had planted their seeds. It had been just before the war when Riddington was an even quieter oasis and the trains still ran along the branch lines. Old steam locos, clouding the sky with white smoke.

In the bright summers of his youth, he used to gather with the other village lads, Cyril Kite, Will Smart, Gordon Jenkinson and the rest, down by the tracks, timetable to hand, ready for each train to roll through. They'd wave to the driver and he'd wave back, and they'd cheer and do cartwheels for the benefit of the passengers. As time passed, their games got more daring and they would race the trains, trying to beat them. Trying to prove themselves superhuman.

Then late in the summer of '38, as the nights started to draw in and the days grew cooler, something happened that changed all that. Will Smart, always the fastest and most daring, stumbled during what they had decided would be the last train run of the summer. They had fallen before many times, but they always ran well away from the tracks where it didn't matter. Except that on this occasion Will had decided to run right alongside the train where the passengers could see him better. Rough stones provided the hard-core on which the sleepers rested and it must have been one of those which turned his ankle. All Williams could remember of that moment was Will's face, flushed and excited, and then his arms going up and his body going down. The scream, so awful even now, cut off suddenly, and horror had exploded on the faces of the passengers who had been smiling at his antics.

They had all rushed over, but he was the one who reached Will first and many times since he had wished to God he had not beaten the others. Will still had some life left in him in those scant seconds before the rest arrived. He remembered the look in his eyes, the realization cutting through the pain, and then the blankness that crept over them as Will spiralled down into the darkness and away. He recalled scrambling around looking for Will's leg, as if he could find it and stuff it back on and make Will miraculously come back to life. And he remembered trying to staunch that horrendous flow of blood from the clean slice halfway up Will's thigh, and only coming to his senses when it stopped of its own accord.

Everything changed after that. The friends slowly drifted apart, their superhuman abilities destroyed by the knowledge that nemesis could be drawn to them like a bolt to a lightning rod. Williams had never escaped the revelation presented to him on that sun-drenched afternoon, and he had spent a lifetime trying to find some way to keep it at bay. It was a war of entrenchment that would never end, but he fought it because there was no alternative, and in that battle Riddington was the high ground.

The rap at the front door was perfunctory, but it served to stir him from his dark thoughts. The clock on the mantelpiece said 11.10 p.m. and he wondered who could be calling so late. The shape through the bottle-glass panel in the door looked little more than a shadow thrown by the streetlight as he drew back the bolt and threw the door open.

There was no need to worry. The man standing with one arm against the door jamb had a pleasant, open face that Williams warmed to instantly, without even being put off by the gold earring in his left ear. The black-haired stranger exuded a winning charisma; Williams could almost hear the pulse of his life's energy.

'I am sorry to trouble you at such a late hour, Mr Williams, but I have some information which I feel is of vital import to your village.'

'And who would you be, young man?'

The stranger's smile grew wider as if he had heard a great joke. 'I am called William Yeats. May I come in?'

Williams stepped aside without a murmur, although he was normally wary of allowing strangers into his home. Yeats slipped by him like a ghost and stood in the hall, his smile now faint and somehow darker. Williams led him into the study and they took up seats on opposite sides of the fireplace. Yeats didn't speak until he was settled and then he said, 'If I may be blunt, Mr Williams, it is a terrible problem you face with these so-called travellers.'

Williams was all ears. 'Oh yes, Mr Yeats! We're all very worried about it in Riddington. Do you know anything of interest?'

'I am something of a trouble-shooter, Mr Williams. Suffice to say I keep an eye on certain elements of our society who could be construed a threat. I do not act, I must stress, but I gather information and point others in the right direction to do what needs to be done.'

Williams smiled knowingly. *Some Government bod. Special Branch or something like that.* 'Everyone thinks they're just a bunch of hippies, but we know better, don't we?' He winked and Yeats winked in return.

'We do indeed, Mr Williams. Long ago I was a farmer myself, and of all the places I could have stayed in this area, I've chosen a farm. I know country stock and I know it takes a stout-hearted man to stand up against the kind of threat these travellers present. I certainly feel you are the man to do it.'

'You know of me?'

'I do, Mr Williams. I do.'

Williams felt a swell of pride, but he tried to maintain a humble appearance. 'What can I do?'

'These are difficult times, Mr Williams. I think the situation is best summed up in a few lines of poetry by ... someone or other.' He smiled and there was power in his voice when he spoke again. '"Turning and turning in the widening gyre the falcon cannot hear the falconer; Things fall apart; the centre cannot hold; Mere anarchy is loosed upon the world, The blood-dimmed tide is loosed, and everywhere The ceremony of innocence is drowned; The best lack all conviction, while the worst Are full of passionate intensity."'

Williams was hanging upon every word. 'Yes, I think I know what you're saying, Mr Yeats,' he said firmly. 'The ceremony of innocence and all that. We have to protect what's ours.'

Yeats nodded. 'The travellers are working to a grand plan. They believe this is no country for old men. On a smaller scale, but equally harrowing, they are going to attack your village. Rob you blind. Sweep through like the Visigoths, attacking the weak and the innocent, and then they plan to be on their way. We cannot allow this to happen.'

'No!' Williams' voice caught in his throat – it was worse than he feared.

'I suggest a pre-emptive strike. Can you muster the necessary force?'

'Well, we have considered something of that kind, Mr Yeats. There are a few of us, a few good lads, prepared to do what's necessary to teach those bastards a lesson. I don't know how many we can count on, but the hard core, well ... there's Bill King, a local builder, and Tim Huxton-Smith – he owns a lot of land in the area ... and, well, Alexander Alcock, I suppose. His heart's in the right place, though he's not really, ah, one of us. Still ...'

'That sounds perfect! You have some time to make your plans, the travellers do not plan to move on for at least a couple of weeks, but when you do strike, strike hard, and swiftly. May I leave it in your hands?'

'Certainly, Mr Yeats, and thank you.' Williams leapt to his feet and shook hands. 'For the information, I mean. We *must* get in first before that scum do their dirty business.'

The visitor drew himself up to his full height, throwing the short, rotund figure of Williams into relief. 'I am glad you have understood me so fully, Mr Williams. It is unlikely we will meet again ... in the short term, at least. I place my trust in you.'

He strode off towards the front door, and Williams hurried behind him, feeling a strange mixture of pride, excitement and anxiety at what lay ahead. At the threshold he held out his hand once more, but oddly Yeats didn't take it. The tall, dark man just smiled and then he departed.

George Newton circled the village one final time, picking out the path he had trodden so many times over the years he couldn't remember *not* walking it. It was 11.45 p.m. and too hot to sleep. As he came up the jitty on to the High Street, he was surprised to see someone standing in the sickly orange light that puddled around a streetlamp. He was stock-still and staring up at Brian Swift's house, George noted. He looked like a shadow suspended in the light and there was something about him which made George uncomfortable.

He thought about crossing the street and passing the stranger on the other side, but there was a steeliness within him which wouldn't allow it. He walked slowly and without making a sound, but as he drew closer the stranger seemed to sense him. He turned and levelled a stare of pure malignancy.

George stood his ground. 'Nice night,' he said.

The stranger looked George up and down as if he was seeing into him, and from his contemptuous expression, George knew he didn't like what he saw.

'"An aged man is but a paltry thing, A tattered coat upon a stick . . ."' the man intoned.

'". . . unless Soul clap its hands and sing, and louder sing, For every tatter in its moral dress."' George completed the quotation effortlessly.

'You know your Yeats then, old man. A literate human being in this village! How surprising.'

'I like to read, aye.' George glanced up at Brian Swift's house. The curtains were open upstairs revealing an unshaded bulb glowing baldly in the front bedroom, but there was no sign of life. 'Seen something interesting?'

'Interesting things are happening, yes. They always do behind closed doors, a lesson I am sure this village has known for years. But there is nothing to see at the moment.'

He looked up and down the street slowly, and although the action was quite normal, George felt suddenly uneasy. The street was empty; there was no one around to see their meeting.

'Are you staying round here then?' George asked.

'A local farm.' The silence between them crackled with tension. The stranger's smile grew wider; he took a step forward.

The scream echoed out from the back of the Swift house like a fire alarm, a male voice pushed up into a high-pitched wailing until it suddenly died.

'What the bloody hell . . .!' George's blood was frozen by that cry. Lights started to snap on in the neighbouring properties.

The stranger looked angry and sighed. 'Scream *louder*, Brian,' he muttered. 'Enough to wake the dead.'

George hurried to Brian Swift's door. 'Are you all right in there?' he yelled and hammered forcefully. He tried again, but there was no reply so he dashed back to look up at the bedroom window. Brian Swift was framed in the glass. His hands rested on the window-ledge as he stared blankly out into the night.

'Are you all right?' George shouted again.

Brian looked down at him, right through him, and in his eyes George saw something dark and scurrying which made him shudder.

He turned and hurried back down the path, but when he stepped through the gate he was surprised to see that the street was deserted. The stranger was nowhere to be seen, and all that was left was a bad feeling in the air like a slowly dissipating black cloud.

'Martyn! Get in here!'

'Not until you tell me you love me.' Martyn swayed awkwardly on the lawn while Annie remained in the doorway, limned in the soft glow of the kitchen light.

She didn't want any distractions; there was too much to worry about, too many plans to make, and Martyn's drunken, lovesick beseeching was exhausting.

'I've been in the pub on my own, *all* night . . .'

'I can tell.'

'. . . thinking about you and me. All the good times. We were made for each other, Annie. You know it's true. You—'

His swaying suddenly took a dramatic turn and he pitched backwards on to his behind and disappeared from Annie's view, his nostalgia replaced by a stream of abuse that floated through the night towards her.

Her laughter was cut short by an anguished cry which echoed dimly over the rooftops from some house further down the High Street. That noise kick-started Annie into life and she sprinted from the doorway to the lawn, grabbed Martyn by his collar and hauled him to his feet before half dragging, half leading him back to the secure world of the kitchen. He collapsed in a heap as she slammed and locked the door.

'See! I knew you cared,' he slurred with a smile.

Severin walked in from the lounge, glanced at Martyn and then said, 'Trouble?'

'There was this awful cry, like someone was in pain. Do you think we should . . .?'

Severin shook his head. 'There's no point running around in the night. Someone else will see to it.' He looked down at Martyn again. 'What are you going to do with him?'

'I can't send him back out after that. He couldn't fend off his own grandmother in this state. If you give me a hand, we'll carry him up to my parents' room. He can stay there tonight.'

Martyn muttered something incomprehensible as Severin complied with Annie's wishes. It took a good deal of cursing to negotiate the winding stairs, but he was eventually dumped unceremoniously on Mr and Mrs Boultons' double bed. Annie laid him on his side in case he was sick, and he mumbled something else and then grew quiet. She switched off the light and left the door ajar.

'He still likes you a lot,' Severin noted. He leaned against the landing wall with his arms folded and watched Annie closely.

'He'll get over it.' She shrugged uncomfortably and looked as if she wanted to change the subject.

His eyes held hers and he looked sad. 'Well, at least he still has a heart. Me, I'm scared of becoming like Wilde. Losing feelings and emotions. Sometimes I can feel that side of me leaking away like water from a busted radiator, making me cold, dry.'

'You'll never get like that.' Her fingers slipped into his hand where she squeezed gently. 'You've just locked everything up inside you. It's still there – I can see it.' Another squeeze; her hands hot, his icy. 'You're a good man, Severin.'

He was going to say something else, but she stopped him with a finger on his lips and then she quickly replaced it with her mouth. And as her hands stroked his back, the passion came through and they steered themselves to the bed in Severin's room.

Their love-making was like a celebration of life as the night closed around them. They both gave themselves to the act as if it would be their last time together as well as their first.

Afterwards Annie lay listening to her racing heartbeat, but as the thump gradually resumed a steady rate, she became aware of another sound deep in the house.

It was like a voice telling her over and over again that she was going to die; the rhythm was insistent, mechanical, a sound that enveloped the house and would not go away. It was the mobile phone. He was calling to her.

Her sweat was cold on her skin as she rolled out of bed, drawn down the stairs to the kitchen which was bright with moonlight that painted her naked body white. There was only a brief pause between the pressing of a button and his voice intoning softly.

'I wanted to let you know, Annie. It has started.' A whisper of a laugh. 'Your little village has begun to wake up to the dark.'

20

Hartley Williams didn't even seem to have a skull. There was just a bag of fat and skin moulded up on top of his shoulders, and most of the time his eyes were as lost as lumps of coal pushed too deeply into a snowman's head. On top of it all was the wax smile, like some token gesture of his humanity. Annie felt quite sick looking at him, a feeling reinforced by her knowledge of his wife's bruises and the way he looked at the young girls around the village, herself included.

'Hello, my dear.'

'Mr Williams.'

On the doorstep he squatted, like an ugly toad.

'Sorry to call so early, my dear, but I'm just doing my bit of community service, and when needs arise, the clock doesn't rule. Are you well?'

'Yes, fine,' she said tartly. Williams' knock had come just as she was preparing to go out with Severin to scour the second area on the map, and she didn't want to waste any time.

'I'm here about young Simon Connor. I'm sure you know his family – good church people.' Annie nodded. 'Well, it seems the lad has taken it upon himself to run away in a moment of high spirits. He told one of his little friends about his plan yesterday afternoon and he hasn't been seen since. Nothing to worry about, of course. Many lads do it. It was a warm night and there are plenty of places to sleep, barns and hedgerows and the like. I expect he'll probably come back later looking for his lunch. Still, if you do come across him today, please give me a call and we'll put his mother's mind at rest.'

'I'll do that, Mr Williams.' Annie went to close the door, but he took a step forward, preventing her.

'I'm calling on everyone in the village because you can't be too careful, can you? Not with those travellers parked up on old Tarrant's land. You probably know that one of them already tried to grab young Simon a couple of days ago. We told the police, but naturally they haven't done anything yet. They never do, until it's too late, do they?' He shook his head with insincere sadness. 'What's the world coming to when scroungers and perverts like that can do what they like? It's no wonder feelings are running high.'

Annie could have said so many things, but she knew they would all be heaped back on her, laced with venom, at some later date. So she smiled as sweetly as she could muster and pushed the door, slowly shutting Williams out of the way, slowly shutting out the possibility that Simon Connor had become Wilde's latest victim.

Scarlet and Kurt sat in the long grass at the side of the road, listening to the lazy buzz of insects in the hedgerow and enjoying the sun on their faces. They had been up since five, wallowing in the quiet pleasures of nature awakening. It was the reason they had given up their dreary life in Liverpool, the dirty flat in the dirty street, the futility of trying to find a job, the air that made you feel nauseous when you breathed it. When life did get a bit hard on the road, it only took one dawn walk through the countryside to convince them they had made the right decision.

Scarlet was the first to stir from their daydreaming. 'Did you hear that?'

'What?'

'Voices.'

'Ah, leave me alone. I'm having mellow thoughts.' Then he did hear it, distantly, like the angry drone of a swarm of wasps. Leaning forward and shielding his eyes against the glare, he peered down the road as the voices grew louder. Eventually he saw movement, the silhouetted smudge slowly coalescing into a small group of villagers who rounded the bend. As they advanced, he realized some of them were carrying branches and stakes like some medieval mob.

'Shit,' Kurt muttered. 'What the fuck's going on here?'

'Come on.' Scarlet tugged at his jacket. 'This looks scary. We should get back to the camp.'

'Chill out. We've done nothing wrong.' But as the crowd

drew closer, doubts began to creep in. 'They can't be heading for the camp, *can* they?'

'Shit, Kurt. You should know better by now. Come on!'

Scarlet hauled him to his feet, but before they could move, some of the marchers had sprinted forward. As Kurt turned to run, hands were already on him, dragging him to the ground, pinning him down. Scarlet was several yards down the road before she realized her boyfriend was in trouble; she could only watch in horror as one of the villagers raised a hefty, gnarled branch above his head.

'This is for Simon Connor,' he said.

It was 10 a.m. as Annie and Severin drove into Blacksmiths Lane. The Mill soon became visible through the trees, an ancient brick building three storeys high with tiny windows that seemed permanently black, even in the bright sunlight. The walls had been repointed, the roof re-tiled, yet regardless of the spit and polish it still seemed the Mill was refusing to be reclaimed. There was a brooding darkness that crept out from deep within it like a bitter old man refusing to dress up for a family party.

'It would be the perfect place for him,' Annie began, braking to a halt. 'It was derelict for years, but then some yuppie bought it and renovated it. He kept the water wheel working, but stuck in a huge bath with gold taps and a kitchen that probably cost more than the bricks and mortar. He died of an early heart attack nearly two years ago, and it's been empty ever since. All that flash décor priced it out of the market, but his estate won't drop the price.'

She glanced up at the Mill and suddenly tensed. *Was that someone at one of the windows?*

'I've got a real ambivalence about the place,' she continued, watching intently, deciding she had been mistaken. 'It's always frightened me, but I have very happy memories of it. When I was little, I used to play here with Robert. It was very run-down then, and became our secret place. Yet I'd never go there alone . . . I always felt there was someone watching.'

'Time to investigate,' Severin said. 'And find out whether there is.'

'Wait,' she said as soon as they got out of the car. 'Can you feel it?'

He could. That same invisible poison in the air that had hung over the killing ground where they had found the Laurence Lucas diary.

'Let's be careful,' he muttered.

They kept to the bushes that lined the drive, but the gravel made it impossible to approach silently. Severin decided to make a break for the nearest window, peering through it, before moving on to another and then another. Satisfied there was no one on the ground floor, he stepped up to the door and pushed. It swung open instantly. Without turning, he beckoned Annie and she ran across the gravel and slipped through the door behind him into a musty odour of dead air and dust.

'Was the door open?' she asked.

'The lock had been forced.'

'Oh.'

The porch opened on to a large lounge with an expensive suite and an enormous Chinese carpet in front of a brick fireplace containing a mound of white ash. It was quite dark and the repetitive lub-dub, lub-dub of the water wheel echoed dully through the walls.

Severin held his shotgun beneath the folds of his coat. He moved quickly and checked through an open door into an oak-panelled study, and then back across the room to a large, bright kitchen. The surfaces were clean, the sink empty.

At its far end was a cellar door that opened on to a set of crumbling stone steps which wound down into thick gloom. A blast of cold, dank air tinged with decay swept up and greeted them.

'That's where Robert and I used to play hide-and-seek,' Annie said quietly. 'Do we go down?'

Before Severin could reply, something banged upstairs. They both jumped and then froze. As Annie's heart pounded, Severin hissed, 'You stay here, I'll go check.'

Annie nodded, but after he had slipped away she found her eyes drawn magnetically back to that gulf of darkness which yawned below her. It was whispering to her, promising that down there, night never ended. She experienced the feeling some people have on the edge of a high drop – against all logic, they are forced to look down.

Another gust of air swirled up, only this one smelled florid and familiar, behind the damp. Her nostrils flared, memories igniting deep in her mind. Aftershave. Unmistakable. Suddenly time flipped and she was back in Blackstone Cottage four years earlier, remembering the bathroom, the steam on the mirror, damp towels, the aromatic trail along the landing ... Her stomach did a twist and knotted. It was Aramis, but like all perfumes it smelled different on each person, and this version hit her like a slap in the face.

Robert.

The smell of her brother, when he was alive. Down there. In the cellar.

She swallowed, but it felt like there was a nail wedged in her throat. She put her foot on the first step, and the darkness rose up to claim her.

For a second or two, Severin stood silently staring at the ceiling. There was a creak in the far corner, and after a spell, another, and then another, the slow, leaden footfalls of someone walking above him. The footsteps stopped directly over his head and did not begin again.

Severin felt the familiar tingle: cautiously, he headed for the open staircase in the corner of the room and with a supple, light step that belied his size, he climbed quickly. At the top was a long landing with five closed doors. To his left was a glass door which opened on to a small wooden balcony above the water wheel and through it he could see the churning white water below.

Quickly he worked out his bearings and selected the door which must belong to the room that contained those measured, almost robotic footsteps. It was the third from the left, the one almost next to the top of the stairs. With the grace of a hunter, he balanced his body as he slipped the shotgun from the folds of his coat and positioned himself in front of the door. He filled his lungs, waited for one instant, then flicked the handle and swung it open.

There was a man sitting in the centre of the floor. At first Severin thought he was asleep; his eyes were closed and his balding head was slumped on his chest. His suit was smeared with mud and filth and what appeared to be blood. And there chunks of bloody meat lay scattered on the carpet in front of him as if some small animal had been torn to pieces. Severin couldn't make out what it had originally been.

The man raised his head and his eyes opened slowly. 'My

house,' he said shakily in a voice that sounded like twigs breaking. 'My possessions.'

As he lifted himself to his feet with an oddly mechanical movement, Severin saw there was something dangerously wrong. There seemed to be no human intelligence in those eyes, just an insectile bulge.

He took one lumbering step and Severin waved the shotgun at him. 'Back off.'

If the man saw the gun, he gave no sign. 'My house!' he bellowed suddenly. 'You're trespassing!'

Suddenly he moved with surprising speed and knocked the gun from Severin's hand with a podgy fist. Severin tried to block him, but it was like trying to stop a runaway train and he found himself caught off balance, then smashed into the door jamb, and on to the landing.

'My house! You can't take it away from me!'

Severin eventually braced himself with his foot and tried to throw the man off, but he seemed resistant to everything and his arms snapped up around Severin's neck. The skin of his fingers felt odd, like dry wood, and he reeked of a foul mould.

Severin found the edges of his vision were starting to go black, and all he could see were the staring, unblinking eyes burning into his face. Forcefully, his knee shot up and buried itself deeply in the man's groin, but although Severin felt the genitalia crush, the attacker showed no sign he had felt a thing; not a flicker of an eyelid or the slightest intake of breath.

The world was going hazy, his life hanging by a thread. In a final act of desperation, he threw himself backwards and used his attacker's force and weight to add to his momentum so that they crashed over together and hit the floor with a bone-jarring impact.

At the same time as he was scrambling out from underneath his attacker, Severin heaved in a tremendous lungful of air and pulled himself forward so he could crawl like a dog for the shotgun. Snatching it up, he cocked, rolled on to his back and aimed in one movement. The other man was already on his feet and advancing murderously.

'Another step and I'll fucking blow you away!' Severin yelled, but he knew what would happen.

'My house! My—!'

Severin fired. The force of the blast ripped off the man's right arm at the shoulder and hurled him back towards the glass door which overlooked the water wheel. He fell to the floor, thrashing madly.

Severin breathed easier. For all of two seconds. Incredibly the casualty case had pulled himself to his feet, his eyes still bulging, not blinking; there was no blood pouring from the wound, just an oily black deposit and a few strips of sinew and tendon slapping against his side.

'Jesus Christ!' Severin hissed. 'What the fuck are you?'

He didn't wait to see any more. This time he aimed for the head when he fired. The face in front of him disappeared in an explosion of bone, gristle and meat and the body attached to it pitched backwards through the glass barrier on the balcony, and descended in a trail of glittering shards.

Before Severin could reach the broken door he heard a loud splash as the body hit the mill pond, and anything else was lost to the eternal heartbeat of the water wheel and the surge of the white water beneath it.

Annie didn't *want* to go any further into that unrelenting dark, but it was beyond her power to turn back. Her mind was awash with memories of what was and dreams of what might have been, all tied up in a neat bow by that faint trace of scent in the cold air. All rational thought had been superseded in favour of something not far from madness.

The steps were steep and well worn and one slip could send her tumbling. Ten steps down and the darkness had claimed her entirely. She had to feel her way and the incessant pounding of the water wheel vibrated through everything, a leviathan off in the wings, obscuring any possible warning sound. Yet in that dark, she knew she was not alone.

The steps wound round ninety degrees, losing the door behind her, and then she found herself on an unevenly flagged surface. Her memory told her the floor plan, but she knew she would soon glimpse it for herself when her eyes grew accustomed to the faint light filtering through a tiny, dirty window just above ground level in the far wall. The cellar was divided up into four rooms, all interconnected, with several pillars in each. This labyrinthine structure was what had made it such a great place to play in as children.

She had expected the smell to be stronger down here, but it

wasn't; still just a ghost of a smell. But her sense of a presence somewhere *was* stronger. During one of the rhythmic breaks in the thunderous lub-dub, lub-dub, she plucked up courage and whispered, 'Who's there?' And then regretted it. Her own voice sounded a dangerous trespasser in the stillness.

Squinting, she struggled to pierce the gloom, but all she saw were the white fireflies of electrical impulses dancing somewhere between her retina and her brain. Uncomfortably, she had the oddest feeling someone else's eyes were on her back. She whirled round. Nothing.

Except a whiff of aftershave. The air buzzed with the feeling of someone moving up close to touch her. The hairs on the nape of her neck tingled as they waited for the brush of a fingertip.

She spun round again, and at the same instant heard the muffled shotgun blast far off in the house above her. She cried out once in shock, her eyelids snapping shut automatically. When she opened them, all she discerned was a fleeting movement near the far stairs, barely more than a shadow slightly darker than the surrounding gloom.

Another shotgun blast above, and then the sound of splintering glass.

'Severin!' she screamed, as the tension within her snapped.

She sensed the hand, rather than saw it, darting out of the gloom towards her throat. Invisible fingers caught in the chain around her neck, a slight pressure, and then it snapped. Her hands went up suddenly, but it was too late; the ankh was gone.

'No!' she cried out, spinning round and round. There was a rustle and a crunch away in the dark. This time the trail had direction.

As Annie followed her ears, there was a change in the quality of the light which signalled the tiny cellar window opening and then she heard the bang of it slamming shut. It was still rocking in its frame when she reached it.

Scrambling on to an old crate beneath the window, she hauled herself up and opened it, then attempted to pull herself through, but it wasn't easy; it would only take someone much smaller without difficulty. But her fingernails dug into the dust and pebbles, and she managed to pull her shoulders through, then, eventually, her hips, and finally she crawled on to the ground outside and scrabbled to her feet.

The water wheel was to her right, turning slowly, and ahead

was the black glass of the mill pond. The only sign of whoever had been in the cellar was a faint tang of Aramis slowly dissipating in the hot air.

Tears stung her eyes. She had sensed his familiarity.

It was Robert.

'You killed a man!' Annie said incredulously.

Severin shook his head and struggled to find the right words, but the only thing that would come out was: 'No.'

'What do you mean, *No*? You just told me you blasted someone in the face and then sent him for a swim in the mill pond. Severin, are you going to explain to me what's going on?'

'I'll tell you as soon as I'm sure myself,' he replied with an edge in his voice.

'Well, play the fucking mystery man! See if I care!' she snapped.

They had already swopped stories and searched the edges of the mill pond, then scoured for yards downstream, but there had been no sign of a body. All Annie understood was that the proceedings had taken an extremely disturbing twist which had brought them no closer to Wilde. Except that now they had to face up to the fact he was probably not working alone.

The tense atmosphere between them had faded a little by the time they made it back to Blackstone Cottage, but the moment they saw Martyn waiting at the door, it returned instantly.

'Thanks for leaving me on my own,' he said sullenly, following them in.

'You were stupid, drunk and abusive last night,' Annie said with irritation. 'Why should I hang around and watch you cope with the mother of all hangovers after that?'

'I see he's still around.' Martyn jerked a thumb in Severin's direction.

'Very observant, kid. You'll go far.' Severin walked straight past Martyn without further acknowledging him.

'Don't antagonize him, Severin,' Annie said wearily. 'It'll only make him worse.'

'Well everybody's in a fine mood, aren't they,' Martyn continued sourly. 'What happened? Lovers' tiff?'

'Look, kid,' Severin snapped. 'You're a loser. She doesn't want anything to do with you. Now quit wasting time on . . .'

'Don't you say what I want or don't want!' Annie shouted.

The knock at the door broke the tension and they all fell silent. The vicar was on the doorstep, looking sheepish.

'I'm sorry to intrude,' he said apologetically.

'That's all right, Father Tony. Come in.' Annie threw the door wide to let him in, happy that the argument had been deflected. They were all too hot and under too much stress.

'I won't keep you long,' the vicar continued. 'I wanted to let you know a bit of bad news. There's been some more trouble in the churchyard. I spent the morning at the crematorium, making the arrangements for Mr Barnwell's service, and when I got back I noticed more damage to one of the graves. Ah, specifically, your brother's.' The blood drained from Annie's face and he instantly threw up his hands to calm her. 'Oh no, it's nothing too serious. The stone had been pushed askew and some of the topsoil turned over. We'll have it right in a jiffy.'

'Was it like the others?' Severin asked, a little too worriedly for Annie.

'It was, which clears Mr Barnwell. I would venture it's all the work of local children who . . .'

But for Annie the coincidence was shattering: her brother's grave and her brother's ghost were suddenly the only two things that seemed real.

What was happening?

Jake Samuels lay on his bed listening to the sounds of his mother and father arguing: it seemed to be all he heard these days, the soundtrack to an increasingly miserable existence. He blamed himself for his parents' problems and he wondered if they would start loving each other again if he ran away like Simon. He remembered a golden time when everything had been fine, before his father had decided to work for himself from home, before his mother had started to complain that they never had money for anything any more, but it was so long ago.

Outside his bedroom window he could hear the reassuring creak of the big old oak tree that soared up higher than the house. His father had threatened to have it cut down, claiming it was too close to the building and a danger to them all every storm, but Jake had protested tearfully and in the end his father had relented. The tree was special to Jake; while it endured everything else would stay the same.

Where was Simon now, he thought dreamily. Jake imagined him standing at the docks waiting to board for America or Africa, or at the airport being given a free seat by a friendly pilot. Simon was braver than Jake – nothing would ever stop him going where he wanted.

His mother and father were screaming now, high-pitched fury. His father: 'If you don't shut up, I'm fucking leaving!' His mother: 'You never listen to a word I say, you bastard!' Anger. Hatred. Jake peeked at his poster of the X-Men above his bed and wished he was Wolverine: fearless, wild, adamantine claws that could drive away any threat, but there was nothing he could do, nothing at all, except listen.

Eventually the screaming died away. Now his father would be watching the TV and his mother would be in the kitchen. He crawled to the edge of his bed so he could dip down to pull a comic from underneath. His head was scraping the floor when he heard another sound, faint but unusual enough to catch his attention. He knew every noise that disturbed the quiet of his room, the creak of the floorboards outside his door as his mother and father went to bed, the wind in the guttering, the rustle of the oak tree, but this was something different. It almost sounded like a voice.

From outside the window.

He slid off the bed and tiptoed over to the curtains, all the monsters of his imagination brought to life. The curtains fluttered in the breeze from the open window and Jake leapt back a pace with a strangled squawk. He held his breath and advanced slowly again, until he was close enough to peel back the drapes, but the bedroom light turned the window into a mirror and all he could see was his own pale face. So he ran over to flick off the light and then went back and threw the curtains open.

There was a man sitting in the branches of the tree on a level with his window.

Jake went rigid with shock. Not an old man like his father, but a young man, barely older than some of the big kids he saw around his village. And he was smiling, very pleasantly, but Jake wasn't fooled because he thought he recognized that face, those staring eyes. And he knew he should run downstairs quickly, but his legs wouldn't move, and then he tried to shout, but all that came out was a hoarse whisper. His eyes ... Jake felt like he was floating in a dark mist. He opened the window wider.

'Hello,' the youth said with a faint sibilance.

'Hello,' Jake croaked mechanically.

He was looking at a sunny, open face, freckles, unblinking eyes and skin that seemed a funny colour, almost grey. As he focused, Jake saw something else, a red smear around the youth's mouth and as he watched, the youth raised his right hand and gnawed on something he held there, something small and furry which made that red smear grow larger. The thing in his hand squirmed and grew still.

'You're a nice little boy, aren't you,' he stated as he chewed and swallowed. 'Do you think I could come in and play? Just for a little while?'

'No,' Jake croaked. 'Please . . .'

'Aw, come on.' The youth pulled a pleading face and then grinned. 'I wasn't supposed to play with little kids like you. I was let loose just to hang around and . . . I dunno, be myself. Well, I am being myself. I'm too strong, you see. For him. He doesn't realize.' He leaned forward and whispered conspiratorially. 'I do what I want. Why, I played with a little kid just yesterday.'

Jake's eyes filled with tears. He *did* know who the youth was. He remembered him from the photo on the front cover of the book his father had downstairs, the one about what had happened in the village.

'Anyway I don't have to have your agreement to come in and play, you know. I told you – I can do what I want.'

He threw away the thing he had been holding, and Jake glimpsed a tail and little feet before it disappeared with a thud. That grey face, smeared with blood like the make-up of a clown, broke into a grin and then began to approach, slowly.

The branch bearing the unwanted visitor ended quite a way from Jake's window, but . . . *he could jump and cling on to the window-ledge and pull himself in.*

Even as the youth arched his back like a panther, Jake slammed the window and with fumbling fingers locked the catch. He had one glimpse of a snarling face, which didn't even seem human any more, and then he whipped the curtains shut and ran back and threw himself on the bed.

He dragged the duvet over his head and shivered in a wash of fear. He wished he could run to his mother and father, but he knew they wouldn't care, they weren't interested. He was on his own.

In terror, he waited for the crash of a body flinging itself at the bedroom window, but when it didn't come, he gradually found the courage to look out from under the duvet. And he heard a sound disappearing off into the night, a terrible mewling like a cat. Only Jake knew it wasn't a cat. It was him.

Laurence Lucas.

21

The travellers' campfire roared away like the furnaces of hell, a beacon of anger in the night. No stragglers hung back in the wagons, tripping or smoking dope and listening to music. Everyone was there, united under threat once more.

As he looked out at the assembled crowd, Tommy realized he had never seen them all so bright-eyed. Their faces were grim though, like bank managers or accountants; it didn't look natural. Angela was at his side and he could feel her 'I-was-right' smile blazing away as powerfully as the fire while, just behind them, Kurt stood as best he could; but the fight had been knocked out of him, he was all cuts and bruises and sagging at the waist.

They had barely recognized him when he'd crawled back to camp that morning. His face was purple and swollen like a football, both eyes had closed up, and three teeth were missing. But there was worse: Scarlet was still missing. Kurt recalled seeing her run when the mob attacked, but she had not made it back before him and there had been no sign all day despite numerous search parties scouring the countryside.

Now all eyes turned to Tommy. They were waiting for him – their unelected leader, the chieftain of the tribe – to speak. Instead, they got Angela.

She pulled Kurt forward theatrically so that he almost pitched forward on to the ashes area that surrounded the fire. 'Look at this! We can all see now that *they're* going to destroy anything which doesn't conform to their own boring, suburban ways with their little fucking houses and their little fucking minds. We thought that if we stayed out of their way and kept on the move they'd leave us alone. But the Criminal Justice Act put paid to those dreams, didn't it? Well, how many more times do we turn the other cheek when one of our own gets attacked?'

Angela felt vibrant and confident. In their faces she could see an opening. She glanced at Tommy, weak Tommy, and she could tell from his expression he knew he was losing out to her.

'And Scarlet is *still* missing,' she continued. 'We all want her back safely, but . . .' Kurt turned his puffy face to her and for a moment Angela thought he was going to cry. Hurriedly, she added, 'They must have arrested her. Stuffed her in some dirty little cell on trumped-up charges. That is an attack on *us* – as a family, as a tribe.'

A piece of greenwood in the fire cracked and spat a volcanic cascade of sparks into the air. It burned so hot Angela's face felt red and prickly. She breathed in the wood smoke, tasted its sourness on her tongue, and then lowered her voice, forcing everyone to strain to hear.

'It's us or them.'

There was a moment of silence and then everyone was speaking at once: *Yeah! Fight back! Don't take it lying down any more!*

'Wait . . .' Tommy interjected, finding it hard to break through the outburst. 'This is crazy!' he snapped. His voice cut through the hubbub this time. 'If we stop being peaceful, it will just give them the leverage they want.'

'Come on, Tommy, we're not talking about burning the village to the ground,' a voice at the back replied. 'Just sending a message.'

It was then that Tommy noticed the male figure standing in the shadows, forming a patch of darkness blacker than the surrounding gloom. He seemed to be listening and watching intently. As Tommy tried to pull more details out of the shadows, he had a sudden feeling of icy cold despite the heat of the fire.

'Who's there?' he called out.

Uncannily the travellers fell quiet. All eyes turned to the figure on the edge of the night. The silence was thick for a moment and Tommy wasn't sure if the stranger was going to speak, but then he slowly took a few steps forward and the tension released audibly when everyone saw it was not a village spy. They all instantly recognized the casual, unrestricted air of a travelling man. He looked around the gathering, noting faces, letting them see he was alone and unthreatening, and then he held out his hands and smiled a smile of pure white that contrasted with his dark hair and olive skin.

'Greetings,' he said. 'Will you welcome me in?'

He was accepted into the tightly knit community with ease, by virtue of the simple chemistry of outsiders recognizing each other. It was just as he knew it would be; in uncertain times like sought the support of like. He introduced himself simply as Wilde, and he was invited into the ranks near the fire and offered tea or cider. His appearance had created a new buzz and, much to Angela's irritation, all talk of confrontation seemed to be forgotten in the short term. The stranger had a mesmeric quality that drew all eyes. And if he noticed Tommy watching him warily, he gave no sign of it.

'Been on the road long?' Tommy squatted down next to Wilde, who already seemed to have gathered an attentive group round him.

'Oh, nearly all my life.' He sipped his tea, still smiling amicably, giving nothing away.

'Where's your vehicle?'

'I travel on foot. I have no need for possessions that burden me. There are always good citizens prepared to help with my basic needs wherever I go, and for that I am grateful. And, as I am sure you find, vehicles bring unwanted attention.'

'Too right,' a long-haired youth with a beret agreed.

'It's easy to travel light when you're alone, but we've got a community to maintain,' Angela said harshly. She was annoyed that the stranger had been accepted so easily, but when he looked at her with his huge dark eyes she felt the irritation replaced by a warm, syrupy feeling of friendship and attraction. She saw the golden flashes deep within those eyes and she had the sudden urge to take off her clothes and make love to him in front of everyone. 'Don't you miss the comfort of people?' she added with uncharacteristic warmth.

'I find it hard to discover kindred spirits. Sometimes I feel I am all alone in the world.'

'You're welcome here,' she said softly. A ripple of agreement ran through the crowd.

'The travelling community is so misunderstood.' His words carried out across the still camp. 'Prejudice is everywhere. You would think in these enlightened times that the simple desire to live how one pleases would not be such a constant battle.'

'Tell us about it,' the long-haired youth said sourly. 'Every day's a fight. Now those small-minded Nazis down there are trying to drive us away. We're not causing any trouble. Yet this morning they beat one of us up and hauled his girlfriend off into custody.'

Wilde looked down the hillside to the lights of Riddington. 'That quaint village there? Surely not?'

'You wouldn't believe what twisted little bastards live in that *quaint* place. I reckon they'd burn us out if they had the chance.'

'And what are you going to do about it?'

There was a long pause and then Tommy said, 'We were just talking about that before you arrived. I believe we shouldn't fight violence with violence.'

'If we sit back, they'll crush us,' Angela snapped. 'We've got to give them a taste of their own medicine. What do you think?'

'Oh, I agree entirely.' This time Wilde's smile was not a pleasant one, but everyone was already so trapped by his spell they didn't notice. 'Some situations call for a forthright response, especially if one is trying to maintain one's security. Fight fire with fire or face eradication.'

There was a lull while everyone soaked up his words, and then Angela said, 'There you are in a nutshell.' Tommy's protestations were drowned out by the raised voices of consensus. And then by a sudden solitary voice.

'Get over here! We need help!'

The cry came from the darkness among the buses and trailers. Some of the travellers leapt up in fear of an attack, but most of them recognized the voice.

'It's Fox,' Angela said, trying to see past the glare of the campfire. She turned to Wilde and added, 'He went out with Skip to look for Scarlet, the girl who went missing this morning.'

'They found her!' someone called out, but any exuberance was instantly dampened when the arrivals stepped into the light.

Fox's bleached hair almost matched the paleness of his face. He was bare chested. Skip was next to him and they were both carrying an unconscious Scarlet, her limbs hanging limply, her skin as white as snow. Fox's grey army shirt was tied tightly around her right foot; the cloth now looked black.

'What happened?' Tommy ran forward and helped to carry Scarlet up to the fire where they laid her down.

'We found her in the woods.' Fox's voice cracked. Everyone could see the tears streaming down his cheeks. 'The bastards!'

Kurt was whimpering through his pulped lips. He stroked Scarlet's face and mumbled, 'She's so cold. Is she alive?'

Fox ignored him. 'We searched everywhere. We thought we'd give up till it got light so we decided to take a short cut through ther wood back to the camp. Skip almost fell over her. She was lying in a hollow ... God knows how long she'd been there. There was a trap, a fucking big metal trap on her foot.' He was trembling like someone in the grip of a fever. 'We prised it off and bound her leg, but she'd already lost a lot of blood. I don't reckon she'll ... I don't reckon ...' He gulped air and almost shouted, 'It nearly cut her foot off!'

'What are we standing around talking for? We've got to get her to a hospital,' Angela said frantically.

Tommy was on his knees examining her. He shook his head. 'Fox is right, I don't think she'll last that long.'

'Perhaps I can help.' Wilde's steady voice cut through the growing panic. 'I picked up some medical experience on my travels.'

'She needs a blood transfusion,' Tommy said resignedly.

'Conventional medicine is not the only answer. I learned certain secrets in Asia which might save her.'

Tommy looked at Angela and then at several others in the crowd.

'Time is running out,' Wilde said.

'If she won't make it to a hospital, there's no other hope,' Kurt said with a sob. 'We might as well let him try ...'

'What do you need?' Tommy asked.

'Somewhere quiet, water, candles, hashish ...'

'OK. This way.'

They picked Scarlet up gently and then carried her over to Tommy's bus. Wilde had them lay her out on the mound of cushions and when the other things he needed had been brought, he asked them to leave him alone. Tommy and Angela stayed behind.

'I am sorry. I must ask you to leave too,' he said. 'I need utmost concentration for what I am about to do. No distractions.'

'What *are* you going to do?' Tommy wrung his hands together impotently.

'I cannot say, but if I act quickly I believe there is a chance. You must trust me.'

'Is it magic?' Angela asked.

'Some would call it that.'

Tommy left reluctantly, barely able to contain his scepticism, unsure he was doing the right thing. Before she followed him, Angela gave Wilde's hand a supportive squeeze and received a confident, seductive smile in return.

When they had both gone, Wilde turned to Scarlet and cracked his knuckles. The curtains at the windows of the bus were drawn so there was no chance of anyone seeing what would occur within. Disinterestedly, he broke off a corner of the block of hash and swallowed it, washing it down with some of the water.

'I may as well enjoy myself,' he said to Scarlet as he knelt down next to her. Then he slapped her cheeks repeatedly until her eyes flickered and a pitiful moan crept from between her lips. 'Good. I would hate you to be unconscious and miss all of this.'

Roughly, he peeled back her eyelid to check the pupil response and when he was satisfied, he placed one hand on each side of her head. Then, with one swift movement, he twisted. There was a sickening crack as her neck broke. Wilde nodded at the success of his operation and settled back on one of the mountainous cushions waiting for the hash to kick in.

When the candle flames glowed and fuzzed, he was ready. Humming to himself, he stood over Scarlet's body and concentrated, focusing on the receding light of her soul. In his mind's eye he waited for the exit door to open, and when the fluttering thing had passed through, he caught it before the door slammed shut again. With a wave of his arm, he summoned and controlled.

Her eyes sprang open.

There was no point in asking the question; he had let the Essential Thing go, and he felt too weary for another disappointment.

217

The important thing was the mortal clay that had been left for him to shape.

'Salutations, Scarlet.' Her eyes had the stupid, empty expression he hated so much. He could barely bring himself to talk to it. Without the Essential Thing, he was speaking to a mannequin which thought it was alive. 'No rest for you, I am afraid. You have a job to do. Can you hear me?'

'Yes.' There was a sibilance to heress.

Wilde stroked her hand which was already growing cool and dry. Her eyes looked into his face, through it, into infinity.

'Where are you now?' he said thoughtfully. 'Have you passed through the Black Cathedral yet?' He shivered involuntarily at the mention of it. 'That place haunts me, Scarlet. In my dreams I see it, soaring up so high its summit is lost. Cold. Silent. It is the seat of all judgement where punishment can be as swift as reward. Sometimes I am standing before it and its mighty door begins to open . . .' He continued more quickly, 'There are two paths beyond that door. One to eternal damnation, the dark side. The other to . . .? Valhalla? The Elysian Fields? Heaven? No one on this planet knows what lies beyond, yet many will discover in time. Except me. It is the only mystery forever denied me. I need to see, Scarlet, yet to pass through it means one thing. Death. And though I wish for the ultimate reward, I do not want to die. And so all the time this hulking, black monstrosity casts its shadow over my life . . .' He suddenly seemed to become aware of his actual surroundings again and lashed out with the back of his hand across the corpse's face. 'Your friends are expecting a great deal from you, Scarlet, as am I. I want you to keep them entertained, at least for as long as you possibly can before the eventual deterioration sets in. They need to see their lively, lovely girl. Do you understand?'

'Yes.'

'Well, make conversation, damn you!' He kicked her angrily in the ribs. No air escaped her lungs; her side merely sunk in and expanded like a well-sprung sofa.

'Yes, I understand. Entertain them. Small talk. Like this.'

He sighed. 'Now, to make you presentable.' He tore some cloth from the wall hangings on the bus, and broke a stick into small pieces, selecting two of them to use as splints for her neck. 'We cannot have your head lolling like a rag doll, can we? I will tell them your muscles were torn during your agony, when the trap snapped shut, and by the time anyone discovers differently it will be too late.' He took a step back and surveyed his handiwork appreciatively. 'I know how it must feel to be in a minority of one, a spiritless lump of meat among these warm, vital beings. Take comfort, Scarlet – although I know you cannot comprehend the term. There are more of your kind near at hand, although I had to work a bit harder to make them presentable. The long-dead are very hard to resurrect, and worms really do damage the complexion. Now, are you ready to meet your public?'

'I'm ready.'

'Good.' The smile fell from his face, and he manipulated his features so that he looked suitably strained from effort. When he opened the door, the waiting travellers crowded silently around, watching anxiously, waiting for him to speak.

A long pause. Then, 'She will live.'

A loud, spontaneous cheer rose up. Kurt ran forward and Wilde stood aside to let him by. Tommy and Angela followed, but he closed the door before anyone else could enter.

Laid out on the cushions in the light of the flickering candles, Scarlet looked like a fairy princess. Her eyes were open and she had a faint smile. A thick rug had been thrown over her to hide her injured leg.

Tommy stared in amazement. 'I'm not going to ask how you did this. Her neck . . .?'

'Injured when she was in the trap.'

Tommy nodded as if that answered it all. Angela had tears in her eyes, and like him, was afraid that to ask any questions would destroy the spell.

Kurt was kneeling next to Scarlet and clutching her weak hand like a frightened animal. He buried his face in the rug on her stomach and cried silently.

'We should leave them alone,' Wilde whispered. 'They should have time to celebrate their second chance.' He laid a hand on Tommy's shoulder, 'And I must caution against moving the young lady, or seeking any conventional medical help. Nothing must disturb her.'

'What about her foot?' Tommy asked. 'Amputation . . .?'

'It was not as bad as it looked. It will heal.'

A momentary expression of disbelief crossed Tommy's face.

'You'll keep an eye on her? Help her through?' Angela asked hopefully.

'Of course.' Wilde smiled at her, and she smiled in turn.

'You know, there's a place for you here if you want to stay,' Tommy said. 'After all you've done, it's the least we can offer in return.'

'Thank you, but no. I enjoy my solitude. I will, however, visit regularly to ensure the young lady's recovery keeps pace. And, of course, to see my new friends.'

Angela hugged Wilde forcefully before turning to the crowd and shouting, 'Scarlet's going to be fine, and we have our friend here to thank for it.'

Wilde was immediately swept away in a tide of back-slapping and hand-pumping, and Angela's eyes sparkled as she followed his progress through the crowd.

'What a skill,' she said softly. 'The ultimate faith healer. What power.'

Angela caught up with Wilde in the thick dark on the edge of the camp. He had stayed for another two hours, telling amazing stories by the dying fire. Everyone had been entranced by his charisma until all the men felt he was their best friend and all the women wanted to have sex with him. When he finally decided to take his leave, he was one of them.

Angela had watched him walk away, and then she had slunk away from the others into the night.

When she was sure no one would hear her, she called out to him and he turned with a faint expression of surprise which changed quickly into that winning smile.

'There's something I wanted to tell you,' she said when she caught up with him. 'There was a girl and a man from the village up here asking about you.'

'Oh?'

'They said the most awful lies. I don't know what they're after, but I had to warn you, you know, because . . .'

'Thank you.'

'And Tommy promised he would let them know if we saw you. So he'll probably get in touch with them tomorrow.'

'Really?' Wilde glanced back towards the campfire thoughtfully.

220

'And I . . . Oh, God!' Angela laughed nervously. 'I just wanted to say thank you for what you did. It was wonderful.'

'I believe you already did thank me.'

'Not this way.' She pushed her arms around his neck and kissed him, a full, passionate kiss that left no doubt what she was offering. It was reinforced with the pressure of her breasts and groin against the contours of his muscular frame. She was almost shocked by how his body felt against her: his muscles so hard, his lips so full they seemed to be bursting with blood. The contained passion of him made her feel heady.

Eventually he broke away. She began to undo her shirt, but he placed one hand on hers. 'Not tonight,' he said. 'There are things I must do.'

'You can spare half an hour, can't you?'

He moved his hand up to her neck and began to stroke it as he considered her question, almost examining it, feeling the delicate bones, the pulse of the artery. After a moment he made up his mind and drew his fingers away.

'No, not tonight. Another time.'

He turned on his heel and marched down the hillside without another word, leaving Angela yearning for him in a way she didn't know she could.

Annie opened her eyes. Flickering torches cast a half-light around her and kept at bay the thick shadows that crowded nearby. She was in a tent; smoke billowed up to a hole in the top from a fire which crackled to one side of a central pole. There were cushions everywhere, all of them covered with intricately stitched designs. Annie's fingertips tingled as she drew them across silk and serge.

Through the tent opening which flapped in the breeze was a flat, grassy landscape which stretched to a few hills on the horizon; it was almost dark with a crescent moon and a thousand stars glittering above. From outside came the musky smell of horses, and intermittently Annie heard whinnying and the stamp of hooves.

'This isn't a dream,' she said to herself. 'It's too real.'

A gust from outside cleared the smoke from the centre of the tent, and Annie saw she was not alone. An Asian man sat upright on the cushions on the other side of the fire. He was wrapped in furs, rough, woollen garments and brown leather.

The face beneath the hood which watched her intently looked Mongolian.

'Where am I?' she asked, doubting that he would understand her.

His dark eyes seemed incredibly sad and when he opened his mouth no sound came out.

Through the hypnotic atmosphere, Annie felt a creeping uneasiness and a faint panic. 'What am I doing here? I should be at home.'

'Theee brays-leet . . .' The words were forced out, but deformed so much that Annie felt she was listening from the bottom of a lake.

'Thee-uh brise-loot hars thee-uh pahr.'

The Mongolian moistened his lips and repeated, 'Theee bracelet hass thee pow-er. Ussse thee bracelet.'

Annie shivered; she understood.

'What do you know about the bracelet?' She felt a note of urgency as the real world began to intrude. 'Are you connected to Wilde?'

He wet his lips once more but this time he didn't speak. Instead he leaned around the fire and held out his hand.

Annie looked at it, but the connection was too terrifying. She shied back into the cushions, and as she did so, the world faded rapidly, the sights, sounds and smells merging into an all-consuming black, and then she was drifting once more . . .

22

'You think it's for real?' Severin asked when Annie told him about her dream as they breakfasted before beginning the day's search.

'It was too lucid to be an ordinary dream. The bracelet is the way to defeat Wilde, that's the message that came through.'

'That's nothing we hadn't already guessed. Couldn't it be clearer? Like, *how* we're supposed to use the bracelet. And,' he continued, 'Who's sending this message? Where's it coming from, for Christ's sake? Your Goddess?'

'Perhaps,' she said tentatively. 'I just know there's a power out there that's speaking to me. And it's undeniably good. I can feel that much, but otherwise I'm shooting in the dark.'

Annie cursed under her breath at the rap of the knocker on the front door. Preparing herself mentally for another confrontation with Hartley Williams, she trudged down the hall resignedly.

'Surprise.' Charlotte stood on the step, smiling wanly, her eyes ready to read the unguarded response in Annie's face. 'Pleased to see me?'

'Of course. Come in.' Annie's heart skipped a beat and she glanced nervously up and down the street before standing to one side quickly. Her immediate thought was: *I hope Wilde hasn't seen her*. She tried not to let it show on her face so Charlotte wouldn't be offended by her caution.

'I've booked into a hotel in Ashby for a few nights so I won't disturb you too much,' Charlotte continued. 'I know you said you've got a lot on, but that way I'm close enough when you do find time to get together. Besides, I couldn't bear to stay at home any longer. The little shit has been ringing me morning, noon and night.'

Annie gave Charlotte a hug and instantly felt better. 'I'm sorry if I sounded abrupt the other day. I didn't mean to. It's just—'

'You don't have to explain.' There was relief in Charlotte's smile. 'I know things have been strange since the train crash. I'm your best friend, you old slapper. I know when there's something getting you down. Want to talk about it?'

'But I'm supposed to be here for *you*. You're the one whose personal life has collapsed.'

'Well, maybe we can do it for each other. Get the tea on!'

They slipped into the lounge in a flurry and Annie silently vowed to do everything in her power to keep Charlotte away from Wilde's sights, and to tell whatever lies she had to in order to keep her out of the shooting gallery.

After brief introductions, Severin left them to it in the lounge, but Annie could tell he was anxious to get out on the road, and she felt time slipping away too.

'So what's happening?' Charlotte asked curiously.

Annie forced a smile. 'It's nothing serious. There've just been a few problems . . .' She lowered her voice to a conspiratorial whisper for effect, '... between Severin and Martyn. The jealousy has to be seen to be believed. If I don't play it carefully, it could get out of hand. And I mean *really* out of hand. Severin has a terrible temper and Martyn's pretty bad when riled. I don't want anybody getting beaten up and at the moment that's a possibility.'

'Oh, The Face That Launched A Thousand Ships. How do you do it?' Charlotte looked relieved that it wasn't anything more serious.

'Yeah, well, it's taking everything I've got to stop another Trojan war breaking out here. Severin should be leaving in a few days and then I'll be free. If you can wait until then, we'll have the time of our lives.'

Though obviously agog about Severin, Charlotte seemed to take Annie's statement at face value, and the conversation quickly moved on to her own break-up with Douggie, including all the sordid details.

When she saw her chance, Annie explained that she had a meeting to keep and promised to get together for a drink in a week's time. *If I'm still around.*

Charlotte seemed happy with that and said she planned to spend her days lazing and 'meeting men, the sweatier and rougher the better'.

They parted with a laugh, but the moment the door had closed Annie shut her eyes and prayed she had done enough.

When Annie drove back through the late afternoon after the futility of the day's search, the two policemen were waiting at the bottom of the High Street opposite the cul-de-sac of new executive houses. They motioned for her to pull over, and one of them came round to her open window.

'Sorry to trouble you, miss.' He bobbed down next to the car and squinted at Severin. He had a baby face that made him look like he was barely out of school. 'Are you local?'

'Yes, I live in Blackstone Cottage at the top of the High Street.'

He nodded. 'Then you may have heard a young lad went missing a couple of days ago. Simon Connor's his name. You wouldn't have come across him, would you?'

'No. I do know what he looks like – I used to look after him at the nursery before he went to school.'

'Well, if you do see him around, please let us know immediately. We need to put his parents' minds at rest.'

Through the open window Annie could hear the cry of a baby; it had been going on so long it had almost become part of the background noise, but now it was starting to irritate her. She wished someone would pick it up and comfort it. It sounded as if it hadn't been fed for days.

'I'll be straight on the phone if I see anything.' She smiled politely to end the conversation and get back to the house, but the policeman hadn't finished.

'There's one other thing. It's about those travellers camped up in Tarrant's field. I've been asked to spread the message that everyone in the village should cool it and not be dragged into any confrontational situation. I know feelings are running high, but . . .'

His voice faded into the background as Annie's attention focused on the baby's crying. It had a wild edge to it, as if it was the cry of an animal, and she found herself searching to see where it originated. As the policeman droned on, she isolated it. There was an open bedroom window at the front of the second house in the cul-de-sac and it became apparent the wailing was coming from within.

Only she couldn't be right. That house belonged to Christopher and Katy Elliot who had lost their only child to cot death just a few months ago. Would they be looking after another child so soon?

'. . . trouble with the travellers, it has to be dealt with by the full letter of the law.' The officer had come to the end of his spiel. Annie smiled again, nodded and wound up the window, but as she switched on the ignition her mind was still struck by that awful crying. It didn't sound normal.

It didn't even sound human.

As she pulled away from the kerb, she felt something creep and crawl in her gut. Bizarrely, the baby's cry had contributed to her growing feeling that something was wrong in Riddington. If villages could have moods, she would have said that Riddington's outlook had grown blacker, almost twisted. She looked at the closed doors and dark windows of the houses on the High Street with a new light, and wondered just what was going on within.

*

The house was alive as they slipped through the kitchen into the lounge. Flies buzzed everywhere. And before Annie did anything else, she trawled through all the downstairs rooms with her second can of fly spray of the week. Finally she flopped wearily on to the sofa and covered her face with her hands.

'I'm afraid we're never going to find him.' It was the first time she had expressed the doubt out loud.

Severin cracked his knuckles loudly. 'I can feel him! He's almost close enough to touch. It's only a matter of time now.'

'And time is one thing *I* don't have.'

She suddenly felt his cool hand on her forehead, stroking the hairs back softly; she hadn't heard him cross the room or felt him sit next to her. She took her hands away from her face and was surprised to see almost tenderness in his eyes.

'Come on, you're a tough kid.'

'You know you like me really.'

'Yeah. I do. You remind me—' He broke off and looked away. 'You're good for me, that's all. Is it too much of a cliché to say you make me feel like a different man?'

'Yeah, it *is* too much of a cliché.' She laughed and got up to make some coffee.

Annie was halfway across the room when she suddenly smelled something beneath the remnants of the fly spray, an unpleasant, meaty odour that made her nostrils flare. She turned back to Severin and asked, 'Can you smell anything?'

He shrugged noncommittally so she progressed into the hall and sniffed again. She called back, 'Will you come with me? I want to check upstairs.'

Cautiously, they climbed the stairs together. The bathroom was fine. So was Severin's and her parents' room.

Her bedroom door was slightly ajar; she always kept it closed. Annie moved down the landing quickly and pushed it open, feeling her breath catch in her throat in a sudden premonition before she saw what lay within.

Blood was everywhere. Gouts of it had splattered up the pastel pink walls where it slowly trickled down to congeal along the skirting board. There were splashes on her books and pictures, her pile of clean clothes in the corner. A pool soaked into the thick carpet, and another, deeper pool in the centre of the brilliant white duvet, next to the body which was sprawled there on its back. She saw instantly it was Tommy from the travellers' camp. His throat had been slit from ear to ear. On the wall above the bed, a message had been roughly scrawled in his blood.

NO ONE IS SAFE. NOWHERE IS SAFE.

All rational thought tumbled into the darkness at the back of Annie's head. It was her room, her safe, secure room, but all it contained was death and blood.

Even though Severin was behind her with his hand on her shoulder, she felt he was a world away. Reality came back in piecemeal fashion like a figure appearing out of the fog and then she turned and buried her face in his chest to blank out the image. 'He didn't deserve it,' she said, desolate.

Severin stroked her hair, and held her in silence.

'It's because we told Tommy to look out for him, isn't it?' she said in a flat voice. 'Wilde's warning us not to get anyone else involved.'

Severin examined the corpse without touching it. 'Maybe the poor bastard had something to tell us.'

Severin left Annie in the lounge while he phoned the police. After a minute or two she closed her eyes and thought about Tommy – a man who never wanted to hurt anyone even when they threatened him. How many more like him would have to pay before it was all through?

Her mind seesawed wildly as guilt and fear merged into panic that dragged her deep within herself. At one point a noise outside the room broke through her brooding; it resembled the soft tread of a foot on the stair, but she slipped back into her inner world in an instant.

The sound of the patrol car screeching to a halt outside brought her sharply to her senses. She met the police at the door. There was a uniformed officer and Detective Inspector Pearson who had interviewed her at the station the morning after Wilde had come to her in the bedroom. He seemed surprised to see her.

'We've had a report of a murder.'

She nodded. 'Upstairs.' Severin joined them from the garden and Annie led the way to her room. For the second time, she knew what she would find before she opened the door.

The body was gone, and all the blood too. There was no pool or even a stain on the pristine duvet, nor was there any on the floor. Annie knelt down and gingerly touched the carpet where the blood had been. She thought she could see a slight outline as if a little of the colour had been leached out, and the area felt harsher than the surrounding softness.

Severin looked like he had been hit with a baseball bat. He walked over and examined the wall where the message had been.

'The body *was* here,' Annie said wearily, but she knew she was wasting her breath.

'So it got up and walked away, did it?' Pearson's face was impassive. 'Now look, I'm not going to take either of you down to the station because that's obviously just what you want – more attention. But if anything like this happens again your feet won't even touch the ground. I've got enough on my plate with this missing kid and I don't need your sort of problem. Do you hear what I'm saying?'

'Yes,' Annie replied, as he turned on his heel to leave, 'I hear.'

Her body ached like it had been through a mangler, but it was the best sex she'd ever had. Angela lay back on the makeshift bed and watched a moth flutter nervously around the hissing hurricane lamp which hung from the tent roof. She wondered vaguely where Tommy had been since mid-afternoon, decided she didn't care, and listened instead to the nocturnal sound of the camp, alive with music and voices. There was a patchwork of blue-black over her torso and legs, livid scratches on her back, bites that burned like wasp stings on her neck. Yet her groin throbbed with a pleasant, fiery pain and she had that bone-weary, content exhaustion that only comes from repeated orgasms and being pushed to the limit in sexual exertion.

Wilde stood naked in the open tent flaps looking out across the dark hillside to the lights of Riddington twinkling in the fields of night below. Angela was surprised to see a black mark on the olive skin just above his left buttock like a cattle brand; it moved as his muscles rippled, a bizarre geometric shape barely bigger than a fifty-pence piece.

'What's that?' she asked dreamily. 'A tattoo?'

'Hmmm?' he mused from the maze of his thoughts. His hand snaked around his back and found the mark. 'This? The fingerprint of God. My passport to a trouble-free life, and the sign of my punishment also.'

Angela laughed and ran both hands through her hair. 'Sometimes I can't understand a word you're saying . . .'

'No, I suppose you would not.'

'I can't believe what an effect you've had since you walked into the camp,' she continued with another lazy laugh. 'You've got them all eating out of your hand. Before, they always went with Mr Boring "Let's Do Nothing" Tommy. Now I think they'd storm that village if you said.'

'Oh, I do not think they will be listening to Tommy very much in the future.' He smiled tightly, but did not turn to let her see it. 'You are in charge now, Angela, as you always wanted.'

'I never—'

He hushed her with a dismissive wave. 'They listen to me because they and I are very alike in some ways. Travelling people, rootless, free. They understand the ache that comes from roaming without direction, from being people of the land with no land to call one's own. Yet we are very different in other aspects. I have a deep loathing of anything which might be considered good . . .'

'I've just been good to you, haven't I?' she laughed throatily.

He laughed too, but with cold mockery; Angela didn't recognize the difference. '*Good* people like artists, musicians and writers,' he continued as if she had not interrupted him. '*Good* people who care for others, who do sickening *good* deeds. That awful, stupid majority who carry with them the spark of the Creator, that bastard deity who in his monstrous arrogance has denied me—'

'Hey, it sounds like you just don't like people full stop.'

He turned, still smiling, and walked over to his pile of neatly folded clothes. 'The ultimate sociopath, I suppose you are right.' As he proceeded to dress himself in front of Angela's admiring stare, he suddenly doubled up and clutched at his stomach, his face contorting in pain.

'What is it?' Angela sat bolt upright in panic.

When Wilde didn't answer and seemed to remain in agony, she leapt up to put a comforting arm around his shoulders. He lashed out with a strength she would never have imagined. It flung her backwards across the tent while at the same time some strangled, almost non-human sound crawled out of his throat.

Angela cowered in fear as the terrifying fit tore through his body, turning his fingers into claws, his limbs into insect legs, but after a minute or so it seemed to subside, sloughing off him like a snake shedding a skin.

'What the hell was that?' Her voice was cracked with tearful shock.

He threw himself up to his full height, a little too soon, she thought, for he seemed to go dizzy. 'Sometimes . . .' he paused for breath, '. . . I become sick if I stay in the same place too long.'

'Christ, Wilde, I thought you were going to kill me!'

His smile returned quickly and he strode over and kissed her hand with surprising tenderness after his rage. 'I apologize most sincerely. It was not my desire to frighten you. Sometimes the pain is so great I cannot control myself, other times it is just a twinge.'

'What is it? Are you *ill*?'

'Consider it as . . . a warning.' He returned to his clothes and continued to dress. 'Like an announcement before a train or plane departs. It tells me I must move on.' He finished buckling his belt and then ran one vain hand through his hair. 'Even so, there is something very important I must do first and it will not see fruition for a few days yet.' He glanced out of the tent again at the village lights. 'Down there. I have set events in motion which will . . . hmm . . . teach a lesson, to one person in particular and to the community in general.'

Angela smiled cruelly and climbed back on the bed where she stretched like a cat. 'Yes, those bastards deserve a good shake-up.'

'Oh, they will be shaken up, Angela, most definitely. I have planted a few poisonous seeds which will transform their lives. They think they are secure in their little world. In their secret hearts they would even love to beat death. Well . . .' his eyes glinted with an arctic humour, '. . . sometimes it is nice to give people their hearts' desire.'

'You'll have to tell me more.' She closed her eyes and started to drift lazily.

'Oh, very soon, you will see it for yourself. This is quite a monumental undertaking for me. There is a risk factor, of course, a danger of being discovered, but then I believe I have been too cautious for too long. And this time, particularly, I feel . . . driven . . .' He shook his head thoughtfully. 'Strange.'

He allowed his soft, modulating voice to lull Angela into a doze. Then he left her and hung on the guy rope so he could feel the warm night air on his face. It reminded him of a hot evening at the summit of the Temple of Quetzalcoatl when the blood flowed like wine and the still-beating hearts had formed small hills all around.

He was talking to himself, clinically weighing the dangers against the need he felt to make his mark. 'I thought I could control everything I created, but he has proved me wrong. I will be forced to dispose of him at the earliest opportunity.'

The scream erupted out of the night somewhere close to the tent. It was a hideous sound which snatched Angela from the edge of sleep.

'Christ! What . . .!' She leapt out of bed and pulled a long coat around her naked body.

Wilde shook his head in mock dismay. 'Oh dear. We are uncovered.'

They both stepped out of the tent to see Kurt stumble from the doorway of the black bus and crash to his knees on the dry ground.

Angela ran to his side and hugged him. 'What is it? Kurt!'

'I went to Scarlet. I love her . . . love her . . . She seemed to be getting better . . .'

'What happened?' Angela said quietly, dismayed by the sucking void within the blackness of his dilated pupils.

'I kissed her. I wanted to get close to her again. She looked at me . . . We spoke . . . She's not . . .' His hand went to his throat, but it was too late and his vomit sprayed across the ground in front of her.

Pounding feet echoed all around as other travellers drew near to see what was amiss. Angela looked to Wilde for help, but he already had a hand on Kurt's arm and was helping him to his feet.

'Poor Kurt,' he said. 'The effects of the attack. It must have been a shock for him.'

'It's more than that!' Angela was frightened by what she saw in her friend.

Wilde hushed her with a finger to his lips. 'A rest will do him the world of good. On his own.' He started to lead Kurt back up the three steps of the bus, into the darkness where Scarlet lay like a fat, black spider in her web. When Kurt saw where he was being led, he started to struggle, but by then it was too late and within an instant Wilde had him inside and the door squeezed shut like the sealing of a coffin lid.

23

In the still time just after dawn before the sun cast its stranglehold across the area, Annie found herself returning to the map on the kitchen wall time and time again. Only four segments of the circle around the village still remained unshaded, a paper clock counting off the days of her life. She felt her heart pounding in panic.

'Are you waiting for it to set on fire like on *Bonanza*?' Severin was leaning in the doorway. 'Before my time, unfortunately,' she gently mocked.

As he moved around the kitchen, Annie watched his supple movements appreciatively and was surprised at how close she had grown to him. She couldn't really describe it as love, it was more a matter of two lonely, frightened people huddling together in the face of the unknown.

When he had finished making the coffee, he clunked the mugs down on the table and pulled out a chair. He waited until Annie was sitting opposite him; it was their morning ritual.

Annie spoke first: 'We're out of our depth, Severin. If he can do what he did with Tommy, you have to wonder what the limits of his power are. What is he? A magician?'

Severin didn't answer.

'You started to think something of the kind after the Mill, didn't you? That guy you shot wasn't helping Wilde, because Wilde always works alone – that's his nature. Was Wilde controlling him in some way?'

This time Severin did speak. 'Let's face it. We don't know what the fuck he's doing. We've just got to put our heads down and walk into the storm.'

'But those dreams I've been having, and . . .' She leant across the table and unbuttoned his shirt so the bracelet around his neck hung freely, '. . . *that*. The two are linked in some way. I think the bracelet triggered the dreams a couple of times when I touched it, and the dreams ... or the last one at least ... pointed back to the importance of the bracelet.'

'OK,' he said, holding it out for her. 'Touch it.'

But when she stretched out her hand to feel it, there was nothing – just cool, corroded metal. She shook her head. 'Maybe the time has to be right.'

'Well, you better learn to fix the clock hands ... quick. Something out there thinks you're up to the job and it's giving you some help to do what you need to do. Maybe you're the only shot the whole world has got of getting rid of Wilde. Just use the help you're getting ... all those dreams and visions ... go with the flow.'

'You talk like I'm preparing for a parachute jump, Severin. This is life or death here.' She paused and the sweat lodge premonition flashed into her mind. 'And I'm afraid what kind of sacrifice I'm expected to make.'

Severin finished his coffee and sat back in his chair. 'There's no point getting screwed up about it,' he said.

'This is a great metaphor for life, isn't it?' Annie resumed with a tight smile. 'Two people fumbling around in the dark trying to find out what's happening while death draws closer.'

'Your college background's starting to show. There aren't any metaphors in the real world. Just a dumb, bone-headed struggle and then the end.'

The phone rang in the hall and with some relief she let her dark thoughs fade away. It was Charlotte, sounding her old irrepressibly happy self.

'Why are you so perky?' Annie asked.

'Because I'm having the time of my life. I didn't realize what a drag Douggie was on my social standing.'

'Sounds ominous. What have you been doing? Or should I say, who?'

Charlotte giggled. 'Well, I was determined I wasn't going to sit around and mope. I've been reading all those books I never got round to while that lump was cluttering up my flat. I did some sightseeing. Ashby Castle. Staunton Harold Church. Shopping in Nottingham—'

'Get to the meat, Charlotte.'

She laughed again at the *double entendre*. 'You didn't tell me the men around here were so wonderful. Everywhere I go some good-looking bloke comes chatting me up. Not in a hassling way, you understand. There's never any pressure. It's nice.'

'Can't say I've noticed it myself,' Annie said with mock sourness.

'There's a couple who I just couldn't turn down, so I'm going to see them for drinks to decide which is best. Maybe you could come along and have my reject?'

'Maybe next week. I'm still pretty tied up at the moment.'

'Even today? I thought I could pop round and run through the vital statistics of the one I think I fancy the most. Well, pretty sure I fancy, actually.'

'Sorry ...' Annie's voice dried up. She was lucky Wilde hadn't discovered Charlotte was around already. 'I really am busy. I'm going to be out till very late.'

'Oh.' Charlotte didn't mask her disappointment.

'I know I'm being a real bitch this week, but I'll make it up to you. Honest.' Her fingers crossed automatically.

'OK. I suppose I don't want you queering my pitch anyway.'

When she had replaced the phone, Annie felt the sudden cold realization that losing her own life was actually the least of her fears. She was more concerned about what Wilde could do to her family, her friends, all the people she had loved and grown up with in the village. She had to stop him for their sakes, and she had to be prepared to sacrifice everything to do it.

'Have you been up to see the enemy recently, my dear?'

Annie smiled at Hartley Williams tightly, but didn't respond to his baiting.

'Because it would really be advisable to stay away over the next few days. The authorities have started to take a particular interest in our little problem, which should ensure a happy resolution very quickly.'

With as polite a nod as she could muster, Annie tried to open the car door to join Severin inside, but Williams prevented her with one podgy hand on the window.

'You should listen to what I have to say, you know. The authorities consider me on the side of right and, indeed, the other night they came to tell me as much, and gave me the authority to take what action I see fit.' Annie found that hard to believe, but Williams was beaming at the confirmation of a status he had always imagined. 'A charming man. We hit it off instantly.'

Something crawled like an insect through Annie's head. 'What did he look like?' she asked hesitantly.

'Actually, he sported an earring,' Williams laughed pompously. 'But it was obvious from his demeanour that he was no gypsy. In fact he didn't even appear particularly British. His skin was almost swarthy . . .'

Annie paused, felt herself sicken inside and then asked half-interestedly, 'Is he staying round here?'

'Funnily enough, he said he used to be a farmer so he's staying on some farm . . .'

'Did he say which one?'

'Not that I recall. You're very interested in him, my dear . . .'

To his surprise, Annie was already wrenching open the door and throwing herself excitedly into the car. She gabbled something he couldn't hear and then roared off with a screech of tyres.

They had made it to a handful of farms during the day, but it wasn't as simple as Annie had thought when Williams had given them their first real lead. Farmers were a shifty, secretive lot, wary of anyone who might be Inland Revenue investigators, environmental regulatory officers, or just plain snoopers. They followed old rules and they didn't want just anybody sticking their noses in. It was an effort to draw any information out of them at all, and for the rest it was left to Severin and his peculiar senses to 'feel' if Wilde was on their land.

Already sombre, both felt their mood darken appreciatively when they pulled back into Riddington at the end of the day, and it wasn't just the unusual sight for that summer of grey clouds pulling ominously across the blue sky.

It was the feeling in the village that hit them almost as if they had run the car into a brick wall. The atmosphere had changed palpably since the morning, as if someone had released a poisonous, invisible gas into the streets. It was oppressive, and Annie feared that the jarring sensations at the killing ground and the Mill had been distilled into a new, potent form.

'What is it?' she asked in a hushed voice, as they cruised slowly around the empty streets in search of what could cause such a powerful yet intangible impression. And as they progressed Annie realized it was stronger in certain areas: outside the Elliots' house where the mysterious baby still wailed hungrily, at the Cockburns' run-down semi and outside Brian Swift's home in the High Street where she had seen, or thought she had seen, his dead mother in the upstairs window.

The storm broke shortly before midnight. Lightning crisscrossed the sky in jagged forks, throwing the night into white relief while the thunder boomed and cracked like heaven was collapsing. A howling wind ripped across the countryside with razor-sharp talons, pulling off slates and loose chimney stacks and uprooting old trees, but there was little for those who had been praying for rain – just one brief downpour and then the stage was left to the wild electrics and the sound effects.

A crack of thunder almost directly overhead woke Severin from his dreamless sleep in the lounge, where he had fallen asleep as he lay on the sofa. The first thing he noted was the darkness; the power had gone off and with the curtains drawn it was almost impossible to see anything. Every now and then a sliver of illumination from the lightning would break through the curtains, creating a white-out for a split-second.

Rubbing his face, he sat up and stretched his limbs, his initial thought of Annie, of sliding into bed next to her, for comfort and for warmth. It faded behind a faint, distracting buzzing in the room; flies; companions for the entire village.

Scrambling over the furniture, he made his way to the kitchen where he knew he had seen some candles. He located them in the cupboard next to the boiler and lit two, leaving one in the kitchen and carrying the other one through to the lounge. The flickering flame brought the flies into a whirlwind of life. They buzzed even more and swooped close to the heat like Icarus into the rising sun. There seemed more than normal. A lot more.

The buzzing was loudest near the French windows. Severin pulled back the curtains just as more lightning flashed across the sky and saw in that instant that the glass was almost black. They were crawling around body to body and wing to wing, too soporific or too bloated to fly off at his presence. There was something sickening about the size of the flies, as if they had fed too well. He closed the curtains again quickly.

He noticed the candle guttered occasionally, and decided there was probably an open window somewhere which had allowed the flies access to escape the storm. He checked the other windows in the lounge and then returned to the kitchen where he noticed the back door was slightly ajar. With his coat wrapped around him in a futile attempt to keep warm, he hadn't noticed the through breeze. He automatically pushed it shut, and then remembered it had been locked from the inside.

There was a corresponding bang deep in the house, too faint and dull to be an echo. *Only Annie*, he thought, but instantly he knew it wasn't. His private radar made the nerves along his spine tingle in warning. Annie was having an early night; she was alone, asleep and defenceless. Someone else was in the house. For reassurance, he ruffled his coat so the shotgun in the hidden pocket banged against his leg.

Another noise upstairs.

Silently, he moved out of the kitchen to the foot of the stairs, pulling out the shotgun before he was on the first step. By the time he reached the top, he had registered another sound, constant and deep in the background like the hiss of a badly tuned radio.

The door of Annie's room was shut. She hadn't ventured into it since the traveller's death, preferring to sleep in her parents' bed. The door to that room was open, and in another flash of lightning he saw her sprawled across the double bed. That left his room.

Hesitantly, he flicked the handle and let it swing open.

It was filled with flies, thousands upon thousands of them, buzzing with one machine-like voice. There was no chaos in their flight. They circled the room in one direction, anti-clockwise, round and round unceasingly, their drone fixed at one tone. At the eye of the whirlpool was a man, seemingly unbothered by the freakish cloud that surrounded him. He was using the torch from the bedside table to peer at drawers and shelves. Eventually he picked up a book. Despite the torchlight, Severin couldn't make out his features through the swirling mass of black bodies, but he could tell it wasn't Wilde; the frame was smaller, lithe and not as muscular.

'I've come for my diary,' said a voice barely audible above the buzzing.

Severin half raised the shotgun, then let it fall again. He reluctantly recognized the face from the photo Annie had shown him on the pub wall. Laurence Lucas. Dead for over quarter of a century.

'You had no right to take it.' Lucas clutched the book to his chest with his left hand and Severin could see he was also holding something in his right. A penknife.

'Christ. Alive . . .'

When Lucas laughed and took a couple of steps forward, the whirlpool of flies moved with him.

This time Severin fully raised the shotgun and pointed it at Lucas's head. 'I don't know *what* you are . . . but you're not going to be in much shape after a couple of barrels between the eyes.'

'I am the Great Deliverer, Eyeless in Gaza.' The intruder showed no sign of being menaced. He was still laughing. 'I'm the man who can do anything he pleases.' So saying, he swept forward, surrounded by the cloud of flies, which threw Severin off balance and then blinded him in a tidal wave of tiny bodies.

They both crashed backwards on to the floor, with Lucas astride Severin, stabbing wildly with the penknife, laughing like a maniac as he brought it down. Severin fended off the blows as best he could, but one tore through his sleeve, temporarily immobilizing his right arm. Lucas screamed with hysterical laughter, and when he struck again, the blade twisted and tore through Severin's cheek.

Through the burst of pain in his head, Severin struck out madly, catching Lucas's wrists by accident. The skin felt hideously dry and it made him think instantly of the man in the Mill. Then Lucas fell forward, until his face was only an inch away and Severin could smell the foul blast of his breath like meat rotting in a hole. But the eyes were the worst; mad, without even the slightest glimmer of humanity. It was like looking into the abyss and seeing the Devil looking back.

'I'd stay and cut you up,' the killer said, 'but you're not really my type. Too old.'

It was then that Annie stumbled in, rubbing her eyes and trying to see what the disturbance was through the gloom.

'Look out!' Severin yelled.

There was another explosion of light. Enough for Severin to notice Lucas suddenly look uncomfortable at Annie's appearance. Then he watched as the cloud of flies gave her bedroom door a wide berth as it surged crazily along the landing and disappeared with Lucas himself down the stairs.

Peter Cockburn's bedroom had become his sanctuary, but there was never any real escape. There had once been a tiny bolt on the door to give him the privacy all nine-year-olds need, but that had been smashed off in one brutish charge. He looked at the splintered wood from his vantage point on the floor, but it made his eyes hurt to stare at such an odd angle and he couldn't bear to move his head, so he closed his eyelids and swam in the pain.

There wasn't one square inch of him that didn't hurt in some way. Fire around the temples, cheeks and ears, cold further down his body. He lay half curled in a foetal position where he had fallen three hours before like an underage drunkard, but the only intoxication that swelled his senses was the abiding belief that life was hell and there was no respite.

Three fat meat flies buzzed around the bare bulb that illuminated his room, sweltering behind the drawn curtains while the storm raged outside. The air was thick with the smell of sweat and an unpleasant green odour of decay.

Some thoughts and memories remained fuzzy. He had a vague impression of committing a horrendous crime that had led to guilt, secrecy and freedom in equal measures, but in the reality in which he was now existing, it had been forgotten. There was only the here-and-now.

He hadn't seen his mother for a while. She hadn't ventured out of her room since Dad had returned, but then none of them did, really. Dad was the warder that needed no keys, roaming the prison-house in a state of permanent drunkenness without ever drinking.

From the corner of his eye he saw a few dog-eared comics poking out from under the dressing table – *The Unexpected*, *Weird Mystery Tales* – and smelled their warm, old paper smell that no longer comforted him. He tasted the iron of blood in his mouth.

Soon it would be his turn for a visit again, but that wasn't the worst thing. No, the worst thing was the sounds that came through the walls from his sisters' rooms, from beautiful Karen who brushed her long, golden hair, from Julie and Ruth who no longer remembered innocence.

239

And here he comes again. The booted feet on the stairs. The fist thumping on the wall. A bitter cycle that would never end.

In panic, his mind flipped back to his early childhood, but even there it could find no respite. 'Clap handies, clap handies, till Daddy comes home . . .'

Annie sat on the grass and hugged her knees protectively. The storm had blown itself out quickly, leaving barely a sprinkling of rain on the pavements, the clouds sweeping away on a wind which disappeared with them. Ahead of her, the hulking body of the church was silhouetted against a clear, star-sprinkled sky, and although she couldn't make out the clock on the tower she knew it must be around 2 a.m. A faint breeze stirred the yews along the perimeter wall, but there was no other sound apart from the muffled clink of Severin's spade. He'd been at work by torchlight for a good half hour and she guessed from how far his head showed above ground level that he must be getting near the bottom.

'We're taking a big risk here, Severin,' she whispered. 'After all the furore when the other graves were disturbed, there might be someone keeping a watch on the place. The police could be here at any minute.'

'I doubt it,' he replied breathlessly. 'The trees shield the grave from the road. Anyone interested would have to walk right into the yard and around the church, and if *you're* keeping watch like you should be, then we'll see them first.'

'I *am* keeping watch,' she stressed.

The pile of earth at the side of the grave had grown quickly. The soil was uncommonly loose so it came out easily.

'Are you nearly there yet?' she asked, for the nth time.

'I'll tell you when I'm there,' he replied exasperatedly.

'Severin, what happens if you find a body down there?'

'I'll fill in the grave, pack away the spade and have a drink to celebrate.'

'Won't you feel bad about disturbing it?'

'I'm only concerned with one thing – finding out what Wilde is doing and stopping him.'

The night was sticky, but Annie still shivered. Lucas's face kept materializing in her mind, and the last place she wanted to be was his burial site. She scanned the rows of stones which glowed in the moonlight, wondering what else was out there in the night. Into her thoughts returned all the horrors of child-hood which had been dismissed by growing up. Those long-gone ghosts and goblins could be drawing closer, moving through the shadows just out of sight, drawing nearer and nearer, stretching out long dead fingers to clutch for her . . .

A twig cracked and Annie jumped to her feet. Severin stopped digging instantly. Together they listened, not daring to move. The trees still swayed from side to side in the breeze, but although they could hear nothing more, Annie could sense someone out there. Her look warned Severin, and he crawled out of the grave as quietly as possible, raising the spade as a weapon.

'You people are fucking crazy!' Annie recognized Martyn's incredulous voice.

'Martyn!' she hissed. 'Get over here!'

He stepped out from behind a crypt, a look of dismay on his face. His mouth gaped and Annie knew he was going to let fly another outburst when Severin ran over, grabbed him and dragged him to the open grave. He shook off the American roughly, and looked from the hole to Annie and back.

'I knew you'd developed some new interests at university, Annie, but this takes the biscuit.'

'What are you doing here?' she asked suspiciously.

'I saw you leave the house. I wondered where you were going.'

'That was about quarter past one in the morning, Martyn. What were you doing watching the house at that time?'

Martyn looked away sheepishly and changed the subject. 'What's going on?'

'We'd better tell him, ' Severin interjected. 'He might be able to help.'

'I'm not helping with grave-robbing! Fuck. You're talking life imprisonment there.'

'It's not grave-robbing, Martyn. It's . . . That man who attacked me on the train. He's here in Riddington, threatening to hurt a lot of people and then to finish the job with me. We're doing this to try and find him.'

'I don't see—'

'I don't care whether you see or not. I'll explain it all to you back at Blackstone Cottage. Just trust me. There's a good

241

chance there's no body in this grave.' A shiver ran down her back when she finally said it out loud.

Martyn didn't look too convinced, but he nodded in reluctant agreement. Severin grinned and held out the spade.

'What's that for?'

'If you want to be in with the in-crowd, you've got to go where the in-crowd go. And get your hands dirty.'

'Oh, Jesus . . .' Martyn took the spade with a look of disgust and then stared blankly into the grave. Before he could have second thoughts, Severin gave him a shove between the shoulder blades and he pitched forward into the hole. He hit the bottom hard and a stream of muffled curses floated back up.

Annie knew why Severin had done it. Martyn had now got his hands dirty metaphorically as well as physically; he couldn't back out. Annie felt sympathy for him. It seemed unfair to drag him into the hell that was slowly taking over her life.

The sound of Martyn's digging echoed hollowly through the night. Thud-thud-thud. Not far off now, she thought. Getting near to that once shiny coffin. Like the one Robert was buried in. Her head snapped around in the direction of her brother's grave: the image of him lying there in the silk-lined casket seared her mind, and she didn't want to think of him that way. Yet when she screwed her eyes up tight, another, more disturbing, thought prevailed. The same silk-lined casket . . . empty . . .

'You OK?' There was a degree of tenderness in Severin's voice as if he knew what was going through her head, and she allowed him to entwine comforting fingers around hers.

As they moved towards a kiss, Martyn poked his head out of the grave and said, 'I've hit wood!'

Severin peered over the edge. 'What state is it in?'

'I don't—' There was a sudden crack and Martyn dropped from view. 'Oh shit! Oh Jesus . . .'

A cry choked in Annie's throat. She ran forward and saw Martyn looking down at his feet.

'It's fucking broken! I've fallen in it! Oh shit!'

'Stop whining,' Severin snapped. 'Do you want to wake the whole goddamned village? Just take the spade and dig around you. Try to clear the rest of the lid.'

Martyn held the back of his hand against his mouth for a second. Gingerly, he probed around with the spade, turning the soil over easily.

'There's nothing here.'

Severin knelt at the edge of the grave and picked up the torch, letting the light play around the insides of the pit. Pieces of broken wood were scattered amongst the earth and at one point the interior of the coffin was visible.

'Whose grave is this?' Martyn asked.

'Laurence Lucas's,' Annie replied coldly. There was no escaping the truth now. No pretending that there was some rational explanation. No fooling themselves that Wilde was human.

'Oh shit!' Martyn said once more as his hand returned to his mouth. 'It's empty.'

Back in the well-lit lounge of Blackstone Cottage, Annie was shocked to see how dirty Severin and Martyn were; grime covered their clothes, hands, faces and hair. While they washed, she made a pot of coffee and fetched a bottle of Scotch from her father's drinks cabinet.

It had only taken them fifteen minutes to fill in the grave, but not a word had passed between them until they were back at the house. They all seemed to be lost in contemplating the repercussions of their discovery: Martyn struggling with the mysteries that had been presented to him; and Annie and Severin trying to face up to the chilling consequences of seeing their worst fears confirmed.

Finally, when they were all sitting tensely in the lounge, Annie told Martyn the whole story. His reactions mirrored her own during the period when it had all happened to her; bafflement, incredulity and then horrific acceptance. Annie wished she didn't have to put him through it – he seemed too immature and innocent, like a boy – but he absorbed the whole nightmare with surprising speed.

'Men can face these things a lot easier than women,' he said when she had finished, 'because we're all kids at heart and we live in the world where Anything Can Happen.'

'That's surprisingly perceptive, Martyn,' Annie said as she poured out the whisky.

'I'm not entirely as stupid as you think.'

'So,' she looked at Severin and smiled humourlessly. 'A rational explanation?'

'The word "rational" isn't in my vocabulary any more. Raising the dead is as far-fetched as you can get.'

Annie looked into the depths of her whisky in silent agreement.

Severin went on, 'You do realize that the dead people are the ones causing that ... atmosphere ...? You saw where it felt worst in the village – the houses of those who had relatives buried in the graves that had been disturbed ...'

'Robert's grave was disturbed too.' Her voice sounded small and shaky.

Severin chose his words carefully before he continued. 'If Wilde had brought your brother back, he'd be here. He's not, so we have to believe that he desecrated Robert's grave just to freak you out.' He paused, then added, 'We *have* to believe that.'

Annie nodded, but they all knew she wasn't convinced.

'It's the biggest taboo of all,' Severin continued hurriedly. 'People can cope with most things, but the one thing they seal up inside and never face, is death. What Wilde is doing is making them look into that dark area in the worst possible way. Take those families who are facing their dead – what they're feeling is spreading out and affecting everyone. The unnaturalness of it is eating away at us all on some sort of psychic level ... causing a pollution that'll rot this place from inside out.'

'Those graves were disturbed a while back,' Martyn said nervously. 'So how come we haven't seen all the dead wandering around like some George Romero film? Why hasn't there been a huge media outcry? If my grandma came back, the first thing I'd do would be to phone up the local rag, at least.'

'Maybe you would and maybe you wouldn't. People never react how you'd expect them to. Who knows, maybe Wilde's done something to stop them bringing it out into the open.'

Martyn put his glass down with a sour face and stood up. 'I don't think this stuff is agreeing with me. I'm off to the toilet.'

When he had gone, Severin said, 'I know how he feels.'

All Annie could think about was her own fear of Wilde. 'What have I done to deserve this, Severin?'

Severin reached for the bottle and filled his glass up to the brim. 'You know what the hippies used to say – shit happens. That's just the way it is in the world. There's pain and tears. People die when they shouldn't. And one day Wilde comes to town.'

A thunderous hammering on the back door made them both jump. Annie dropped her glass which bounced, but didn't break, spilling whisky all over the carpet. She glanced at the clock – it was nearly 4 a.m.

'Do you think someone's found the grave?' she whispered.

The hammering erupted again, a slow, rhythmic bang.

She stepped into the kitchen. A tall figure could just be seen through the frosted glass; she was relieved to see it wasn't wearing a policeman's uniform.

Annie took a few steps forward and then paused. The figure didn't move. It could have been a wax dummy out there. Suddenly, a cold wave of fear came over her. *Who the hell is it?*

She sensed Severin behind her. He pushed past her to answer the door, but she caught at his arm. 'Don't.'

He took one look at her desolate face and then dashed upstairs where he had left the shotgun after he had washed himself, leaving Annie clutching her hands as she watched the rigid shape through the frosted glass. It looked familiar, the shape of the head slightly to one side, the long, lithe legs, the skinny chest. If she opened the door would she smell Aramis?

It is him, she thought.

And then: *Of course it isn't. Don't be stupid!*

It would be Wilde's ultimate blow, sending her dead brother round to see her when she was at her lowest ebb. Yet another part of her *wanted* to see him, just once. To bring back the past and hold on to it for as long as she could.

No! That would be madness!

Annie took one more step towards the door and that hazy shape outside. There was one vertiginous moment as she reached out for the handle and then the dark outline melted away from the glass. Through the top of the door, there was a new lightness in the sky; dawn was not far away.

Severin clattered down to the hall, breaking open the shotgun and thumbing in the cartridges as he ran. It snapped shut with a dead click. Annie felt her world falling away from her and she clutched on to him for support.

They stood together and stared at the empty glass silently, until Martyn emerged looking pale and shaky. 'Who was that at the door?'

'You don't want to know,' Severin replied.

He stood with his fingers on the door handle for several seconds and then he yanked it down and swung the door open. The garden was empty. But on the threshold he paused, stooped down and plucked something from the doormat. He held it in front of him where it spun on the end of a chain, glinting in the kitchen light.

It was a silver ankh.

'I lost that,' Annie said. 'At the Mill. Someone ripped it from my neck.'

She felt dazed as she took the ankh and held it on her palm for a moment before fastening it back around her neck. Then she looked up at the sky and the dawn light was blurred by the tears in her eyes.

24

There was a clear blue sky that Saturday, a very special day in the calendar for the people of Riddington. It was the day of their fête, a rowdy party when all the disparate elements in the village came together to celebrate the wonderful place they called home.

The stalls were being set up in the grounds of the school long before most of Riddington was awake. And Alexander Alcock was preparing to open the pub early, as well as a special beer tent for the traditional breakfast and complimentary beer. This was none too soon for the band who arrived in time for a quick tune-up next to the marquee before adjourning for a pre-concert libation. The brass section and the woodwinds entered into an impromptu drinking contest which did not bode well.

Tony Aris wandered down from the rectory to chat to those present and express his belief that the fête would allow them to put all the *unpleasantness* of the previous few days behind them. He had prepared a short speech for the grand opening which also included a prayer for the speedy return of Simon Connor. Everyone was worried about Simon. It had gone beyond a boyish prank and now people were starting to fear the worst.

Some of the people who had promised to help did not turn up on time. Few were surprised at the non-arrival of Brian Swift who still seemed to be having trouble getting over the death of his mother, his sole companion for so long, but Christopher and

Katy Elliot were always reliable. Tony Aris realized he had not seen them since that day at the rectory when Mrs Cockburn had collapsed. He resolved to call round in the near future to see how they were doing.

A good-sized crowd had arrived for the grand opening at eleven, hoping the speeches would be short so that they could get on with the festivities. When Hartley Williams took the microphone there were a few groans and then a few cheers from those who considered the parish council chairman the backbone of the village. Surprisingly, Williams kept his speech concise as he briefly trumpeted Riddington's strengths and successes, with only a few vitriolic words reserved for the travellers who were posing such a threat.

When he declared the fête open, everyone rushed to the stalls and beer tent where Bill King and Huxton-Smith were already well down their first pints. They were in good spirits. An early morning trip to Tarrant's Wood had resulted in the discovery of a gin-trap covered in blood, smashed up and dumped in a nearby field with some of the other traps. They had laughed all the way back.

And so the mood of rejoicing began. It was a time to celebrate life and the sun, and to stand up and say we are not scared of darkness and death; they hold no sway over us.

After only a few hours' sleep, most of which had been disturbed by terrifying nightmares, Annie was weary and drained when she made it to the door to answer a sharp rap just before 11 a.m. She felt like a robot.

'Jesus, Annie, are you sick?' Charlotte greeted her pale, drawn face with concern.

'I just had a bad night, that's all.' Annie tensed instantly and tried to keep her friend on the doorstep in the hope that she could swiftly send her back to her hotel, but Charlotte squeezed by into the kitchen.

'You're not keeping me out, madam. I know there's something wrong. You've been trying to hide it from me and I've given you your way for a while, but it can't go on any longer. Look at you!'

Annie pushed Charlotte into a chair at the kitchen table and brewed up a pot of tea. *More lies*, she thought. *Where will it end?*

'I'll tell you all about it later,' she said, 'when we're alone.'

'We're not alone now?'

'Severin and Martyn are asleep upstairs.'

'Oh, you dirty bitch,' Charlotte joked, but her eyes were serious as she tried to read Annie's face.

Severin emerged in the doorway, looking bleary-eyed and sallow-skinned. 'I thought I heard voices,' he muttered.

'Charlotte dropped round for a . . . er, why exactly are you here?'

'To tell you that I managed to decide which man I want.' she laughed as Severin retreated uncomfortably. 'We arranged to meet up for the day at your village fête so I thought I'd drop by and take you along with me.'

'What a staggering coincidence, Charlotte,' Annie said sarcastically.

'OK, I admit it. I engineered it so I could drag you out for the day. I couldn't let my best friend wallow in whatever she's wallowing in, now could I?'

Annie realized she wasn't going to shake Charlotte off easily. 'I'll be back in a minute,' she said suddenly.

In the lounge, Severin was pacing around like a tiger in a cage. Annie explained the problem. 'If I don't go with her, she'll jsut keep bugging me, and every time she turns up on the doorstep there's a chance Wilde might see her, wherever he is.'

'Then go ahead, spend the day with her. Don't worry about the search. I can do it just as well with Martyn. All I'll say is, keep your wits about you. I don't think Wilde will strike before the day he said, but keep with the crowds, OK?'

After a moment's thought, Annie reluctantly agreed. She wished Severin luck, and then hurried Charlotte quickly out into the street where there were already several people making their way down to the school grounds.

'It didn't take much to change your mind about going out,' Charlotte said as she fished her Raybans out of her pocket.

'Oh, I decided to seize the opportunity,' Annie lied. 'Let's have a good time.'

'You said it!'

Charlotte maintained a light-hearted banter right up to the fête which was swarming with what seemed like most of the village. They grabbed a couple of beers and then watched a group of ten-year-old cheerleaders running through their routine.

'Oh boy, Annie,' Charlotte said sympathetically as she rested back on the grass and looked up into the infinite blue. 'Do you look . . . hunted.'

Annie almost laughed at the irony of it. *Hunted? No, just backed up into a corner with a Dobermann snapping at my neck.* She clutched at the ankh as she always did in times of stress and then looked down at it and realized what she was doing.

'You did a Comparative Religion module on your course, didn't you?'

'Oh yes, right bundle of laughs.'

'Anything in it about paganism or wicca? Or the triple goddess?' She thought she heard a whisper of acknowledgement on the edge of her perception, but it could have been just the breeze in her ear.

'The three-in-one aspect of the Mother Goddess, is that what you mean?' she replied in a puzzled voice. 'Mother-maiden-crone?'

'That's the one.'

'If you wanted to change the subject, I'm sure you could have found something a little less heavy!'

'I'm not changing the subject. It's just something that's been on my mind.' From the spot they'd chosen, she could look out over the village to the gently rolling hill where the travellers' camp was based, and Tarrant's Wood, thick and dark against the fields of green and gold.

'Yeah?' Charlotte searched her friend's face doubtfully for a moment, but then responded to the seriousness she saw there. 'I always said you had a strange mind, hon. What do you want to know?'

'How it all started.'

'Nobody knows that: the worship of a Mother Goddess goes back to the dawn of time. Cave paintings and all that malarkey. The current theory is that man started worshipping woman as the giver of life, which seems about right to me.'

'Go on,' Annie said quietly.

'Well, there are elements of Mother Goddess worship throughout all major societies right up to modern times,' Charlotte replied hesitantly, as she struggled to see where the conversation was leading. 'Some scholars point to the Madonna as an example of it which has been swallowed up by the Christian faith. And now it's been taken up by the wiccan religion, or witches to you and me.' She furrowed her brow as she tried to remember. 'God, it's amazing how quickly you forget all that stuff they pump into you at university. OK, how about this? In wicca, the Triple Goddess represents birth, love and death – the only important things in life, right? As I recall, among wiccans there are three schools of thought. Some say the Triple Goddess is a symbol, others that she actually exists, while the rest say it's a good old Jungian archetype, a primal image that we all carry around with us in our heads.' She took a breath and added, 'Is that enough? I've taken my exams now, Annie. You don't have to test me any more. What's all this about? A crisis of faith? Because if that's the case, I'm not really the person you should be talking to.'

'I'm just trying to make sense of my life. Do you think there might be something in it?'

'What are you asking me for? The last time I went to church I had water poured on my head. I don't know, Annie. There's probably something in all religions. Maybe it depends on how much you put into it. Why? Are you thinking of converting?'

Annie looked at the ankh once again. She thought of Robert and wondered where he was. She considered the three women and their silent beseeching. Finally she thought about the premonition in the sweat lodge. Suddenly she understood that there were strands joining all three things, a complex web that had her firmly trapped at the centre.

Her thoughts were disturbed by Charlotte fumbling for her hand. 'Annie, I'm so worried about you; you've got to let me help you. You know I'll do anything, anything at all. All you have to do is ask.'

Annie gave her hand a squeeze. Under normal circumstances, Charlotte's words would have been reassuring.

'Thanks,' she said. 'But this is something I have to face on my own.'

'Can't you feel it?'

Esther Barnwell hugged her arms around her and rocked gently backwards and forwards on her heels. Since her outburst in the pub she remained fairly restrained, although there was no doubt in anyone's mind that the shock and grief of her husband's death had unbalanced her. The cremation had passed without incident, and her close friend Muriel Smith had thought the village fête would be the perfect opportunity for her to get out and about once more. Now she was not so sure.

'I said, can't you feel it?' Mrs Barnwell repeated. Eyes closed, head back, she clutched on to the side of the Women's Institute stall so tightly it shook when she moved. A handful of onlookers watched her nervously.

'Feel what, love?' Muriel asked sympathetically.

'There's something rotten in the village, like a bad smell, only you can't smell it, you just feel it. It's everywhere, Muriel, but it's worse near some houses than others. The Cockburns'. And Brian Swift's, and the Elliots'.'

'There might be something wrong with the sewers.' Muriel tried to divert her friend's attention to the tombola. 'Why don't you—'

'It's going to destroy the village. It's changing people. Whenever they come into contact with it. It makes them worse, Muriel, nastier, angrier. It brings out all the horrible things shut away deep inside, all the bad thoughts and feelings.'

'I can feel it too.'

The voice made Muriel jump, and she turned to face Hilly Pitt who had crept up behind them. If anyone else had interrupted Esther in full flow, Muriel would have been relieved, but Hilly was almost as unbalanced. She had never really recovered from the trauma of losing her only son to that awful child-killer more than twenty-five years gone.

'This is a terrible time, Esther. Something strange is happening,' Hilly continued. 'Anyone with half an eye on life in Riddington can see it. Folks have been acting plain bad.'

'If you ask me, it's those awful people up at that camp,' Muriel whispered conspiratorially.

She suddenly noticed Mrs Barnwell's eyes had gone as glassy as marbles and there was a ripple across her face like the first tremors before an earthquake. Before Muriel could steady her, she had stretched out her left arm towards Hilly and was snapping her fingers open and closed rhythmically.

'The sheep *have* no shepherd,' she stressed. 'All faces turn when the walker passes by, and now he is among us. Nature rebels. The anomaly warps the fabric.'

'I've heard those words too,' Hilly said in a distant, dazed voice. '"The anomaly warps the fabric." We have to stop it, don't you see? Before something dreadful happens.'

'Nothing dreadful's going to happen!' There was an edge in Muriel's voice as she tried to stop a scene.

'It already has!' Mrs Barnwell cried. 'They've found the boy!' She looked out past the school, across the fields. Softer this time: 'They've found the boy.'

Hilly Pitt followed her gaze and tears filled her eyes. Then she began to sob repeatedly until she could barely catch her breath, a despairing sound that brought stares from all around.

'Yes, they've found him,' she said in a gasp of utter horror.

'Do you really think this is going to work? Because it just seems too random, if you ask me.'

Martyn was red-faced and there were huge sweat patches under the arms of his white t-shirt. He drove with the window right down and one arm hanging out of it.

'Nobody is asking you.'

Severin stared out of the passenger window, his overcoat pulled tightly around him. They had already tried three farms that morning and he had sensed no sign of Wilde at all.

'Don't you get hot in that coat?' Martyn fired a sideways glance and ground the gears as they went round a corner.

'I'm fine.'

'Look, I'm trying to fucking help here,' he snapped. 'I've never been so scared in my life. The least you could do is fucking talk to me.'

There was a long pause when Severin didn't seem to have heard him, but then he said, 'OK, I'm sorry.'

'Look, I'm worried about Annie, y'know. I didn't think she was in this kind of shit. What are you . . . we . . . going to do if Wilde comes for her?'

'I'm going to make sure I'm in front of her.'

'You'd give up your life for her?'

'Yes.' As Severin said it, he realized it was true. 'I've got nothing to live for. My family's dead. I've got no home or job. All I've got is the nightmare, day in, day out, dogging Wilde's trail. So if it comes down to giving everything up to take him with me, yeah, I'd do it in an instant.'

Martyn said shakily, 'I'd do it for Annie too. I love her.'

'I know you do.'

'Have you slept with her?'

'I'm a gentleman. I don't talk about anything which impinges on a lady's private life. Go ask Annie.'

'You have. You fucking have!'

'What's the point getting wrapped up in all that? The important thing ... the only thing ... is that we make sure she comes out of this safe and sound. Whatever it takes. Deal?'

Martyn nodded and scrubbed the back of his hand across his face. 'OK, deal.'

They fell silent as the relentless hedges and fields rolled by, both feeling they had passed some kind of point which would change their lives for ever.

Hartley Williams' sausage fingers closed around the plastic glass and crushed until it exploded in shards, spraying beer all around. 'I can't stand it any longer,' he hissed. The veins stood out on his forehead like cords.

'Calm down, dear,' his wife said with embarrassment. She placed a hand on his shoulder and he spun round as if he had been burned, fists bunching, cheeks as red as hot coals. His wife recoiled, her hands going to her face automatically.

'Yes, calm down, Hartley,' Bill King said drunkenly. 'I told you we'd get one of them. There was blood on that gin-trap. Lots of it. In fact, it looked as if they might have bled to death.' He guffawed. 'Poor bastard.'

He drained his pint and stacked the plastic glass on top of the growing tower on the ground in front of him. Bill King liked his beer, but even he hadn't been so drunk in a long time, and he felt the urge to get even drunker.

Nearby, Tim Huxton-Smith was oblivious to everyone else in the beer tent – apart from Jane Sutherland. His skin tingled every time he looked at her.

'How long have we been seeing each other now, Jane?' he asked.

'Eighteen months. Seems like longer.' Jane sipped her gin, forgetting her responsibilities as a teacher to be sober and upright in the eyes of the community. She felt breathless, aroused; although she controlled it better than her lover who had a familiar pre-coital flush to his cheeks.

'And we still feel as passionate, eh,' he continued, putting his hand on the small of her back and then slipping it down to her buttocks where he began to squeeze rhythmically.

Jane knocked his hand away. 'Tim, not here,' she whispered in his ear; her lips brushed his lobe. 'Your wife and children might be around.'

'I doubt it. I'm sure they've got something far more dull to do back at the farm.' He licked his lips. 'Where then?'

Jane blushed, but she looked at him expectantly.

'I know,' he said. He took her hand and winked at King and Williams before leading her out of the beer tent and around the back. It had been erected close to the wall of the school building, but there was enough space for a love-nest. He pushed her against the wall, and his hands were all over her body before their lips had met.

Inside the tent, Hartley Williams had started to rant about the travellers to anyone who would listen. His normally well-modulated voice rose and fell like some Bible Belt preacher as flecks of his saliva showered everyone in the vicinity. His wife tried once more to calm him down, but he shrugged her off roughly, the back of his hand catching her sharply on the chin. She pitched backwards on to the grass, as Bill King laughed so heartily it seemed as if he would burst a blood vessel. Williams just cast her a contemptuous glance and then returned to his rant.

Near the bar, two men in their twenties, friends for life, started to argue and quickly moved to throwing punches at each other. A few half-hearted attempts were made to separate them, and then they were left to roll around the ground in mutual combat while everyone else skirted them to fetch their drinks.

All around the fête, at the Christian bookstall, at the bandstand, arguments flared, snide comments were made and tremors began to spread out across the school grounds, breaking up the civilized façades cultivated over a lifetime, and releasing that dark primal thing deep within.

Behind the beer tent, Huxton-Smith and Jane Sutherland were lost in their passion. He had almost ripped her clothes from her. Her knickers and bra were missing somewhere and her dress was rolled in a coil around her waist. His trousers were around his ankles and he had turned her to face the wall so he could enter her from behind, roughly, as he liked.

'Daddy? Miss Sutherland? What are you doing?'

The small voice stopped him like a bucket of ice water. Jane was still moaning for him to carry on. Huxton-Smith was too terrified to turn and look.

His eight-year-old son Daniel was standing in the end of the gap watching them. His face had turned crimson and he looked on the verge of tears. A second or two later, Huxton-Smith's wife Sally appeared and instantly her expression became one of someone who had seen a terrible car crash; the blood drained from her face in a second and her eyes froze wide in shock. To add to the effect, she gave a shriek.

While one of the lovers fumbled with his trousers, the other pulled on her dress as best she could and ran out into the field, realizing in shame that half the people there were watching to see what was happening.

When Huxton-Smith finally emerged, his wife slapped his face in full of view of everyone, and then walked away with their son clinging to her skirt, looking as if the sky had fallen in on him.

For a few moments, the charged scene disrupted the tension that was flooding out across the village fête and at that point, the travellers arrived.

Annie was the first to notice them massing at the gate, a small, ragged army filled with righteous anger, and she watched in horror as they trooped up from the direction of Colthorpe Road.

'Shit,' she hissed. 'There's going to be a war.'

Charlotte broke off her ramble about the latest man in her life who seemed to know her thoughts before she thought them, and gaped in the direction of the approaching crowd as Annie ran towards them. Angela was at the head of the mob, and Annie guessed she was now the unelected leader.

'Don't do this!' Annie pleaded breathlessly when she reached the silent, stoney-faced contingent. 'They'll tear you apart. There're some real psychos lurking in that beer tent.'

'Let them try.' Angela continued to walk, barely deigning to look at Annie. 'If they want to cause trouble it's up to them. We're not here for that. We're just making a point – that we can go anywhere and do anything we want. The law's on our side here. We're not going to be outsiders any more.'

Out of the corner of her eye, Annie saw Hartley Williams and Bill King step out of the shade of the beer tent, King blinking stupidly, Williams' face the colour of a summer sunset.

'It's not going to achieve anything,' Annie warned.

This time Angela did look her full in the face, but it was with a sneering expression of contempt. 'What the fuck do you know, townie.'

Annie tried to find a way of communicating. 'Look, about Tommy—'

'That shit-head! If he won't back us, he doesn't deserve to lead.'

'You don't know, do you? He's dead, Angela. He was murdered.'

Angela looked at her incredulously for a moment and then shook her head, sneering again. 'You'll say anything to protect your own, won't you? Yes, Tommy's dead. That's why I saw him walking around the camp twenty minutes ago.'

Her words brought Annie up sharp, and as she marched on the travellers surged around Annie towards the beer tent and stalls.

Hartley Williams strode out to meet them. 'What the *hell* do you think you're doing?' he blazed.

'Whatever we want to,' Angela replied coldly. 'And you give us any aggro we'll have the cops down here in an instant to break up your little party. We've had enough of you lot trying to destroy our lives.'

The whole ground was silent; conversations died away and the band ground to a halt. Annie felt everybody was holding their breath and waiting for someone else to make the first move.

She could have guessed who would do so even before she saw the flickering stupidity on Bill King's face develop into vague comprehension and then rage. He let out a drunken roar and ran forward with his head down like a bull, his giant builder's fists like sledgehammers. The travellers parted to let him enter their midst and then closed ranks around him so that he was hidden from public view. Annie saw at least three burly youths at work and there was a murmur of concern from the villagers when King didn't appear again.

But the fate of Bill King was soon forgotten as a swooping, anguished cry echoed across the grounds. Simon Connor's father was standing near the gate with his son's body in his hands, and all eyes turned to take in this new spectacle.

'I found him down near the stream,' he said. 'He'd been dumped there.' He looked into his son's dead face and sobbed.

There was a scream from Mrs Connor who had been standing near the band. She crashed against the microphone and then pitched forward on to the ground.

Her husband didn't seem to notice. 'He's been murdered,' he gasped.

The cry from Hilly Pitt went up like a siren, carrying out over the silent school grounds to the village beyond. She tore at her hair and then fell to her knees sobbing hysterically, beating the grass with her fists.

'It's starting again,' she screamed. 'After all these years, it's starting AGAIN!'

25

Simon Connor's death transformed the fête. There was a genuine explosion of shock and grief which affected the travellers as much as it did the villagers and any negative emotions were frozen as the honesty of human affection came through. The travellers drifted away slowly and uncomfortably while those who knew Simon's parents huddled round them to give support.

The police and ambulance came quickly, although no one knew who had called them. And when Simon's mother and father had crawled into the back of the ambulance with the body of their son, and it had pulled away, leaving a field of staring, white faces, grief slowly changed to anger.

Annie gathered her own feelings with an effort and hurried across the grass to an open door in the main school building. She knew she had been on the verge of hyperventilating, and she needed to compose herself on her own. Away from Charlotte, away from all that distress. It was cooler within, and the stillness of the empty corridors eventually began to calm her.

As the echoes of her own footsteps died away, she heard

another sound, faintly, from behind a classroom door. Crying. A woman, not a child. Tiptoeing along, she peeked in through the glass of the door and saw Jane Sutherland sitting at a tiny desk, head down. Annie couldn't decide if she should go in to offer comfort, and find out what was wrong, although she guessed Jane's Neanderthal lover had something to do with it. After a few seconds, she made up her mind and went to tap gently on the door.

With no warning, the hand clamped across her mouth and her yell of shock was stifled in her throat. Another hand grabbed her arms and then she was dragged backwards with her heels kicking. Before she realized what was happening, she had been pulled into the opposite classroom and the door slammed shut. The speed of the backward movement kept her off balance as she was dragged across the length of the room and into a storeroom at the back.

Darkness.

Annie could hear the deep breaths which ghosted warmly on the back of her neck. She kept telling herself not to panic, frantically trying to remember all her rape training, her body rigid, ready to move, fight back, in an instant.

And then she smelt him.

Through the chalky atmosphere, his special aroma: olives and honey and spices. His hand brushed her nose, releasing the natural fragrances of his skin; as unique as a signature. She didn't need to hear him speak to know who had taken her prisoner.

'Hello, Annie.'

Wilde's body was hard against hers. She could feel the muscles of his arms, his chest, his thighs, his embrace almost like a lover's. The power and charisma that radiated from him paralysed her; all she could do was listen to his voice.

'Do not worry. Your time has not yet come. This is just a report on the current situation, shall we say. I feel I should keep you informed as, after all, I am doing this all for you.' A faint smacking noise as he licked his lips. The hairs on the nape of Annie's neck tingled. 'Have you learnt anything over the last few days, Annie? Nod if you have.'

She thought for a moment and then decided it was best not to antagonize him. She nodded once, sharply. She could barely breathe from the pressure of his hand across her mouth; his fingertips bit into her cheek.

'You are a clever girl! My good work is not in vain, then. I have left my little pellets of poison in a few select homes and they are already starting to pollute the pool. You know what I am talking about?' She nodded again. 'Poor Malcolm Hughes has, unfortunately, returned to the ether. He was in a terrible state after your testosterone-crazed friend Mr Severin went wild with his shotgun during their encounter at the Mill. And Malcolm was so happy to be back in his old home, so lovingly converted. I could have reconstructed him, of course, but it seemed unnecessary once he had been exposed. The other little maggots in your village are doing their work well, however. But I would caution you against trying to remove them. You would only cause untold psychic damage to the relatives so happy to have their loved ones back.

'And always remember,' he continued. 'Against the burning heat of my long life, your brief existence is a snowflake that fizzes and is gone.'

His arms were wrapped tightly around her, but not painfully. It was almost as if he was hugging her, but his muscles were so rigid she felt bound, claustrophobic. She could feel that he sensed her fear and was excited by it.

He breathed in deeply and told her, 'You misunderstand death so totally. That was the first thing about you that annoyed me. And then you spoke of this village of yours as somewhere perfect, an Eden. Well, everyone will soon see your village is no Eden, Annie. Understand? And that brings me on to the real reason for our little chat. That ridiculous scene outside with the boy has upset my plans. Lucas has become a liability – I presume you guessed he killed the boy – he seems to have developed a life of his own. Perhaps his evil was just too strong for death to contain. Soon I will be forced to eliminate him, but who knows what damage he will cause in the meantime.'

Annie felt his body tense even more. It was just a subtle shift, but the muscles in his arms felt like cables, and she realized he was more concerned than his words made out. Strangely, it gave her the briefest feeling of hope.

Slowly, he removed his hand from her mouth and at the same time took a step back from her. She couldn't tell if he had moved away several feet or just a fraction of an inch; it was an odd sensation which left all her nerves tingling in anticipation of an accidental touch.

'Have you . . .?' Her mouth had grown too dry to speak. She tried again. 'Have you brought Robert back? I've got to know.'

'If I told you now it would ruin the surprise.'

She bit her lip to stop herself from crying.

'Is he here or is he not?' he mocked in a sing-song voice. 'Would you like to see him again, Annie? Dear Robert. Your little brother.' He leant closer to her ear and whispered seductively. 'Death holds no dominion, Annie. You can have him back if you want. All you have to do is ask.'

She wanted him, yes, she *wanted* him, but it wasn't right! Could it work? Was it possible Wilde was right, that everything could be as it was? Her head was spinning madly between the two extremes, and she knew whichever one she chose would destroy her; on the one side lay damnation, on the other the rest of her life spent knowing she'd had the chance to bring Robert back . . . and lost it.

'Your time is up, Annie.'

'Wait . . .!'

Another mocking laugh. 'Oh, no, you obviously do not want it enough if you have to take so long thinking about it.'

'Wilde . . .' she pleaded.

'Hush. Perhaps I will ask you again, some time before the end. In the three days remaining to you, think about it. Dwell on it. So when the moment comes you will know what to say.' There was cruel humour in his voice; he was enjoying himself. 'Pleasant dreams, Annie.'

The sunlight almost blinded her as he swung open the door. She caught one brief glimpse of him, a shadow slipping through the gap, and then the door slammed and she heard a chair being slipped under the handle. All the tension rushed out of her like steam from a fractured pipe. When she had recovered a minute or so later, she grabbed the handle and rattled it furiously, but it wouldn't budge. She was trapped.

Scrabbling madly in the dark, showering herself with boxes of chalk, Annie set about investigating every inch of her prison. Just as Wilde had known she would.

Only a few minutes later she had reached the top of the shelves that segmented the cupboard and had sent their contents tumbling to the floor. Light streamed in, and for a moment she had to shield her eyes. When they had adjusted, she saw the window that was barely the size of her head and which allowed a view on to a small, private grassed area.

A movement outside the window caught her eye. Wilde was walking slowly across the grass and he turned to give her a cursory mocking wave. It was a fleeting acknowledgement and then he turned his attention to someone she couldn't see, beckoning them to join him. In his hand was an old radio which he switched on and turned up so loud she could hear The Beatles singing 'Ticket To Ride'.

Annie watched, mesmerized. This charade was for her benefit. She held her breath; there was a sudden tension in the air. Wilde's companion finally responded to his summoning and sauntered across the grass to join him.

It was Charlotte.

Ice and fire flooded Annie's system as everything came together in an instant. Charlotte's new boyfriend! The man who knew her thoughts before she thought them.

She felt herself erupt inside and threw her body across the top shelf so she could bang ferociously on the window. She continued until her hands were sore, but Charlotte couldn't hear over the radio. Just as Wilde had planned.

When he held out his arms with a grin, Charlotte ran across the lawn and threw herself into them in a mock-romantic gesture. He picked her up and swung her in the air, and then, laughing, she put her arms around his neck and kissed him.

Annie felt dizzy. She tried to bury the memory of how she had felt the first time she had seen him, but watching the two of them together it surfaced again with another edgier emotion. Jealousy?

Now Wilde was holding out his hands, taking Charlotte's. Then he was kissing her again, passionately, and Charlotte was responding. Slowly he began to massage her breasts. Charlotte didn't try to stop him.

Annie grabbed her hair and tore at it in frustration. One thought ran through her mind in a loop: *Wilde is going to kill her.*

And behind that, another, almost hidden, thought: *And it's my fault!*

Wilde was pulling Charlotte on to the grass, tracing his

tongue down the curve of her neck, down to the top button of her blouse which he tenderly unfastened.

Annie covered her head with her hands, unable to look for a minute. When she forced herself to watch again, the pair were in the throes of passion, Charlotte's legs round Wilde's waist, her hands clawing at his back, her eyes closed tight in passion. And Wilde was pumping, powerfully, skilfully, teasing every ounce of desire out of her. There was no love in what he was doing; it was an animal act for Annie's benefit, whether Charlotte wanted it or not.

Annie felt intensely sickened. Even when she closed her eyes, she could still see the image in her head. Every now and then she peeked between her lids to see if it was over; until, finally, Wilde had finished. He rolled off and kissed Charlotte flamboyantly before helping her to her feet. They dressed quickly, with Charlotte glancing nervously towards the marquee, then hand-in-hand they started to walk away, an innocent picture of two young lovers. Just as they were almost out of Annie's field of vision, Wilde looked back at her and flashed her a grin.

Then, as Charlotte walked on ahead, he raised his hand to his neck and drew his finger across it in a cutting motion.

Annie yelled until her throat was raw. Finally, when she was at her lowest ebb of energy, she heard a noise outside. The chair was being dragged away. Before whoever was outside could open the door, Annie snatched at the handle and did it for them with such force it slammed into the shelves and rebounded.

Jane Sutherland was outside, her eyes red from crying, 'Oh, Annie, you frightened—'

Annie thrust her to one side, sprinted across the classroom and down the corridor, her footsteps echoing like firecrackers. *Faster. You can do it. He hasn't got much of a lead.*

She burst out into the hot afternoon and glanced around, frantically searching for anyone who could give her a lift. The school grounds were almost deserted as the last few revellers drifted away in shock. So she ran along The Hollows and up to the High Street where she managed to flag down a car. She mumbled some story about an emergency in Ashby which secured her a lift to Market Street. Once there, she scrambled out of the car almsot before it had stopped and ran across the road to Charlotte's hotel.

'Please let them not have gone,' she prayed under her breath. Her eyes burned with tears of exertion.

From the receptionist's reaction, she knew she must look a state, but she managed to garble Charlotte's name.

'I'm sorry, dear, she's already checked out,' the receptionist said sunnily. 'Just ten minutes ago.'

Annie's heart plummeted and she gripped on to the desk as if the hotel was going to tilt away from her. 'Did she say where she was going?'

The receptionist smiled again. Annie wanted to shake her until she understood the importance of the situation. 'No, dear. She left with a young man. A very handsome young man.' She winked, and then glanced down at her book. 'Oh, she left this. Are you Annie?'

'Yes, yes, that's me,' Annie said as she snatched the envelope and tore it open. Inside was a single sheet of hotel notepaper with a couple of lines scrawled on it:

'Annie, if you call I've asked them to give you this. I've gone to stay with my new man for a few days! Yes, what a slut! But I couldn't resist him. I'll be in touch. Love, C.'

'Bad news, dear?' the receptionist asked sympathetically.

It was early evening when Annie made it to the travellers' camp, the sun low and blood-red in the sky, patches of midges dancing above the hedgerows. After the heartbreaking episode at the hotel, she had made her way back to the village, knowing instinctively what she had to do, what she should have done all along. She only hoped it wasn't too late. She left a note for Severin and Martyn at the house, and then set straight off for Tarrant's Field.

The atmosphere among the vehicles and tents was solid enough to cut with a knife. And the few travellers who spoke to Annie were subdued, many had already retired early for the night.

She located Miranda sitting on the step of her Bedford van, a birthday cake in pink and white with the jarring symbol of a pentacle painted on the side. She had her eyes shut and her head back, catching the last few rays of the sun as it travelled towards the western horizon. It would have been a peaceful moment, but for the deep threads of strain in her face. She stirred as Annie approached, and nodded when she recognized her.

'Do you know what's happening?' Annie sat down next to her.

'All I know is the crisis we all feared is here. It's only days away, or hours, and it's going to take a lot of us with it.'

'You can sense that?'

'The power of the Mother Goddess is strong. Sometimes I can feel her presence just behind my shoulder. So whatever's out there, it's important enough to bring Her close to this world. And, like I say, it's getting nearer.' Her eyes wandered over Annie's face, trying to see something that would help her. 'I'm scared.'

'Me too.'

'You're at the heart of it. Don't *you* know what's going on?' Miranda was almost pleading.

'I can tell you this, the threat we all sensed in the sweat lodge was a *man*. One who kills people just because he can. And now he's got my best friend.' Her voice shook as she said it.

'Did he kill that little boy?'

Annie shook her head. 'Someone connected to him did that.' She couldn't bring herself to discuss Laurence Lucas and the hideous thing that Wilde did with the dead. But she did tell Miranda that not long ago she had seen Tommy's dead body, covered with blood.

'Our Tommy? When did it happen? How?' Miranda looked more puzzled than upset. 'I'm sure I saw him earlier today wandering around the camp.'

'That's what Angela said this afternoon. Believe me, I saw the body. You don't get much deader.' As the words left her lips, the cold realization of what Wilde had done hit her. Of course they'd seen Tommy, because he was back, polluting the atmosphere in the camp in the same way that Wilde's other acolytes were tainting the village.

'Shit. Poor Tommy!' Miranda closed her eyes for a moment, in grief or remembrance, and when she opened them again, she had forced all her emotions back in. 'Do you think this weirdo's going to come here? To the camp?'

'I don't know. He could do. You'd soon know him if you saw him – tall, dark hair, beard, dressed in black. Goes by the name of Wilde . . .'

'The stranger!' Miranda's eyes widened in surprise. 'He's been here already. He seemed really cool. Chatting, friendly, a traveller . . . he helped us. He healed Scarlet after those townie bastards nearly did for her with a gin-trap.'

'You've been taken in. He's everybody's friend – and he'll kill you as soon as look at you.'

Miranda was staring blankly at the ground. 'Shit.'

'He might be back. If you see him, you get in touch with me straight away.'

Annie looked up and saw a pasty-faced youth with a mohican watching them. When he realized Annie had seen him, he made a pretence of disinterest and drifted away.

Annie had a sudden feeling of guilt that she had just made Miranda a target. 'Look, if you don't want to get involved—'

'I'll do anything that will help.'

Annie took a deep breath. 'I need to contact the Goddess. Christ, that sounds like you could just call her up on the phone! But you mentioned something about a ritual before . . . and since then she has been speaking to me. I've had visions, dreams, and I think it's the Goddess trying to nudge me in the right direction. Miranda, this could be my last chance.' Her voice broke and she swallowed to steady herself. 'I don't know why She chose me, but I'll do whatever's necessary, if it'll save my best friend.'

'You can't make deals with the Goddess, Annie. You have to take what you're given. Somehow you've got what it takes to fight this thing, but I can help by focusing you, giving you more power.'

'How?'

'There's a ritual called Drawing Down The Moon. It's empowering. Tonight would be a good time to do it. We've had a full moon and now it's waning which is just right for sealing the ending on something that ought to be brought to an end.'

Annie shifted uncomfortably. 'I'm not a pagan, or a wiccan, or . . . or a believer in anything. I used to be a Christian, but then my brother died.'

'It doesn't matter, Annie. None of us know what lies on the other side, but it's whatever you feel when you shut your eyes, and listen to all the thoughts and feelings rushing around your head. When you stand on a mountain or in a deep forest. Perhaps there's room for all our gods and goddesses. Trust me, do the ceremony.'

'When do we begin?'

'When it's dark.'

Annie looked at the sun. It moved too quickly, sliding down the sky like a car light speeding away. She felt insignificant, and at that moment what she feared most was that her final spark of hope would disappear with the light.

The night was there before Annie knew it. From the camp it was possible to look out across the landscape and see what marks humanity had made: the glow of Leicester and Birmingham far off in the distance; the lights of Ashby near at hand and the snaking luminescence of the M42; and at the foot of the hill, Riddington, just a handful of streetlights and uncovered windows isolated in a sea of black.

'You've made your point, Wilde,' she whispered to the still night air. 'Why don't you stop now and leave me alone?'

It seemed cooler than it had done for months, and Annie shivered then walked back to the hissing hurricane lamp which hung on a wire outside Miranda's van.

Miranda had given her some water and a few odd biscuits – that was all that was allowed – and she was starting to feel hungry, and a little weak. Miranda was staring up at the old moon as Annie approached, an old shawl wrapped tightly around her shoulders.

'It's time,' she said before Annie had chance to sit down. 'There's a clearing in the woods. We'll go there.'

'I don't know. That's where those creeps were laying gin-traps.'

'Don't worry. After Scarlet was hurt, we found them all and destroyed them. It'll be OK. We won't be disturbed.'

She picked up the hurricane lamp and a packed rucksack and started to trudge up the hillside towards the wood. She was so lost in her thoughts, she didn't even check if Annie was following. The barbed wire fence around the wood had been broken down at one point and Miranda passed through it before picking a steady path among the trees. The lamp caused the shadows in the immediate vicinity to dance and twist oddly, yet further out the darkness among the trunks was impenetrable. All Annie could think was that a bright light in the woods made them an easy target.

'Don't you think it's a bit ... isolated?' she said, trying to peer out beyond the circle of light.

'If you're worried about him, don't be,' Miranda's voice floated back. 'Once the ritual has started, the Goddess will protect us.'

The clearing lay almost at the centre of the wood. It looked like Tarrant had cut down a few trees for firewood. Miranda stood the lamp on the ground and took a handful of candles and small, brass candlesticks out of the rucksack. She lit them and placed them in a circle aoround her before turning off the lamp. Annie felt ghost fingers on her spine as the darkness swelled; the flickering flames seemed poor protection against it. After that, Miranda removed some white cloth which she unfolded slowly. It was covered with strange, black symbols that were incomprehensible yet at the same time menacing. When it was laid out it made a complete circle with Annie, Miranda and the candles within it.

'I'm nervous,' Annie confessed as the wind picked up and tore through the trees. 'I've seen *The Devil Rides Out* one time too many.'

'Don't believe all the bad press. We're not calling up the Devil, whatever He might be. We're communing with a caring spirit.'

She began to take off her clothes and motioned for Annie to do the same. As they stripped, Miranda elaborated in a clear voice, 'We identify the Maiden, Mother and Crone with the changing aspects of the moon,' she said. 'Waxing, full and waning. The ceremony we're about to do is designed to bring the moon's power down to Earth, and therefore some of the Goddess's power too.'

Annie didn't know if she believed in what Miranda was saying or not, but there, in the dark of the forest, it did seem more tangible than on the sunlit step of Miranda's van.

'Drawing Down The Moon is the key rite in our belief system,' Miranda continued. 'Normally we carry it out with a few of us present to maximize everyone's energy, but tonight it's just going to be you and me.'

'Will it work with just the two of us?'

'Every ritual I've done since camping here has been like lighting sticks doused in petrol when you're used to them soaked in water. Supercharged.' She paused and then added, 'I'm almost afraid of how well it will work.'

When they were both naked, Miranda stood in the centre of

the circle and raised her head to the heavens. Annie followed her gaze and was surprised to see how light the sky appeared next to the silhouetted tree tops; she could see a smattering of stars, and in the centre, the old moon.

As Annie went to remove her ankh, Miranda said, 'Leave it on. Silver is the moon's metal.'

'It was my brother's,' Annie replied, almost to herself.

'When I draw down the moon and the power of the Great Mother enters me, I will become, in essence, an aspect of the Goddess,' Miranda said. There was a slight tremor in her voice. 'When that happens, ask me three questions to find out what you want to know.'

'Have you done this before?' Annie asked timidly.

'Of course. Normally I just go into a trance . . .'

'And this time?'

'We'll see.'

Miranda took two ornate goblets from the rucksack and filled them from a plastic bottle of water. 'The water is the moon's element and it will capture the power,' she said. 'It will become charged and afterwards I'll ask you to drink from one of the cups.'

Then she stood with her feet apart and her arms raised to the sky, one goblet in each hand. Slowly she let her head fall back, her long hair flowing loose around her shoulders. Annie sat cross-legged at her feet and waited.

For a long time there was silence, but then Miranda started to mutter something over and over, a mantra that Annie could not discern but which had its own peculiar, infectious rhythm. It seemed to match the pulse of the blood in her head, and Annie felt it begin to drive away rational thoughts, replacing logic with an easy, soothing darkness where images appeared and disappeared at random.

This is it. It's really happening, she thought lazily.

Slowly, she looked up at the sky. The stars seemed to burn like beacons and the moon glowed with an unnatural, steady power. She felt something respond deep within her, the heat flowing down from her stomach into her groin. The ankh on her breastbone seemed to weigh a hundred tons and was at the same time as hot as a furnace and as cold as the Arctic.

Miranda's head was moving lazily from side to side. She was chanting a little louder now. Annie still strained to hear the words, only her ears were filled with the rushing of a sudden wind, until she realized the trees were not moving and the rushing was coming from somewhere else.

Whatever it was, was affecting her eyesight too. Out among the trees she could just make out a movement, lost to the shadows at first, but as it grew closer she seemed to see lights, like fireflies in the branches, and then they became the slow fall of luminescent flakes that she had experienced in the pub in Leicester. Beautiful but at the same time frightening, they moved towards the circle, shimmering and shivering, occasionally coalescing into some kind of shape before breaking up on the verge of completing any form. And the rushing turned into a deep resonant hum that vibrated at the base of her skull.

Miranda seemed to be painted cream, the reflected light from the moon glowing on her breasts, her belly and her thighs. Annie was transfixed by the strands of silver that appeared and disappeared all over her body like hoar frost. This continued for minutes and just as Annie was wondering if that was all there was, the candles guttered and extinguished, and then sound and light vanished as if someone had thrown a switch. Next she heard a crack like thunder.

An arc of pure white light seemed to streak down from the moon itself to blaze on Miranda. She shook like an epileptic and then grew calm. As the arc disappeared, the candles suddenly flickered back into life.

Annie held her breath. Gradually, Miranda's head came forward, her eyes still closed. They remained that way for a second and then they snapped open and looked directly at Annie with shiny, black pupils which seemed to fill the entire socket. Her face was awe-inspiring, yet at the same time beautiful.

Annie trembled before her, mesmerized, but she realized it was her moment and she had to force herself to speak. The words clung in her throat like fish-hooks, but they came out clear enough. 'Who is Wilde?'

Miranda opened her mouth, and her voice boomed hollowly, a disjointed second after her lips moved. 'A man, that is all.'

Annie shivered; the spirit was there, speaking to her. She had the sudden, awful sense of being in the presence of something unimaginable. For a second or two, she gaped stupidly, but then she thought: *Idiot. You have to be more specific with your questions. Don't waste them.*

As if sensing her frustration the voice continued to speak. 'His true name is not to be spoken here. If you listen in the right place, you will hear. He has as many names as there are people. But his abiding name is "The Eternal", for he cannot die even though he was born of woman, and he has lived the span of many mortal lives.'

Annie still felt she had been short-changed. 'Yes, but what are his powers?' The instant she had spoken, she regretted it. She had been looking for more detail on her first question, and had inadvertently wasted another. She felt so dwarfed by the power in front of her she wasn't thinking straight.

In the still between her question and the answer, there was a faint humming like the sound of overhead power cables. And Miranda's face altered slightly, as if in response to an inner quality that seemed to gather the muscles of her features in a different way.

'All things within Nature must pass,' she began. 'But he does not know death and so he exists outside Nature. He is an anomaly, and all his works are anomalies, poisoning and transforming any natural things with which they come into contact. Death has no jurisdiction within his sphere, so he has rule over life and death. That is his abiding power – at his will, dead things can live and living things can die. Nature rebels at his passing like a cancer in the body, and like a cancer he must be cut out. From the birth of mankind he has been The Enemy. From the Dawn he has been opposed.'

Annie thought the power had finished, but it began again suddenly, with passion. 'He is the essence of Man and we are the essence of Woman. He is brutal, cruel and logic. We are caring and intuitive. In the war between Man and Woman he is the Sun, we are the Moon. He is born of the Man-God, you are the Chosen of the Woman-God. He cannot meet death, but he is against life. You must champion life. Find the balance.'

Outside Nature. Supernatural? Annie was dazzled. Nevertheless her mind turned to the final question. But she immediately realized there were *two* things she still needed to know: where he was *and* how to stop him.

She dug her fingernails into the dry soil and forced herself to

270

think. She had to make a choice. Which was the more important?

Come on, you stupid bitch. Choose.

But there was no real choice; closing her eyes, she said, 'How can I defeat him?'

'You may not defeat him. He bears the mark that protects him from the wrath of men. Another will commit the final act. But you have the means of leading to his defeat, and you must first learn his essential name. The solution will spring from that. You must listen to your woman-power, heed the inner voice and follow the signs it lays out. Follow the moon-path through the mind. Salvation will require sacrifice. Accept it, and know the greater good, that life will benefit. When the door opens, call his name.'

When Miranda's voice ceased, the humming died slowly away. 'That's not enough,' Annie protested. She had learnt nothing of use. Tell me more!'

She could see from the silver and white dappling Miranda's skin that whatever had entered her was still there, but from the yawning silence she knew no more information would be forthcoming. For a second or two, everything hung in stasis and then the white light seemed to fizz along Miranda's arms to the two upheld goblets which glowed briefly.

When Miranda spoke again, the strange quality to her voice had disappeared although the altered aspect of her face remained.

'I who am the beauty of the green earth, and the white moon among the stars, and the mystery of the waters, and the desire of the heart of man, call unto thy soul. Arise and come unto me.'

Annie was being summoned. She stood up and Miranda offered her one of the goblets. Nervously, Annie took a sip. Although she knew it was water, it tasted like nothing on earth. As it trickled down her throat it burned its way into her stomach and she felt as if she was being filled with that same white light. It was an unnerving sensation, both ecstatic and frightening.

'What's happening to me?' she asked.

'The sacrament.' Miranda's voice was now huskier, as if it had been strained, but completely her own once more. 'You've been given some of the power.'

271

And then the essence disappeared, fading out like a star at dawn rather than repeating the slow, strong build-up with which it had arrived. Miranda crumpled to her knees, drained by her experience.

'Are you OK?' Annie asked, slipping an arm around her for support.

Miranda nodded, but kept her head down as she regained her breath. After a second or two, she managed, 'What was it like?'

'Don't you remember?'

'Nothing. Just . . . dark. Warm dark.'

'If I wasn't a believer before, Miranda, I am now. There was a presence here, in you.' In the new calm Annie felt exulted by the knowledge that there was something beyond the mundane world. She felt transformed; no longer the old, weak Annie Boulton, beset by doubts and fears, worried by darkness and the unknown. Any despair at asking the wrong questions had gone too, so that she felt only strength and confidence. She had no idea what was to come, but there and then she felt like a star glowing in the night.

Miranda sat back and listened to Annie's account.

'It told me things, but they didn't seem to make much sense. They were like riddles.'

'That's the way the moon-power works. It speaks directly to your subconscious. You've got to forget logical thought processes if you want to understand. You must use intuition, make connections, everything will fall into place.'

I don't have time for things to fall into place, Annie wanted to say. 'It would have been nice to learn something that would have been useful right now.'

'Have patience. Trust. It will come.'

Annie's head was spinning, her contact with the Goddess already seemed distant, but one impression shone uppermost in her mind. She shared it with Miranda. 'What's all this about the war between men and women?'

Miranda nodded weakly. 'It's been going on since the beginning of time, Annie. It's not a war between gods and goddesses – it's a struggle among the people who follow them. But at its heart, it *is* a war betwen men and women – between the way men act and the things women believe. My religion has been beaten down for too long, forced into submission by the sun-power. Now it's coming back. Not to fight for dominance,

272

that's a man-thing. To return to the natural order ... to find the balance.'

'Yes, a balance ... that's what I was told.' Annie looked out into the darkness, comprehending in a way she had never done before. This was about more than Wilde and his threat to her. It was about even more than ridding the world of a force for death. It was about changing things on an enormous scale, realigning power in a world that had been one-sided for too long, and it was all supposed to start with *her*.

Meanwhile she had two full days before he came for her, that was all. In panic, she decided she ought to get back to the cottage to tell Severin what she had experienced.

As both women dressed quickly, there was a chill in the air that Annie had not felt since spring and a wind was blowing, sweeping the odd streak of cloud across the patch of sky above them. She had the sudden belief that there was going to be another storm.

Against a constant feeling that they were being watched or followed, they hurried back through the lonely dark of the woods. When the lights of the camp appeared Annie felt relieved, but she didn't rest until they were at Miranda's van. Miranda was still looking pale and all she wanted to do was lie down, so Annie thanked her and quickly slipped away.

As she moved among the quiet vehicles, the sensation of being watched returned, forcing her to stop and look around. At that moment, she heard her name whispered so softly it might have been a sigh or a breeze. And the winding paths among the various trucks, buses and vans seemed to be deserted.

Then she saw it, a man's figure standing far away near the edge of the camp. He was enveloped by the dark so she couldn't make out his features, but she was sure she knew him. He watched her without moving or speaking, and for a second Annie almost went over to see who it was.

Then some familiar aspect or stance brought back memories, and Annie turned and hurried away as quickly as she could. She was sure she had just seen Tommy.

He entered the camp precisely three minutes after Annie had set off for home, whirling from the dark of the night as if he had been brought in by the howling wind and the approaching storm. There was no one there to see his entrance; all were sheltering in their tents or homes on wheels. But if anyone *had* seen him stride into the circle of vehicles, they would have seen a face filled with hate and eyes which seemed to glimmer with mad, dancing fireflies. His destination was never in doubt.

Miranda's van rocked gently from side to side in the gale. Inside, in the converted sleeping area, she lay face down on her bed, pondering by the light of the hurricane lamp what had taken place that night. His knock on the door was met with a curt, 'Go away.'

The lock splintered like matchwood as he tore an entrance for himself and marched in. The damaged door banged like a death-drum in the gale.

'Do not cry out,' he said simply. 'Or I will kill you. Painfully.'

The haze of the ritual still hung about her and Miranda had to force herself to grasp what was happening. 'What do you want?' she asked.

'Your kind have always opposed me,' he replied bitterly. 'For as long as I can recall, you have been there snapping at my heels like annoying little dogs. For millennia. And you have not achieved one jot. Yet still you try. It becomes wearying after a while, and I find I cannot maintain my tolerance. Women, eh? Cannot live with them – so why not kill them? You are always so much better when you come back from the other side.'

His fingers flexed and closed as if he was fighting with himself. His gaze never left her face, and Miranda could see in the depths of his eyes he was weighing up his options.

'I do wish Annie would learn her lesson. I told her the last time. If she does anything stupid, other people pay the price. Tonight she did something very stupid. Many people will pay the price.' He crouched down beside the bed so he was inches from Miranda's face and smiled cruelly. 'Starting with you.'

She wanted to struggle, but there was something in his eyes which held her fast, like a mouse before a cobra. No words came forth when she tried to speak, but her thoughts seemed to play out on her face for he nodded and then said, 'Get down on your knees before me. Pray to your Goddess. Ask her to save your soul. Who knows? Perhaps She will answer.'

Before Miranda could move, Wilde grabbed her by the hair and dragged her off the bed and on to the floor. She howled in pain, but he didn't let go until she was kneeling.

'I do so love to see women in this position,' he said mockingly.

She looked up at him fearfully and then lowered her head and closed her eyes.

His fist went up and came down so hard her skull shattered instantly. But it wasn't enough to sate his anger. He did it again and again and again, and he didn't stop until the body before him was unrecognizable.

Blood coated him from head to foot, slick on his face and his arms, soaking deep into his clothes. For a moment, it was the old days again. That thought made him fulminate even more.

Ten minutes later, he left the van and moved through the camp, fighting to keep the level-headedness on which he prided himself. He chose his victims at random, as death always did. A bus here, a van there. A tent over there. Men, women, children. He used his knife or his hands as the mood took him, often forgetting that any death would have to look like an accident. He allowed his anger such monstrous vent, that at times what remained didn't resemble anything human at all.

When his rage had run its course, he had to go back and reclaim his victims from the other side, recreating their bodies. By the time he had finished a full fifty per cent of the camp were changed for ever. They waited in their makeshift homes, thinking different thoughts, living different lives, letting the poison of their anomalous existence pollute the fabric around them.

26

The house was thick with buzzing flies so Annie, Severin and Martyn sought relief in the garden, but there seemed no respite anywhere. The storm of last night had blown itself out quickly, and the land seemed fresher for all the rainfall. Despite the circling, bloated insects, Annie felt uncommonly positive. But Severin seemed to have returned to a sullen, emotionless state. Martyn, on the other hand, looked nervous and pale as if he was permanently on the verge of throwing up. Annie could tell he was feeling increasingly out of his depth, but she gave him credit for fighting his fears.

They sat on the garden furniture and ate fried egg sandwiches while they discussed a new strategy. On the previous day, Severin and Martyn had worked until late, covering every farm in the area without discovering any trace of Wilde. Two days ago Annie would have been distraught at the news, but after her experience in the woods she had a new-found optimism.

She spoke firmly. 'I feel sick every time I think of Wilde and Charlotte, and of what she must be going through, but we've got to stay positive.'

'But what are we going to *do*?' Martyn protested. 'Jesus, we haven't got any options left.'

Distantly, they heard the ring of the mobile phone in the kitchen. Annie was moving before either of the other two and she reached the house in a matter of seconds. She had expected a call that morning; Wilde wouldn't miss another chance to taunt her.

'Where is she, Wilde?' Annie snapped before he had time to speak.

His laughter sounded unusually tense. 'No time for any pleasantries, Annie?'

'Where is she?'

'Oh well . . . Your good friend Miss Ames is quite well and has been enjoying my charming company. And she is such a vixen, Annie. So passionate in bed, so—'

'Have you hurt her?'

'There would be no point, would there? What would that achieve? No, I find it more effective for you to know that she is with me and that I could kill her at any time.' He laughed again. 'You have forty-eight hours before I come for you, Annie. I would hate you to waste your last two days worrying needlessly about your friend. So here we are . . . you have my word that I will not harm her until two days hence. I have arranged for her to meet her maker at the very time I come to teach you that final lesson. I should warn you now, however, that Miss Ames is not with me at this particular moment. She is staying somewhere safe and secure where she can enjoy pleasant surroundings. That means, of course, that if you put your energies into finding *her*, you will not be able to devote your time to looking for *me*. What a terrible choice, Annie!'

Annie felt a cold fever. 'Give me a clue, Wilde.' She crossed her fingers and closed her eyes. 'Make me work for it. There's no point if it's hopeless.'

His laughter was brighter and she knew her ploy had worked. 'Why, Annie, so nice to see you getting into the spirit of things! Let me think. You already have a thin hint at Miss Ames' location ... somewhere safe and secure. But here is another one, just for luck: she is surrounded by old people.'

There was a click and the line went dead, but Annie was already buzzing with adrenaline. She replaced the phone and turned to see the others standing anxiously in the doorway. After she told them what Wilde had said, Martyn moaned, 'An old folks' home. Jesus, we're getting the same old runaround. First farms and now this!'

'No, you've got it wrong, Martyn,' Annie said with a tight smile. 'Remember he has my diary and my fax. He knows everything I've done in the last five years. So he knows that I used to help out at Westwood Retirement Home ... And he has a thing about farms. Well, The Westwood was one before it was converted.' She glanced at Severin. 'What do you think?'

'Sounds feasible.'

Annie crossed her fingers one more time for luck. She thought back to the moon ceremony and, when she concentrated, she could still feel that alchemical power which had surged through her at the end of the ritual.

'I want to be prepared for Wilde when I face him,' she said. 'We know the bracelet is the key, and somehow I've got to find a way to unlock whatever power it has over him. Severin, why don't you let me carry it?'

Severin went to take it off his neck and then let it drop back with a puzzled expression. 'No.'

'Why?'

He shook his head, white-faced. 'I just can't. I'm afraid to remove it.'

'Well this is great,' Martyn said sarcastically. 'Annie's the weapon, the bracelet's the trigger, and never the two shall meet.'

Jake Samuels' parents still hadn't broken the news to him that his best friend had been murdered. They had told him not to venture out of doors alone at any cost, of course; but without any adequate reason to stay inside on such a great summer day, Jake simply ignored them as he had done so often before. They were too preoccupied with their own problems anyway; their arguments disturbed his sleep every night, and he was increasingly worried they were going to get a *divorce* like Julie Hendon's mummy and daddy. The word was mentioned too may times, even when he was there. Before it had only been discussed when they thought he wasn't listening. Night-time wasn't much better. His nightmares had been terrible ever since he had seen the monster outside his window, and he knew that there was something horrible waiting in the dark. Once he had tried to explain that he had seen a ghost, but his father had laughed so much Jake had not mentioned it again. The nightmare he'd had the previous night had been the worst, and the ghost wasn't even in it. He had dreamed about a huge, black building, and when its doors had opened he had been sucked in and swallowed alive.

School had shut down early for summer for some reason, so Jake was skirting the village looking for someone to play with – the churchyard, the oak tree with the rope swing, the playing fields, all the usual haunts – but everywhere was deserted. Riddington was quieter than he had ever seen it.

Eventually he wound up at the stream, just across from the school. Floating sticks and then bombing them with rocks soon proved boring, so he decided to build a dam. The last time someone had done that, it had brought the wrath of everyone whose home backed on to the water. But Jake didn't care; he felt like doing something bad.

Some broken planks and a few old bricks liberated from the edge of the playing fields provided the basis for the structure, and it was just beginning to take shape when he heard a voice calling his name. He looked around, but couldn't see anyone. It was eerily calm; the back gardens of the houses opposite were all empty, sun loungers, towels and balls scattered around as if everyone had dashed inside after a storm warning. The school grounds were empty too, and there was no one on the road.

'Jake!'

The sun glared off the water and made it difficult for him to see anything. The Lovers' Bridge. Someone was on it? He squinted. No, *under* it.

'Yes?'

'Come here, Jake.'

'I'm not supposed to talk to strangers.' He returned his attention to the dam. A couple more bits of wood and he would be able to flood the whole area.

'I'm not a stranger, Jake. I'm a friend of Simon's.'

Jake squinted again, and this time he could see a man hunched in the shadows of the bridge. Jake couldn't see his face, but what he could make out suggested he was as old as the youths who hung around the phone box. He could hear something too, a buzzing which seemed to echo in that dark beneath the bridge.

'I know where Simon is,' continued the voice. 'He's been staying with me. We've had such a good time.'

'I'm not supposed . . .' But he *did* want to see Simon.

'Come on, Jake.'

'Oh, OK.' He threw down the wood he was holding and started to splash through the water in the direction of the bridge. When he got closer, the pale, grinning face leapt out of the shadows and Jake went rigid with terror. It was the ghost!

By then it was too late. The ghost, who resembled a teenager with a nice, friendly smile, was staring at him with wide eyes that didn't seem to blink, and Jake suddenly felt he was wading through glue. His mind was telling him to run away, but his legs wouldn't obey. One tear slipped slowly out from beneath his leaden eyelid and trickled down his cheek.

'Where is he?' Jake asked in a dreamy voice.

'In a secret place, Jake. Come with me and I'll show you. He's under the bridge in a great den which no one else can find. You'll be able to play there to your heart's content. Come on, take my hand, I'll show you.'

Laurence Lucas held out his hand. To Jake, it looked strong and supportive, but when he took it the fingers were as cold as ice.

Westwood Retirement Home stood at the end of a short, winding lane on the outskirts of Ashby. It had once been surrounded by green fields when it was a farm, but the previous owner had sold off his land to builders who had thrown up masses of boxy houses on all sides. It still had a couple of acres of green space around it, though, and from the top floor of the old farmhouse it was possible to glimpse the ruins of the castle near the centre of the town.

Annie left Martyn and Severin in the car and banged on the weathered oaken door with a big iron knocker. She felt ready for anything. There was a second or two before she heard the sound of hurrying feet and then the door was thrown open by

Sarah Kirk, the home's owner, who had given Annie her Saturday job in those distant times before Robert had died.

'Annie!' she said with surprise. Her cheeks were flushed and she had a harried expression; Annie knew what a handful the old people could be.

'I'm sorry to trouble you, Mrs Kirk. I know how busy you must be, but I wondered if I could pop in for a minute or two.'

'Of course you can, Annie.' She stepped aside and made a theatrical sweep for Annie to enter. 'We have missed you since you went away to university. You were such a hard worker. And always a smile . . . even when Don Richards was getting a little frisky!'

'I suppose it's changed a lot since I was here?'

'Well, you know how it is in this business, Annie. I could fit a revolving door. Oh, that sounds callous, doesn't it, but you know me!'

Annie dipped into her pocket and pulled out a photo of Charlotte taken just before their exams. 'I wanted to ask if you'd seen my friend Charlotte Ames, Mrs Kirk. I was told she was staying here.'

'Here? Oh, I don't think so, Annie. Not unless she's aged a lot since the photo was taken!' She put her glasses on the end of her nose and examined the picture for a second or two. 'She's a nice-looking girl, but I can't say I've seen her around.'

'How about a man, good-looking, tall, curly black hair with a close-cropped beard? A single gold earring?'

'Well, he sounds more my type, but I can't say as I have, unfortunately. What's this all about then?'

'It's hard to explain.' Annie's mood started to drop. Was she mistaken? 'I had a garbled message that they may have been calling round here. Is it possible they dropped in when you were off duty?'

'Well, I'm not around all the time, as you know. Why don't you ask around? I'll trust you not to pinch the silver!'

Annie thanked her and headed into the lounge where the residents sat silently, watching some game show with glazed eyes. There was a stale odour in the air that seemed to cling to the dull décor of brown and orange. It reminded Annie of a scene from *One Flew Over the Cuckoo's Nest*; she almost expected Jack Nicholson to storm in and insist everybody reject their medication.

Charlotte's picture met with little response – a few half-hearted glances, a mumbled comment or two. She knocked on closed doors, peered into the empty rooms and questioned the antisocial ones who preferred their own company, but no one had seen any new faces.

The final room was built partially in the roof and was reserved for any resident agile enough to negotiate three flights of stairs. The door was open and there was a man with a wizened, brown face and silver hair, sitting at the window smoking, against Mrs Kirk's rules. He looked up nervously when Annie tapped at the door, then summoned her in with a weak smile when he saw it wasn't the matron, as Mrs Kirk called herself.

'Having a break?' Annie asked.

'Oh, aye, just lost in my thoughts. I was watching the birds land on the castle, and thinking about when I was a young 'un.' He glanced back out of the window, and Annie thought how sad he looked.

'I was wondering if you'd seen a friend of mine,' she began, not sure if he was listening. She described Charlotte, but he shook his head slowly and continued to watch the birds swooping in the clear, blue sky. He seemed to have forgotten she was there, and she was in two minds about leaving when something prompted her to ask about Wilde. As she began the description, she was met by a pair of frightened eyes.

'Aye, I've seen 'im. He came up here yesterday. We had a chat . . .' He broke off to cough hard. 'Never thought I'd see him again . . .'

'You've seen him before?'

'Back after the war. He didn't remember me, but I wouldn't forget that face. I was working up in Manchester at the time, and there was a bloody great fire at the factory just before knocking-off time.' His eyes glazed over as his mind drifted back to the horrors in his memory. 'Hundreds of people died. Hundreds! I was lucky to get out myself. As I was climbing out through a window, I saw him walking through the flames like he didn't care if he got hurt. He had a jerry can of petrol and he was swilling it around everywhere, spreading the fire. I thought it was some bloody insurance job, but it wasn't.' He shook his head bleakly. 'George Smithee who was my buddy . . . we worked on the same bench . . . he was trying to get out of the smoke to reach the window where I was. That bastard grabbed

281

old George and threw him back into the flames. It was horrible, bloody horrible!'

He sucked nervously on his cigarette. 'And you know what?' he continued in a sandpaper whisper. 'He hasn't aged a day between then and now. Here's me old and weak, and there was he, just as fresh as he was then.' He looked back at Annie. 'I didn't tell him I'd seen him in the fire.'

'No,' Annie said sympathetically. 'That was probably for the best. What did he say to you?'

'He told me somebody'd probably come asking about him, and if they did I should give 'em this.' He got up creakily and walked over to his bedside table where he rummaged around for a second before handing Annie a folded piece of paper.

She undid it with trembling fingers and read the single line written across it:

Wrong! You are wasting time!

'What's it all mean?' the old man asked as he slumped back into his chair. He looked as if he had a sack of coal on his shoulders, and there were tears in his eyes.

'I'm going to stop him,' Annie said quietly. She screwed up the paper in defiance, and then repeated with more force, 'I'm going to stop him.'

'I wish someone would,' the old man said, before turning his attention back to the black specks soaring across the cloudless sky.

'Who do you think you are?' Martyn stormed around the kitchen, rattling the dinner plates before dropping them in the sink. 'Swaggering around with your shotgun like you're fucking Clint Eastwood or something.'

Twilight was drawing in and Severin sat at the table cleaning his gun sullenly. 'It's a tough world, kid,' he muttered. 'Sometimes a gun is the only answer.'

'That's just what I'd expect from you! What a macho git! And I'm no fucking kid, you old bastard.'

'Well, what are *you* going to do when we run into Wilde? Slap him across the face, and ask him kindly to leave the country?'

'That's about as effective as your approach, isn't it? Just how smart is it to go after a guy who's immortal with a gun?'

'At least it'll hurt him. And when he's in pain his defences will be down.'

'You wish . . .'

Severin threw the gun on the table and stood up so suddenly his chair went flying backwards. Martyn moved backwards too, until his back was pressed against the fridge. 'You're starting to irritate me, kiddo,' Severin hissed. 'With your whingeing and your nothing's-ever-right attitude. "This won't work, that won't work." Why don't you do something positive for a change and get your ass outta here before I shove this shotgun up it and pull the trigger.'

'Mr Emotionless loses his rag,' Martyn jeered nervously. 'Why don't you—'

'Will you two knock it off!' Annie stormed into the kitchen and confronted them with her eyes blazing. 'You've been going at it hammer and tongs ever since we got back from Westwood. Do you think this bickering is doing any good?'

Severin grunted something under his breath and picked his chair up before focusing on his gun as if neither of them were there.

'We just don't know what to do next,' Martyn said, glancing at the clock. 'The more desperate we become, the harder it is to think. And we're all knackered after driving round every old folks' home in the area.'

'We had to do it,' Severin muttered. 'There was a chance . . .'

'Not much of one!'

'Martyn,' Annie cautioned.

He sighed and started to wash up. 'Christ, I don't even know why I'm doing this. What's the point of having clean dishes when he has your friend, and when you . . .'

'Only have a few hours to live?'

'Sorry.'

'Severin was right about one thing, Martyn. We've got to be positive. Otherwise we'll just dig ourselves into an even deeper hole.'

Martyn moaned, 'Well, you're the one who's been having all the dreams and visions. Why don't you go and have a kip? Something might come to you.'

'Maybe I will.'

He looked at her askance for a moment, but instead of retorting he froze at a strange noise outside the kitchen door. A snuffling and a dragging sound, vague the first time, but drawing closer and closer. They all fell silent and looked at each other questioningly. No one went to investigate. Snuffle-snuffle. Kritch. Kritch. Kritch.

There was something obscenely unnatural about the noise that made it impossible to place.

The blood had drained from Martyn's face. 'Don't open the door, Annie.'

She had a sudden ringing thought: *What has he done now? What atrocity is about to enter this kitchen?*

In the tense atmosphere, the click of Severin closing the shotgun sounded as loud as if he had fired it; Martyn and Annie jumped together. The noise was a few feet away from the door now. Whatever it was must have dragged itself along the path from the gate that opened on to the road – the locked gate.

'Don't open the door, Annie,' Martyn repeated. It was a plea, not an order.

Severin was at her side, exuding strength. The shotgun, his prop and talisman, was ready; she had rarely seen him without it over the last few days. He went to open the door, but Annie pushed past him and swung it open herself.

The light from the kitchen cast an oblong of illumination across the patio and into the garden, and framed in it was a dog crawling on its belly towards the house. The mongrel's eyes rolled and foam flecked from its mouth as it struggled to heave its body forward by its front legs. Its rear legs were impaled on a piece of wood which went through its haunches from one side to the other. Almost half of its head was missing, exposing what was left of the brains which glistened in the light. There was no way it could live with such injuries, yet it was alive, after a fashion. It snuffled and then whimpered pitifully.

Annie's hand went to her mouth. She heard Martyn rush through to the toilet where he retched loudly.

She turned away as the tears welled up in her eyes. 'It's Flash.'

'What?' Severin's gaze was firmly fixed on the dog.

'My pet . . . our pet . . . Robert's and mine. He died after he was hit by a car. He was thrown on to a piece of wood supporting a sapling at the side of the road. Dad buried . . .' She bit on her knuckle as the snuffling sound filled her head. 'Dad buried him at the top of the garden.'

Snuffle-snuffle. Kritch. Kritch.

Severin swallowed loudly. 'The bastard! Talk about twisting the knife!'

'He's showing us what he can do. This is what happened to all those people ... those dead people ... in their old homes. How can their families live with it?'

Gently, Severin put his arm around her shoulders and led her back into the stark light of the kitchen.

'You can't leave Flash . . .'

He nodded.

A minute after the door closed behind him, she heard the retort of his shotgun and then again, and a few seconds after that, twice more. Then he returned for a box of matches and some lighter fuel.

In their run-down house, the Cockburn family screamed. When his mother refused to leave him alone, Brian Swift muttered, then howled. Christopher and Katy Elliot tried to enjoy their newborn, but the crying wouldn't stop, and then they were crying too, screeching. One voice, one pain.

The darkness had come into the village, seeping out of the night and into homes whose electric lights could not dispel it. And it went further, into the hearts of the people, a deep, liquid darkness that poisoned all it touched.

Wilde's time had come.

There was darkness and there was warmth, and then there was light from two flickering candles and a faint chill in the air like autumn. Annie could smell dampness and a touch of mould. She shivered a little and pulled her arms around her, wondering where the bed had gone, feeling an odd sense of disorientation spinning through her head. Slowly she looked around.

She was in a cramped room with a low, beamed ceiling. The walls were covered with bookshelves packed with huge leather-bound tomes fastened with a clasp, pocket-sized monographs and squat, chunky references, jutting out haphazardly as if they had been thrown on to the shelves without any thought. There were maps and charts, some hanging half-open so Annie could see ornate yet simplistic views of the world and intricate studies of the constellations. Odd artefacts choked àll available shelf space and covered a rough-hewn table in the centre of the room:

a blackened, desiccated severed hand, a crystal ball, a small carved box, statues, jewelled daggers, a globe, and much more.

The man watching her from the far corner of the room was lost among the clutter so she did not see him at first. He had large sad eyes that looked as if they had seen the suffering of thousands. Hollow cheeks and greying skin made him appear cadaverous, but he had thick brown hair. His clothes were Elizabethan, a doublet and off-white ruff.

'Another dream,' Annie muttered.

'There are no dreams,' he replied in a faint, echoey voice. It shocked her alert.

'Who are you?'

There was an unusual displacement when he replied; he moved his lips and a split-second later the words appeared like a soundtrack running out of synch with a film.

'The son of the snake is eating himself. Can you see?' He held up his left hand. The fingers were snapping shut into a fist and opening out again, too fast and jerkily as if he was not controlling the movement himself. 'Nature rebels against the transgression of the natural order. He is an anomaly that warps the fabric.'

'Are you talking about Wilde?'

'He has the ear of John Dee. I am out of favour. The jewelled crown bows down to listen. No good will come of this.'

'I don't understand.'

'Many have opposed him along the twisting road of time. Oh, my mind fragments. The words are not in tune. Can you hear my voice? So hard. So hard.'

'Who is he? Tell me something I can use.'

'He made murder. The sheep have no shepherd. The name is the spell.' He closed his eyes and his lips trembled.

Annie felt uneasy; the dream was too real. She shivered again; it was getting colder. She wanted to go.

When the Elizabethan opened his eyes, he seemed to have found renewed strength. 'Life and death are one to him,' he said in a clearer voice. 'He has been taken out of the cycle and the old rules do not hold. The Eternal is his taken name, but not the one the shepherd knew. I cannot say it. The bracelet is the key. All who have opposed him have given our souls to unleash its power. Each one a drop that fills a mighty cup. Still not full but almost. His punishment is humanity's suffering – the test

286

was made for both. He carries the mark that orders man not to slay him. You must know this and heed it or suffer. The true solution lies elsewhere.'

'I'm afraid that he's going to destroy everything I love.' Annie bit her lip and felt the pain. 'How can I find the solution?'

Slowly, the Elizabethan raised his left hand and held it out to her; the fingers were still opening and snapping shut. She knew that he wanted her to take his hand, but she was too terrified.

'The graves are empty,' he said, smacking his lips like an old man with no teeth. 'Men will fall like chaff. You stand on the edge of the chasm.'

His hand jerked open and closed more frantically for her to take it. The fear was building in her. She wanted to scream.

'No!'

27

The news of Jake Samuels' disappearance was around the village by 8 a.m. By 9 a.m., his distraught parents had conferred with the police and drawn up detailed plans for a search of the area using volunteers. Hartley Williams somehow managed to place himself in charge of co-ordination.

Annie heard about it from the paper boy who relayed the news with breathless excitement. She immediately hurried to tell Severin and Martyn who were drinking coffee in the kitchen.

'Lucas has got another one,' she said baldly. 'Jake Samuels. I used to babysit for his mum and dad. He's a really nice lad.'

Severin and Martyn both looked as if they'd had so much grim news they couldn't digest any more. Martyn placed his forehead on the kitchen table in resignation and crossed his hands on the back of his head. 'It's like the end of the world or something. One disaster on top of another as everything falls apart.'

'There's going to be a search,' Annie continued. 'I wonder if we should . . .'

'More shooting in the dark,' Martyn sighed.

Severin looked at Annie curiously. 'What is it? Have you thought of something?'

'I feel that we should go up to the camp.'

'*Feel*? Oh no, it's Witchy Annie and her crystal ball.' Martyn threw his hands in the air theatrically.

'What's to lose?' She picked up the car keys from the side and headed towards the door. 'We're going to the camp.'

Martyn carped on for most of the journey until Severin threatened to open the door and roll him out, which seemed to have the desired effect. Annie felt too tense to get involved. The clock on the dashboard was ticking away the minutes of her life with such a loud mechanical click it was all she could concentrate on.

They left the car in the field next to the campsite and wandered over to where the coaches and vans were parked. Annie was disturbed to see how much the camp had changed since that first day when the travellers had arrived. There was no music thundering from the sound system now, no children playing, no one cooking or chatting. The colourful spark of life that had crackled incandescently among the community had gone and all that was left was a flat, dead atmosphere that made her feel she was looking out across the surface of an inhospitable planet.

Severin tensed the moment he stepped out of the car and surveyed the jumble of vehicles.

'What is it?' she asked.

'We shouldn't go in there,' he warned. His eyes were black slits in his stony face.

'Is Wilde in there?'

'I can't tell. Whatever's in there is so bad it's swamping any sign of Wilde. It's like an oil slick on the water, suffocating anything in its way.'

Annie took a few steps and then she felt it, like she had crossed some invisible barrier. It was the same atmosphere of despair and hatred that radiated out of the homes in Riddington where Wilde had seeded his revenants, but it was much, much stronger. She almost fell to her knees and gagged. 'What the hell's in there?' she whispered.

'Let's just stay away.' As Severin pulled her back, Annie saw Martyn was deathly pale and trembling. She grabbed his hand and squeezed it.

An angry cry cleaved the still air and they all spun round to see a tight-knit group of people emerge from the vehicles and start to head towards them. There was only a handful of them, but they seemed fearful and hunted, and they clung together as if they expected attack from any side. Angela was at the head, her sallow complexion even paler, her face filled with fury.

'Get away from here!' she yelled as they drew closer. Her furious shout was taken up by one or two of the others, men Annie had had friendly conversations with only a few days earlier.

'Maybe we should head to the car,' Martyn ventured. As he spoke, Annie saw that most of the group were carrying lumps of wood and two of them had metal bars.

Severin grabbed Annie's arm and hauled her back, and then all three of them were running to the car with the travellers in pursuit. Severin pushed Annie into the back seat first, but there was no time for him or Martyn to clamber in before the group was upon them.

Martyn cried out in pain as a steel bar crashed across his back, slamming him into the side of the car where he slid down. Annie watched in horror as his pained features were crushed against the glass by the blow of a fist. He disappeared from sight, but before anyone else could get to him, Severin pulled out the shotgun.

Annie's initial alarm subsided when she realized he wasn't going to blast away. The shock of seeing the weapon halted the travellers for a moment, but Angela's fierce hollering in the background stimulated them to resume their attack. One raised a lump of wood over his head to bludgeon Severin. The American's response was quick and forthright; he whirled the shotgun round and cracked the butt in the traveller's jaw, putting him out like a light. Then the gangling youth who had already attacked Martyn brought his crowbar down sharply on Severin's shoulder. Annie winced when she heard the impact which she guessed had shattered the bone. But to her surprise, there wasn't a flicker of pain on Severin's face; he might as well have been hit by a feather duster.

The traveller was surprised too, which allowed Severin to use the shotgun once more and bludgeon him to his knees. At that point the others backed off despite Angela's protestations and, to maintain his advantage, Severin cocked the gun and blasted it into the ground where it raised a torrent of dust. In the shock of the retort, the travellers ran back a few yards, giving Severin time to help Martyn into the passenger seat and throw himself behind the wheel.

They lurched forward from a standing start with a screech of tyres and a shower of dirt, and then Severin put his foot to the floor as the car skewed across the field towards Blacksmiths Lane.

Annie put a hand on his shoulder as he drove. 'Are you OK?' He nodded.

'Aren't you going to ask about me?' Martyn whined. 'Well, for your information, my back's agony, but I'll live. As if you care.' But he calmed noticeably when Annie gave his shoulder a squeeze too.

'What brought that on?' she said. 'They've never been that violent before, and it's not as if we're strangers.'

'Their minds have been poisoned,' Severin replied coldly. 'Wilde's evil is strong in that camp now. Just as it is in the village.' He paused and then added, 'It's worse than we thought.'

As Angela wandered back into the camp, she tried to work out what had come over her. However angry or wary of strangers she had felt in the past, she had never acted like that. What was happening to them all? The camp was not the same since Tommy had left, although she was loath to admit it. In fact, she wasn't entirely sure he *had* left. She had glimpsed him a couple of times walking among the vehicles, but when she had shouted his name and chased after him, he hadn't waited. Well, if he wanted to avoid her, that was his problem. Typical, childish male. He couldn't cope with the fact that everyone now turned to her for advice, since that night at the campfire when Wilde had arrived. She felt a sudden rush of sexual excitement in her groin at the thought of her lover, and it was followed by images of his tongue on her skin, his teeth, his nails. Her desire was so powerful she had to repress it forcibly. There would be time for all that later tonight, when he returned as he had promised.

The communal atmosphere had changed, hadn't it? That sense of fun and spontaneity had somehow turned sour. People rarely ventured out of their vehicles or tents. The evening campfire was a sparsely attended affair, just a few of the old acid-heads smoking dope and reminiscing. There was no buzz, no passion; it was just flat.

She stopped next to Tommy's old black bus where Scarlet now lived, and listened. The door never opened; the inhabitant was cocooned in her own little world with Kurt whom Angela occasionally glimpsed through the window doing whatever he did inside. Didn't they eat any more? There was no music either. There was *always* music.

Angela continued her meandering path around the camp, faintly depressed that her ascension to leader had not been met with round-the-clock partying. As she moved in from the edge of the camp, she came to a small, secretive area formed by three parked buses where a few teenagers who harboured dreams of a music career used to jam. She was surprised to see it was filled with bodies, around twenty-five, lounging on the grass. A small fire cracked and sputtered in the centre.

Only there was something not right. No one was jamming, or talking, not even laughing; there was just a cold, stony silence.

Angela walked up to the fire. 'Come on, it's not that bad!' she said with what cheeriness she could muster. 'We showed them all at that pathetic little fête! They're not going to run us off this land!'

There was no reply, not even a flicker of interest. Staring into their blank faces for the first time she was disturbed by what she saw: their complexions, never brilliant, were almost grey; their hair uniformly lank and greasy; but it was their eyes that really unnerved her. They were all heavy-lidded and stupid as if they were on smack. All of them. Men, women, children: silent, stupid and staring.

'What is it? What's wrong?'

No response. It was *really* starting to unnerve her now. One of the hundreds of flies that had descended on the camp over the last few days landed on the face of a young, shaven-headed woman, crawled right across it without a hint of irritation from her and then disappeared into her half-open mouth.

'Don't treat me like this,' Angela snapped, trying to mask her alarm. 'If you'd rather have Tommy in charge, you only have to say.'

At that instant, the eeriness of the scene finally broke through her defences and she turned quickly and marched off, only looking back when she was several vehicles away.

No one was following her. Through the gap she could see them all watching her, still blank, still stupid. Chewing her nails, she hurried back to her own van, wishing Tommy was around.

'We should help,' Annie said firmly.

'Sure,' Severin said sarcastically. 'And consign you and your friend to the morgue. We just haven't got any spare time.'

The thought of Charlotte brought a swell of emotion, but she couldn't let it deter her. She had to trust her intuition and she felt it was vitally important they join in the search for Jake Samuels. On the way back from the camp, they had almost crashed into a van with the unfortunate legend 'Jake's Quality Meats' in bold black letters on the side. Then at the house, Martyn had switched on the radio just as a news report about the police hunt for Jake was about to start. And when she had glanced out of the window, in the briefest instant as her eyes focused, she could have sworn the shadows on the lawn formed a strange pattern which seemed to be an exact likeness of Jake's face. When she looked again, it was just an incoherent jumble of light and shade. *Coincidence*, Severin would say, but Annie knew it was more than that. *Synchronicity*. Jung and Robert Graves were hailing her across a gulf of time and space.

'I'm telling you guys, it's the right thing to do. I sense something will come out of us helping to look for Jake.'

Martyn stopped fiddling with the bandages Annie had bound around his chest and back and said, 'We're just worried about you, Annie.' He bit his lip. 'I'm more than worried, I'm terrified. What's going to happen when that bastard comes for you tomorrow? We'll do anything we can. Fight till we drop. Die even! Christ, I don't want to lose you.' His voice broke, and he swallowed. 'What I'm trying to say is, I don't want to waste any time when we could be doing something to find Wilde. Lord, I think I'm more nervous than you are.'

Annie gave him a hug and he flinched when her arms fell across his back. 'I love you, Martyn,' she said, and gave him a kiss, too. 'But I'm not being stupid. I know what's at risk here and I'm not about to throw Charlotte's life away on a whim. Or my own, for that matter.'

'You really think this search is going to help us?' Severin asked.

She nodded. She felt on a roll, as if she was in a quiz and her intuition was a voice shouting out the answers that only she could hear. She had ignored it for so long, and now it seemed like everything was coming up trumps.

'OK,' Severin said. 'You're the boss. Let's do it!'

The search had lasted for nearly three hours and Annie was soaked in sweat and feeling nauseous from the blazing heat of the midday sun. Almost all the village had turned out, the bitterness and anger that had manifested itself at the fête now replaced by a quiet concern that masked a real fear. Jake's parents hovered in the background like zombies, occasionally fighting back tears, while everyone else formed short, quiet lines combing the fields, or small groups roaming the lanes and the banks of the stream.

No one could bring themselves to voice what they secretly felt; that Jake had been taken by whoever killed Simon, and he would not be seen alive again.

Some of the villagers seemed surprised to see Annie and Severin involved in the search, but their offer of help was accepted without any bad feelings. Annie remarked how Wilde's plan was backfiring on him if he was trying to foment trouble in Riddington; Jake's disappearance, and Simon's death, had actually brought everyone closer together. Only Hartley Williams kept his distance, firing mistrustful looks in their direction.

Annie, Severin and Martyn joined a small group scouring a cornfield behind the church. The hot, laborious search sapped her energy, but it relaxed Annie's mind and she found herself drifting back to the moon ritual, until connections started to appear out of nowhere.

Swish, swish, went the corn.

Her dreams, all the men with outstretched hands. 'When the door opens, call his name.'

Swish, swish.

Esther Barnwell talking about the sheep without a shepherd. The Elizabethan in her dream saying the same.

Swish, swish.

The Elizabethan saying, 'He made murder.' And the thought that she was only one step away from his name, just a step, just a . . . and then it disappeared again.

Swish, swish.

And then . . . and then . . . Wilde's voice on the mobile phone. '. . . surrounded by old people.' Westwood Retirement Home? The old man on the top floor who was still haunted by Wilde's atrocity. *Old people. Old. Man.* She looked up from the corn and at that moment she had a perfect view across the sun-drenched roofs of Riddington to Blacksmiths Lane and the travellers' camp, to Tarrant's Farm, and next to it the brooding, dark mass of Tarrant's Wood. Where she had experienced the moon ritual and been transformed. Where she had lost her virginity and been transformed. Which she had written about in her diary . . .

She turned suddenly and grabbed hold of Severin's arm, her eyes blazing bright, the adrenaline pumping so hard she could barely control herself. 'I know where he is!' she gasped.

Severin looked at her askance. Martyn dropped the stick he was using to search the corn and ran to her side.

'There's a hut in Tarrant's Wood, near where I went for the moon ritual. I used to go and play there with my friends. Martyn, you remember it?' Their smiles sparked memories. 'Tarrant keeps all his woodcutting and coppicing tools there. Wilde was playing a game with me . . . *surrounded by old people.* Listen, the hut is next to a group of really old oak trees in the middle of the wood. There's a myth that they turn into men under a full moon and hunt for children. They're called The Old Men of Riddington.'

There was a breathless moment as three minds sparked and fired as one and then they were all running across the field to the road.

The wood was as still as the Arctic wastes. No birds called in the tree tops, no breeze rustled throught the branches. Silent, unnatural.

Annie, Severin and Martyn stood at the broken barbed-wire fence which had been put up to keep out trespassers and watched silently among the trees. The air was filled with the dry, musky scent of leaf mould and the acid tang of fern and willow herb.

Severin already had the shotgun under his arm. Martyn had his air rifle, a pathetic substitute, but he had spurned the chance to carry a knife. 'I'm not getting in that close,' he'd said honestly. Annie carried no weapon.

'Are we ready?' Severin asked.

'As we'll ever be,' Martyn replied, wishing he was a world away.

Annie was oblivious to them both. Her mind was fixed firmly on Charlotte, replaying images of her face, keeping her alive by the power of thought, dreading what Wilde would do if he was there when they broke in. Over the past days, they had discussed this eventuality over and over again, addressing every possible scenario. In the end they'd agreed that if they ever did crack his hideout, they had no choice but to try to steal up and use the element of surprise to keep Wilde at bay while they snatched Charlotte back. Martyn had argued consistently for them to seek the police's help, but Annie and Severin made it apparent that that wasn't an option.

Severin was the first to step past the fence into the shade beneath the trees, with Martyn close behind. Annie followed, tense, but remembering everything she had been told in the moon ritual. She listened and watched, but she used her intuition most of all, shutting down her logical thought processes to the bare minimum.

The flies were there too, as they were everywhere, but at first there were not as many of them. Severin picked a path that offered the most cover and soon the bright white light of the afternoon sun was far behind them, as they were plunged into the wood's inner world. The further they progressed, the stiller it got, an absence of all life apart from the flies which were growing in force, zipping here and there, diving down at their heads so all of them were repeatedly swatting the air.

Lord of the flies, Annie mused. *The Devil Himself.*

They didn't see the shack until they were almost upon it. It squatted low among the trees: a simple structure of rough wood, daubed with creosote and dirty windows which had been covered with roof felt on the inside since Annie's last visit.

Severin paused behind a massive oak tree, one of the original Old Men, and watched the hut surreptitiously. Martyn stood behind him, his ragged breathing loud in the silence. Annie could see it had taken tremendous courage for him to accompany them, and she knew he was only doing it for her. She wished, for his sake, he was a long way away.

'Do you think he's in there?' Martyn asked nervously.

'Can't tell.' Severin watched and listened intently. 'There's no sign. I can't sense him, but that's no guarantee.' He looked at Annie. 'I can go in alone.'

She shook her head. 'We do it together, or not at all.'

'Remember, we've got surprise on our side,' he said, more as reassurance to Martyn than anything. 'Our main objective is to get Charlotte out. If that's all we do, that's all we do.'

'No more talking,' Annie urged. 'Let's do it before I faint.'

He nodded, bent low and ran for the side of the hut where there were no windows. Martyn and Annie were just a step behind. The chemical stink of creosote filled the air, but they could hear no sound.

Severin slunk around the corner and took up a position next to the door with Martyn on the opposite side of the entrance. The atmosphere was so charged all Annie could concentrate on was the thundering of her heart.

He's waiting for us in there, she thought. *He'll just pick us off as we go in.*

Severin nodded to Martyn and then he counted down from three on his fingers before stepping back and kicking the door hard. The flimsy, old wood burst off its hinges with a resounding crack and Severin was into the dark interior before it had hit the floor. Martyn lunged after him as Annie ran forward.

A second later, Severin was back in the doorway trying to keep Annie out, his face contorted. But it was too late. She had seen past his shoulder.

Charlotte.

Annie roughly shoved her way in, the shock locking her emotions into some kind of stasis. All she could do was stare.

The inside of the hut was swarming with flies. They crawled through all the shadows that clung to the corners, fat and lazy and not even buzzing. The hut had soaked up the heat and it was as hot as an oven. There was a smell like vomit and ripe fruit that permeated everything.

Charlotte hung from the beam that supported the roof, the noose taut around her neck. Her face was swollen, her eyes wide and staring. And all Annie could focus on was the creaking of the wood and the rope as Charlotte swung gently from side to side, *creak-creak-creak*, until it seemed to fill her whole head. A sound that would never go away.

There was a note pinned to the wall. On it was scrawled in big block letters: 'I LIED'.

Severin stared at the body aghast. 'He's lost it,' he muttered. 'He was always so careful to leave no trace. This is pure venom! He's gone insane.'

Severin put a hand on Annie's shoulder and tried to pull her away, but she shrugged it off. She couldn't take her eyes off her best friend. There were no tears at all, just a horror that burrowed so low into her being it felt a part of her. And still that awful creaking carried on.

Finally, she did let Severin lead her out of the stink and the flies. Martyn had already collapsed against the outside wall, looking as if he had been hit in the face. Only Severin was anything near normal, an automaton, going through the motions. Annie could see the signs in his face though; something was broken there.

'How long . . .?' she asked, as he made to re-enter the hut.

With a handkerchief over his mouth, he climbed on a workbench and leaned over so he could cut the rope with his knife. Charlotte fell to the floor with a sickening thud. Outside, Martyn heard and winced.

When he had climbed down and removed the handkerchief, Severin reappeared. 'A while. Probably since he snatched her.' He swallowed loudly before continuing. 'I think he wanted you to crack that clue because he knew you'd come here geared up . . . positive . . . so it'd hit harder this way.'

Annie muttered, 'He was right.'

She felt the panic begin to rise through her; the knowledge that time was running away, and found herself sobbing uncontrollably.

Severin pulled her tight to him and dragged her well away from the hut into the still, dead air of the wood. 'We've got to keep going,' he said quietly.

She choked back a sob and added, 'To the bitter end?'

They both became aware that Martyn had walked up to them, his eyes not resting on anything for more than a split second. 'I never thought anything like this would . . . It's all beyond me . . . all this. Shit! I'm not strong enough, Annie. I'm sorry. I just haven't got what it takes. I need a break tonight. On my own, at home with my mum. I'll be back tomorrow, when I feel a bit better . . .' He started to walk away. His voice floated back weakly. 'I'll see you, y'know, tomorrow morning. Before anything happens. I'll—'

They watched him go and then Annie clutched at Severin's lapels and pulled him so she could look into his dark eyes. 'Oh, poor Charlotte.'

'I know, honey. But you've got to think of yourself now. That's what matters. Getting through the next day.'

'I can't. Charlotte's dead.'

Martyn stumbled blindly back through the wood, not really sure if he was going in the right direction, not aware of anything apart from the fact he had to get away. His head was fizzing and blinking like a beat-up TV.

Trees loomed into his field of vision and he careered off them, looking for the sunlight that would draw him out of the shadows. Over there. No, over there. No ... He broke into a jog, his chest tight, his breath coming in gasps.

The man had stepped into his path before he knew it. In fact, it was a few seconds before his brain registered anything apart from the fact that a patch of darkness had briefly obscured his vision. Then the details came: black, curly hair, beard, piercing eyes and a wide, wide grin.

'Your turn now, Martyn.'

Severin phoned the police anonymously and left details of the whereabouts of Charlotte's body, claiming he had stumbled across it while looking for a romantic hideaway with his girlfriend. They couldn't afford to get tied up in questions and accusations. Let the police do what they wanted. Annie only had hours left.

He watched her through the doorway as she sat at home with her head in her hands. She seemed to have lost all fight. Wilde had chosen the perfect way to knock her down. All the way back from the hut she had talked about the premonition she'd had of her death; it was as if she was determined she was going to make it come true.

The light was fading and night was creeping in.

28

First Robert, an innocent who died for nothing. Then Charlotte, the same.

The clock ticked. It had been ticking at sun-up and now it was still ticking at 9.03 a.m.

What was the point in getting up? Charlotte was dead, and she would be next; let him come. Downstairs, clank and clatter, the slam of doors, Severin trying not to seem tense. His gun banging against door jamb and walls. Good old Severin.

The room was too warm and there was a troupe of dust motes spinning a complicated dance in the sunbeam that squeezed through the half-drawn curtains. Outside, another fine day. Her last day. The small window was open and she could smell the countryside drifting in. No exhaust fumes like there had been in Manchester. Annie closed her eyes and opened her eyes and closed them again.

Severin coming into the room once, twice, three times, more, bringing breakfast which remained uneaten on the tray, trying to pep her up, using threats and cajoling. Nothing worked. She hardly knew he was there.

All her thoughts turning inward, spiralling down inside her, where the shadows crept and crawled.

Down inside.

Down.

Annie didn't realize anything was happening until it was well under way. One moment, she had her eyes closed trying to recall the first time she had met Charlotte; the next, she looked up at the clock and into a distorted room which seemed to have had all the colour leached from it. The monochrome effect made her feel distinctly queasy.

Curious, her thoughts came together for the first time that day as if she was swimming out of murky water. In the sense of calmness that descended on her, she knew what was happening.

It was coming.

There was a sound like a rushing of wind as doors opened then slammed throughout the house, progressing towards the bedroom. Finally, her own door opened and crashed shut and a stillness descended on her black-and-white world. A whispering began on the edge of her consciousness. Annie couldn't make out what was being said, but many voices seemed to be circling her, questioning, doubting, worrying.

She felt no sense of panic; her emotions seemed to have been cauterized and she felt she was an outside observer looking into a room where a bizarre scenario was being played out. Her wandering gaze fell upon her parents' dressing table, a mahogany antique topped by three mirrors at angles to each other. The startling reflection showed a female presence hovering in the room just beyond the end of the bed. Annie looked back; the space was empty. With a shiver, she focused on the mirrors, each of which showed a different aspect of what was there, but not there. In the first, there was a lovely young girl, raised in the air, turning slowly, eyes closed. The second showed the well-rounded Mother performing the same action, while in the third, the wizened Crone followed suit.

As she watched, Annie felt a tingling sensation in her toes which spread slowly along her legs, to her groin, her womb, her breasts, and then to her mind until she felt herself aflame with some inner power. She seemed to be floating an inch above the bed, but the sensation was lost when she heard the whispers echo around her head.

'Accept death.'

'Draw strength.'

'Accept death.'

Three different voices giving the same message. Annie's muscles relaxed and her eyes closed as she gave herself to the silvery-white light that now seemed to be burning within her.

'Draw death into your heart. It is not an ending.'

'It is one of the three.'

'Death, rebirth, life.'

Yes, I understand, Annie replied, although she couldn't feel her lips moving.

'Death.'

'Rebirth.'

'Life.'

She opened her eyes to look at the wondrous sight which now filled the bedroom; a snowstorm of light, white flakes shimmering and falling in a never-ending cycle from ceiling to floor, and in the mirror, the three figures whirling faster, dancing with life and passion. She knew instinctively what it was: the Spiral Dance, the invocation of Everything That Was.

She seemed to be suspended in it as if time meant nothing, and in it she was being cleansed and renewed, made ready. She found herself rising and growing, ready to face the trial that lay ahead.

Down into the snowstorm she plummeted, then up, up. And out.

Severin jumped up in surprise when Annie walked into the lounge. 'Are you OK?' he asked hesitantly.

'I'm fine.'

'I thought you weren't—'

'Let's not talk about it.' As she put her arms around him and rested her head on his chest, the smell of him brought back all the times they had spent together, talking, making love, and in those memories she found a comfort and strength.

'I don't want to lose you, Annie.'

'Don't worry,' she whispered.

'We could always stay here and barricade ourselves in,' he suggested half seriously.

Annie shook her head. 'Sooner or later he'd get to me. And now that Charlotte's gone, we've got to concentrate on little Jake. We're the only ones who know Laurence Lucas has him.'

'If he's still alive.'

'And if he is, we've got a responsibility.'

'What about you . . . and Wilde . . .?'

'I'll face up to that once Jake's OK, or at least once his parents know one way or the other.'

Severin shook his head irritably. 'We haven't got the faintest idea where he is.'

'Look, Lucas has probably taken him where he took those other kids all those years ago. Habits like that are difficult to break if you're a psycho.'

'So where is it?'

'I don't know,' Annie replied. 'But I know who will.'

Severin didn't look convinced. Annie knew it was his nature to rage against the night, but it was her life, and her death, and the choice had to be hers.

*

The Green House on Starling Lane was a fine old Riddington home, rambling and with an enormous garden filled with nooks and crannies that were perfect to hide away in. Annie remembered visiting it as a little girl and she had never forgotten it. *The perfect children's garden*, she thought. And then she realized the dark irony: it was a long time since it had been filled with the laughter of children.

Hilly Pitt answered the door and ushered Annie and Severin in as if it was as natural as day that they would be standing on her doorstep. Annie knew her well enough to say 'Hello' on the street, but it was her reputation she knew better: sad and pitiful in the eyes of the adults, a witchy madwoman to the children. Since the loss of her son, Hilly had walked a fine line of sanity, sometimes pitching one way, sometimes the other. Annie remembered her mother explaining, 'Death does strange things to people.'

'We're sorry to trouble you, Mrs Pitt,' Annie said, turning down the offer of tea and biscuits.

'Oh, no trouble, my dear,' she replied amiably. 'My Derek's out for the afternoon and it's nice to have company. Is this your young man?'

'Ah, yes, I guess it is.' Severin introduced himself.

'I suppose you've come about my Kenneth,' Hilly said. There was a glimmer in her eyes when she spoke his name which cut through the fuzz that seemed to enshroud her.

'How did you know?'

'Oh, quite a few people have mentioned Kenneth recently. Since the killings started again, and poor Simon died and little Jake disappeared. He's been gone so long, and forgotten by everybody but me until now. It's funny, really, when you think about it. Do come with me.'

She led them upstairs to a small room at the back of the house. It was a boy's bedroom, specklessly clean, the bed made, the toys positioned carefully as if the owner would be back to pick them up at any moment. Airfix model aeroplanes hung from cotton across the ceiling. A small pile of yellowing *Superman* comics stood in one corner and on the bookshelf there were hardback annuals, *Eagle*, *Lion*, boys' books that Annie had only ever seen in jumble sales.

'I come up here every day, sometimes twice a day,' Hilly said, sitting on the edge of the bed. 'Derek doesn't like it so I try to wait until he's not around. He doesn't think it's healthy. But you can't forget your own son, can you? You can't pretend he never existed. I try to imagine what he'd be doing now. What kind of job he'd have, a good one, of course. What his wife would be like, and what little grandchildren there'd be for me.'

As Annie knelt next to her she tried to comprehend exactly how much Kenneth's death had taken away from Hilly – Lucas had destroyed two lives. And now Wilde had brought him back so he could do it again, to other families.

'Hilly, I'd like to ask you a few questions,' Annie began. 'It might be upsetting for you so tell me if you don't want to answer them, but it's about Laurence Lucas, and Kenneth.'

Hilly Pitt composed herself and then said, 'You ask away, dear.'

Annie glanced at Severin for support and then continued. 'When Lucas snatched Kenneth, do you know where he took him? Did he have somewhere special that he went?'

'Oh yes, he did. His lair, he called it. Or his den, one or the other.'

'I think I remember now. Did it have something to do with the bridge? When anybody talks about Lucas, they always mention the bridge.'

'That's right, dear. The Lovers' Bridge. Underneath it, he found a hole when he was a boy, and he dug it out and found this cave place under the road next to the stream. I don't know if it was natural, or if the builders had put it there when they were making the road. Anyway, that's where he used to go. The police had the entrance all filled in after it came to light. After he killed himself.'

Severin was nodding to himself. It seemed likely that Lucas would return straight to his old haunt if he had returned from death. They thanked Hilly and slipped away.

Back at Blackstone Cottage, Annie called the police to tip them off about Jake's likely location. But after speaking to a harassed desk sergeant, she was told that the bridge had '. . . already been searched, thank you madam.' Not satisfied, she then called Jake's parents, but the phone rang without answer.

Severin was standing at the door, and she could see he knew what she was going to say. 'We've got to do it ourselves.'

'You're crazy! Can't you understand – this is your last day.

303

Wilde's not going to give you an extension just because you're playing the Good Samaritan.'

'And Lucas isn't going to give Jake a stay of execution either.' She sighed wearily. 'Forget me for the moment – Jake is a little boy. You saw what Kenneth's death did to Hilly. If I can do anything to prevent that happening again, I will do.'

'Even give up your life?'

She paused so she was sure of what she was saying. 'Even give up my life.'

As Annie stood on the banks of the stream and watched it rolling under the bridge, black as glass, she had a moment of startling clarity. 'The black river runs and never stops,' she whispered.

'What?' Severin was at her side, following her gaze.

'It was something Mrs Barnwell said in the pub that night she went crazy. She was talking about this.'

'What else did she say?'

'Something about talking in the voice of a clown, and about small feet not waiting. She was seeing Lucas, Severin! She was in touch with things like . . . like I've been.'

There was a sudden rustling in the branches above their heads as if something had moved among them. They both looked up and saw only green leaves and blue sky, but Annie shivered.

'Nature is rebelling,' she whispered.

'It's great that everybody's getting help from the other side,' Severin said cynically. 'It would be even better if we could all understand the messages.'

'Shall we go?' she asked hesitantly.

'Yeah, it's now or never.'

Severin led the way down into the water, splashing along the middle of the stream over the gravel shoals where it was barely more than a summer trickle. Annie followed, momentarily noting the sensation of the cold seeping through her boots. The shadows beneath the bridge seemed impenetrable at first, but then dissolved to reveal details in the darkness.

They had to stoop to get under the archway with its atmosphere of dank cellars. Severin kept banging his head on the brickwork and he cursed in a whisper which echoed louder than he expected.

About halfway down, there was a dry bush which seemed to be growing out of the bricks. It wasn't until they were parallel to it that Annie glimpsed the blackness behind it. She motioned to Severin who grabbed it and pulled it free easily. Behind was a gaping hole in the wall, a few clumps of new cement still clinging to the edges where the bricks that had filled it in since the sixties had been chipped out. Through the hole was complete darkness.

Severin hovered on the edge for a second and then in one movement, turned and kissed Annie gently on the lips. Then he slipped through like a fish swimming into the mouth of a shark. Annie didn't hesitate; she was behind him, inches from the soles of his boots.

The hole led on to a tunnel in the packed earth, shored up every now and then by old crates. Severin's body filled the cylindrical space almost completely. As Annie inched after him, she had to fight a sweaty claustrophobia that amplified her fears. And she could not shake off the image of Riddington's young boys being dragged down there by feverish hands.

Severin suddenly disappeared from view, and the darkness was replaced by a flickering grey. It provided enough illumination for Annie to realize the tunnel ended with a slight drop into a much larger area. She felt Severin's hands helping her out before she saw him, and then they were side by side in an area about the size of a double garage with a ceiling about six inches above Severin's head. Hilly Pitt had been right: it was impossible to tell at a glance if it was man-made or natural.

The faint light came from a stubby candle in a saucer which flickered in the far corner and sent shadows licking around the walls as if they were living things. The first thing that struck Annie was the smell; a florid stench of rotting meat. Then she slowly became aware of the scattered animal corpses, like the ones they had previously discovered: rabbits, birds, a fox, a badger – some decomposed, some placed on spikes. Their carcasses were piled across the floor as well as hanging from the ceiling.

Strange muffled sounds came from a small boy at the back of the cave, who was almost lost in the sick heaps of decay around him. It was Jake Samuels, bound and gagged, lying on an old, dirty mattress. Lucas was nowhere to be seen.

They rushed forward together to free him, but as they closed on him, he suddenly began to struggle, thrashing against his bonds with his arms and legs as his eyes grew wider.

'It's OK, Jake. We're here to help,' Annie said soothingly.

Even when he could see who Annie was, the young boy didn't calm down. He started rolling about, the grunts behind his gag more frantic.

'What's wrong with him?' Severin said gruffly.

'He's just scared.'

Annie stood back while Severin took out his knife and dropped to his knees to cut the oily rope tied around Jake's hands and feet. Up close, they could see the boy was filthy and covered with numerous cuts and bruises.

'Poor bastard,' Severin hissed.

The bonds cut easily, and the moment he was free, Jake tore at his gag. 'Look—!'

The pile of rotting animal corpses next to him erupted before he could finish his sentence. Laurence Lucas pivoted up from the waist, covered with the grue of the creatures which had been burying him. His arm went upwards and then down in an arc, the penknife glinting in the candlelight.

Annie screamed. Severin tried to fend off the blow with his right arm, but he was off balance and on his haunches. The blade penetrated deep into his chest just above his heart. And at the same time, the flies that had been lying with Lucas swarmed angrily.

As Lucas struggled to drag his penknife out, Severin lashed out with the carving knife he had pocketed from the kitchen at Blackstone Cottage. It tore across Lucas's throat, and produced a gush of something black and foul-smelling which burst out and showered Severin.

In that instant, Severin threw himself forward and dragged Lucas down and then they were fighting like wildcats among the rotting carcasses, both knives slicing into flesh in a frenzy of cutting.

Before Annie could move to help, Severin yelled, 'Get the boy outta here!'

She forced herself to move, grabbing Jake by the arm and pulling him back to the tunnel.

As they slithered in, she was sickened to hear the sounds of butchers at work gathering momentum back in the cave. She prayed it was Lucas who was being cut.

'I'll be back, Severin,' she whispered. 'Just hang on. Hang on!'

306

They fell out of the other end of the tunnel into the cold water. Jake was crying in distress by then and Annie hauled him to his feet and quickly helped him under the bridge into the light.

'Just run as fast as you can, Jake. Scream and shout! Someone will come. Make them take you to the hospital.'

Annie knew it was futile asking him to bring help back. He looked hysterical and on the verge of collapse. She should have stayed with him, but she had to get back to Severin. She couldn't bear it if he died too. She watched Jake for a few seconds as he splashed along the stream, screaming and crying, and then she turned frantically to go back to the cave.

Wilde was standing in the shadow of the bridge next to the water's edge. He grinned as the shock on her face slowly turned to horror.

'Time to go, Annie.'

His fist came down swiftly and hard, smashing into her face, and the last thing Annie remembered was falling backwards into the cold, black water.

PART THREE

Journey's End

All I seek, the heaven above
And the road below me.

ROBERT LOUIS STEVENSON
'The Vagabond', *Songs of Travel*

29

Music filled the darkness. Drizzling rain easing into the spangle of keyboards, then bass and drums, pulling her into the whirl-pool. When the vocals began, Annie succumbed to the flow of memories. She was reassuringly warm in a drifting dream; she was behind glass, hot plastic seats, motion, soothing, the deep rumble of an engine. She was on a train. Christmas, so close she could smell the tree, the baking mince pies. Happy times just around the corner. The music, relief from a bleak world.

The Doors. 'Riders on the Storm'.

She opened her eyes.

'Pleasant memories, Annie?' Wilde leaned deeply into her field of vision until he was all she could see; his stare was so hot she could barely stop her eyelids from snapping shut. He brought a cassette recorder in front of her face and clicked the off switch. The music stopped.

'Severin?'

'Let us not concern ourselves with that sad, bitter man. You are the woman of the moment, Annie. It has been so long since we had the opportunity for a really good talk. And here we are—' he gestured around, ' – the perfect opportunity.'

They were sitting at the back of a bus, fifties vintage, driving through the open countryside. There were a couple of pasty-faced young travellers lounging in the front seats and a slightly older man driving. Annie's disorientation was difficult to con-trol; her head was thundering from Wilde's blows and there was a throbbing around her right eye.

'You bastard,' she said. 'Charlotte.'

'Ah, yes. Miss Ames. Poor, troubled girl. An energetic lover, however.'

'There was no need—'

'There was every need. Besides, she will not be missed.'

With a tremendous effort, Annie suppressed her anger and

grief; he wanted her to break down and he was pushing all the correct buttons, but she wouldn't allow herself that weakness.

'How is your little Eden, now?' he continued. 'Still a gloriously simple and secure place of caring, open-hearted people? Or have I succeeded in opening your eyes?'

Annie ignored his question and looked out at the vaguely familiar countryside. 'Where are we going?'

'Around. I instructed our driver to tour the area for a while. It calms me, you see. I have to seize whatever opportunities I can for peace of spirit. My curse is to remain constantly in motion, tarrying never long enough to form any deep relationship with another being. If I stay too long in one place I soon feel I have swallowed a poison. The alternative, this ceaseless travelling, this restlessness, is—' he curled his lips distastefully, ' – also unbearable.'

'I hate you.'

'My teachings have not been entirely in vain, then.'

Annie wanted to fly at him, to wreak vengeance for all the suffering he had inflicted. But when she half moved, there was a bolt of pain in her wrists which were roughly tied together with baling wire. It had cut into her flesh and blood was smeared over her hands and forearms.

'I must apologize for causing you any discomfort,' he offered. 'I had no intention of causing you *physical* pain. Psychological, of course, is an entirely different matter.'

'*Why*? Why am I so important?'

He laughed. 'You are not important, Annie. Not at all. It was just something you said on the train, something which touched a nerve . . .'

'It must have been quite a nerve!'

'Oh, it was. The rawest nerve of all.'

'What was it?'

'That would be too much to reveal. Because of it, however, I felt the need to teach you a very important lesson – an illustration of the futility of human existence. You do not appreciate, Annie, and you do not perceive. You and your kind squander, you complain; nothing is ever right. I, with the life I lead, can see the riches you possess.'

'You're talking gibberish again, Wilde.'

'Most amusing of all is your constant search for security. You build little communities, create illusions, to show that death does not conquer all. Even when individuals die, society continues, and so you feel you have in some way beaten the reaper. Created immortality in a few tiny shacks. My little task before I move on my way is to expose that lie, and to show the reality behind it. You live, you die and you do not know if there is anything beyond. That is the true horror.'

'You're obsessed with death, Wilde. You should get a life.'

These words stung him. 'Get. A. Life.' He formed each word carefully and spat it out. 'You have a saying in this era: life is a bitch and then you die. For me, life is a bitch and then you do *not* die. Life remains a bitch for all eternity. Obsessed? Certainly. I think I am justified.'

He completed his diatribe by slipping his hand into his pocket and pulling out something which he kept hidden in his palm. Annie couldn't tear her eyes away. She caught a glimpse of an ivory handle, and then she heard a click and a blade shot out. Wilde held it towards her like a branding iron, turning it slightly so the light glinted off the razored edge.

A cold heat rose from her belly but she didn't flinch. She looked through the blade into Wilde's face with as much defiance as she could muster. A faint smile ghosted the edge of his mouth; he liked his games.

Slowly he brought the blade forward until its tip teasingly touched her cheek. Despite herself, Annie's breath caught in her throat. Then, with a flourish, he spun the blade round and plunged it into his heart. Annie cried out and felt the flow of her own blood speed up as Wilde's gouted across the aisle between them and splashed across her t-shirt. With horror, she watched as he sawed at his flesh with a grimace, chipping at the rib, making the hole ragged and meaty. The blood pumped out in spurts with every beat of his speared heart as Wilde made his point.

He left the hilt of the blade protruding from his chest. Annie could tell from the angle and depth that it was puncturing a ventricle, severing an aorta. Her head swam. When he pursed his lips and said mock romantically, 'Be my Valentine, Annie,' she had the fleeting impression he actually meant it.

There was a slurping gulp and then the scrape of metal on bone as he withdrew the knife. Surprisingly the bleeding had almost stopped, and there was the oddest impression that his life-fluid was actually flowing backwards into that gaping wound. He was bursting with vitality, but his face left no doubt that his demonstration had caused him pain.

'That hurt,' he said dispassionately. 'You might have to pay for making me do that.'

There was a flinty rebellion in her voice. 'If you thought that display would shock me, you caused yourself pain needlessly. After the last few days, there's nothing more you could do that would disturb me.'

'Really?' In his smile, there was an icy void. Annie thought of Robert and shivered.

Wilde pressed the meat of his chest together and held it. 'I can suffer but I cannot die. My body heals itself. This is my punishment for one moment of thoughtlessness, a punishment which has now far, far exceeded my original crime. In your civilized society criminals are given remission for good behaviour. Their sentences are finite. Not mine.'

'Some people wouldn't consider eternal life a punishment.'

'Then they would be very stupid. Do you recall our discourse on death on the train? Its importance in bringing meaning to existence? Tying up loose ends, ending a story so that it can be understood? That is forever denied me. I remember when the continents were a different shape. I recall stalking across the land when the earth was in its infancy, scrabbling for food at a time when death never left one's elbow. I have stood in the shadow of half-built pyramids, participated in the sacking of Troy, watched the murder of Caesar, dabbled in the court intrigue of Elizabeth the First and the Palace of Versailles. I have felt every possible sensation, tasted every food, smelled every aroma, heard every sound, read every book, experienced every form of sexual gratification. Nothing is new. I know everything. Except one thing. And you wonder why I am obsessed with death?' His voice was almost lost in a whisper. 'It is a futile existence which would have destroyed lesser beings. I have survived by finding my own rationale.'

'Which is?'

'Why revenge, of course. I upset the status quo, ruin the Grand Plan as best I can, sweep the pieces from the board whenever the game gets interesting.'

'That sounds very childish.'

'No, it is very considered. The Master Chess Player, the Lord of All He Surveys, has imposed his definition of goodness upon this world. Well, is my punishment *good*? Is it *just*? I think not. And so I strive to eliminate the sickly stain of goodness wherever I encounter it, to show the essential truth behind His grand lie. There is no good. No bad. Just people.'

'You're striking out at God?'

'In all His forms. Wherever He has left His mark.'

Annie looked out of the window across the sweep of the green countryside. 'You're mad,' she whispered.

Wilde laughed. 'Ah, but I cannot be punished any *more* for my actions, Annie. I carry my hell round with me.'

'Why were you punished? Who are you?'

'I told you,' he said, 'names have power.'

Annie glanced down at Wilde's wound. It seemed smaller, the exposed meat had all but disappeared. 'You were human before your . . . your punishment?'

'Yes.'

'What about the powers you have . . . the dead coming back?'

'My punishment was eternal life, but a great deal of baggage came with that. It took me out of Nature, where nothing is immortal. I break the laws of the planet. I am an anomaly. I am like a hole in reality. I found I could manipulate the laws of nature. Life and death became tools to wield. I am a magician; I can pull the recently dead back from the brink of eternity while their essence still burns brightly. The long-dead are more problematical. It takes great concentration and it leaves me exhausted, but I can normally find a trace in every corpse, a memory of what was, that allows me to recreate them. They are never quite right, though. Too much has departed – the goodness – and all that is left is the base.'

'Tommy in my bedroom . . . all that blood?'

He nodded. 'A simple trick.' He smiled. 'When you know how.'

The bus began to slow down. Annie could see the orange, blue and white of a panda car parked further down the road and two yellow-jacketed policemen standing before it. It was a road block, obviously random searches for the child-killer. She glanced sideways at Wilde, but he was already on his feet, scanning the obstruction.

'Time to move, Annie!' He grabbed her upper arm and hauled her to her feet. She cried out as the baling wire bit her flesh.

Wilde barked an order and one of their pasty-faced fellow-travellers lurched blankly down the bus. When he reached them, he dropped to his knees and flicked up a hidden trap door in the middle of the aisle. There was a small, dark hole beneath it.

'Where they used to hide their drugs.' Wilde nodded towards the black space.

It took a second or two for Annie to understand. 'In there? You've got to be joking! It's barely big enough for a dog.'

'No time to argue!'

Wilde's fist crashed into the base of her skull and she slammed forward on to the floor. There were flashes of purple and pink, and she was dragged backwards and thrust roughly into the hole. She noted obliquely that it smelled of hash and dogs and that there wasn't enough room to turn even half an inch, and then the lid went down and she was suspended in complete darkness.

Claustrophobia engulfed her in seconds. It was difficult to breathe and for a while she was sure Wilde would leave her there until she died in choking agony, finally tying up the circle that had begun with the premonition of her death. But just as the panic started to claw its way into her throat, she told herself it wasn't Wilde's way to let her die like that. When her moment finally came, he would want to be there, lapping up every bit of suffering.

That calmed her enough to focus on the muffled sounds coming through the floor. The bus had pulled over, the doors clanking open, and she guessed one of the policemen had climbed on board. The voices were too dim to make out words and they ended too quickly; there was the mechanical clunk of the doors once more and the engine restarted.

After the bus set off on its way, Wilde didn't free her and that brought another wave of panic, but she rode over it and gave herself to the drone of the engine and the thrum of the wheels on the road. It was twenty minutes before she heard a change in the surface noise and realized the bus had pulled on to rougher terrain. A few minutes later, it stopped with a judder.

She was almost blinded when the lid flew up, but the sunlight was quickly blocked by Wilde's body as he leant in, grinning.

'Journey's end,' he said.

He pulled Annie out of the compartment without any concern for her well-being, cracking bones and bruising flesh until he had her standing shakily. She recognized instantly where they were.

'Jack Tarrant's farm,' she said.

'That is correct.'

'I came here—'

'I know. I watched you. And that lump of deadwood, Severin. I enjoy watching you, Annie. You move with a certain grace that belies the weight you have placed on your own shoulders.'

'What's happened to Tarrant?'

'Dead. Both him and his shrew of a wife within minutes of my arrival. I brought them back immediately; so as not to draw attention by their absence. Their home gave me a perfect base.'

He herded Annie up the bus and out into the dead heat of the yard behind the farmhouse where flies swarmed and the choking dust blew in billows.

'Of course, I knew Severin would be searching for me. He never rests, does he? I had to perform some strenuous magick to cloud myself from his perception, and give me the time I required. It worked better than I could have hoped.'

Their destination was one of the disused outbuildings at the back of the yard, the only one with a complete roof. The inside was filled with the fruity odour of sheep dung and damp, but it was cool.

'Your new home,' Wilde said, taking a pair of shears and snipping the wire around her wrists.

'How long are you going to keep me here?' she asked, although they both knew the real question – *how long until she died*?

'Enjoy each day as it rises, Annie. When the time comes, it will come.'

He pushed her on to a pile of dirty straw near the wall. A rusty chain with a manacle hung above her, and he fastened it round her seeping right wrist, saying, 'This is a new stage in your life, Annie. My work in the village is almost complete, and I will allow you to see it before you die. Now I have business elsewhere. In the meantime, someone will come and prepare you for your imprisonment whilst you await my personal tuition.' He smiled cruelly. Annie didn't ask him what he meant.

30

'I'm dying.'

The thought reverberated through Severin's head like a footfall in an empty mansion. All his senses were heightened, and he wondered if it was the same for everybody in those minutes or hours before death came; the sound of the stream was unfeasibly loud, the smell of the dank hole and the loam into which his face was pressed was overpowering, a foretaste of the grave. The most prominent sensation was his burning wound but it wasn't just his injury which was killing him; some of Lucas's foul essence had found its way into his veins and was spreading out across his body in a lethal wave.

And Annie, sweet, lovely Annie? She had touched the part of him he had kept safe since Marj had died and she would be back for him soon. There was still a chance. Unless Lucas had got to her.

Or Wilde. He felt unconsciousness creeping up on him, flashes of light in the dark of his head, and wondered if it would be for the last time.

'John. John. Listen to me.'

The words were gossamer-thin and floating in his mind, but they had an emotional pull. The voice was familiar. Every nerve in his body was on fire in a network of agony. And the only other feeling was the bracelet pressing against his chest like a block of ice. If only its cold could stop the heat consuming him.

'John.'

Again, the whisper, tugging insistently. It gave him the strength to roll on to his back. There was only a little light in the hole, but in one corner the luminescence seemed to gather in a veil of dim stars. It shimmered and gathered shape until he could almost make out details: a face, a hand, eyes, hair. A pre-death hallucination?

'John, my love . . .'

'Marj?'

It was her, or some strange reflection of her. The tears welled up into Severin's eyes. 'Marj, I'm sorry . . . for Annie . . .'

'John, you can't stay here. You have to get out.'

The words seemed to come from within the hole as well as from within his head. He could not ignore them.

'I'm sorry Annie . . . Marj . . .' He was losing it again, drifting back into the dark.

'John, you've been kept from me for too long. We'll be together again.' The voice was harsher, urging him to hold on to the real world. 'You have something you must do.'

'Are you there, Marj?' he said in a moment of sudden lucidity. Severin couldn't tell if he had actually heard her voice, or if it was his own, rattling around his head, and when he squinted at the stars they became just flashes on his eyes that leaked away in a glitter trail.

He didn't have a body; he had a latticework of pain that glowed radioactively. But he had to think beyond that, focus his mind and energies. He had to move.

Severin's concept of time had skewed so badly he had no idea if he had been in the hole for hours or days, but when he eventually managed to crawl out from under the bridge, it was twilight.

The sky was pink and gold and blue and for a while he thought he was in Monterey, then Nashville, then Florida, moving east towards the darkness. His mother and father, both long dead, sat on the newer bridge further down the stream. He stopped for a while, reminiscing over old times. They laughed just like they used to, and his father promised to teach him how to strip down a gear box one day soon.

Then his mother turned to him and said something which made him take his leave: 'The Cathedral doors were open to you so long ago. Why didn't you come through?'

No one saw his half-walk, half-crawl along the road; Riddington's residents were shut up in their homes with their own personal nightmares.

Severin's thoughts trickled out of his head like water from a rusty bucket; nothing made any sense any more. Night came like a clap of thunder, or so it seemed, the sudden darkness swallowing the sun and filling the landscape with murky shadows that closed in so tightly around him he could only see a long, oddly lit tunnel ahead of him.

At one point he was convinced someone was following him, and he snapped his head around every ten seconds to scan the empty road, his lips muttering some half-remembered mantra to keep the evil at bay.

In a field next to the Old Lodge, a large white horse that he had never seen before snorted and whinnied and whisked the air with its mane, and he decided obliquely that that was what he had heard behind him, the sound distorted by the trees and hedges. He had never seen the horse before. It glowed a spectral white in the gloom, and its eyes seemed to flicker like red coals in a furnace. Every now and then it would raise its front hoofs and pound the ground, and Severin seemed to hear pathetic squeals of pain as if some tiny, defenceless animal was being repeatedly hammered into the grass in a sadistic torture that kept it permanently on the edge of death.

In the shadow of a nearby tree Severin noticed a man he had not seen since the first few weeks of his long, weary search for Wilde. His last recollection was of the man lying in a bath of the most brilliant red with an expression of such bovine stupidity at his fate that it was almost comical. Wilde always did have a sense of humour. The man's wrists had been opened in twin parallel lines from the heel of his hand for three inches towards his elbow. The right way. Impossible to stitch. He would have known his death was inevitable from the moment Wilde started to wield the razor and he would have had to lie in that lukewarm water and wait for his life to seep out of him. It had been in an upmarket room in a ranch hotel on the outskirts of Palm Springs. He had been waiting for his wife, an in-patient at the nearby Betty Ford Clinic where she was being treated for drink and drugs addiction. His wife had checked out an hour after the news had been broken to her, and she was dead of an overdose the next day.

All of these things Severin knew instantly. In a section of his brain still working correctly was a grim repository of death, the log of Wilde's awful tally, names, backgrounds, the way they went; as much as he could possibly store. Above all else, Severin wanted them to be people. His greatest fear was that he would become like Wilde, counting carcasses as they shuffled through a never-ending abattoir.

'Still walking?' the man asked.

Severin nodded. 'I've miles to go before I sleep. You're Glynn. Mike Glynn. Is this Palm Springs?'

'No, we're a little further down the road.' He took a drag on a cigarette; the skin hung in tatters from his wrist. 'Nice night.'

Severin shook his head. 'Too cold. I haven't been able to get warm for five years. How's your wife?'

'She's OK. It wasn't suicide; just an accident. There's a different place for suicides.' The smoke wasn't expelled from his mouth; it just drifted out and was caught by a breeze. Severin watched it with fascination. 'You've travelled a rough old road, friend,' the man continued. 'You shouldn't have had to do it. It's not right. Not fair.'

'Shit happens.'

'It does indeed. You deserve your rest, but after coming so far it would be a shame to turn away before the job is done.'

'I'm so tired.'

'I know you are.'

'And there's Marj, and Matty . . .'

'They've got all the time in the world, John.'

Severin could no longer feel his pain; he was floating above the ground, insubstantial, ready to be carried along by the merest gust of wind. 'I can taste the dust of the desert on the breeze. The mountains look so huge, blocking out the stars.'

'Stay focused, John. Annie needs you. You remember Annie?'

'Yes. I love her.'

'She doesn't need your love, John, but she does need your help. She's important. She's been chosen. She's got the moon-light shining out of every part of her. They want her to do a big, big job, but she needs the key to open the door. You know what key, John?'

Severin thought for a moment and then fumbled in his shirt and tugged out the bracelet. It burned with an icy fire in the lambent rays of the crescent moon. 'This one.'

'That's the ticket. You get that to her, John. You get that to her as soon as you can. Don't worry about the consequences – everything's going to be fine.'

Severin's head was swimming; Glynn was fading in and out of focus. 'Why should I trust you?'

'Trust your heart, John. That's what's kept you going.'

There was another cloud of cigarette smoke and this time Severin could almost smell it. It swirled around Glynn's head and when it had cleared he had gone, stepping back into another world or time. Severin searched for the Californian

321

desert and the mountains, but there were only green fields and trees, and soon even that was fading. He plunged along the shrinking tunnel into the night without a second thought.

Somewhere high above himself, Severin saw himself locate the house and lurch through the gate into the garden. The meat puppet looked too awkward, a graceless beast which he wanted nothing to do with. It stumbled and fell, crawled and rolled, like it had no mind of its own, yet somehow it found the keys, and then it was in and he was back in himself, then out, then in once more. Somehow he made it to the lounge where he lay face down on the carpet, trying to recall what he was doing and what he *had* to do. There was pain so excruciating he felt he was engulfed in flames, and then there was the sweet respite of nothing.

Voices echoed all around him. Some he understood. Others seemed to be talking gibberish. Some he recognized as old friends long gone, people he thought had died. And intertwined among it all were the voices of three women, discussing if he had the resistance to succeed, if there was any strength left in him, if his end was near. At times it sounded like just one woman who changed from being very young to very old.

And then the voices were gone too, and there was just him, deep within the black hole of his head, and getting blacker all the time.

He was dying.

'Come on, lad. You'll be all right. Come on now.'

Severin's eyes flickered open, squinted against the too bright light. A face, silhouetted at first with a halo behind it. Movement, then detail.

'Stay with me, lad. I'll clean the wounds, then I'll call an ambulance.'

An old face, lined by years of happiness and pain, wispy, silver hair, eyes that had the sparkle of joy and humanity. A kind face. Severin relaxed.

'No ambulance.'

'You need one, lad.'

'No ambulance. You help me.' A deep, painful breath. 'Who are you?'

'George Newton. I'm a friend of Annie's.'

Severin closed his eyes. It was going to be all right.

31

At least Wilde had the courtesy to send in two *female* travellers to prepare Annie for the period of torment that lay ahead. They came in the evening and made her stand against the wall on the dirty straw, the manacle hanging heavy against her leg like an umbilical cord. In a base parody of handmaidens preparing an old-time bride for her wedding, they stripped her before scrubbing her skin with icy water from an old pail. After they had finished, they left her naked and wet and did not return until an hour later.

This time one of them held something pointed and silvery which made Annie's stomach churn and she feared the worst. They moved in quickly and one of them grabbed her hair, yanking her head back so that her slender throat was exposed. All Annie could manage was a gurgle of shock, and then the second one wielded the scissors and began to hack at her hair. She struggled and swore as her jet-black locks fell around her in a frenzy of snipping.

When they had done, they shoved her roughly to the straw and departed silently as if shamed by their act. Annie ran her fingers across her head; they had trimmed it so severely that it was almost a stubble. Her tears were hot and painful.

She remained alone with her thoughts for almost an hour, by which time the outhouse had grown completely dark apart from one shaft of moonlight shining through the dirty window. When she rolled over, Wilde was sitting against the wall near the door, watching her. His eyes were like hot coals in the shadows.

Annie started, and then rolled over on to her stomach so he couldn't stare at her body. 'You won't break me,' she said defiantly.

'Such an indomitable spirit. How attractive. Tell me, Annie, does it excite you to be naked and debased before me?'

'Fuck off and die, Wilde.'

'Oh, but it is *you* who will die, Annie, and soon.'

There was a rat in the outhouse with her. Annie could hear it snuffling in the dark, rustling through straw, its tiny claws click-click-clicking on the brick floor as it scurried back and forth. And where there was one there was probably more.

Annie rattled the chain. No hope of moving far if it came for her. Did rats attack people? If they were hungry enough, she guessed, and then she thought of 1984 and Room 101, and she pulled up her legs and pressed her face against her knees.

Even though it was a warm summer night, her nakedness had left her chill and wracked with occasional convulsive shivers. Her bladder ached so much it had started to burn. The straw was her bed, though, she couldn't do it there; she wouldn't allow him to debase her that much. Soon she would have to see if the chain would stretch far enough for her to relieve herself to one side. But the rat was still scurrying around and she was afraid it would come when she was in that vulnerable position. She would have to try. Soon.

The rat circled a little closer. Click-click-click.

First light streamed through the dirty windows, filling the outhouse with a pale glow that grew stronger every moment and chased the shadows away. Annie woke suddenly as if she had been shaken. Her body was a frozen log; she couldn't feel her skin and her joints seemed to be locked in place. As she opened her eyes and reality crashed in, her first thoughts were of despair and tears and hopelessness; somehow she managed to hold it all back.

The door swung open and Wilde walked in. 'Good morning! Did you sleep well? Pleasant dreams?'

He shrugged when she didn't answer him and took up his cross-legged position against the far wall.

'There's a rat in here.'

'Really? How unhygienic. I'll have to see what we can do about that. Anything to make your stay as enjoyable as possible. Your breakfast will be in shortly. Please do not expect too much. This isn't a hotel, after all.'

Annie glowered at him, surprised at how much hate she felt. 'Is today the day?'

The door opened and one of the traveller women entered with a bowl and a spoon. She placed the bowl on the floor where Annie could reach it. Cornflakes. She could smell the stink of sour milk from two feet away.

At that moment Wilde suddenly lurched to his feet and clutched at his stomach. He had to steady himself against the wall to block out whatever was gnawing at him.

'Something you ate?' Annie mocked as the traveller rushed over to his side.

Wilde glared at her, but he turned his anger on the other woman. His fist smashed into her face, and as Annie watched in horror he whipped out his switchblade and plunged it upwards beneath the woman's ribcage, ramming it, twisting and turning it with such frenzy that his hand disappeared into the wound. The woman on the receiving end coughed blood and collapsed on the floor.

'God!' Annie cried out.

'What has God got to do with it?' Wilde roared as he struggled to pull both his hand and his blade from the body.

When he stood up, he looked capable of anything.

'Do you want to see what else I can do?' He turned to the body and concentrated for long minutes until the woman's leg started to shiver. The ague spread up her body and as it did, the pool of blood that surrounded her started to grow smaller. Eventually, Wilde waved his hand and the woman sat upright, her eyes unfocused but filled with agony.

'God,' Annie whispered again.

'Will you stop saying that!' he shouted.

Next, he grasped his victim about the throat with both hands and forced her head back roughly. 'Tell me what you saw. Tell me about the Grey Land and the Black Cathedral.'

'I walked the land of howling winds, along a path of stone,' she began. 'I saw against the sky, a building, huge, black. You could fit a hundred cathedrals inside it. There was no way round it. A big wooden door. I knocked on it. It opened.'

'Did you see what was on the other side?'

'No. You brought me back.'

His rage exploded once again, unquenchable and violent. He threw the not-living woman to the floor and began to kick her repeatedly, so hard the toe of his boot disappeared into her unrecognizable flesh.

Annie covered her eyes, wondering if such a bloody death was to be her own fate.

Finally, his anger dissipated, he spoke to her almost as if he was explaining himself.

'I need to know what is on the other side of death,' he said. 'The Black Cathedral marks the boundary between here and There. All men pass through it.' He laughed. 'And women too. On the other side are two paths, one to the Dark Side, one to the Light. Beyond that? God, goddesses? The essential mystery. No one has ever returned with the information. It is the only thing left for me to know, and the only thing forever denied me. Unless, one day, I can reclaim someone who is just at the point where they can see everything, before their rational mind breaks up. And then I *will* know!' He paced over to the window and wiped the dust away so he could see outside. 'And that is where you come in. I have high hopes for you, Annie. The charge of life and intelligence in you is so strong.'

'How will you kill me?' The moment the words came out, she wished she hadn't asked.

'Gently. A nerve in the neck, a little trick I learned in China long ago. You will feel no pain. There will be no disfigurement.'

'Well, that's a relief,' Annie said ironically.

He bent down and tore off a strip of the traveller's clothing.

'You were concerned about rats, I recall. Well, we must do something about that.' He strode across the room and tied the rag roughly across her eyes. 'There. Now you will not have to see them. I will arrange for one of my people to come in and adjust your chains so you cannot remove it. Rest easily.'

Lunch and dinner were even less substantial, and by evening Annie was starting to feel weak and sick. As Wilde had promised, they had come to fasten both her hands up against the wall so she couldn't remove the blindfold. Now she was completely defenceless, and though it would have been easy to give in to despair at that moment, she kept going. Even when she heard the rat snuffling closer, even when it went silent and she waited tensely for what seemed like an eternity for that sensation of whiskers against her leg.

Wilde visited her twice, taunting her, hinting at the nearness of her death. And then he would speak about some incident from his past, during the Depression in New York or with the

326

conquistadors in South America, illustrating some act of brutality before trailing off into a long silence so she never knew if he was still there watching her or if he had slunk out and left her alone. And behind it all was a constant, rambling discourse about the Black Cathedral. It figured largely in his life; Annie could tell it terrified him and filled him with wonder at the same time. As he described it to her, she felt an echoing *frisson* in her own heart.

She tried to ask him about Robert, but Wilde refused to answer any of her questions. He was teasing her, dangling the carrot and then snatching it back so she couldn't tell if he really had brought Robert back or if it was another of his psychological torments.

When the little light that filtered around the edges of her blindfold had disappeared and .darkness was everywhere, she heard his voice inches from her face. She had not realized he had entered once more.

He said quietly, 'And when I do finally come for you, it will be like this. Silently. You will not know I am here until you feel my hands on your neck.'

Time lost all meaning in her cold, dark world and she could only nod off and wake, nod off and wake, until her weariness summoned unwanted hallucinations out of the dark.

Into that ball of confusion, the scratching intruded like the sudden jab with a blade. Her first thought was that it was a rat, clawing at the wall next to her, but gradually she realized that there was what sounded like human endeavour behind the steady labour.

'Who's there?'

The scratching stopped immediately. After a second or two there was a reply in a weak, flat voice that only just managed to penetrate the wall. 'Annie?'

'Martyn!' Annie recognized his voice immediately. The knowledge snapped her out of her drifting state. 'Jesus, he's got you too!'

'Yes.' His minimal answer told her all she needed to know about what he had been through.

'Are you OK?'

'Tired.' A long pause. 'He moved me in here earlier.'

'When did he get hold of you, Martyn?'

'After I left the hut in the wood ... after Charlotte ... He brought me up to the farmhouse ...'

Annie thought his voice was going to break completely. Hurriedly she said, 'Well, now we're together, we can help each other. Are you with me?'

'Yes, Annie. I'm with you.'

32

When Katy Elliot looked deeply into the mirror, she almost recognized the person she used to be, behind the sallow skin and blue-ringed eyes of someone who wasn't allowed to slow down for even a second. How long was it since she'd slept? It didn't matter. She had adapted to her new life in the same way that Christopher had. Caring for the baby came above everything, and so what if they had no energy for their own relationship, at least they didn't argue any more.

The baby *never* slept (for some reason she had stopped calling it Saul). Instead it cried all night, all day. No bottle would satisfy it, no amount of rocking or singing, no rattle or cuddly toy, no cooing or bouncing. It ... he ... it cried incessantly, wailing like a warning siren. It cried and it cried and it cried.

Christopher hadn't been to work for days. The phone rang intermittently but on the occasions when they heard it beneath the baby's crying, they never answered. Christopher busied himself with the endless cycle of dirty nappies and bottle cleaning, and lived the life of a drudge.

Recently it had got worse. Much worse. Katy couldn't understand it at all; was she doing something wrong?

'Katy?'

Christopher was at the kitchen door, a changed man with stubble that had blossomed into the early stages of a beard and greasy, unkempt hair that was badly in need of a cut. His shirt was stained with milk posset and baby shit; he had given up changing himself when he realized he was getting through six shirts a day.

'What is it?' she snapped.

'There's something wrong with the baby.'

Katy almost laughed at the ridiculousness of the statement; as if there had ever been anything right with it. But then she forced herself to listen to the cry that had become so constant it was part of the accepted background noise, and she realized it *had* grown more manic, raw, almost wild like an animal.

For the first time in days, her emotions came alive and she pushed past her dead-eyed husband and hurried through to the lounge. In the centre of the room, the Moses basket was rocking from the baby's frantic kicking. Suddenly panicking, Katy rushed over and peered in. The crying stopped instantly. It was so unusual it made her catch her breath.

The baby looked up at her, almost serene as its eyes searched her face. It seemed to be waiting for something. A shiver of anticipation ran from its left eye to its mouth.

'I think,' Katy mused, 'I might call the doctor.' But somewhere deep inside her, the forgotten rational her, a voice was screaming, *No! He'll find out the truth! What you've denied to yourself in order to live this lie!* 'Just to be on the safe side,' she added. But already the thought was dying; breaking out of their cocoon into the outside world was too much to contemplate.

She stepped away and the baby suddenly erupted in a monstrous howling so inhuman it made her blood freeze. Already at her limits, from the dazed state she had occupied for the past few days, the strain told instantly.

'Pick it up!' she yelled at Christopher who hovered near the door. 'Comfort it, for God's sake! Stop it crying!'

Christopher dawdled for a second, but when he saw the blaze ignite in her eyes he ran forward and plucked the child from the basket. Its cry died in its throat. With relief, Christopher held the boy up before his face and made gurgling noises, trying to elicit something, anything, that would bring the warmth back into the family.

The baby wriggled in his grasp and with a cold intelligence that belied its age, it grabbed hold of Christopher's cheeks. He laughed briefly at this sudden show of playfulness, but then he jumped as nails bit into his flesh.

'Ow! You'll have to get his fingernails cut. He's got a right little grip on him.'

The baby paused, its nails digging into the little tucks in

Christopher's cheeks, while its eyes ranged over his features. Christopher looked into them lovingly, but what he saw there disturbed him and he had to look away.

The baby released its grip. Christopher looked back, smiling once more. But it was no longer his son that he held there. In its place was a demon; placid, innocent features transformed into a snarling, spitting morass of venom and hatred. Before Christopher could move, the baby's hands were lashing out at his face, a whirlwind of raking by tiny nails that tore through skin and raised blood. Christopher howled in shock, but he was drowned out by the baby's own maddening screech of hunger which now seemed to be a blood lust.

Although he tried to put the baby down, it was wriggling too much and somehow it managed to bob its head forward and plant its mouth on his face where it sucked with its horrible hard gums. With horror, Christopher realized it was slurping up the blood which flowed from the numerous tiny cuts and tears.

This time he threw the child away from him. Katy yelled out and tried to grab it, but it hit the floor with a squeak. Strangely, the cry didn't change to one of pain. That animal scream of hunger remained as loud as ever. It flipped over on to its stomach and dug its fingers into the carpet to drag itself forward like some hideous pink slug.

'It's not old enough to crawl!' Katy cried out stupidly; it was the only thing she could comprehend.

The baby moved forward inch by agonizing inch, its eyes rolling, blood smeared round its open mouth like jam.

Christopher and Katy Elliot could only hug each other in mute horror and watch the beast approach them.

Peter Cockburn's mother lay dead on the bed. At some point during the last twenty-four hours, her madness had won its guerrilla battle and driven all sanity out of her mind. A glass tumbler was broken; the jugular was cut. The carpet still squelched underfoot.

Peter sat on the edge of the bed near his mother's head; her expression was peaceful for the first time in years. Beautiful Karen with the long, golden hair sat at the foot and Julie and Ruth were on either side, their eyes a little too wide with the first taint of their mother's madness. Only Peter was wholly sane, but his suffering had been purely physical and that could be overcome through force of will.

Their mother's death was a catalyst which had brought them partially out of their dominant dream-state and back into each other's company. At first Karen hadn't recognized Peter's swollen, battered face, but then the tears came and had released some hidden store of strength.

The house was silent. It was one of the increasingly rare lulls between the monster's rampages. It was downstairs somewhere, slumped like a clockwork toy that had run down, brooding before it ran through its machine desires once more. Somehow the silence was worse. The quiet amplified the degradation that was waiting to such a degree that in the back of all their minds there was a voice praying for it to start up again, so they didn't have to endure the awful anticipation.

'What do we do now?' Karen asked. She couldn't find her comb so she pulled at her hair with her white, clawed fingers.

'We can't do anything!' A sob punctuated Julie's comment.

'We don't have to stay here for Mum,' Peter interjected quickly but calmly, before the hysteria came. 'Not any more. We've just got ourselves to think about now. We can go.'

'What? Leave the house?' Ruth said incredulously.

'Why not?'

Saying it out loud suddenly made them wonder why they hadn't thought about it before. It seemed so obvious. Yet the magnetic pull of the horror still had power, controlling them in ways they couldn't see, and was hard to break.

'Where would we go?' Julie said with another sob.

'Anywhere we want. We could have adventures.'

'You and your adventures!' Julie stood up and then sat down again heavily. Her mother's body bounced on the rippling bed springs.

'We've got to break the spell,' Peter continued. 'And it is a spell, if you look at it. Sit and think about it, about—'

'No!' Karen was adamant. 'I'll do whatever you say, Peter, but don't make me think about *it*.'

'Come on then! Let's go now. Everything's quiet. We could slip out.'

'Now?' the twins said in unison.

'Yes, *now*.' Peter jumped from the bed and ran as best he could to the door. Pain filled each limb and joint, but he knew he shouldn't give in to it. The girls were slower, but they followed his every move. Out on the landing, they carefully avoided each creaking floorboard, memorized from the long-lost days of their youth when they didn't want to wake their father from his drunken sleep. Peter wasn't even sure that their father did sleep any more, but he didn't want to risk a sound.

At the bottom of the stairs lay an abyss that continued right into the bowels of hell. That was where it had happened, an age ago, it seemed. The stink of beer and flatulence. That roar and the echoing slap of a meaty palm on the side of Karen's face, with the threat of more to come. That was the moment when the dam wall had come crashing down. When they'd all leapt on their father as one, clawing and hitting and screaming while their mother stood back and watched through the one eye that hadn't closed up.

And then their father closing his hands around Karen's neck and Peter rushing forward to throw himself at the wobbling bulk of muscle and fat. The figure teetering on the lip of the stairs, and then plunging backwards. The crashing from top to bottom. The sickening snap of the neck when he came to a halt.

Peter put his foot on the top step. Good. It didn't creak. Karen held his arm so tightly her nails dug through his shirt and into his flesh. The second step, then the third. One of the twins started to whimper. Karen hushed her rudely. Then they were halfway down and Peter was breathing a little easier. It was just a matter of slipping through the kitchen and out of the back door, and then they'd be free, all the horror and pain behind them.

The door at the foot of the stairs burst open so roughly one of the hinges tore away from the jamb. They all screamed together as his monstrous form lurched through, eyes glazed as they had been as long as they had known him, hair lank to his head, oozing a trail of sweat and piss and booze. His roar was almost familiar, but there was a new dimension to it, one that didn't have any roots in humanity.

Peter turned and tried to scramble back up the stairs, but the twins had frozen, mouths gaping as the beast advanced. *Thoom.* His foot hit the first step. *Thoom.* His fist hit the wall. And the roar grew louder, and the girls' screams joined it, until Peter thought he would go insane. He tried again to get upstairs, but he couldn't force his way past the others on the narrow staircase. With tears of fear in his eyes, he turned back. He was the man of the house; he had to protect his sisters.

Karen was screaming something which he couldn't understand at first. It came to him a second late because the sound was out of sync with her lips.

'Do it again! Like we did before!'

Do it again.

When his father had advanced enough to be within range, Peter ducked under his flailing arms and planted his foot heavily in that marshmallow stomach. There was a hideous moment of *déjà vu* as his father wobbled comically on the step, waving his arms above his head.

The crack when he hit the bottom was as loud as it was before.

'You broke his neck!' Karen squealed gleefully, clapping her hands.

Peter's proud smile disappeared a second later as their father began to drag himself up, head lolling grotesquely. This time Peter didn't hesitate. He ran down the remaining stairs and kicked his father full square in the face, flooring him again. Peter jumped on top of him and yelled for the girls to run.

There was a whole second when he thought they were going to ignore him, but then he heard them screaming as they scrambled past over the body and out into the kitchen. He made to follow them when he felt the clamp of iron fingers around his ankle. Peter clung on to the door jamb, but his broken-necked father was yanking him back.

The girls were watching in horror, frozen. Peter could feel himself losing the fight. The pain in his ankle was unbearable.

'Go on!' he shouted. 'Get out!'

The twins turned and ran, throwing open the kitchen door and screaming into the night. But Karen remained, staring at him, looking like a ghost with her white skin, and for a second Peter thought she had cracked, like his mother.

Then she moved, snatching the shovel from behind the door and bringing it down hard on her father's wrist, hard enough to win a prize at the fair. Peter pitched forward as he was released, and when he glanced back he saw a hand twitching on the kitchen floor.

He didn't wait to see any more. Grabbing Karen, he dragged

her out of the door as their father finally managed to pull himself to his feet.

'He's going to get us,' Karen sobbed. 'And he's going to drag us back like he always did.'

Peter knew she was right.

Brian Swift closed his eyes and tried to pretend she wasn't there. It was impossible. His mother was everywhere. Really and truly everywhere. And at night when he cried himself to sleep, he prayed for the time when she had only run his life, not tried to live it. Now, he thought, it seemed she was actually trying to get inside his skin.

For a while after she returned, she had only followed him around. It had been unbearable, but nothing like now. He winced. She would be beside him on the sofa; a few paces behind when he walked to the kitchen; outside the door when he went to the toilet; at the side of his bed, the ever-vigilant sentinel, all night long.

She had finally cured him of his habit of talking to himself, as she had tried to do all her life, because her constant presence gave him no space. She was like a juggernaut bearing down on him and all he wanted to do was get out of her way.

And then she had started to get closer. Sometimes he would stop suddenly and she would bump into the back of him. Other times she would leave barely a millimetre between them. Once he had sworn under his breath and she had pinched the nape of his neck so hard tears sprang to his eyes.

That was when things really started to get bad. When he went to the toilet, he had to struggle to force her out, and then she hammered on the door and screamed and wailed like a mad woman until he could bear it no more and he had to let her in. To his embarrassment, she would stand there almost between his legs while he sat down and tried to complete what he had to do. Then at night, she got in bed with him, her dry skin pressing against him so that he couldn't get to sleep. And bit by bit, the madness began to eat away at him.

That morning she had started to touch him. When he got out of bed, she rested a hand on his shoulder. He shook it off, but she replaced it instantly, the nails digging into his skin. And that was how it had remained all day. One hand on his shoulder,

334

her body behind his, the stink of too much perfume in his nose. And he wondered what chance of escape there was now.

Brian tried to scramble upstairs, but those needle fingers were hooked into him and in the end it was like dragging a dead weight up with him. At the top, he turned on the landing and slammed backwards, crushing her against the wall, but there was no response from the awful, dry thing. Her arms simply folded around his neck and her legs around his waist, an albatross much worse than the Ancient Mariner's.

The sensation of her hanging there drove him into lunacy as he barrelled along the landing into his bedroom. As his screams tore at his throat he careered from wall to wall, trying to throw her off. Somehow she managed to swivel round until she was facing him, her lips as close as a kiss.

In the shock of the moment he tried to throw himself away from her, overbalanced and crashed backwards. His head hit the floor with the force of a boxer's punch, and as he faded into unconsciousness his last thought was of her weight on his chest and her dry fingers pulling, pulling, pulling at the flesh of his stomach.

33

Annie could tell when dawn came by the faint light that broke through her blindfold like a ghost slipping into her dark world. She had spent most of the night talking to Martyn, and she had been horrified by his state of mind. There was no fight, no life, no light. Wilde had worked his torment like a master.

It only served to make Annie feel she had to be strong for both of them. There was a way out – there had to be. Shivering, she tried to focus on Wilde's weaknesses in the hope that she could find some chink. And he did have weaknesses, that was obvious. For someone so powerful, he had all the flaws of man – arrogance, pride, anger and, despite his vast experience, the immaturity of a boy who had never grown up. It was that combination of childishness and monstrosity which made him so dangerous. And there was one other weakness which she was almost afraid to consider. His attraction to her. Although he denied it was anything more than a sexual allure, Annie could sense it was more than that. Almost – dare she admit it? – a form of love.

He's not a god or a demon. He's a man, she told herself. And he loved her.

'Good morning, Annie. No trouble with rats, I hope? Now, my dear, I have brought someone to see you.'

There was something in his voice that made Annie shiver; it was the sound of a trap being laid. She heard the door slam and then soft, slight footfalls unlike the tramp of Wilde's boots. She listened for the sound of breathing, but she could hear nothing. And the dirty stink of the outhouse swamped any other smell.

'Don't you know who it is, Annie?'

He was just out to humiliate her even more. What other point was there in bringing someone to see her naked, chained and blindfolded?

'No idea? Will you not even try to guess? Please, let us have a little fun. Here's a clue. Who have you been dreaming about seeing again for years?'

Did he mean Robert? Was it him?

Wilde was twisting the knife deeper and deeper and she felt on the verge of a full-scale panic attack. Then the figure with Wilde took a few laboured paces forward. She cringed.

'Oh, my little surprise is not appreciated? Maybe some other time.'

Annie felt a blast of warm air as the door swung open and at the last moment she couldn't control herself any more. 'Was it Robert?' she called out.

Wilde stepped over the threshold and this time there was triumph in his voice. 'You will never know, will you?'

After he had gone, images of Robert, dead and standing just a few feet away, haunted Annie's thoughts. It was too much to bear and she hated Wilde for perverting the memory of her brother.

The stress took its toll and her head started to nod forward. As it did in that hazy state between sleep and waking, she realized something was calling to her and she gave herself up freely.

The sky was filled with bursts of light and the sound of distant thunder. It took Annie a second or two of orientation to realize it was no storm. She was standing in the middle of a field at twilight, the acrid smell of burning on the wind, the scream of the Valkyries in her ears.

She looked up at the slate-grey sky that threatened rain and realized it wasn't the Valkyries; it was planes sweeping in from somewhere behind her. The thunder was explosions just beyond the hillside on which she stood. Boom, boom, boom. A relentless beat. Where was she this time? What era was reaching out to her for help?

The presence seemed to call to her long before she saw it. Turning in a slow arc, she surveyed the landscape until she saw him, standing under an ash tree, dressed in the uniform of an American World War II GI.

He raised a hand to her in greeting. Like the others, his face was filled with sadness, crumpled from suffering. Without fear, Annie walked over to him.

He looked up at the clouds. 'Storm's brewin'.'

'I can understand you! I couldn't really tell what the others were saying.'

'You're getting the hang of it. Lettin' your subconscious do the work.'

'Why are you doing this? Who are you?' Annie shook her head in frustration. 'I've got so many questions.'

He nodded thoughtfully and pulled a pack of Lucky Strike from a band around his helmet. Flicking a cigarette into his mouth, he lit it and inhaled deeply before answering. 'We're doin' this because we want you to finish the job we all started. He was too good for us. You can beat him.'

'You're very confident.'

He dismissed her with an irritated wave of his hand. 'C'mon, let's walk.' He began to trudge slowly up the hill and Annie moved to his side with a double-step. 'Who are we? Just human beings tryin' to do the world a service. Your man's been around a long time, I guess you know that by now. All that killin' he's done wasn't gonna pass unnoticed. Down the years, there was always gonna be one or two people who came across him and realized what kinda monster there was loose in the world. They got a real raw deal. Nobody'd believe them. They had to shoulder the burden themselves. And what a fuckin' burden. It crushed too many good men. Everybody who stood up to him

337

was dedicated to the job and they all gave a little part of their soul to the fight.'

'Is that what you are? A little part of a soldier's soul?'

He drew on his cigarette and continued without answering. 'The bracelet holds the souls. Each one gives a little bit more magic to that shitty hunk of iron and now it's got enough in there to be filled with the power you need. When you have to make that final journey, it's got what it takes to get you where you wanna go and to keep your mind whole. That's the trick. Most people lose their mind straight away, but you need it when you open the door. You've gotta have the bracelet with you, y'hear me. Without that you're lost.'

'Severin's got it. I don't know where he is. He might even be dead.'

The soldier shrugged. 'Somethin' will work out. Anythin' can happen where magic's involved. An' there is a lot of magic here, you know that. Woman-magic. The Old Religion has opposed him since the start. The Craft has got its heart in nature and he's been against Nature from the beginnin'. Because some women had been instrumental in tryin' to destroy him, he's never had much time for them, as a sex. In fact, he's treated them pretty bad, but like all men he's drawn to them too. Crazy, but that's life. Anyways, it's not gonna be men's ways that will stop him – guns or swords or bombs. It'll be women's ways, subtle ways. That's why you're so important.'

They had reached the top of the hill and had a clear view across miles of countryside which looked like a scene from some Boschian painting. Far ahead of them a town was burning scarlet and gold with new blasts flashing every few seconds, its thick, black smoke filling the sky and bringing the night down early. The lush fields were pockmarked with craters. Annie could smell death.

'Where are we? What battle is this?'

'It doesn't matter. There's only one war that concerns you. The one that's been goin' on since the dawn of time.'

Annie turned to him and looking closely realized he was only in his twenties, although whatever he had experienced made him seem much older. She reached out a hand to his shoulder, but he shied away. 'Who is he?' she asked. 'You've got to tell me.'

'You know your Scripture?' he said with a humourless smile.

'The old Book, the fire and brimstone stuff. He's in there, right at the start.'

Annie's brow furrowed in confusion.

'OK, I'll help you out. I don't recall the exact words, but I know enough. Two brothers, one of them a keeper of sheep, the other a tiller of ground. One of them gives an offering, the good Lord loves it. The other one, well, his gift's not quite up to scratch. He's bitter and jealous and he goes out into the field and rises up and beats out his brother's brain with a rock.'

'Cain.'

As Annie whispered the name, the bombing erupted to a crescendo and the wind seemed to rise, filled with strange voices that whispered hideous things.

'"And the good Lord said, *Where is Abel?* And Cain replied, *I do not know. Am I my brother's keeper?* And the Lord said, *What have you done? Your brother's blood is crying to me from the ground. Now you are cursed from the ground, which has opened its mouth to receive your brother's blood from your hand. When you till the ground, it shall no longer yield to you its strength. You shall be a wanderer on the earth.*"'

'Cain!' Annie cried out this time.

'"And Cain said, *My punishment is greater than I can bear. I shall be hidden from thy face, a fugitive. Whoever finds me will slay me.* And the Lord said, *Not so! If anyone slays Cain, vengeance shall be taken on him sevenfold.* And He put a mark on Cain, lest any who came upon him should kill him. Then he was driven out from the presence of the Lord, east of Eden."'

'The first murderer!' Annie was overcome.

'Maybe that story's not true. Maybe the Bible's just based on what really happened. But you better believe me, he *is* Cain, and he's got a helluva sin to wipe out. He's been wanderin' the earth ever since 'cause he's refused to look for his own salvation. That's his punishment, to keep on walkin' until he comes to his senses. Only he's too stupid to learn so he keeps on repeatin' his mistake like some spoiled brat tryin' to thumb his nose at authority. He can't stay still for long because he gets sick in the gut. He has to keep movin' on and on till Judgement Day, or until he finally repents.'

'God did this?'

'Whatever you want to call that power that's over us. That ain't for me to say.'

'But all the suffering he's caused. All the killing. How can that be just?'

'The Lord moves in mysterious ways.' He smiled grimly. 'That's an old saw, but it's true. Maybe it was a test for all of us, as well as Cain. They say you don't appreciate anythin' unless you struggle to get it.'

'But if the Bible's true, we're not allowed to kill him. He's got the mark on him and anybody who tries—'

'There's another way. That's where *you* come in. You've got to use the bracelet. It's important to Cain 'cause it reminds him of what he did. He's bound to it in some way, but he's terrified of it too 'cause he knows it's got the power to finish him off.'

'Why doesn't he just destroy it? And if he's so scared of it, why didn't he take it back from Severin when he had the chance?'

'He can't do either.' The GI flicked his cigarette butt into the wind and turned to face the storm. 'You and me, we're just normal folk. But he lives by rules we'll never know. He can't destroy the bracelet, that's for sure. It's part of his curse, to carry the seeds of his destruction around with him. An' for some reason, once he's lost hold of it he can only take it back when it's given to him freely. Don't ask me why. That's just the way it is.'

There was still much for Annie to grasp. 'The bracelet—'

' – belonged to his brother. It was drenched in his blood when Cain murdered him. There's a lot of power in blood.'

'I still don't understand where I come in. What do I have to do?'

The GI took a few steps away from her and held out his hand, just as the others had done. Annie looked at it nervously. After a few seconds she reached out and took it.

'That's what you have to do,' he said. 'You make a leap of faith straight into the abyss. You have to take a hand across the divide. Once you do that, you'll know exactly what to do next.'

He tugged at her arm and as she tumbled towards him, the dream began to break up and fall apart. The bomb bursts grew unnaturally loud, then faded. The wind eased off, and the last thing she recalled was a whisper in her ear: 'Sacrifice all to fetch him back.'

*

'Wake up!'

A palm crashed against the side of her face. Annie's head snapped to one side and she yelped as fingers slid down the front of her blindfold and tore it away roughly.

Cain.

Annie considered taunting him with his real name, but what if that pushed him over the edge? He might kill her there and then if he knew she had the secret he valued so much.

Names have power.

His face was only inches away from her and in his eyes were basic instincts which dated back to his earliest days. He seemed to be regressing to the thing which lay at the heart of him. The true identity. The one he would never escape, however much he pretended. A raw, brutal murderer.

There was an instant when he looked as if he had reverted completely and was going to tear her limb from limb, but his civilized side regained control at the last second and pulled him back. The animal retreated inside him and the mask returned. With some difficulty, he attempted to restore his dignity.

'I am so sorry,' he said as if he had made some social *faux pas.* 'As you can see, the pain is very great and sometimes I find it hard to keep it within me.'

'If you're in so much pain here, why not just move on?'

He laughed. 'Please do not tempt me, Annie. No! After I have risked so much it would be such a waste not to see it through to the end. And we are getting *very* close now. I want you to see what has happened to your little village before it is all over.'

Our own little Garden of Eden. It came back to her in a rush that left her feeling sick and dizzy. One throwaway comment, a few stupid words. Coupled with the *goodness* he said he sensed inside her, that was all it had taken to trigger his hatred and set all the ghastliness in motion. He had killed and destroyed on a whim because he didn't like her choice of words. Eden, in his eyes, the place where his punishment began.

'Listen to this. The revenants I have seeded around your beautiful little home have been spreading their malignancy far and wide over the last few days. All your neighbours have altered. The true nature of humanity, the dark, twisted side, has been brought out from beneath the pathetic veneer of civilization. But that is not really enough. I do so hate to leave a job half-done. The revenants are flawed, you see. They are like little

341

time-bombs. Without that essential element of goodness which has been lost to the other side, they deteriorate rapidly – psychologically at first, then physically. And as they do so, they become like beasts. They kill, Annie! They maim and destroy. Once that starts, your home village will be eradicated in hours and the perpetrators will disintegrate into the remains from which I created them. It will be a mystery to be celebrated for years – who murdered an entire community? And quite a conundrum for your parents on their return. I have left many mysteries in my passing, but I will be particularly proud of this one. Such a hideous, provincial place, too. I do not know how you can feel so strongly about it.'

He bowed mockingly and left.

The sickness was almost too powerful to control, but Cain couldn't allow it to show on his face. Weakness would be his downfall. Focusing himself, he marched down the steps of the farmhouse to the cellar and he smiled when he opened the door.

Laurence Lucas sat in the corner, his dead flesh a patchwork of cuts and gouges. He looked up sullenly when Cain entered.

'You're not going to stop me,' he sneered in his educated, accentless voice. 'I'm too clever. My essence is too strong.'

'I normally admire confidence, but yours is badly misplaced.'

Lucas sniggered like a schoolboy. 'You know I'm not like the others. I'm not going to deteriorate – I'm here for good! You never expected me to come back so powerfully, did you, you old fool?'

'Say all you want, little dead boy – you are still just worm-fodder. I admit I made a mistake with you. You are a loose cannon, drawing attention to my plans. You have forced me to act hastily, make errors . . .'

Lucas sneered. 'You're losing control. And all because of a girl! You should develop a taste for boys, old man.'

Cain watched him coldly. He still couldn't quite understand why Lucas had come back so different from the others – more intelligent, more aware, almost human in his aspect. It made him wonder if it was the work of whatever force lay on the Dark Side. Perhaps he was being used by that power to bring a concentrated evil back into the world. Well, *he* would not have it, *he* would not be manipulated.

'Your ego is out of control,' Lucas continued, enjoying his moment. 'You're too sure of yourself.'

'A human trait.' Cain smiled cruelly. 'And like all humans, I am bitter and vengeful. There is a price for disobeying me, and even dead flesh can be made to suffer.'

In the screaming halls of Lucas's mind, a glimmer of his near-forgotten humanity reignited. Cain saw the trace of fear in his unblinking eyes and nodded. 'Time to pay the piper, little man.'

Without the blindfold, Annie knew Cain was not listening in on them and she couldn't stop talking. To her surprise, Martyn responded in kind and she was taken aback at the strength of her affection as they relived old times. It hit her with such force she had to tell him.

'Martyn,' she began hesitantly, 'I want you to know that I love you for standing by me and helping me through that nightmare after Robert's death, even when I treated you like shit. I love you for trying now when I've been such a bitch for the last three years. The truth is, you're as much a part of my life as my family, and I don't want you ever to go away. And, no, I'm not just saying this because we're trussed up in a dirty outhouse, waiting to be killed like lambs. We're going to get out of here, Martyn, and when we do I want it to be you and me against the world.'

Then it came through the wall, his reply. 'That's all I ever wanted.'

She slumped back and felt so good she almost forgot there was a monster lurking outside who was preparing to slaughter her without mercy.

34

George Newton never left his side. And Severin was grateful for the old man's administrations. George was the one who'd found him after he'd somehow lurched back to Blackstone Cottage, and at present he was Severin's only anchor to humanity.

He recalled the fight with Lucas, Annie ushering the boy out, a backward glance and then she was gone. His torturous journey back to the house with his dark partner beside him. And then?

He looked at the old man who rested in a wooden chair next to the sofa where he lay, a blanket over his legs. 'Annie?'

George Newton shook his head. 'There's something terrible happening in this village, lad. I felt it long before I saw it in people's faces, when it just seemed to be in the air, like a bad mood. But now it's on the streets, in our houses . . .' He sighed wearily. The last time I saw Annie, she seemed to know what was happening so I thought I'd come round here, talk it over with her. Work out what's best. And what do I find? Your poor self looking like you've been combine harvested.'

Severin tried to sit up, but he wasn't quite ready for it. The pain lanced down his side.

'You take it easy,' George said. 'By rights, you should be dead. All those stab wounds, all that blood . . . I've never seen anything like it. You must have some bloody constitution on you.'

'Actually I feel like hell,' Severin croaked.

'Aye, well, you should be happy you can feel anything at all. Do you want to tell me about it?'

Severin tried as best he could to outline the nightmare that had crept into the village, and the old man nodded sagely as Wilde's doings were unveiled.

'Do you think he's got Annie?'

'I can't think where else she is. She'd have come back for me otherwise, I know she would. And today,' – he glanced at the clock on the mantelpiece and tried to guess how long he'd been out – 'no, two days ago, that what when he was coming for her.'

'Then we'd best go and get her back,' said George Newton without a trace of fear.

'Easy to say. I've spent days looking for the bastard and not got even close.'

'Well, it seems to me he's been thick as thieves with those travellers; we should go there first, when you're fit.'

'I'm fine.' Severin levered himself on to his elbow and almost pitched off the sofa.

'Aye, you look like it.'

Severin protested, 'Annie's what's important. I'm getting better all the time. You help me along, I'll be fine.'

George didn't argue. 'We'll see how we go, ay? And if it's too much I'll drop you off somewhere and go up on my own.'

'What's an old man gonna do against Wilde?'

'About the same as an invalid, I'd say. Now, listen, there's one thing I'd ask you.'

'What's that?'

'That on the way we call in those houses where the dead folk are and try and sort them out. They're the ones that are causing all the rotten stuff.'

'We haven't got time.'

'We've got time. If he came for her two days ago and he hasn't done anything by now, we can afford a few extra minutes. Won't take long if you're as good with that shotgun as you make out. At least that should stop things getting any worse down here.'

Severin agreed because he didn't have the strength to argue.

Everywhere Severin looked in the once pleasant and ordered streets of Riddington he could see Wilde's face leering back at him. George had already described the transformation that had overtaken the village, but now it was plain to see for himself.

At the corner where the High Street met Church Street, two boys were attempting to set fire to a hissing cat; a stone's throw from the church gate, a man lay in the gutter, battered to within an inch of his life; through a window further down Church Street, they saw a woman hanging by her neck from the light fitting in her lounge. Nobody had bothered to cut her down, even though she was illuminated for all to see by the spotlight above her.

And the black cloud of negative emotions lay so thick and heavy, it seemed impossible to breathe. A band tightened across Severin's damaged chest and when they reached Brian Swift's house, he could see that old George was wheezing.

'Are you ready?' the old man asked as they stood outside the door.

Severin rested his hand on the shotgun in his hidden pocket. He nodded.

It smelled unpleasant, like someone had left an open dustbin in the kitchen for a week or two. Not wishing to announce their presence until the last minute, they had slipped in through the unlocked back door. All the lights were blazing and the TV was playing to itself, yet there was no sign of Brian Swift. Or his returned house guest.

'We'd better try upstairs.' Severin's heart was beating wildly as George helped him to the foot of the stairs. The lights were on up there too, a glaring attempt to drive all shadows out of the house.

Cautiously, Severin scanned the open doorways that lined the landing as he made his way upwards. At the top, he turned to George and whispered, 'I can hear something.'

It was in the bedroom at the very end of the landing where the door was only half-open, obscuring most of the interior. Slowly he approached, easing the door with the barrel of the gun. It butted up against something that was making the noise behind it. Steeling himself, Severin peered around the edge.

Brian Swift lay spread-eagled on the floor, his clothes pulled from his naked, obese body. The dead thing that used to be his mother sat over him, her face grey above a dress as black as night. Her head turned slowly as Severin barged in and he saw the blood smeared around her mouth. She grinned, revealing yellowing teeth stained bright red.

Although he fought against it, Severin's gaze was drawn irresistibly to Swift. With a gulp of nausea, his first thought was: *Oh my God, she's been eating him*. But then he realized this wasn't entirely true. She had been *at* the corpse, yes, but it seemed she had been clawing and gnawing at the flesh simply to pull it away from the bone, to strip it down. Like nothing more than a crow pecking at carrion.

He raised the shotgun and fired. Reloaded and fired again. And again and again until George Newton yelled at him to stop.

Although it was part of their eradication policy, Severin felt sickened by what he had done. He kept telling himself it was just a carcass, but it haunted him as much as if he had murdered a real person. And the next one was going to be worse.

They were about to try the door when Severin had a sudden sense of being watched. He looked round and saw Christopher and Katy Elliot sitting in the front of their car. They looked awful, as if they hadn't slept or eaten for days. He walked back to them and waited for Christopher to wind down the window which he seemed reluctant to do. He noted there was no key in the ignition. They weren't going anywhere, they were just waiting.

'Are you two OK?' he asked, squatting down to their level. They looked at each other and then back at him, but neither was prepared to speak first. 'I know what's wrong,' Severin continued. 'It's that thing in there, that thing that's pretending to be your little boy.'

They glanced at each other again and this time, after a second, Katy burst into floods of tears. Christopher looked both ashen and relieved. 'Thank God,' he gasped. 'We thought we were going mad. Inside the house, we seemed to ... accept it. We came out here to get away from it after it ... after—' he swallowed. 'And then we didn't know what to do.' He put an arm around Katy and pulled her next to him.

'Leave it to me,' Severin said coldly.

Now he had started talking, Christopher couldn't stop as the tension forced everything out. 'We prayed for Saul to come back, constantly, but God ... we never wanted it like this! It's like that story, the monkey's paw. We keep asking ourselves why *us*? Why should we suffer? We've done nothing wrong.'

Katy leaned towards the window. 'We know we shouldn't have kept praying for him. We should have mourned him and moved on. Not let this thing pervert his memory. We loved him. God, if there's a way out of this, we'll learn ...'

'There's a way out,' Severin said. 'Just don't think of that thing in there as your son. It's not. It's a monster. Your son died and his spirit is happy. Remember that.'

'What are you going to do?'

Severin didn't reply. He pulled away quickly and headed towards the door, his hand already moving to the shotgun in his pocket.

George caught at his arm as he opened the door. 'And *you* remember too, lad,' he said. 'It's not a baby. It's not a baby.'

Severin felt on the verge of being sick, but he stepped across the threshold and into a world ruled by those hideous wails.

'I can't get the smell of that smoke out of my nose.' Severin coughed and hawked, deliberately focusing on the aftermath of the deed rather than the deed itself. 'It stinks like shit.'

George examined Severin's hunted expression. There was too

much white around the pupils; no man should have to do what he'd done. 'It was the only way, lad. We couldn't leave it for that couple. They've been through enough.'

Severin rubbed at his hands. He could still feel the awful, dry skin of the tiny corpse as he had scooped it into the dustbin bag. It had only taken a few seconds to burn. It went up like tinderwood.

'Just one more now ...' George urged, as they walked onwards.

The sound of screaming children echoed through the night towards them. They both moved as fast as they could in the direction of the cries and met the Cockburn twins sprinting out of their front garden, eyes wide and panicked. George knelt down and blocked them in mid-flight. For a second they scrambled and tried to fight him off before they saw who it was.

'Back there!' Ruth screamed. 'He's coming!'

As Severin stepped forward, Peter and Karen crashed out into the garden too, and stopped dead. Then Peter gasped, 'You've got to help us. He's coming!'

Severin herded the boy and his sister in the direction of the others and carried on. Immediately, he saw a dark shape lurch from the house and start towards him. He waited until it came into the streetlight before he fired. The blast crashed against its sternum and knocked it off its feet, but it was up with surprising speed.

Severin fumbled to reload and by the time he had got the cartridges in, it was on him. Its bulk hit him like a truck, and flattened him. From that position, and with a tremendous effort, he pulled the shotgun free, planted it upwards, turned his head away and pulled the trigger. The flare burned his face and blinded him but by the time he had climbed to his feet, his work was done and the Cockburn beast lay supine.

The twins clung to George's legs while his arms rested around the shoulders of the other two, comforting them.

'Is it over?' Karen asked, disbelieving.

He nodded wearily. 'You better get back inside to your mother.'

'Mum's dead.' Peter stepped forward, his expression serious beyond his years. 'We've got nowhere to go.'

Severin had already turned in the direction of the travellers' camp. He wondered if he would have the strength to make it up there.

'We can't leave them here, lad. Not with all this madness going on.'

'What do you suggest we do? Take them to meet Wilde?' Severin snapped as he fought against the strain.

'They can wait at the camp till it's all over,' George continued. 'There'll be plenty of people to look after them.'

'Yes. Take us.' Peter walked forward and looked up into Severin's face.

For a second, Severin felt he was looking down at his own son and a sweeping desire to hug the boy came over him. He controlled it and replied emotionlessly, 'OK. But no talking.'

Peter's pleading gave way to relief, and he turned to give his sisters a hug.

George came over and patted Severin's back. 'You did well, lad. That part's over.'

'Sure. Now we've only got the hard part left.'

Out beyond the streetlights, the night seemed impenetrably dark as if it was yet another black beast waiting to devour them. At that moment, all Severin could think was that he might never see another dawn.

As they made their way slowly along Colthorpe Road and then up the winding lane towards the camp, Severin began to think the travellers had moved on. There was no distant thrum of bass-heavy music, no glow of a campfire cutting through the darkness. Everything was deathly still and unnervingly unlit. Only when they stepped around the hedgerow and into the field did they see the jumble of vehicles was still there, lifeless, as if the inhabitants had been spirited away the moment dark had fallen.

'Young folks. They probably all fancied an early night,' George said wryly, but both adults could tell the poisonous atmosphere was denser and more caustic than it had been in the village.

Severin surveyed the buses and trucks and vans and eventually glimpsed the odd chink of light behind tightly curtained windows. 'They're here,' he said, trying to sound confident. 'Come on.'

There was no reply from behind the locked doors of each

vehicle they hammered on. They could hear movement within, fearful shuffling, the occasional whimper, but no sounds of chat or music. No one responded to their calls.

As they moved slowly through the camp, the oppressive atmosphere became more and more powerful, and eventually the children were huddling so close to their legs the two men found it difficult to move. Not far from the burnt-out remains of the campfire, Severin recognized the old black bus which had belonged to Tommy. He guessed it was abandoned now, after the traveller's death, but some sixth sense drew him towards it and he decided to knock on the door.

There was a long pause and then a quiet voice replied, 'Who is it?'

'A friend of Tommy's. From the village.'

There was another long pause and then, 'It's open.'

He yanked open the door. The inside smelled of candle smoke and sweat like some Turkish brothel. It was gloomy, with the only light coming from one stubby candle which guttered and almost went out. It took a second or two for Severin to recognize the occupant. Angela sat cross-legged on the voluminous cushions, her face chalk-white yet puffy here and there with bruises. She wore a large pair of sunglasses despite the gloom. There was no one else around. George and the children crowded in behind Severin, desperate to get out of the night, but she didn't look up.

'Where is everybody?' Severin asked.

'Inside their homes. Nobody goes out much any more.' There was an edge to her voice.

'What's happened?'

She laughed bitterly and looked up, although strangely she seemed to be staring off to one side as if she could see someone else behind his shoulder. '*What's happened*? Just the end of the world!' Then she added in a tiny voice, 'Everything's fallen apart. We're just waiting.'

'For what?'

'To die.'

The words fell like stones and Severin heard a whimper from one of the children behind him, and saw Angela look up at the sound. 'Wilde?' he asked.

She nodded. 'We . . . I had no idea what he was . . . what he could do. He's a monster.'

'I know. Annie told you that when we asked you to look out for him.'

'I didn't listen.' The three little words were filled with regret.

Severin walked over and squatted in front of her. 'What did he do here?'

'It started when he first visited us. Scarlet had got her foot caught in a gin-trap left by some of those bastards in the village. She was nearly dead from the shock and the blood loss, but he said he could heal her. She wouldn't have made it to a hospital so we gave him the chance, and it *seemed* like that's just what he did . . .'

'But he killed her and brought her back to life?'

She nodded. 'We were so happy! Everyone was celebrating and he . . . was so hypnotic . . . powerful. Everyone liked him.' She was having trouble continuing, and when she said *everyone*, Severin guessed she meant herself. 'After he went, there was a bad atmosphere here. Like arguing and fighting – we'd never done that before. We were a family. It was Scarlet that caused it, or whatever it was that was in Scarlet's body. Then he returned, the night of the storm, and he *killed* people, right through the camp, from home to home. Men, women, children . . . he didn't care. And next, he brought them back to life. Of course we didn't realize what he'd done, until those he'd killed started to change. At first they were almost normal, but then they became violent, out of control. That's when we started to spend more and more time inside.'

'Why didn't you try to get away?' Severin asked incredulously.

Angela looked as if she was trying to search for the reason herself. Eventually she said, 'We couldn't. It was like something was stopping us. At night we'd hear them roaming round the camp, terrified they'd try to break in. Recently, though, they seem to stay inside too.'

Severin looked back at George. 'Wilde's lost it. He was always so careful not to leave any trace of his passing. Now his sticky handprints are everywhere.'

'He's in pain,' Angela interjected. 'And he can't cope with it. It's like he's breaking down.'

'It's because of Annie.' Severin stared into the candle flame and focused, 'Did he give you any clue where he might be?'

'Yes, he told me,' Angela replied angrily. 'He doesn't care any more. He's at the house of the farmer who rented us this land.'

'Jack Tarrant!' George said. 'It's just up the lane.'

Severin jumped to his feet and immediately regretted the sudden movement; he still felt weak and he had to steady himself.

'You better take care,' Angela said. 'He's got some of us on his side. It's like they've fallen under his spell, despite everything he's done. He's very charismatic . . .' Her voice trailed off.

'Y'know, I'd have thought if anybody had gone with him, it would've been you.'

She thought for a long moment and then said, 'I wanted to. We shared . . . we were together for a while. Then something happened with Kurt which really disturbed me. He seemed to go crazy and he was spending all his time in this bus with Scarlet. I wanted to know what was happening, so I made Wilde explain. He did that all right.' She laughed bitterly. 'Even after he'd told me, it didn't bother me, not really. You know, I just wanted to be with him and I guess I came on to him. But he got angry and said he'd had enough trouble already with that Annie girl. Then he did this.'

She took off her sunglasses. Behind them, her sockets gaped blackly, the flesh around the holes torn and bruised where he had ripped her eyes from her.

'Jesus . . .!' Severin swallowed, and his face rippled at the thought of her agony.

'You've got to stop him,' she said with a heave. 'I can't even cry any more, you know?'

Severin gave her hand a squeeze, but it felt dead in his grasp and he had to let it drop. 'I'll do my best,' he whispered. He turned to Geroge. 'You better stay here with the kids. Give me until dawn.'

'You're not well enough to go up there on your own, lad.' George looked at him sympathetically.

Severin was glad the old man was there, and told him, 'I've got to, for Annie's sake. I can't lose any more time.'

Then he was gone before George could answer, moving into the darkness which seemed to grow deeper in the direction of Wilde's lair.

One solitary light glowed in the Tarrant farmhouse as Severin made his way along the lane. A beacon for the dead, he thought. The shadows seemed to lick out from it, crossing the fields, swamping the trees and the hedgerows, spreading the message that Death Lives Here.

All he could do was stand and stare at it as a convulsive shiver flooded through his body. For the first time in five years he considered turning back, giving up.

35

'Good evening, Annie.'

Cain's sickness had not let him go. It made him appear more terrifying than ever, stripping away the urbane mask that hid the beast within.

He wandered over and touched her shaven scalp with surprising tenderness. 'I shall quite miss you.'

'You don't *have* to kill me, you know.'

'Oh, but I do. You have to understand my perspective. Even if we became ... friends ... you would soon be gone from me in the wink of an eye, on my time-scale. You may as well die now as later.'

'Well, I'd appreciate it if you freed me from these chains. My arms really hurt. And you've made your point.'

'And what point would that be?'

'That I'm powerless in the face of all the grand forces that control life, and that I should understand that and not fight it.'

He smiled in the way a teacher would do to a bright pupil.

'Very Zen,' she continued, encouraging him.

He paused only for a second, and then pulled a bunch of keys from his pocket and unfastened the chains. Annie almost fell forward on to the straw, surprised at how weak she felt. Her joints cracked and her skin buzzed with pins and needles as she pulled herself into a sitting position. Strangely, with the chains gone she felt acutely conscious of her nakedness again, but Cain gave no indication that he was aware of it.

'In a short while I will show you your village again,' he began. 'Perhaps then you will finally appreciate the true meaning and importance of death. It is a vital force; without it, there is nothing. Chaos. No meaning.' He paced the room and then stopped to add quietly, 'Therefore do not hate death.'

'And I thought you liked me, Wilde.'

'I have told you I like you, Annie.'

'But you won't admit to yourself how much.'

His face grew tight but he said nothing.

'Here you are trying to teach *me* things and in all your years, you haven't learned your own lessons. Burying feelings doesn't make them go away, Wilde. They're still there, working beneath the surface, forcing you to do things that you don't understand. Over the last few days, you've broken your own rules. Because of me. I'm that important to you. That should tell you something.'

He turned away from her and when he spoke his voice was almost unrecognizable. 'But I walk a lonely road, Annie. That is my punishment. There can never be anyone to accompany me.'

'Don't you want to know how I feel about you?'

'I know how you feel.' Another deep breath. Annie wanted him to turn round so she could see his face, but he kept his back firmly to her. 'I can see it in your eyes. Despite who I am and everything I have done to you to break that connection between us, the spark is still there in the heart of you.'

People would say I'm perverse . . .'

'Then they would not understand human nature.'

'You don't have to carry on that way. There has to be a way out for you.'

He turned round so she could see his familiar rakish grin, but it seemed false, another mask, but his skill at hiding himself was collapsing before her eyes. 'Oh, it is too late for me, Annie. I am beyond salvation . . .'

'Nobody is—'

' – beyond redemption? I will simply carry on as I am, venting my spleen at my unjust punishment, because, as you so truly pointed out, anything else would be too horrible. Now do you understand why I have to kill you?'

Annie nodded.

He looked into her face and saw something there which surprised him. 'I have indeed been successful.' His voice grew hushed, almost reverent. 'You have been transmuted, here in this dingy shed, from base lead to gold.'

'Changed? How?'

'Can you not feel it? You have given up the shadows.'

He was right! *Transmutation*. The final stage and her last chance. As she looked into Cain's black eyes, her stomach did a nervous flip; she knew instinctively the time was hers. 'You don't forget anything, do you?'

'I remember everything. That is part of my curse, too.'

Annie swallowed; her throat was too dry. 'Then add something here to your memories. An experience you can take with you.'

He shook his head.

'If you don't, you'll regret it. And regret, for you, must be a terrible thing.'

She caught her breath. Had she said enough? Were they the right words?

Then his hand reached out and the fingertips brushed her cheek. They remained there for a second and Annie felt they were like a conductor building up the power between them until her flesh burned. His tongue flicked on to his full lips leaving a sheen of saliva and Annie felt hers do the same almost simultaneously. She could smell his scent as if he had suddenly exuded it in a cloud, olives and warm sand, enveloping her. So close. His mouth opened slightly and she could see his straight white teeth. Their noses were almost touching.

Then, he moved suddenly and touched his lips on hers. Her head almost shot backwards with a gasp, but instead she forced it forward until she was locked in his kiss.

And at that moment she *wanted* to kiss him. She could have given herself up to it completely.

Instead, she reached behind, fumbled for the chain against the wall. Then, in one swift movement, she pushed herself back so she could fling the links around his neck in a noose. There was an instant when his expression shifted from shock to profound betrayal and Annie had to force herself to break away from the powerful despair in his eyes before it crushed her.

He was rooted; she moved quickly. The chain flicked up and around itself. Annie jumped up and yanked hard on it, pulling it tight to his neck. Spitting like a tiger, he put his hands to his throat, but it was too late; she was already wrapping the chain in a knot which he would pull even tighter unless he calmed down.

Then she was backing away across the outhouse. She couldn't

355

afford to wait. She needed enough time to free Martyn and make some kind of getaway. But she did turn at the door and told the raging figure, 'I'm being true to my nature too ... Cain.'

His name hit him like a blow. But Annie didn't wait to see any more. The moment was hers and she had taken it.

Severin had found a few drugged and sleeping travellers upstairs at the farmhouse, but there was no sign of Wilde himself. Yet the place stank of him, of decay and death, as if his presence had left a psychic trail that corrupted each room.

He had heard movements in the dining room, but what he found was the dead farmer and his wife tearing madly at the carcass of some animal. Their eyes loomed up at him in the gloom like the lamps of an approaching car and he slammed the door and pushed a chair under the handle before they could make a move in his direction.

The only place he hadn't searched was the cellar. He looked down the steps into the dark and had a sudden flashback to digging out the grave in the churchyard. There was something down there; he could sense it. Not Wilde, but something just as monstrous. As his eyes adjusted, he could see there was a door at the foot of the steps and a thin strip of faint light glowed beneath it.

Steeling himself, he descended, shotgun at the ready. Hearing no sounds, he kicked the door open, brandishing the gun before him.

The stench almost turned his stomach. In the glare of the bare lightbulb, he noted six bodies heaped around the walls in various states. One of them was barely more than a bloody carcass. But as he took a reluctant step into the room, it moved like the coils of a snake unfurling, making him catch his breath in shock.

It shifted again slightly and then looked up with white, round eyes from a red-smeared face. A thin giggle escaped what was left of its lips.

Severin stared in horror until he saw through its injuries to its true identity. 'Lucas!' he hissed, pointing the shotgun at its head.

'I can help you,' the bloody thing replied. 'I know how you can hurt him.'

356

Severin looked down the barrel unflinchingly.

'Sorry I cut you up, old man,' Lucas giggled, 'but I paid the price for my sins. Look at me. It's taking everything I've got to heal myself. He doesn't know I can do that, but I can.' A gash suddenly knitted above his left eye. 'He still can't believe I'm not like the others.'

Severin began to pull on the trigger. Lucas noticed the slight movement and held his hands up.

'I can help you,' he repeated, a little more earnestly. 'Get me out of here and I'll show you how to pay him back.'

Cain's anger was almost elemental in its power. He tore at the chain, throwing himself back so it ripped at the flesh of his neck, but the pain didn't slow him down. Again and again he wrenched, until his hands were slick with blood, and finally the manacle burst free from the soft brick of the wall. He rolled over and straight on to his feet, making for the door with the chain still trailing from his neck.

By then, he had expected Annie to be halfway across the next field, but there she was, standing naked near the next outhouse door, sobbing softly with her head on Martyn's chest and her arms around his neck. She looked up when Cain burst out into the night, her tears suddenly lost to her fury.

'You bastard!' she screamed.

Cain laughed.

'Why?' She scrubbed a hand across her eyes to clear her vision. 'Why did you kill him?'

His laughter grew richer and tormented her more than his words ever had. 'Annie! You have ruined my final surprise!'

Annie touched Martyn's cheek and tried to find, beyond the dry skin and glassy, pained eyes, some sign of the boy she had loved.

'I killed him for you, Annie,' Cain spat maliciously. 'I did it purely for the moment when I could bring him back and distress you. It takes a seasoning of hope to make the dish of futility so much more potent.'

Annie leaned forward and gave Martyn one final kiss on the cheek before forcing her emotions back in. Cain looked at her curiously, and a little anxiously. She knew what he was thinking, that his control was slipping away. That she was growing stronger.

357

'Annie!'

Severin was standing at the back door of the farmhouse, resting on the jamb with the shotgun held loosely in his hands; he looked like death. Next to him, half stooping from a raft of terrible injuries was Lucas.

Annie didn't have time to work out what the two of them were doing together. She ran over before Cain could get between them, but to her surprise he didn't move; instead, his mocking laughter followed her across the courtyard.

'Yes, run to Severin!' he shouted. 'You will soon find how useful he is to you.'

Annie threw her arms around the American and hugged him tightly. But he felt almost frail against her. For a second she was supporting his entire weight until he lurched upright and took off his long coat to cover her nakedness. She turned back to face Cain as he mocked them and Lucas slipped off into the shadows.

'And what are you going to do now, my little hen? It does not appear that Mr Gentleman Severin has the energy for a pursuit.' Cain stretched out his arms theatrically, then pulled his switchblade from his pocket and began to march towards them.

The rain came out of nowhere, pouring down from a clear night sky on to Cain. He raised his head curiously and stretched out his hands, searching for its origins. Only it wasn't rain. Annie could smell the chemical stink of fuel on the breeze, so strong it made her cough and cover her face.

A high-pitched giggle drew her attention to the edge of the courtyard where Lucas hopped up and down on the spot with malicious glee. He was standing next to an archaic petrol pump, holding the nozzle up and spraying tractor fuel into the breeze to rain down on Cain.

'Get ready to run,' Severin whispered in Annie's ear, clutching something in his closed palm.

He struck a match and threw it. It went out almost before it had left his fingers. Severin tried again. The match didn't light. He struck it once more and the instant it flared he let go of it.

The fire roared across the courtyard in a second, a lake of flames that almost knocked Annie off her feet with the heat. The inferno reached Cain and soared up him in one roaring blast.

Annie glanced back for Martyn, but she could see no sign of

him, as she gathered up the folds of the coat and made for safety with Severin. They half stumbled, half fell away from the conflagration. By the time they had made it round into the lane, the fire had spread to the farmhouse and there was an enormous pall of thick, black smoke blocking out the stars.

'That won't stop him!' Annie shouted above the thunder of the fire. 'Nothing can!'

Severin shook his head. '*You* can stop him. I've just bought you some time.'

36

Bill King sucked on his Silk Cut and filled the van with another cloud of smoke. It was followed by the usual bout of coughing from Alexander Alcock, who, Bill thought with irritation, should have been used to smoke after running a pub for so long. Bill considered smacking him in the mouth, just once, to make his point, but then he saw the warning glare in Hartley's eye and controlled himself. How did Hartley always know what he was thinking?

'How much longer have we got to sit here?' Alcock whined.

'These things are all about timing, Alex. You know that,' Hartley Williams replied with a tone that was intended to be calming, but had the opposite effect.

'They should be settling down now. Drugged up. Getting off with all their women.' Tim Huxton-Smith leaned over the wheel and peered out into the night. The camp was just over the rise. He had known exactly where to park the van so they were just a stone's throw away, yet could not be seen.

'They won't know what hit 'em.' Bill King chuckled throatily. Next to his feet were several cans of petrol, enough to burn the whole camp to the ground. They all had shotguns, but they were for last-ditch protection. They didn't want any evidence that would lead the police to them, although Bill had argued that no court in the land would convict them even if they were caught red-handed.

'That's funny,' Huxton-Smith said, peering out of the window, 'I reckon I can see smoke over Tarrant's farmhouse.'

'The old bastard's crazy as a loon,' King said dismissively. 'He's probably burning off a pile of old tyres and hoping nobody will report him.'

'I don't think there'll be many folk mourning, even if it *is* the farmhouse on fire,' Hartley Williams said with a supercilious smile. 'After all, he was the one who invited this shower on to his land in the first place.'

'Aye, that's right,' King said. 'Burn, you bastard!'

Alcock checked his watch nervously. 'Come on, Hartley. Don't you think it's time? I've got a lot to do back at the pub.'

Williams thought for a moment and then smirked. 'All right then, lads! Let's do it. Let's give that scum a taste of the Lord's cleansing fire.'

Bill King whooped and kicked open the van's back door with his huge steel-capped boot. His enthusiasm died in his throat; he was met with twenty pairs of staring, emotionless eyes.

The travellers were gathered in an arc around the rear of the van. Normally King would have waded into them, arms flailing, without a second thought, but there was something about those unrelenting stares and rigid postures that unnerved him. None of them moved, not even the twitch of a muscle. They looked like waxwork dummies. *Or corpses.*

'Tim!' He turned and barked at Huxton-Smith in the driving seat. 'Let's get the fuck out of here!'

But it was too late. The driver's door was wrenched open and King watched as a pair of arms flashed in and dragged Huxton-Smith from his seat.

As King turned back, he already knew it was his turn. The travellers' frozen expressions were gone, replaced by bestial snarls as they surged forward with one mind, one animal desire.

'What do we do if they come for us?' Angela faced the blazing campfire to feel the heat on her face, as if that could make up for not seeing.

'We fight, lass. To the bitter end.'

George felt tired, but proud. The remaining travellers had responded to his orders with surprising compliance, when, backed up by Angela, he had convinced them to emerge from their homes. Buses and vans were hastily moved to form a circle around the central area. The campfire had been stoked to provide light and, if necessary, ammunition. And then they had gathered in their circle of hope, like a few frightened natives, praying to their various gods and goddesses and staring into the east as if it would hurry the sun along.

'It's a bit like a wagon train, isn't it?' Peter Cockburn stood close to George.

'That it is, lad.' *Only the enemy on the outside was much more terrifying than a few Red Indians*, George wanted to add.

The old man was surprised at how quickly the boy had shaped up; he seemed to have an inherent psychological hardiness that could cope with anything. His sisters had taken it worse, but that was only to be expected. They were being cared for by a couple of traveller women close to the fire.

'How many of us are there?' Angela asked.

George looked round. 'About thirty.'

'So few.' She hung her head. 'It's all my fault.'

George stepped up to her and hugged her shoulders. 'It's nobody's fault, lass. This would've happened whatever any of you lot did. And whatever you might feel, you're making up for it now. You're brave coming out here after what you've been through.'

'What else could I do? Hide in the bus until they came for me?'

'Well, yes, you could have done that. But you didn't. You came out here and told me what's what and helped me organize the others. And now you're facing up to it shoulder to shoulder with everyone else.'

His words seemed to have some effect for her muscles grew less tense and she allowed herself to sink next to his body. He turned his attention out into the night and wondered when the attack would come. He had seen the madness of the dead things in Riddington and he feared nothing would stand up to it in force, but he kept his thoughts to himself.

'Can you hear anything?' Peter asked.

George shook his head. 'My bloody ears are not much cop these days, lad.'

'I thought I heard something just beyond that rise. Like a shout or a scream.' Peter had a sudden yearning for his mother and he thought he was going to embarrass himself with tears, but he managed to hold on.

361

'This is a terrible time,' George said quietly, 'but if we come through this we're all going to be stronger and happier. And we'll all look at life in a different way.'

He put his other hand on Peter's shoulder, and pulled Angela closer to him, and then the three of them stood and waited.

A soft wind had blown up and whistled among the vehicles, fanning the campfire into a surge of crackles and sparks that almost drowned out the sounds of the things prowling just beyond the buses and trucks. George felt exhausted. In the past hour, they had repelled numerous assaults and the effort was taking its toll.

Some of the travellers had managed to get over the shock of what had happened to their friends; others seemed unable to cope. But the only way the dead could be kept at bay was by fire, and George had everyone armed with burning faggots from the campfire to torch anything which tried to clamber over the vehicles. The revenants burned as if they were stuffed with dry wood and straw, flaring up brightly for a moment before collapsing in a heap of blackened bones. Yet to the travellers who stood on the bonnets brandishing flaming torches, the things out in the night were still their friends, and each time one of the dead fell in a conflagration, George could see the terrible price paid on the faces of those around him.

None of them could deal with the children, though. They still looked too innocent despite the cold gleam in their eyes. In the end, as child hands crashed and clawed at the perimeter vehicles, George had taken the decision simply to contain them. They were herded towards an open van. Then they were driven in like rabid dogs and the doors slammed shut. George could hear them crashing around madly inside. They were aged about eight to fifteen, six of them, and ready to tear anyone else limb from limb.

Now, as he looked out over the bonnet of a van, one of the travellers came over. He was a bearded man in his thirties. Of them all he seemed the most in control.

He nodded to George grimly and said, 'I think you should see this.'

He led the way around the campfire and into a bus, so they could look out across the night-dark fields through the windows. A stone's throw away, one of the dead was wandering aimlessly in circles, first one way, then the other, as if it had forgotten where it was. Occasionally it would drop to its knees and press its face against the soil.

'Jack's been ... it's been doing that for five minutes now. What do you think's wrong? It looks like a clockwork toy that's winding down.'

Suddenly, it started moving quickly as if it had received a jolt of power, arms and legs jerking randomly before it opened its mouth in an awful, silent scream and started to tear at the flesh of its face.

'Look, it's gone mad!' the traveller whispered.

'It was mad before,' George replied. 'It looks to me like it's breaking down.'

There was an instant when it froze, its face contorted, and then it crashed to the ground. They both held their breath, but it didn't move.

'Now it's dead ... or whatever you want to call it!' There was relief and wonder in the traveller's voice. He looked at George. 'Bloody dead!'

Before George could reply, there was a sudden burst of angry shouts from the campfire. They hurried back to see four travellers wrestling with a young man who was fighting like a wildcat. He was spitting and snarling so much it was difficult to get a look at his face. But when the young man saw George, he stopped his struggling and grinned maliciously. George felt the heat drain from his limbs as an icy horror swept over him.

'Well, look at you. George Newton! You've grown *very* old, George, and I'm still young. Aren't you jealous?'

'Laurence Lucas.' The hushed words felt poisonous on George's tongue.

'Do you bloody know him?' one of the men holding him snarled. 'Somehow he managed to sneak into the circle. We caught him trying to drag one of the kids away.'

His injuries almost healed, Lucas looked as fresh as the day George had last seen him – just before his terrible crimes had been exposed. 'You can't fight it if you're wired that way, George,' he said with a snigger.

'He's one of them,' George said disgustedly. 'He should be dead and buried and forgotten. He killed three boys back in the sixties.'

'But he's different to the others,' the bearded traveller said curiously.

'Better,' Lucas snapped. 'Soon they're all going to go back to the shit from which they were formed. They're deteriorating all the time. Me, I'm here for good. I've got another chance.'

George shook his head fearfully. 'God forbid.'

'What do we do with him then?' someone asked.

The bearded traveller stepped forward and said quietly, 'I know. Bring him this way.'

They dragged Lucas around the campfire to a van on the far side. He fought to begin with, and then drew himself up and walked contemptuously to the rear doors.'

What *are* you going to do? Lock me away?' he sneered.

The traveller didn't reply. He grabbed hold of the door handles and then nodded to the men gripping Lucas's arms. When he ripped open the doors, the six children within were caught unawares for a second. On seeing them Lucas's expression began to change from curiosity to fear, and just at that point he was heaved into their midst and the doors slammed shut.

The van started to rock and a frenzied noise began immediately. Rending and tearing, an abattoir sound that was soon intercut with the screams of Lucas. No one could bear to listen and they all hurried away to the other side of the fire until the screaming was suddenly cut off.

'Poetic justice,' the bearded traveller said darkly.

'Still and all, a horrible way to go,' George replied.

They walked over to the perimeter together and looked out. The other sounds from the night seemed to be dying down.

'If he was right, it could soon be all over,' the bearded man said.

George thought of Severin and Annie and said nothing, but in his heart he was praying.

37

Annie and Severin moved as quickly as they could down the lane towards Riddington, but they were hampered by his weakness and by Annie's bare feet which were raw and bleeding from the sharp stones on the road. As they went, she told him how her dream had led her to Wilde's true identity, and how she confronted him with it. He was staggered at the revelation and that she had lived to tell the tale.

Behind them, the farmhouse burned brightly and the air was filled with the sulphurous smell of dense smoke.

'We've got time,' Severin said. 'It's gonna take the bastard a while to recover from that. Maybe weeks.'

Annie wasn't so sure.

Then the bus lurched into view. Before they even had time to consider what the rumbling sound was. It slewed about on the stony road as it rounded the corners at full speed and fought to stay out of the hedgerows.

Annie didn't have to see through the darkened windscreen to know who was behind the wheel. *The angel of death*, she thought as it hurtled towards them.

They both moved in different directions, throwing themselves aside. But it was Annie that the bus went after, ploughing through the undergrowth to pursue her.

Severin was nowhere to be seen as she bolted towards a gate into a field further up the lane. She estimated she would have just enough time to reach it. The snarling, misfiring engine roared louder as the bus bore down on her from behind, its twisted bumper almost barrelling against her fragile legs.

Reaching the gate, she threw herself over it, hitting the grass hard, rolling and then up and running again. It was the right thing to do. The bus didn't stop; it came too.

The retort of Severin's shotgun brought Annie up sharp and she looked ahead. There he was, bracing himself, shotgun raised, to fire again. She ducked and the blast frosted the window, but the bus kept coming. Severin calmly fired the other barrel. This time the glass was completely shattered.

A second later the vehicle spun out of control and crashed to a sudden halt. A dark shape was jettisoned out of the broken window. It landed with a wet sucking sound.

As they both made to regain the road, giving a wide berth to the wreck of the bus, Annie's attention was drawn again to the strange slurping sound. And then she saw it, a black smudge silhouetted against the night sky, and she realized what had happened. A fence stake had impaled Cain from crotch to shoulder and he was writhing on it like a skewered fish. He turned his head grotesquely as they skirted him, and watched them in silence. Then he started trying to heave himself off the stake.

Severin had stopped. 'There's no point running,' he said as he reloaded the shotgun. 'That way, he's gonna get us sooner or later. I might as well see if I can blast him into jelly.'

Annie grabbed hold of his arm. 'But it's not up to you. I'm the one who's got to end it, and this isn't the time or the place.'

'How do you know?'

'I just do.' And she did; the thought was suddenly there in her head like a shaft of moonlight in a dark forest. They had to get back to the village.

Severin resisted for a second and then allowed her to lead him.

Annie felt their destination intuitively. 'The church,' she replied confidently. 'That's where it's got to happen.'

Before they could set off, the squelching intensified and ended with a sudden plop. When they turned the fence stake was empty.

'Shit!' Annie whispered. 'Where the hell is he?'

She scanned the hedgerows and the fields beyond, but it was too dark to see anything; and at that moment she remembered the message Cain had scrawled on the wall of her bedroom: *No one is safe. Nowhere is safe.*

A second later, he emerged around the edge of the bus, making no pretence to hide, a black shape darker than the surrounding shadows. He was bent double from pain, but he dragged himself forward.

Severin didn't waste a second. His shot hit Cain's right knee, blasting it apart and flinging him backwards. But only seconds later, Cain had reached the side of the bus and began to climb up it.

Severin fired again and hit the other knee, sending Cain crashing to the ground once more.

'Christ!' Severin exclaimed incredulously. 'I've seen him

injured much less than this and he always scurries off like some dog to heal himself.'

'Come on,' Annie said, giving him a push. 'We can't afford to wait.'

As they stood at the lych-gate and looked up at the enormous black bulk of St Martin's, Annie saw the moon come out behind the steeple and she found it within her to continue.

Inside the churchyard, she felt better. It was the right place, the only place. Where two religions met; the solid, reassuring masculinity of Christianity, evident in every stone block of the church; and the wild femininity of the pagan belief which preceded it and on whose sacred site the church was built, with its yews and ivy and nature symbols hidden in the architecture. Here the two powers melded into the stew of whatever dominated human existence. The site was rich with magick, and Annie, who in her time had straddled both religions, could draw upon it.

Severin, who was on the verge of collapse and who had not said a word since they'd left Cain by the bus, now whispered, 'Don't take any risks, Annie.'

She slipped her arm around his waist and rested her head on his shoulders. 'I'll do what I have to do.'

'I don't want you to get hurt any more,' he continued falteringly, 'I love you. Even with no hair.'

'I know. And you'll always be dear to me, Severin.'

The church door was always left open, so they slipped in wearily and switched on the lights, then walked up the aisle to the altar. Annie faced the cross and bowed her head in respect.

'It's going to be hours before he gets here,' Severin said weakly, collapsing in a pew.

'No,' Annie replied. 'It won't be long. He'll force himself to heal, even if it takes every last drop of his energy.'

As if in answer, the door creaked open like a gunshot in the stillness. He was there.

Annie turned and glimpsed a magnificent ebony statue, its blackness so deep it was almost a shadow slipping in through the door. But then she saw its eyes, wide and white in black bone sockets, and the stench of charred meat wrapped itself around her. Wilde was barely recognizable except as a charcoal crust. Nothing could survive that and remain a person, she told herself.

And there *was* insanity in those huge white eyes, but there was also a cold intelligence still trying to fight its way through. And, as if in response, his body was starting to put itself back together, even though wisps of yellowy-grey smoke were still rising from his limbs. It was as if he was out of focus; there was a blurring all around him where the cells screamed and fought and pulled themselves together in a mockery of the tramp of life across millennia, knitting across liver and spleen; wrapping themselves lovingly around bone, rebuilding eyelids and ears and lips.

A strange mewling noise filled the church and Annie realized it was Cain trying to speak without lips. 'Ahhh – nieee.' The sound was like a knife in her spine.

'Ahh-nnniee. Ah-nie.' A pause. The half-regenerated lips were almost there. 'Annie.'

His grin was triumphant. 'You really are a masochist, Annie.' His voice crackled drily. 'You insist on doing things which you know will anger me.' He paused and his whole body seemed to tremble. 'We are linked so closely, you and I. I dance to the tune of my trinity, my God of ultimate judgement and ultimate mercy, my masculine God of the sun and science and logic. And you have your own trinity, just as judgemental, just as merciful, the feminine Goddess of moon and magic and intuition. But there are two differences, and let us not forget them. I have power and you have none. And I cannot be killed . . . *and you can.*'

There was a sound like creaking leather as he took a few steps forward. His bulk was growing before her eyes, sinews increasing in power so they could strangle the life from her. Annie felt she was looking at a machine with only one impulse: murder.

This is it, she thought. *It's nearly time.*

But Severin had somehow found the strength to step in front of her. He swayed a little as he took out the shotgun and pointed it at Cain.

Those reformed lips said softly, 'You have never been a threat, Severin. Not from the first day you decided to pursue me. I have humoured you because, to be honest, I enjoyed the company. There was something ... reassuring ... in the knowledge that you were always there, a few miles behind.'

Severin looked as if for the first time he realized his own impotence. His finger squeezed on the trigger and then relaxed; Cain smiled triumphantly, his point made.

'It's time, Severin.' Annie put her hand on his shoulder and eased him to one side. 'Give me the bracelet.'

Cain's reaction was instantaneous: he darted forward. But Severin already had the bracelet out of his shirt and the sight of it stopped him dead. It seemed to glow.

'You do not know what you are doing, Severin,' Cain warned. 'If you give up the bracelet, your life is over.'

Severin grunted dismissively, but Annie was unnerved, 'What do you mean?'

'What I mean, little girl, is that the trinket may be the only way to destroy me, but it is also the only thing keeping your dear lover alive. Tell me, Mr Severin ... I know you are not one of the world's greatest intellects, but did you never wonder how you survived that plane crash?'

'I was lucky.'

'Lucky? I do not think so. The truth is, Mr Severin, you died on that day.'

Severin shook his head, but Annie saw the doubt there; he was suddenly starting to find the answers to questions he had asked for a long time.

'Think, Mr Severin. Think hard. Do you not feel different now?'

'Cold ...'

'Deathly cold, all the time. And that strange empathy you have for me? That ability to track me, to know where I am at any given time? Why, it is almost like the empathy that I have for dead things and which dead things have for me.'

'No!' Severin was vehement. Annie gripped his arm, not wanting to believe it either.

'The only thing that has kept you going is that bracelet, Severin. It has tremendous power, you know that. It is filled with life, with souls, and you have drawn on that to continue on your single-minded mission. There is no reason why you cannot go on for many, many years to come. Enjoy what is left of your life. But if you give up the bracelet, you will lose its power. You will return to your natural state.'

Cain could smell victory. 'If you walk out now, and take the bracelet with you, I will allow you to go, and I vow that our paths will never cross. But if you hand it over, you will die, Severin. And this time it will be permanent. Can you do that? Can you give everything up?'

Annie turned to Severin and she knew it was all true; it was etched in his terrible expression – the knowledge of the horrific damnation of a lost soul.

She tried to hold him, pull him back from the brink. 'Severin,' she whispered. 'Remember Marj and Matty. Remember why—'

Her words caught him. Slowly he came back to her and forced a weak smile. 'Crazy world,' he tried to joke.

Cain was enjoying the pain he had caused. 'You see, Severin. You have life *now*. Taste it! Acknowledge its value, its brightness. And what is there in death? Just a cold, hungry nothingness.' He laughed. 'Who would want that?'

Severin turned briefly to him, defiant to the last. 'I don't need you to tell me what I do or don't value, *Cain*!'

Annie's eyes were wet, but Severin didn't try to wipe them. 'I'll miss you,' he whispered. 'You were the one who gave me life.'

Annie knew he had made his choice. She waited as he slipped the bracelet from his neck and handed it to her. She threw her arms around his waist and kissed him once, then she pulled her head back, watched the light die in his eyes. A flicker, bright at first, then diminishing. His smile remained, even when the light was long gone.

As he grew heavy and limp in her arms, she let him slide downwards and gently brushed his eyes closed. There was a new weight in her heart that she would have to bear for ever. But she gripped the bracelet tightly and turned back to Cain, who looked stunned, disorientated.

'You don't understand good people, do you, Cain?' she asked softly. 'You think everyone's like you. All those years and you haven't learnt a thing.'

He could not take his eyes off the bracelet. Annie knew he was wondering if she knew what to do with it; she asked herself the same question.

'I have learnt many things about *you*, Annie. I have read your diaries, and I know what you want, more than anything.' He closed his eyes and concentrated, flexing the muscles on his forearms as he opened and closed his hands. After a few seconds, the wind outside rose and whipped against the side of the church, and when it subsided, Annie heard a movement just beyond the door. She watched, but no one entered.

In the lull, his voice sounded hollow. 'Your brother is out there. You only have to give me the bracelet and call his name. He will come and you will be together again. That is what you want, Annie. Do it.'

Even after everything she had seen and experienced of his foulness, she almost gave in.

'The choice is yours, Annie,' Cain continued. 'Say yes, and he is yours. I have the power to make sure he will not deteriorate like the others. He will be no different to how he was in life. Your family will be whole. The happy days will return. No sadness, no mourning, no darkness. Your choice, Annie.'

So easy. Just say yes.

But it *wouldn't* be the same, would it? She was changed. Those golden days when Robert was alive were like an island far out at sea, and that was how they should remain; a shining, perfect place. Never to be tarnished.

She shook her head, and felt her heart sink in despair as she did so. 'No, Cain.'

'A bad choice, Annie Boulton. Now you have lost everything.'

He began to advance, never taking his eyes off the bracelet as if he feared it would leap out of her hands and destroy him. Annie's head was whirling, her breathing grew short and laboured.

What do I do? She looked at the bracelet, then at Cain. *What do I do?*

'I'm not scared of death any more,' she said confidently, and it was true. She remembered the premonition from the sweat lodge and she knew it was only seconds away from becoming reality. She did not shrink from it. But she did grip the bracelet tightly, whispering a prayer she had thought long-forgotten.

He drew closer and closer, and then he was there. She could taste the ozone in her mouth from whatever process was rebuilding him. He placed a hand on each of her cheeks and drew her face up until she was looking directly into his eyes. He smiled.

'Time to die, Annie.'

His hands slipped down to her neck, fingers searching for the

371

pressure point. They caressed her skin for just a second, and then he pressed sharply. There was one brief instant of pain, and then Annie was falling back into herself. Head over heels, whirling and spinning, away from the light, away from Cain's grinning face into death.

38

Annie felt at peace for the first time in her life. No fears, no tension, just a softly suffusing golden glow that filled her entire being. It was the feeling of rolling over for another doze when it wasn't really time to get up, of sunshine on the face, of being next to the ocean, of those seconds immediately after an orgasmic rush.

Much to her dismay, it started to fade too quickly. And she started to recall the queasy disorientation that had overcome her at the point of passing over.

Slowly, she scanned the landscape without really being surprised there *was* a landscape. She was standing on a windswept plain. In the distance, purple mountains brooded beneath a sky which moved from the deepest blue, overhead, to a fiery red on the horizon. The gale whipped granules of dust into her exposed skin and she could feel a raw power glowering behind her, sullen and oppressive. She turned to face it.

The Black Cathedral.

The main block of the building rose up in a majestic fusion of spires and columns, cupolas and towers, gargoyles and friezes, all in the blackest marble which seemed to glow with an inner light. On either side, a black wall, as tall as three men and topped with spikes, ran from horizon to horizon. There was no way around it. The only way through was via an enormous black door with a mighty iron knocker at its centre.

Annie understood then in the hum of the Cathedral's presence, why Cain's life had been dedicated to discovering what lay on the other side. It was a mixture of three motivations: that simple human urge to discover secrets forever denied; a masochistic desire to see the light that would always be beyond him;

and a plaintive attempt to find some meaning to his existence. She had none of his needs, just a desire to get where she had to go.

Her old life hadn't been forgotten; it had simply faded into the background like one of those hazy, happy memories of childhood, there to warm her if she wanted.

She glanced down at her wrist and noted, curiously, that it was encircled by a strange bracelet. The sight threatened to free a whole host of less happy memories and emotions, and Annie quickly shook her head to dispel them. They would only drag her back; she had to move forward. Inhaling a deep lungful of the arid air, she marched towards the Cathedral and kept her thoughts to a minimum.

The journey felt arduous, but Annie had no sense of time passing. She simply walked and walked and then she was there.

A heavy chill encompassed her when she stepped into the deep shadow of the cathedral. Her breath caught at the immensity of the edifice. She strained back and looked up once again, feeling like an ant outside the home of a colossus. She couldn't begin to imagine what hands could have built it. Before her was an ebony door that towered over her head, yet strangely the wrought-iron ring that served both as a knocker and a handle was at the correct height for her. Cautiously, she reached out to it and hammered.

The sound far exceeded the action; Annie thought her ears would burst as it thundered like cannon-fire. For a few seconds, the air tremored and then the immaculate stillness returned. She had just reached out for the knocker once more, only to hear a response deep within the Cathedral. It sounded miles distant, yet she recognized it as the toll of a mighty bell.

A second later, the door started to swing open. Cool air seeped out around her, scented with subtle fragrances which smelled of lime and nutmeg. With it, came an almost tangible magnetic feeling, like invisible hands trying to pull her in. When the gap was wide, Annie peered inside, but she couldn't see because something like a searchlight was glaring directly at her. She shielded her eyes, and as she did so the bracelet jangled against her cheek. Suddenly the restrained thoughts burst free and exploded in her mind like fireworks.

In an instant she remembered everything: her death; Cain; Severin; and all the killing that she wanted to leave far behind her. *Forget it all. Go on – into the light.* But however much she tried, she couldn't keep the thoughts down. Her mission came first. Her reason for existing.

The name is the spell. The bracelet is the key. Annie recalled the words of her dreams. 'Call the name,' she whispered dreamily. 'Call the name.'

The writing on the inside of the bracelet which had previously been impossible to decipher, now burned with a red fire that spelt it out: 'ABEL.'

'Abel,' Annie whispered. And through the light, deep within the Cathedral, she thought she heard the tolling bell reply. The air seemed to fizz with an electrical charge. Everything was suspended.

She grasped the bracelet with her other hand and repeated in a much louder voice, 'Abel!'

The bell was louder too and the light shimmered, its rays seeming to bend unnaturally. Deep within it, she sensed some-one was coming.

As she waited, Annie had a powerful feeling that there were others in the light, just a step or two away from her. She could feel them watching her. She tried to take a step forward, but something was holding her back.

'Severin?' she said tentatively. And then, 'Martyn?' And finally, 'Robert?'

There was no reply, but Annie registered their presence so strongly that if she closed her eyes she could see them. A sudden, overwhelming feeling of love and strength took her by surprise and she couldn't stop the tears streaming down her cheeks. Right then, Annie knew everything that she needed to know and all the hideous black thoughts were washed from her mind. She knew she wouldn't be allowed to see her loved ones now, but there was time. She could wait.

Several sudden changes came next, all happening at once. The atmospheric pressure dipped as the static crackled in blue lights around her. It was accompanied by a sound like a jet taking off, muffled at first but growing louder, coming towards her from the depths of the Cathedral. After a minute, she had to cover her ears as the roar grew almost unbearable. The very foundations of the Cathedral seemed to shake and the ground appeared to tilt and keel as if it was being rippled by an earthquake. Annie fell to her knees, terrified of what would happen next. Then she saw it, advancing rapidly, a light even brighter than the glare in the Cathedral, a blinding golden glow in the shape of a man. It was hurtling towards her, arms outstretched.

She waited a moment and then realized what she had to do. Tentatively, she held out her hand. She was the bridge. She was going to bring him back.

There was a moment of vertigo as the light rushed towards her and then its golden hand touched her fingertips, her palms, held tight.

Annie opened her mouth to cry, but no sound came out. The roaring encompassed everything. The light filled her vision and sucked at her senses, and then she felt herself being ripped away and up into space.

Her eyes snapped open. In the second it took for her to orient herself, the details of the Black Cathedral melted from her memory like frost in the sun; but the feelings of love stayed with her, as powerful as if she was still standing at the threshold.

She realized everything had been transformed again. Her first sensations of the real world were so intense she could hardly bear them: everything she saw was crystal-clear, super-focused, almost too real to be real. The air was filled with a hundred different scents, and her fingertips seared with the touch of every minute contour on the flagged floor beneath them. She could hear so many subtle sounds it was like an orchestra playing. Annie had never experienced life like it before.

She was back in the church, lying on the floor where Cain had killed her. The thought made her body go rigid. He *had* killed her. She recalled his hands on her throat searching for the correct nerve, and that dizzying sensation as the life rushed out of her. Now, something had brought her back from the other side of death.

Cautiously, she raised herself on to her elbows and looked around. Severin's body was slumped in the pew where he had fallen. She felt a tremendous sense of loss, but surprisingly no bitterness or despair.

Cain was further down the aisle, leaning on another pew with his back to her. He was trying to heal himself, but he looked broken. A hunched, fragile, old man.

Annie pulled herself to her feet as quietly as she could, but he must have heard her for he spun round to face her. The fear in his face when he saw her was so powerful, it shocked her.

'You've returned?' he whispered almost reverently.

'I did what I had to, Cain,' Annie replied calmly. 'I was chosen to stop you and all the damage you were doing to the natural order. And that's what I've done.'

Cain glanced around him as if he could hear something. 'What have you done?'

'I think you know. I've brought back the only thing that could stop you. You've got the mark on you which prevents any man killing you, but it won't stop this.'

'My brother . . .'

'You killed him in the field. Crushed his head with a rock. The Bible says you introduced murder into the world, Cain.'

'My punishment has far outweighed that crime!'

'But you've compounded it, over and over again. You could have sought salvation . . .'

'No!' He was looking around him fearfully, now.

'You never learned the lesson, Cain. And now your time is up.'

Annie sensed the arrival of the light, growing behind the altar, before she saw it. Cain was staring at the door and he didn't see what was happening until the glow had filled the whole church like a magnesium flare. He turned suddenly, but the light in the shape of a man was already advancing along the aisle towards him. Annie stepped into the pews to let the power pass her.

She expected Cain to run, but he remained fixed to the spot as if he knew anything else was useless. The fear disappeared from his face and was replaced by a longing that was searing to see. At that moment Annie thought she didn't really know him at all.

She heard his whisper as clearly as the rustle of autumn leaves on a still day. 'Forgive me.'

There was no reply. The light bore down on him slowly but relentlessly, and only at the last instant did it seem he was about to break away. But by then it was too late. The quality of the light changed slightly and Annie felt a tremendous heat. She had one last sight of Cain's face – frightened, scared, a small boy lost at night – before the light engulfed him completely and the heat pushed the temperature in the church up to that of a furnace. There was a sound like sizzling meat and then the light imploded silently, leaving the church to the brilliant white glare of the sun.

When Annie woke, dawn had broken outside and the sun streamed through the stained glass windows, painting colours on the flagstones. There was no sign of Cain or the light that was the essence of his brother. Further down the aisle, a dark smudge marked the stone floor like a soot deposit.

Whatever had taken place, it had been traumatic enough to leave her unconscious for at least two hours. She stood up and experienced an almost overpowering sense of relief that it was all over. Looking into the dawn light, a smile slipped to her lips, but it faded as she recalled the price that had been paid. So much death piled high.

And then she walked over and sat next to Severin who had proved his humanity was stronger than death, who had made the ultimate sacrifice without a single thought for himself. Annie leant and kissed him on his cheek before whispering in his ear, 'Rest easy, John. Your long years of wandering are finally over.'

She cried a few tears for him and then walked slowly down the aisle towards the new day.

39

They left just after dawn, the tattered remnants of an army heading for safer climes. Pole position was borne by a black single-decker bus of fifties vintage, still bearing the dust of Stonehenge and the mud of Glastonbury. The windows were blacked out and only the driver was visible, an unshaven forty-year-old with dreadlocks. A few other vehicles followed, but many had been abandoned at the camp, on the edge of the village, which still smouldered with the remains of several funeral pyres. There was no one around to see their departure.

In the back of the black bus, George Newton thought fleetingly about seeing his old house one more time, but he dismissed the idea almost as soon as it arrived; there was no point holding on to the past when a bright new future beckoned. He smiled to himself and pushed his hat back on his head, everything that had happened during the last twenty-four hours already driven to the back of his mind. He didn't *know* if that Wilde character had been defeated, but he *felt* deep in his heart that this was the case. Somehow the American had won through, just like his compatriots did back in the war. And Annie had been involved too, as sure as sugar. There was one sour-lemon twinge of sadness that he would never see her again, but he was happy in the knowledge that she had her life ahead of her, ready to be filled with wonder and magic and experience.

'Where are we going, George?' Peter Cockburn was perched on a voluminous serge cushion next to him, watching his sisters play cards further down the bus. The girls were still numb with shock, their dark eyes occasionally slipping into vacant stares as they recalled snatches of the horror. But those snatches were breaking up slowly and dispersing like oil on the sea, and George knew the worst of them would be swept away by a tide of hope.

'I don't know, young Peter,' the old man said. 'What do you say, lass?'

Angela slumped back in a large bean bag like a broken doll, sunglasses pressed tightly against her puffy face. Although her injuries had been monstrous, the scars on her psyche were less than those suffered by the girls, and George was confident that soon *she* would be leading them all.

Her voice when she replied was paper-thin. 'North. Scotland, if they'll let us get that far. There's a community up there, in the Highlands, where we can rest for a while. Build up our strength. Get over all this . . .'

'Scotland, eh? What do you say to that?' George interrupted before Angela got maudlin. He scrubbed Peter's head playfully and the boy ducked away with a laugh.

'Great. Can we see Loch Ness?'

'You can see anything you want, lad. There's a big world out there and you've got plenty of time.'

George lounged back in his marshmallow cushion and pulled his hat down low. He wondered what the strange feeling was that made his stomach tingle, and then he remembered: excitement. How long had it been since he'd felt that? But there it was. *Excitement*. The sun burned like a clear white light through the windscreen, illuminating a dazzling array of dust motes in a way he had never seen before. He closed his eyes and thought perhaps he might have a little sleep after their long night. And when he opened his eyes, well, he might not even know where he was. Now wouldn't that be a thing?

Annie took one last look around her room and put her good memories to bed, tucked up safe and tight where they couldn't be harmed. Her suitcase was full and fastened, her Walkman was round her neck, and her feet were itching.

The click of the door disturbed her from her thoughts and she looked round to see her father, tanned and smiling.

'Now you're sure you're making the right decision?' he asked.

She nodded. 'London will be great. Just the place to grow my hair back! Gill's happy for me to stay with her until I can find a place of my own. And if it doesn't work out, I can always come home, can't I?'

'Of course you can. What do you think we're going to do? Rent your room out the moment you're through the door? It'll work out fine, don't worry. You just make sure you do well at those interviews.'

He picked up the suitcase and held the door open for her. She was still getting used to the lightness in her own step. The days after that final confrontation in the church had been hard, but she was over it now; her emotions had ranged through triumph and mourning, joy and suffering.

Sometimes on those crisp, warm nights as summer had wound down towards autumn, she would sit in the back garden under the apple tree and look at the stars, waiting for the moon to emerge from behind a cloud. At those times, the memories would creep out and present themselves like ghost images on the silver lawn. Severin and Martyn and Charlotte. It was hard to hold the tears back, but they weren't the black, acid tears she'd cried after Robert's death. They were more like the rain that came after the hot spell ended, cleansing and refreshing. She missed her dear friends and she sorely regretted the way they had been driven from the world, but their sacrifice had not been for nothing; they had achieved something transforma-tional. The world was a better place, for the first time in millennia, and Annie knew that when her time came she would see them again, beyond the black door, deep in the glare of a better place.

The scars were more evident in the village where everyone had suffered to some extent; they all felt a gritty, painful despair at what had happened. There had been a flurry of newspaper headlines as the police tried to make head or tail of the deaths that had occurred on that long, sleepless night, but then other events took centre stage in other parts of the country. Most people Annie encountered seemed to be in shock, as much from what they had seen within themselves, as what they had experienced. She was doubtful that Riddington would survive; several homes had already gone on the market. Young Jake Samuels and his parents had left for a new life in Australia – still a family, though no one knew for how long.

Her father hurried out to put the suitcase in the boot, while her mother fussed around in the lounge, primping herself in the mirror before joining them for the trip to the station. Annie sat in the kitchen and thought about what the future held, while in the background the radio played some song she didn't know. There were so many new records she had to catch up on now.

She knew she was a changed woman. The white light of the moon radiated out of every pore and she felt magical whispers in her head, telling her secret things, hinting at a network of power and connectivity she had never glimpsed before. Although her struggle had been a tremendous one, Annie guessed another longer and different one lay ahead, where her new perceptions and strengths would be needed. She was ready for it.

When the music ended and the news came on, her attention suddenly focused. 'And the headlines this morning . . . a plane carrying two hundred passengers has gone missing *en route* from Heathrow to Paris. Air traffic—'

Annie didn't hear the rest. There was a rushing in her ears as her stomach did a flip.

She closed her eyes and instantly she could smell olives and warm sand, hear his charged, charismatic voice. Her body filled with ice water.

Of course, it could have been an accident. Planes did crash and for all sorts of reasons – not just because Cain made them do so. But suddenly she couldn't be sure. She hadn't seen his body. Was he still out there? Would she carry with her, for the rest of her life, the faint fear that one day he would return?

His own words came back across the void: *No one is safe. Nowhere is safe.*

With a shiver, she looked down at the two bracelets on her wrist, the old corroded one which her parents could never appreciate, and the new silver one engraved with the symbol of the moon.

She could never be sure, but she wouldn't let that stop her enjoying her life to the full. If the darkness was going to come back, she would face it then.

She plugged her headphones into her ears and switched on her Walkman. The Isley Brothers launched into 'The Highways Of My Life' and music filled her world once more.

Nocturne

MARK CHADBOURN

He woke up on a New Orleans trolley car. He was wearing his best suit and carrying a walletful of travellers' cheques, a reservation at a smart hotel and a suitcase full of bloodstained clothes.

But David Easter had no idea how he got there. The last thing he remembered, he was working in a south London record shop.

Somewhere in the city is a girl who holds the key to what has happened to him. As David sets out to find her he is drawn inexorably into a darkness that stretches back to the dawn of the jazz age – and now threatens not only David but the city itself . . .

£5.99   0 575 05793 9

PEEPING TOM

has published stories by MARK CHADBOURN - BRIAN LUMLEY - RAMSEY CAMPBELL - STEVE HARRIS - IAN WATSON - GRAHAM JOYCE - CHRISTOPHER FOWLER - STEPHEN LAWS - STEPHEN GALLAGHER - BEN LEECH - GUY N SMITH - MICHAEL MARSHALL SMITH - NICHOLAS ROYLE - MARK MORRIS - BRIAN STABLEFORD - SIMON CLARK - JACK PAVEY - KEITH BROOKE - JOEL LANE - CONRAD WILLIAMS - D F LEWIS - MADELEINE FINNEGAN - DAVID RILEY - PAUL PINN and a whole brood of new horror writers.

TWICE WINNER OF THE BFS AWARD FOR BEST SMALL PRESS MAGAZINE

"PEEPING TOM remains a showcase for uncompromising horror fiction. It boasts a printing schedule that has yet to fall behind" - **Dementia 13**

"PEEPING TOM draws the reader into the magazine, playing to our inquisitive nature and the darker, more illicit side of our character" - **BBR**

"One in the eye for those who perceive such titles as ghettos for the sub-literate... there's no denying the professional approach to its written content." - **The Dark Side**

PEEPING TOM magazine costs £2.10 (£7.50 for a four issue sub) from David Bell, Yew Tree House, 15 Nottingham Road, Ashby-de-la-Zouch, Leicestershire LE65 1DJ. Cheques payable to Peeping Tom Magazine.

Forthcoming Vista paperback
horror titles

The Blue Manor   Jenny Jones   0 575 60010 1

Black Rock   Steve Harris   0 575 60082 9

Vanitas   S. P. Somtow   0 575 60051 9

Dark Terrors   edited by Stephen Jones and David Sutton
0 575 60024 1

Fevre Dream   George R. R. Martin   0 575 60005 5

VISTA and Gollancz paperbacks are available from all good book-shops or from:
    Cassell C.S.
    Book Service By Post
    PO Box 29, Douglas I-O-M
    IM99 1BQ
    telephone: 01624 675137, fax: 01624 670923

VISTA